A LAND OF MIST AND LOSS

THE DANDELION CHRONICLES
BOOK FOUR

A.S.R. GELPI

SILVER RIVER PUBLISHING

Book cover design by germancreative
Cover images: DepositPhotos
Other images: Canva
Map by Cartographybird Maps
Fan Art Illustrations by @colouranomaly, @saramirza_art, @jemeny69, Duy Phan, Sam Balgruuf, and yours truly.

Silver River Publishing
P.O. Box 1272
Santa Maria, CA 93456

E-Book: 979-8-9991473-2-5
Paperback: 979-8-9991473-3-2
Hardback: 979-8-9991473-4-9
Audio Book: 979-8-9991473-5-6

First Edition: February 2026

To my daughter, Sarah—my future.
To my sisters—my mirrors.
To my mothers—my roots.
The world begins and blooms again through women like you.

a LAND of MIST and LOSS

A.S.R. GELPI

AUTHOR'S NOTE

This is the fourth installment in *The Dandelion Chronicles* epic fantasy series that delves into the story of Kharis, a woman bound by an ancient curse that enslaves her and her sister.

- Book One: A Land of Shadows and Moss
- Book Two: The Dandelion Tree, Part One
- Book Three: The Dandelion Tree, Part Two

To enhance your reading experience, a comprehensive glossary of terms and pronunciation, along with detailed explanations, is provided at the end of the book.

The land of Hegra is a male-centered world in which gender roles are firmly established within its social structure. This is the world Kharis must navigate as she questions every aspect of its culture and seeks to understand who she is.

This story addresses a variety of adult themes and situations that may be sensitive for some readers, including but not limited to:

- The death of a spouse, parent, sibling, child, or mentor;
- Alcohol consumption;
- A near-drowning experience;
- Violence within a fantasy context, using magic and medieval-inspired weaponry, sometimes potentially graphic;
- Wounds and injuries, with some descriptions potentially graphic;
- Themes of physical abuse, torture, and verbal harassment. Acts of abuse and torture do not appear on the page, but their effects are referenced, and characters may witness or tend to the resulting injuries;
- A terrifying fire that destroys forests and villages;
- Content of a sexual nature, never graphic but open door;
- Mental health struggles caused by past trauma, such as panic attacks, night terrors, and nightmares;
- There is in-world cursing, but no modern cursing is used in this book.

I value you as a reader and encourage you to consider these elements before embarking on this journey through Hegra.

Thank you for choosing this book. I hope this fantastical tale captivates and inspires you as you accompany Kharis on her quest for truth and identity.

A.S.R. Gelpi

QUICK GLOSSARY
OF PRONUNCIATION

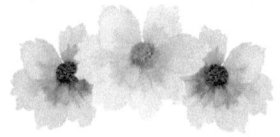

A more thorough list of terms is available at the end. However, here's an initial list to get you started. How you sound the letters in your head will be close enough, so don't sweat it. Go forth and confidently read this book. Welcome to Hegra.

- Andaheimur: and-HAY-moor
- Benkhi: ben-KEE
- Cuileagh: kooh-LEE-ach
- Darragh: DAH-rach
- Drieadh (Manor): DREE-ad
- Djinnshirukh: GEEN-shee-rook
- Eilidh: eh-ee-LEED
- Hrag: HAH-rag
- Kharis: KAH-rees
- Mahabhal: mah-ha-BAL
- Neagh: nee-ACH
- Poliormos: poh-lee-OR-mos
- Sahrit: sah-HA-reet
- Saigham: SAY-gam
- Saya: SAH-eeah

- toirmeasgh: tor-MEH-ach
- Tung: toong
- Välissa: bah-LEES-sah
- Zahar-Ghak: sa-har-GHAK

Quick Explanations:

- **A mark** is a unit of measurement similar to a foot. It is used to measure length and height. One cliffmark equals three thousand marks.

THE REALMS OF TÍR

PROLOGUE: THE
WATER PORTAL

Kharis held on, dangling from a branch above a water behemoth. The waterfall unleashed its power with a roar, its force and intensity rendering it terrifying. Rising in luminous tendrils, mist draped everything except her sister's panicked golden eyes.

Dread made them glow.

Saya inched her way along the slippery tree trunk toward Kharis and stretched her arm, fingers barely brushing against Kharis's hand.

Loss.

That had been the theme in her life—loss of freedom, of choice, of people that mattered to her. But love had also painted her canvas with exuberant strokes, like the hues of a majestic sunrise coloring the soul of her kind, loyal, and dependable sister.

The tree trunk steadily dislodged from the rock wall, each root releasing its grip one by one. Saya's added weight simply accelerated it.

So, to save Sayah, Kharis let go of the branch.

When her feet shattered the churning surface, the waterfall's massive weight slammed into her like a giant fist and pinned her to the rocky bottom. Then, a flashing burst erupted beneath her, splitting the chaos. The ground vanished, and a force yanked her into the hole. The world twisted inside out—then hurled her through to the other side.

Her head broke the surface, and she gasped for air. Her limbs flailed, clawing at the water to stay afloat. Her legs kicked wildly, lungs burning for breath.

Every contortion brought fresh pain, flaring white-hot through her body.

"*Stop fighting me,*" a soft, silvery voice uttered. "*I won't let you drown.*"

"Farrádh!" she gasped, the name breaking on a gurgle as she struggled to keep her head above the surface. His calm certainty cut through her panic, and she stilled.

"*That's it,*" he said, steady and controlled. "*Let me do the work.*"

Something long and silken coiled around her limbs, holding her afloat. The current shifted, carrying her upward as if this river obeyed Farrádh's will.

"*Dhordan...*" A quiet sigh drifted through her thoughts. "*I choose this moment to fulfill my promise to you.*"

Her memories.

"Do what you must and take them." Perhaps it was best to float into infinity and leave everything behind. *North.* The sensation settled deep in her chest. The sight of midnight stars caught her attention, and for a moment, she almost forgot the pain consuming her.

"Where am I?" she whispered.

"*I am taking you to where you were always meant to be.*" A warmth spread beneath her ribs, guiding rather than pushing. Northward. Always northward. "*The waters remember that path,*" he murmured inside her. "*So will you.*"

Farrádh's voice rippled through her mind like moonlight over dark water. "*I have brought you to my home, my realm, and here, I shall care for you.*"

The stars above shuddered, their reflections bending as the current brightened beneath her.

"*Now rest,*" he said.

Her heart drummed in her throat. "Don't leave me. Please."

"*Never,*" came his answer, his voice tenderly warm. "*Now that I have found you, I shall be with you until my very last breath. Close your eyes and rest.*"

The ache in her limbs loosened; her body grew weightless. Her mind began fading.

"When will I see you?"

A soft laugh brushed her consciousness. "*When you open your eyes.*"

A quiet smile tugged at her lips. Her pulse slowed. The world dimmed, stars collapsing into shadow.

"*Rest, my beloved,*" Farrádh whispered, his words dissolving into her thoughts.

Names and faces vanished. The pain dulled. But his voice lingered even as her mind emptied.

"*Until my last breath…*"

Like a veil descending, darkness rose to claim her, and she drifted with the currents toward the world that awaited her.

PART I

THE RIVER OF FATE

1

LEÓGHAM AND THE GIRL

I will find you. I will look for you in every universe and every timeline. Because if you are worthy of my love, my devotion will be boundless. - Poliormos

When she opened her eyes, daylight pierced her vision, feeding the dull headache throbbing in her head. Her thoughts drifted, her vision swimming in a thick haze, but something in her chest tightened, a thin thread pulling northward, though she had no idea why. A silhouette moved near the fireplace, adding wood in silence. She wasn't sure where she was or who *he* was.

A potential problem.

A restless thought stirred, pressing at the edges of her mind. She had to do something, but what? A pressure gathered behind her ribs, sharp enough to urge her to rise, to move, to go. Her left leg felt heavy, not her own, tugged by some steady, unnatural weight. She shifted—or tried to. Pain knifed through her thigh, ripping a gasp from her lips.

The figure turned at once and hurried toward her.

A blurry face leaned over her. "You're awake."

A pleasant male voice. Resonant and silvery. Oddly familiar.

Her body loosened at the sound, and that made her uneasy.

Water splashed nearby, and a cool rag patted her face, the sensation divine against her fevered skin. *This blasted heat...* Her body burned like a forge, as if fire lived beneath her flesh.

"You've been out for a while," the man said. "I was—" He paused, uncertain. "I'm glad you're awake. My name's Leógham, by the way. I've been taking care of you."

She squinted, but his face remained behind a hazy veil. And why was she so hot?

"Thirsty?"

"Yes," she rasped.

A gentle hand lifted her head; a cup brushed her lips. The water slid down her parched throat like mercy made liquid. She drank greedily, the taste clean, sweet—heavenly. When she drew breath again, the world felt steadier, the light less harsh. That odd tug northward remained, insistent beneath the haze.

"How are you feeling?"

"In pain." As if someone had kicked and punched her relentlessly. The kind of pain that pressed tears into the eyes.

"I'm not surprised. You suffered serious injuries, but you're safe now."

Thankfully, he didn't add, *You almost died.* Though... perhaps she had?

"Where am I?" Her voice scraped her throat.

"Hegra."

The name tugged at the edge of her memory like a loose thread. She reached for it, hoping for a face, a voice—anything—but nothing came.

I... Why can't I remember?

Her pulse quickened—hot, dizzying. She tried to rise, but pain exploded through her leg again, stealing her breath. Her gaze shot downward: linen and leather wrapped her left leg, suspended by ropes and weights.

"What did you do to me?" The words shot out of her. "Why did you tie me to the bed?" Her heart beat fast. Who was this man? Where was she? How—?

"You were injured," Leógham cut in gently. "This contraption," he gestured to it, "keeps your leg still so the bone heals properly."

Injured? Her mind stuttered. *How? Where?* She searched her mind: nothing but a pounding headache. With an unsteady breath, she forced herself to sink back. Her voice came out small.

"What happened to me?"

"I don't know. But right now, you need rest." A pause. "I'll help you find answers." His tone broke the dark spiral of her panic. Her heartbeat slowed.

"You promise?"

A heavier pause fell between them before he took her hand and squeezed it. "I'll be back with medicine. It'll dull the pain and help you sleep, but it tastes unpleasant."

Whatever.

Pain rolled through her; heat seared beneath her skin. Her mind churned like a nest of chaos. The taste of some remedy was the least of her concerns.

What happened to me?

The question lingered, one of many fluttering through her mind like a murmuration of starlings. The clink of metal striking pottery drew her back. Leógham lifted her head and held a cup to her lips.

The taste? Vile. Her lungs seized. Her tongue swelled. Facing death would be preferable to ingesting this repulsive concoction.

"Try not to spit it out." He sounded apologetic. "Please?"

Easy for him to say. Her eyes teared, but she obeyed, and like a brave soldier, drank it all, urging her stomach not to send it back up.

"The worst part is over," he murmured.

She doubted that.

That faint pull brushed against her ribs once more. *A reminder?*

With a cloth, he wiped her mouth, then eased her upright. He brought something else from the hearth.

"Hungry? I made broth."

The aroma reached her first, and her traitorous stomach growled its approval.

A soft laugh. "Let's feed you."

He held a spoon to her lips. The warm, savory blend coated her tongue with the taste of mushrooms, root vegetables, and tarragon.

"It's good." She thanked the Blessed Mother and opened her mouth, waiting for more.

Leógham chuckled. "I'm glad you like it."

Soon, her eyelids drooped, yet that odd pull north lingered in the back of her mind. Leógham fed her until her pain finally drifted away and sleep claimed her.

Leógham sat with the empty bowl in his lap.

He'd found her three days ago, nearly dead.

She'd somehow crossed into his realm, an impossible breach. The wards woven into its borders recognized only him, a legacy of centuries of magic meant to bar intruders from every direction. If an outsider had slipped through, the magic had shifted.

He shuddered at the thought.

But there was a more imminent danger—one no less deadly.

By Hegran law, he was bound to report her. Harboring a stranger was treason against the Crown and a threat to the kingdom, punishable by death. And yet, something in him resisted. A quiet certainty stirred beneath his fear: An inexplicable sense that her arrival was not an accident, but the continuation of something long set in motion.

Turning her over... The idea unsettled him deeply.

The realization sent a shiver through him.

He looked at her—this stranger he'd pulled from the lake —and couldn't shake the feeling that she was both a warning and a key; something lost returning at last. Regardless of whatever force had carried her here, one thing was certain: his next choice would decide both their fates.

Now, she slept, her breath even and calm. Three days ago, she'd been barely breathing, her pulse a whisper beneath his hands. He remembered the weight of her in his arms, her body cold, her life slipping from his grasp. He had not expected her to last the night.

The idea of her death had affected him more than it should have.

Yet here she was, color returning to her face, wounds closing at impossible speed. The cuts that had once gaped raw were now faint silver lines. The deep gash on her thigh —he'd seen bone—was nearly gone. Even the purple bruising, dark as ink when he found her, had faded to green and gold. It meant that in a matter of days, she could leave.

Magic unknown to him was healing her. In a land where magic was dying, this was no minor miracle.

Her wounds... Had it been an accident? What had done this? Someone? *Who would dare—?*

The surge of protectiveness startled him.

He unclenched his fists and forced a breath to steady himself.

Her left side bore the brunt of the damage, including a broken leg, a severe concussion, and bruises everywhere. He couldn't imagine anyone beating a woman, then the image of *that* revolting man, Saigham, came to him. Some men would do something like this. And Saigham, most of all, his smug grin stretching farther than it should while doing it.

He shook his head to dislodge the images; it was better to forget than to linger in his hate for Saigham.

When Leógham gathered the woman's black hair to plait, muscle memory took over. His hands moved as they once had for Elinor. She had always teased him for his obsessive precision. The memory struck hard; his fingers faltered. He forced them to move faster, as if speed alone could smother his ache. He tied off the braid and let go.

Drawing a slow breath, he held it until his hands steadied.

Leógham scratched his beard. He didn't know her name or where she came from, and the mystery only deepened. So would the danger.

Her eyes had startled him, though. Dreams from his youth surged back. A maiden stood in the mist, her gaze piercing it, a silver starburst radiating into a field of sapphire. He had woken from those dreams countless times with his heart racing, carrying her image with him throughout the day.

Back then, he had asked his mother about the dream's significance, even told her he thought he loved the girl he saw there. Her warning had never changed: "Never let your father know you dream of a blue-eyed girl."

A coincidence, he told himself. *Nothing more.*

She'd finally awakened after days of unconsciousness—a small but significant victory.

The bracelet with the green stone caught his eye.

When he'd found her at the lake, tangled in watervines and half-submerged, the gemstone had pulsed desperately as though calling for help on her behalf. It stopped emitting light when he pulled her from the water.

"You're her good luck charm," he muttered to the trinket, fastening it around her wrist.

He frowned at the black markings, though. *What are you?*

They coiled up her arm, torso, and legs like serpents—permanent, inked in a method he didn't recognize. *Healing magic? A protection spell?*

He traced the curve of one with a hesitant touch. It shimmered faintly under his fingers, power humming beneath them, prickling against his senses in warning. From afar, the markings looked solid. But up close, they were tiny, tightly packed letters, forming seamless patterns in a language he didn't know.

"What are you?"

The question was dangerous, but the answer, sadly, would have to wait. He tucked her arm back beneath the coverlet, lingering, then sat back, aware too late of how gentle he'd been.

There would be time for questions—and regret—when the answers came.

2

MY NAME IS KHARIS

The stars may wander, the oceans may shift, but every step has always been toward you. - Poliormos

That unsettling urgency rose again, dulled but persistent. Something important waited beyond the fog in her mind. She had to go somewhere, though the certainty arrived without direction, tugging at her all the same.

She opened her eyes. The world around her felt slightly tilted, as if some invisible current kept sweeping past her. Faint light spilled across the cabin, revealing a space both simple and spacious, with wood floors and stone walls. Furniture seemed sparse: a bed, a worktable with mismatched chairs, and shelves with leather-bound books of different colors. The gilded lettering told her these were expensive. Mortars and pestles, utensils, pots, books, and parchment cluttered the table, along with a few empty glass jars.

Leógham slept on the cot by the fireplace.

Beyond the window, treetops blurred into a sky streaked with rose.

Bundles of dried flowers hung from beams, and their scent infused the air with the aroma of sun-kissed meadows. She took a deep breath to enjoy it... Her lungs exploded. A violent cough tore through her chest. Pain crushed her lungs; her ribs screamed.

Leógham shot up and rushed to her. He lifted her upright, one hand steady on her back, rubbing slow circles.

"Take slow breaths. Don't force it."

She focused on the hand rubbing her back, and the motion anchored her.

"In... and out," he said. "That's it."

The phrase settled into her chest as if it had been placed there before. Her body settled into the rhythm, but she did not understand why.

Bit by bit, the coughing eased.

Her lungs were on fire. Her ribs throbbed. That breath had beaten her into submission. *Broken ribs?* Heat surged from deep within her, coiling tightly around her ribcage. The blaze she'd believed extinguished flared to life once more.

When she met his gaze, she realized her vision had cleared. Soft, brown curls framed his face, glinting copper. A short beard framed a well-defined jaw, full lips, and an angular face with balanced features. A man not much older than her. His unbelievable emerald-green eyes stole her breath. Common sense slapped her out of the spell.

"How do you feel?"

His voice, silvery and steady, thrummed through her. Her mind stirred in answer. He still held her in his arms, the warmth steadying her pulse.

"I hurt everywhere."

"I'll brew more tea for the pain." He released her and offered a wry smile. "Honey helps the flavor."

She doubted it.

The coughing scare, however, had dissipated some of her mental fog. Right. She had questions. Lots of them. She didn't know where she was, who he was—or who *she* was.

Curious *and* alarmed, she searched the chaos her mind had become. Fragments of memory flickered and died before taking shape.

What's my name?

And then, like a lightning strike cutting through a darkened sky, a word came to her.

"Kharis!"

Leógham stopped and turned, brow furrowed.

"Kharis," she said again, softer this time, tasting the truth of this word.

"Your name?" he asked.

Kharis wasn't entirely sure, but it resonated with her. "I think it is."

A bright, unguarded smile softened his features. "Beautiful. You're named after the Hegran flame flower— *kharisot.*"

෴

They shared breakfast by the window. Her appetite had returned with alarming force, as if Kharis needed to devour the world to quiet this hunger, gather her strength, and go north.

The thought snagged. She stilled, spoon hovering halfway to her mouth.

Why north?

An annoying contraption held her left leg hostage. It was a crude system of ropes and pulleys affixed to the rafters. A stone hung from one end, swaying gently as she shifted her weight to lean against the headboard.

"When does this come off?" Her head jerked toward the ropes suspending her leg.

"I'll check after breakfast. If the bone doesn't set right, you'll limp for life."

She hummed, gaze unfocused for a beat. That would complicate traveling to wherever she needed to go, so she kept eating. *Strength first.* She eyed her nearly empty bowl. A third serving sounded necessary.

"Do you remember how you ended up here?" he asked.

Kharis sifted through her memories, but those pages were eerily blank. "I…" She drew a shaky breath, looking down. "I don't know."

"You remembered your name. In time, it'll all come back to you."

She didn't think it would be *that* easy. "I don't even know how I got here."

A frown flickered across his face, then vanished. "Eat. Rest." He smiled. "We'll figure it out, and before you know it, you'll be going home."

Home… The word should have comforted her; instead, it hollowed her out.

"Hey."

Her eyes shot to his face.

"Eat before it gets cold." He tilted his head toward her bowl, a playful grin making the green in his eyes gleam.

Her heart somersaulted.

The reaction startled her. Her pulse skidded, then steadied. He was a stranger. It was ridiculous to feel anything at all for someone she barely knew. Yet, his voice tugged at something in her mind, insistent and unresolved. And if he knew her, wouldn't he have said something already?

She picked up her spoon and obeyed, forcing her attention back to the bowl, though her eyes kept straying to him, drawn by a nagging sense that she was missing something important.

Sunlight glanced off his hair as he served himself more. *He's handsome—*

She pressed her lips together and looked away, annoyed with herself, and dismissed the thought.

"I hope you like it," he said as he sat, breaking the odd silence. "I don't often have visitors." His chuckle hinted that she was his one and only visitor.

"It's good," she said between spoonfuls. "Keep this up, and I may never leave."

At her comment, his gaze lingered, unreadable.

"Would you like more?" Which sounded more like "you eat like a famished wolf."

"Yes, please." Heat rushed to her cheeks.

He rose, ladled another portion, and set it before her with a grin. It felt strange—how easily the care slipped past her guard. Stranger still, some part of her had been waiting for it, and she didn't know why.

❧

The days blurred into a haze of bitter medicine and meals. She learned Leógham's habits through fragments: the creak of floorboards when he rose before dawn; the aroma of porridge in the morning, and broth in the afternoon; his steady voice reminding her to breathe, to eat, to live.

She grew stronger; he grew watchful. Their words found an easy rhythm—light teasing, soft laughter that startled her each time it escaped. At night, she sometimes woke to the sound of his quill scratching on parchment, his silhouette lit by firelight.

Then the nightmare seized her.

"*North, north, north,*" the voices shrieked.

She jolted awake, gasping, sweat clinging to her skin. The word *monster* echoed in her mind, paired with the memory of a finger leveled at her in accusation. The need to leave hit her like a blow. She had to move. Now. Pain shot through her hands. Red sparks snapped across her fingers.

Leógham threw off his blanket. "Kharis—?"

"I'm fine." The lie came quickly. She curled her fingers into her palms and hoped the sparks had guttered out.

He brought water and sat beside her. "Here."

She hesitated, afraid the sparks might betray her, but took the cup with trembling hands. "Sorry. I woke you."

"No need for apologies. Bad dream?"

She nodded, unwilling to meet his eyes. Her throat was raw. Had she screamed in her sleep?

"Often, residual trauma can resurface as nightmares. Your mind is working through what happened to you." He paused, his eyes searching hers. "If you wanted to talk—"

"I'm fine," she blurted, sharper than intended.

An awkward hush fell between them. Leógham's lips tightened into something that resembled a smile. He clapped his hands lightly against his knees and stood. "Good to hear."

"I'm sorry," she said quietly, fidgeting with the end of her braid. "I don't know what came over me."

His gaze gentled, the shadow in his eyes gone as quickly as it came. "I know what it is to suffer nightmares." He stretched his chest and rose. "The offer still stands if you ever want to talk."

He returned to his cot, moving with quiet strength. If only she could remember whether anyone had ever cared for her like that.

3

A FLICKER OF ENCHANTMENT

> *The most brutal battles are fought within, every scar conveying a story of strength and resilience. - Poliormos*

"Fire," Kharis blurted over breakfast.

Leógham shot to his feet, chair legs screeching against the floor. His gaze swept the cabin—corners, rafters, door—searching for the threat. *Huh?* He blinked, frowning. "Where?"

"Sorry. In my nightmare," she said softly, color rising to her cheeks. She bit her lip, as if deciding whether to explain. "I'm standing on a peak," she finally said, "watching everything burn." Her fingers tightened around her bowl. "I hear the screams. I feel the heated wind. And there's nothing I can do but watch."

Leógham sank back into his chair. The words settled uneasily, echoing his own fears. He studied his porridge for a long moment, steam curling up between them. Pain was never easy to share. He picked up the spoon and stirred once, then set it down.

He could have dismissed the subject. Change it. But she

had shared something personal, and such an exchange demanded fairness.

"Sometimes," he said at last, "I dream of the civil war."

Her head tilted, curiosity flickering in her eyes. He went on, the words arriving with a weight that often left him breathless except in the morning.

"I fought when I was younger," he said. "The details are always vivid. The stench of blood. The sound of metal striking flesh. Friends gasping their last breath."

He paused, rubbing at his jaw. "It never fades."

She went very still. Her eyes widened, then her lips parted. "You... fought?"

"A long time ago." *An eternity ago.*

She glanced at him, probably wondering how long "long ago" was for a man of twenty-five.

He rose, unwilling to linger in that darkness, and gestured to her bowl. "Would you like more?"

She shook her head.

He set his on the table. "May I examine you?"

She shrugged and nodded.

It unsettled him how calmly she'd accepted the request. Any Hegran woman would've flinched. Touch carried consequences in Hegra, but Kharis simply accepted it. Was it because she trusted him, or was she unaware of how dangerous the act was?

He checked her thoroughly, fingers moving methodically to assess her progress. His focus wavered despite himself. Touching her had rattled him more than it should have.

"How did you learn to heal?" she asked.

Her question snapped him back. "My uncle." He kept his eyes on her leg. "He taught me everything I know."

When he looked up, her blue-gray eyes were on him—curious, luminous. Getting lost in them was undeniably tempting. The immediacy of the thought alarmed him. He stiffened and glanced away, closing his eyes for a moment.

"I'm removing the leather casing," he said gruffly.

21

She observed him loosen the cords and lower the weighted leg.

"Any pain?"

"None." She smiled.

His lips twitched. Her left femur had shattered—an injury that should've taken months, not days, to heal. Even then, she'd limp for life. *Did I misjudge the break?* His gaze slipped to the black markings coiled around her legs.

He stepped back, one hand stroking his chin. She'd breached his realm, healed with impossible speed, and bore magic inked into her flesh. And yet her memories remained blocked.

Who are you?

Once she left, so would the danger of having her here. He untied the last strap. The counterweight thudded to the floor. "Everything seems to have healed, especially the left side of your body. It took the worst of it. Do you remember how?"

She furrowed her brow. A lull, then, "I fell."

Leógham's curiosity sharpened. "From?"

Her features strained, as if she were chasing a memory. "From..." Her face tightened. "All I see is water, crashing on me. A river... maybe?"

Her explanation didn't add up. His realm lacked a river with swift rapids. "An unfortunate accident, then," he said. "It's a miracle you're alive. Thank the Infinite."

His gaze caught on the markings again. Clearly an enchantment, but what kind—and for what purpose? "What are you?" The question slipped out before he could stop it.

"Huh?" Kharis's gaze snapped to him.

Fires burn me.

"Sorry. I was thinking about the markings on your skin."

Confusion flickered across her face. "You see them?"

Her question startled him. "Yes," he said slowly.

"I'm glad, then." Her shoulders eased. "I thought I was imagining things." She grinned, and his heart stumbled.

Days ago, her face had been a map of bruises. Now, it stole his breath—and that startled him.

He clenched a hand, caught off guard, and cleared his throat, dragging his attention back to the markings. "Aren't you afraid of them?"

Her brow furrowed, lips pursed in thought. "I think I've always had them... or maybe not?" She shrugged. "I thought you'd inked them—"

"I'd never do such a thing."

"Sorry!" She lifted her palms. "Ignore the comment."

Leógham glanced away, jaw tightening. He was about to say something when a shrill neigh split the air. His head snapped toward the door, his breathing suddenly difficult.

Flames take me now. He pressed a trembling hand to his mouth. *How could I have forgotten him?*

Kharis's smile vanished, her eyes following his every twitch.

"I'll be right back. Promise me you'll stay quiet. I must send someone away." He snatched his long black coat from its peg, slinging it over his shoulders in a jerky motion. "Better yet—lie down. Rest."

Cold air hit like a slap. It didn't help. He clenched his jaw until it ached. Down the path, a young man in riding livery dismounted. Leógham drew a steadying breath, forced a smile, and went to meet him, every step an act of will.

No one—*absolutely no one*—could ever know she was here.

4

A LINE DRAWN,
A LINE CROSSED

> *Sometimes, the smallest act of rebellion speaks the loudest. - Poliormos*

When Leógham returned, the afternoon light streaming through the window bathed the interior in gold. He quietly closed the door behind him, brow tight, and dropped into the nearest chair, massaging his temples to forestall a headache.

"Leógham?"

He flinched. "I thought you'd be asleep," he said, forcing calm into his voice.

"I was." She rubbed at her eyes. "But you were gone so long I—" She stopped herself, lips pressing together. "I was worried."

Flames above.

"You must be hungry." He'd forgotten Hrag's arrival, and his carelessness had almost cost her. "So sorry." His hand lifted to the back of his neck—an old habit—and he squeezed against the tension there to shake off all these *what ifs.*

She only watched him, the quiet between them awkward.

Finally, he sighed, leaning back in the chair. "I didn't

mean to be gone all day. I forgot my nephew comes out when Sharan is full. I had to send him away."

"Why?"

Her question hit him harder than expected. "If he knew you were here—"

"Why would that matter?"

"Because I can't have you here." He stared at her, expecting the "you're right" from her that never came. "An unmarried woman..." No reaction. "Under my roof?"

Her eyes widened, then narrowed just as quickly. "I'm injured." The corners of her mouth twisted. "What would you have me do? Crawl into the woods?" She even flicked a hand toward the window.

"Well..." He scratched the side of his head. "A woman should care for y—"

"Nonsense." Her nostrils flared. "In Zahar-Ghak, healers tend men and women alike."

He froze. "Zahar-Ghak?"

"Yes." Her arms crossed. Her chin lifted. "What of it?"

Leógham's pulse stumbled. *Where in the mighty fires is that?* Not a Hegran province or outpost, not even a scribbled note on a map. He rubbed his temples, attempting to slow the thoughts racing through his head, when the realization struck.

He shot to his feet. "You're not from Hegra, are you?"

She frowned. "I don't even know where that's on a map."

Her words hollowed the air between them. The floor seemed to tilt beneath him, and he sank into the chair. Harboring her meant treason. *Execution for both of us.*

Against the tense silence, the fire crackled and popped. Kharis exhaled sharply. "If you only care for men, I'll become a man."

Despite himself, he nearly laughed. Disguising herself as a man wouldn't change the fact that she was still a foreigner. It would be weeks before Hrag returned. She would be gone by then. *Problem solved.*

A slow breath escaped him—resigned, weary, too full of things he'd rather not think about.

"We'll eat soon."

The fire hissed when he added a log.

He said little after that.

5

MIST AND LOSS

> *Mist may obscure the way forward, and loss can carve deep wounds, but kindness and compassion lead the way and heal the heart. - Poliormos*

L eógham brooded as he peeled, chopped, and stirred. His hands moved by habit while his mind churned with tangled thoughts about the girl he'd rescued.

What was he supposed to do with her? How would he shield her from Hegra? Hide her—protect her—when her otherness was so blatant? And what excuse would he offer his nephew when he returned?

He'd hoped—naively—that by now she would've remembered something. That her rapid recovery meant she was nearly whole. That she'd be on her merry way back to wherever she came from. But now…?

If found, Hegra would execute her on the spot—her fate sealed by centuries of blood and history. His gut twisted. He'd rescued her, healed her, only to send her to her death.

Outside the window, stars emerged. Two at first, then more, until the sky shimmered with them.

Soon, he served dinner.

Leógham reached for a bowl, his mind still snagged on their argument, and handed it to her. Kharis frowned, turning it in her hands. She looked at him with a questioning gaze, eyes sharp and searching. He glanced away, another knot forming in his stomach. When he started eating, she said nothing beyond a breath and a small shrug.

The tension loomed like a giant shadow. He hated this rift but didn't know how to bridge it, so he kept his eyes on his stew, chewing each spoonful slowly.

When Kharis finally spoke, her voice startled him. "Is this your hunting lodge?"

He blinked, slow to register the question. "Come again?"

Her mouth quirked. "Glad to see your eyes again." The bite in her tone warned him to tread carefully. Thorns covered his path ahead.

"Is this your hunting lodge?" she asked again.

"Ah—yes, it was." He caught himself. "No. I mean, it is."

One of her brows lifted. "Is or was?"

He shifted in his chair, the motion strangely sluggish, his limbs heavy. "This is my hunting lodge, yes." He stabbed at a piece of meat in his stew. "But it's also my sanctuary."

The confession had slipped out so easily. It surprised him.

She tilted her head, curiosity flickering across her face, but to his relief, she didn't press. He swallowed the last spoonful and tried to stand, but the movement took more effort than it should have, like pushing through water.

"My wife died in childbirth," he heard himself say. "Along with the baby—our son."

He had never spoken the words aloud. Now, he stared into his empty bowl, fighting the sudden, violent urge to hurl it against the wall. A year gone, and the anger still burned.

"With their deaths," he continued, "my every hope vanished. Nothing else mattered anymore."

The edges of the room blurred. He sank back into the chair, shoulders slumped, one hand rising to his brow. The tight armor he wore had cracked. He didn't even know why he was speaking so openly, but he was so exhausted: the burdens of his life, the strain of outrunning them, the constant pressure of expectations he no longer knew how to meet. He felt so heavy he wondered if the chair would buckle under him.

"I came seeking solace and found myself unable to leave."

He stared at his hands, things that no longer felt like his own. He'd never spoken of Elinor. The heat behind his eyes stung. He was on the edge of collapse when her hand came to rest on his shoulder.

"I'm sorry." Her voice was quieter. "Truly sorry."

He lifted his head.

She stood beside him—quiet, unarmed by words, one hand braced on the chair, her weight kept carefully off one leg.

Hegran law forbade touching except under strict conditions, and this moment certainly wasn't one of them. He was vulnerable. She held power now. A single, careless touch, and she could draw out a lifetime's worth of secrets. And if Hrag returned unexpectedly and found them like this…

He should've stepped away, but her hand—so gentle, so warm—held him fast. It startled him to realize that he didn't want her to let go. Even more startling was the truth beneath it: a simple touch wasn't enough.

He took her hand, cradling it between his palms, quietly grateful for her kindness. But even as warmth spread through his fingers, Elinor's final moments tore him apart. Gods, how he wished to close that door forever and pretend that night had never happened.

Why had he told Kharis? Why had his heart betrayed him like this?

He sat, torn between the urge to flee and the need to stay. Then Kharis enclosed her hands in his. "I would've died without you."

Every dark thought stilled.

"You chose to go hunting *that* day," she continued. "Had it been a day early or a day later, I would've died. But you went out *that* day."

Leógham looked up and held her gaze.

"Because of you, I received a second chance, as if the gods had tipped the scales in my favor. So, I'll honor whatever reason they had for sparing my life and ensure they never regret placing you in my path."

Her smile broke like a sunrise after an endless night.

"I'll never understand why they take those we love, but I'll defy them if I must." Her eyes glinted with a fierce stubbornness. "Even if I can't remember, I'll live to honor those I've loved." Then she squeezed his shoulder. "You must do the same, Leógham: honor her, make her dreams a reality."

Her words struck deep, the truth in them immutable. Escaping had never been the answer. This woman, born in a place he'd never heard of, had brought him clarity, parting the fog that had clouded him for far too long.

To honor Elinor.

To remember her love, her kindness, and carry forward all her dreams and hopes.

The walls around his broken heart cracked. It had been a year without tears. A year living suspended in numbness. And he couldn't keep this grief locked away forever. The release terrified him, and yet...

"I..."

He hesitated, struggling to find words and shape his emotions into language.

"I..."

Tears blurred his vision, but this time he didn't hold them back. Hegran men didn't cry, least of all in front of a woman, but he no longer cared. He was done with Hegra's laws and his duty and responsibility toward a place that didn't appear to care about him.

"I... loved her so much. All our dreams of a family

together... Gone in a single night." He drew a shuddering breath. "The toys and clothes, all the little things we'd gathered for our child—taken away as if they'd never existed."

He swallowed hard, the taste of salt coating his throat. "I was forced from the room, denied even the smallest mercy. I wasn't permitted to hold them, to say goodbye. I bit my tongue. I obeyed. I endured until..."

A strangled sob tore from him.

"Until I couldn't take it anymore." He shook with each ragged breath. "I came here to escape it all, because I couldn't imagine a world without her."

And then it all broke loose: the sorrow, the anger, the helplessness that had carved itself into his bones.

"Elinor..."

It hurt so much.

A wail tore from him—a sound that had been locked inside him since the night she'd died.

Before he shattered completely, Kharis leaned over and wrapped her arms around him. He stiffened at first, but the strength in that hold—that quiet promise that she wouldn't let him drown—kept him anchored so the powerful release of emotions he'd long buried wouldn't sweep him away.

And so, he wept.

Bitterly. Deeply.

For Elinor and the child he never got to hold.

For the life fate had stolen from him.

For the grief that Hegra had never allowed him to mourn.

6

CHASING THE WIND

Every challenge offers a glimpse of who we are and who we might become. - Poliormos

The next morning, Leógham reached for his bowl and stopped short.

Her name was carved into the wood.

His fingers tightened around the rim. He had taken the wrong one and eaten her portion. Sleeping herbs, pain draught, and all. The memory rushed back with unwelcome clarity. The loosened tongue. The grief he had never meant to share. He set the bowl down as if it had burned him.

When Kharis joined him, he didn't meet her eyes. He greeted her with the crisp courtesy of a man who had dropped something fragile and didn't wish to confirm it was broken.

Kharis neither teased him nor asked questions. She took her seat across from him and ate quietly, her posture now easy, her shoulders no longer drawn tight as a bowstring. When their gazes brushed by accident, she... smiled.

His pulse quickened. He lowered his head, fixing his attention on the porridge.

With the passing of days, the tight knot in Leógham's chest loosened. The grief was there, but quieter. His mental fog had given way to clarity. He'd never let go of Elinor, of everything she'd meant to him, but he was learning to make peace with the whims of fate.

Kharis grew stronger as well. She had also apparently declared war on weakness.

Each morning, she moved through strange, disciplined exercises, holding rigid poses, springing from the ground, repeating the cycle with fierce focus. He tried not to stare. He really did. But her odd contortions made it impossible to look away.

Then she began climbing trees for eggs.

"Don't you dare fall!" he shouted at her.

"I won't," came from the woman swinging among the highest branches like a squirrel.

Why is she doing this? His heart lurched with her every leap from one branch to another. Then, an unmistakable "Oh-oh" followed a loud crack.

"Kharis?" He shielded his eyes from the sun and searched the canopy. "Where are you—?"

The branch gave way with a splintering snap. She plummeted through the foliage in a shower of twigs and pinecones. He caught her just in time, the impact knocking them both to the ground.

"Are you all right?" he asked, breathless, running quick hands along her arms and legs. She was a spectacular mess covered in sap and pine needles.

There was an awkward silence before she burst into laughter. "Fires of Ifran, that was intense."

"You could've killed yourself," he scolded.

Kharis studied the stump above them, biting her lip. "That looked a little different in my head." A trickle of blood slipped from her nose.

"You're bleeding," He wiped it with his sleeve, cupping

her neck to keep her head still. "You're mad. I should tie you down."

Kharis simply chuckled.

He frowned. "You think I'm joking, don't you?"

She smirked, leaning in close. Leógham struggled to maintain his composure, doing everything to resist the magnetic pull she radiated.

"Do you think I'd let you?" Her grin turned wicked. "First, you'd have to catch me. That won't be easy."

His eyes narrowed. "Are you daring me?"

Her grin widened.

He gritted his teeth on a groan. "I'll catch you, tie you to a chair, and leave you out in the rain."

"Such promises," she purred.

That irritated him even more.

"Kharis...? You're still bleeding."

"It'll stop." She tilted her head back, her mouth suddenly so far from his. "Use the moment to rest. You'll need it if you're going to chase me."

He glared at her. "I cushioned your fall."

"And for that, I'll always be thankful." Her smile transformed from sharp and seductive to radiant and disarming, and Leógham found himself at a loss for words. He let the moment pass through him, unsettled but no longer resisting it.

A gust lifted plant debris in a playful swirl, spinning it through shafts of light.

"Your right palm," he said after a moment. "There's a scar there." Unlike her other injuries, already healed, this one seemed permanent.

She hummed, eyes tracing the X etched into the skin. "I don't remember how I got it... only that it's meant to ensure I never forget." A dry chuckle. "Ironic, no?"

He frowned at her—on principle, perhaps—but inwardly, a smile stirred. He leaned back, rough bark pressing into his back, while the wind teased the edges of his thoughts.

Later in the day, she was back at it—again. Stretching her legs and swinging her arms wide, limbering her neck and shoulders as if some invisible force drove her to prepare for war.

Leógham stopped chopping wood. Curiosity had finally gotten the best of him. "What exactly are you doing?"

She lifted a brow. "You've seen me do this day in, day out."

"Yes, but *why?*"

"Well…?" Kharis frowned, searching for an answer. "Why not?"

He dropped the ax, crossed his arms, and arched a glaring brow.

"Fine." She planted her hands on her hips. "Don't laugh, but I feel this is something I must do. That my life"—she pursed her lips—"depends on it."

Her conviction mirrored a fact: Kharis moved with a constant readiness in her limbs, like someone trained for war. Had she escaped this Zahar-something? Or worse, had she been sent here? His fingers curled at the errant thought. *An assassin…?*

"Have you remembered something?" It was worth asking, his attempt to strip the truth from her. Because if she remembered, even a fragment, it might explain why his gut screamed that her training wasn't for sport alone.

Kharis pondered this, eyes closed, a faint crease between her brows. Her shoulders sagged. "Nothing."

Then, with the kind of stubborn resolve he was quickly coming to recognize, she moved as though to chase the thought from her mind. While maintaining the stretch, she flashed him a dangerous smile.

Leógham knew he was in trouble.

"Run with me."

"Why?" His stare sharpened.

She shrugged with a taunting smirk. "Rather than watch, do. Or are you afraid I'll outrun you?"

Leógham huffed. "I'll make you eat dirt."

"I can't wait." Her tone was all Leógham needed for his competitive spark to ignite like a raging fire.

"Dirt," he muttered at her as he settled beside her. "If I win, I *will* tie you to a chair."

A corner of her lips curled, hinting at danger. "And if I win, you'll cook for me."

"I already do that," he said dryly.

"Then take me hunting. Deal?"

He gave her a bland look. She smiled as if the victory were already hers. *The nerve.*

"We'll go on three," she said sweetly.

He groaned. "Kharis, really, you—"

"Three!" She bolted.

"You cheated!"

Her laugh rang through the trees, bright and wild, and he found himself chasing the sound as much as the woman. He hadn't expected her to be wind-fast, nor the heat that surged through his limbs, fierce and reckless, carrying him forward. He didn't understand the feeling—only that it had momentum now, and resisting it felt pointless. The pursuit ignited the urge to catch her, to tumble with her in the grass, breathless and laughing, and feel that wild spark close the distance between them.

7

WHEN THE WILD AWAKENS

When the wild awakens, it shakes free what you thought you'd buried forever. Be ready when it does, for once kindled, its fire will reveal everything—the whole and the broken alike. - Poliormos

Leógham lost the bet.

Being a man of his word, he took her hunting— grumbling to himself about unfair advantages and vowing never to wager against her again. As they hiked through the woods, his thoughts crowded in, restless and unwelcome.

Who is she?

Ever since he'd found her, that question had gnawed at him. Her eyes were blue, but Kharis lacked the pale, almost translucent skin and blue hair the Water Kin clan was known for. She wasn't Forest Kin, lacking both the silver hair and green eyes. And without wings, she wasn't a Wind Walker. That left Hegra, where a few noble families still sported black hair, but she didn't behave like a Hegran. *Not even by a long shot.*

And there was the *oh-so-minor* issue of her entry into *his* realm.

"Aren't these pretty?" Kharis shouted, waving at him from a sunlit copse where wildflowers swayed in the breeze.

Her joy never failed to bring a smile to his face. But if they were caught...

She bent to smell the flowers, radiating the confidence of someone ready to conquer the world. With a bow slung across her back, she certainly looked the part.

Hegra would strip away the wildness that made her extraordinary.

He tried not to think of it and enjoyed the moment. *She'll go home soon*, he told himself, a smug smile creeping onto his face. No one would ever know she was here. With that thought, he walked toward her.

۞

Kharis brushed her hand against moss-cloaked bark, her smile as permanent as it was possible. Only days ago, she'd watched this world from a bed, leg-bound and useless. Now she stood here, steady enough to walk. Winning the bet had been satisfying. Hiking beside him was better.

She caught his muttered complaints on the breeze and smiled wider, careful not to gloat.

Around her, the trunks creaked in the wind. Sun-dappled leaves shivered overhead.

Leógham, scanning for wild pig tracks, crouched beside a patch of disturbed earth. A cluster of hoofprints pressed deep into the damp soil—fresh, still holding their edges.

"They passed through not long ago. Wind's turning. We'll come downwind of them."

Kharis nodded and slipped between shafts of late-afternoon light as she followed him. A faint rustle stirred the silence. Then a low, guttural grunt drifted from behind nearby bushes. Leógham motioned her to remain silent and crept closer, peering through the foliage.

A small herd rooted beneath the oaks, hides mottled with mud. The largest, a boar with a torn ear, snorted and shouldered the others aside to reach a bed of acorns.

Leógham drew his bow. His breath steadied.

The arrow flew—clean and fast.

It struck high on a pig's flank and tore through, the fletching vanishing as the shaft burst out along the other side. The sow's squeal shattered the hush, sending the rest of the herd crashing into the brush. The beast spun, staggering, before lurching into the thicket.

"Fires." Leógham burst into motion, bow still in hand.

Kharis darted after him, pulse quickened, branches whipping her arms as they plunged through the undergrowth. Ahead, the animal crashed through ferns, leaving a jagged trail of broken stems and dark spatters.

"Keep to the left!" Leógham called.

She veered, eyes locked on the sow. The forest roared around them—birds scattering, insects buzzing.

Then a massive shadow leaped from the gloom and fell upon the pig. The creature screamed—high, strangled. A wet, bone-deep crunch followed.

"Leógham...?" she whispered.

He raised a hand for silence. His expression had gone taut; his eyes flicked toward the trees. He moved closer to her, boots silent against the grass. "Come," he said through clenched teeth, gripping her elbow, urging her back.

The breeze shifted, rushing from them toward the carcass.

Leógham swore under his breath.

A guttural moan rolled through the undergrowth. The creature rose onto its hind legs, towering above the brush. Blood dripped from its muzzle in slow, viscous strands. Kharis froze, mind struggling to comprehend the goliath before her: matted fur streaked with brown-and-gray stripping, muscles rippling beneath the thick pelt. Two pairs of molten-yellow eyes glowed beneath a heavy brow. Its paws were the size of her skull, its claws long and black as obsidian.

Its four eyes locked onto them with the feral focus of a creature defending its claim.

"That's... a bear?"

"No," Leógham whispered grimly. "A mathan. Much bigger. Much worse. Don't move."

The mathan's breath came in huffing bursts, vapor curling from its nostrils. Then it unleashed a deep, primal roar that rattled her ribs.

Leógham shoved her behind him, scanning the shadows for a way out. The beast lowered to all fours and stomped the earth. Each vicious snarl stripped away another layer of her courage.

Blessed. Mother. Of all.

"Stay close," Leógham said. "We move on my mark."

Kharis nodded, her heart hammering in her chest like a loud drum. The creature's eyes seemed to bore into her, promising a swift and brutal end.

The mathan lunged.

Leógham yanked her aside as the ground erupted under the beast's charge, dust and leaves exploding around them. The force knocked her sprawling, palms skidding over damp leaves before she scrambled back to her feet.

"Close your eyes!" Leógham shouted.

"What—?"

Leógham shoved her head down. Out of nowhere, a brilliant flash of red split the air. It burned behind her eyelids, searing its color into her mind.

"Over here, you lug!" He waved his arms. "Come and get me!"

The beast rounded on Leógham.

"Run!" he roared to Kharis as he drew his hunting knife.

The beast thundered forward, claws tearing up the soil.

Leógham ducked aside, driving the dagger up beneath its shoulder as it barreled past. Another scarlet flash tore through the shadows, followed by a burst of heat that scorched the air between them. The mathan bellowed, staggering back, its fur smoldering.

"I said, *run*," Leógham shouted.

But Kharis didn't.

Fear burned out of her in a single breath. She moved without a thought, guided by a rhythm ingrained in her muscles. She found his bow jutting from a bush. Scattered arrows lay half-lost beneath the leaves. Her fingers closed around one before she could question herself. She nocked it. The string thrummed under her touch. Her muscles tensed. The world narrowed into a single bright line.

She released.

The arrow flew straight and struck the mathan high in the haunch. The creature howled and twisted to bite at the shaft, branches cracking beneath its weight. She stared at her own hands, stunned that she'd known what to do.

She reached for another arrow—

Leógham grabbed her wrist, his hand hot with sweat, and bolted, dragging her along.

They raced through the forest, jumping and dodging, twigs snapping against their bodies.

"I know how to use a bow!" she shouted.

"Get ready!" Leógham never once glanced back.

"Ready for w—?"

"Jump!"

The ground vanished beneath her. His grip tore away. For a breathless moment, she was weightless—then the world dropped out, and she plunged into a lake.

8

WHEN FEAR OPENS THE DOOR

Fear unseals the doors where memory keeps its most dreadful beasts.- Poliormos

The air swallowed her scream.

She hit the lake in an explosion of light and sound and plunged beneath the surface, the icy waters crushing the breath from her chest. Bubbles burst around her face, spinning silver through the dark. For a heartbeat, she didn't know which way was up.

Her muscles locked, then jerked free.

Faint shafts of light teased the way up, distant and taunting. She flailed toward them, limbs tangled in fabric. Her fingers clawed for purchase. Her body still sank. And at that moment, memories spilled out of her like the bubbles streaming out of her nose.

A woman's voice shouting, *"Don't let go."*

A formidable rush of water.

Plunging into the white churn.

The memory fractured as her lungs began to burn. The world became cold pressure. Darkness edged into her vision.

She surrendered to this liquid world, fate dragging her into its frigid depths.

A rough yank wrenched her upward.

Her head broke the surface in a shattering gasp. She inhaled greedily between coughs and desperate gasps, but the reprieve lasted only a moment before she slipped under again. Terror surged anew. She seized a figure, clinging to flesh, and the added weight dragged her down. She let go, hands clawing at the water in futile attempts to climb out of it. The lake seemed infinite, giving her nothing.

Then arms found her again, gripping her from behind, and she was rising again. The world exploded into air and light as she broke the surface together.

"Stop fighting me," Leógham shouted. "I won't let you drown."

The words struck deep, cleaving through her panic. She'd heard them before, the command familiar. Her limbs obeyed before her mind could question it, and she went still enough for him to keep them afloat.

"That's it." His voice was steady, controlled. "Let *me* do the work."

Those words...

With one arm, Leógham swam, towing her along. When they reached a series of boulders, he pushed her up. She hauled herself onto the sandy shore, coughing up water, every gulp of air a reminder that she was alive.

Leógham dragged himself up beside her, chest heaving, the two of them sprawled on the shore—soaked and shivering, but breathing.

"How are you doing?"

Kharis didn't answer at first. She rolled onto her side, coughing up water, trying to wrestle her breath back under control. Her throat ached. Every inhale scraped like glass.

"Thank you," she rasped.

"Sorry." Leógham sat up and wiped his face. "I knew the

drop was nearby. I should've warned you." A slow frown creased his brow. "You can't swim, can you?"

The question hit deep. A frisson of fear passed through her, far colder than the lake's water. After a long beat, she muttered, "No."

He sighed, shaking droplets from his hair. "No shame in that. I can teach—"

"No."

He blinked at her, brow furrowing as her refusal sank in. "Why not? You would've drowned if I hadn't—"

"I said no!" she snapped.

He recoiled, startled. But she was already pushing herself upright, shoulders tense, water dripping and pooling around her waterlogged boots. The heat beneath her skin rose, pulsing with her heartbeat. She was angry at herself. At the weakness that had gripped her. At the panic that had stolen her reason. At the way her body had *frozen.*

The memories had struck without warning, like assassins in the dark: her hand clutching a slick branch, the endless drop waiting to swallow her whole.

"Don't let go," that voice had begged her. "Please, hang on."

So why did she let go? The air seemed to thin.

The visions clawed at her like phantom hands, desperately tugging at her sleeves. They dragged her back into the lake of memory: the glimpse of desperate golden eyes through the spray, and the scream that was both hers and not hers.

She found it hard to breathe, her pulse drumming in her ears, until fear became fury.

"Stop!" The word tore from her like a heated spark, demanding the onslaught to end. The lake rippled outward, waves lapping against the stones.

"A waterfall." She clutched her head, seeing it clearly now. She'd fallen down a waterfall, and it had been her choice to let go of the branch. But why? This truth struck her like a blade. Why had she chosen this?

"Kharis...?" Leógham sounded far away, muffled by the pounding in her ears.

A surge rose inside her, burning away the cold. The helplessness that had strangled her moments before loosened its grip. That old hunger rose instead: a fierce need to reclaim control of her life, her fate, even the moment of her death.

Never again. The words rattled through her like stones in a current. Never again would she feel small or powerless—

Poisonous voices flared in her mind, crashing together like a stampede of wild horses.

Weak. Useless. A fool.

The accusations seeped through the cracks in her mind. They twisted her deepest fears into certainty. Her hands trembled as the need to silence them rose in a violent swell. She'd crush, break, and burn them to oblivion. She'd destroy everything to silence them once and for all.

The lake heaved. Pebbles quivered beneath her boots.

Something hovered at the edge of memory. What had she forgotten? What task waited for her? She had to go somewhere, but where? And why was it so urgent? Her fingertips prickled with pain as the questions pressed harder. Heat climbed her arms. Tiny red sparks flared to life across her palms.

Her thoughts spiraled.

All at once, a wall slammed down, caging the beast. The memories, the voices, the anger vanished in a frozen hush.

"You owe me, little sister," crooned a resonant male voice.

Kharis spun, searching for its owner, but the world twisted with her. Trees blurred into streaks of teal and jade.

"Kharis!"

Leógham caught her by the arms. The touch grounded her, steadying the tilting world.

"Look at me." His face swam into focus, the only solid

shape in the haze that had scraped her mind clean. "Are you all right?"

Tears pricked her eyes. He drew a breath. "I'm sorry," he said.

She lowered her gaze. "Take me home. Please."

Leógham's expression softened. He exhaled slowly, a breath weighted with understanding. "As you wish."

Without another word, she followed a few paces behind him, her feet cold and numb, her boots squelching. The silence between them sank its teeth and bit, sharp as the few memories that had come to torture her.

9

DREAMS AND DECEPTIONS

Dreams often echo a truth we dare not face in the waking world. - Poliormos

That night, Kharis tossed in bed, her mind like a restless tide. Behind closed eyelids, the mathan loomed, waiting to get its revenge on her arrow, but the plunge into the lake jolted her most. She shuddered at the memory, at the frantic struggle to reach the surface and not sink into the dark.

Her eyes flew open, and the visions dissolved. She pressed her palms against her eyes when a sudden arc of red sparks leaped from her fingers.

What—? She cringed, clenching her hands. Cautiously, she turned them over, searching. *Nothing.* She bit her lip. *Did I imagine it?*

Across the room, on the cot near the fireplace, Leógham slept soundly, and she was glad. The last thing she wanted was to add to his growing concerns. Her presence here had already upended his quiet life.

Still asleep, Leógham turned and settled on his side.

It made her smile.

He was soft-spoken, adorably shy, and kind-hearted. And when it mattered, this man rose to the occasion, brave and ready to take charge. Had men in her past done the same? Somehow, she didn't think that was the case.

Lost in the chaos in her mind, a memory whispered of unbearable loss. Had she lost someone she loved? Was the loss good or bad? Should she cry or be happy? Was it better to forget and live unmoored to the past? To begin anew... *With Leógham? On her own?*

Unable to sleep and desperate for a distraction, she rose. A vague unease tugged at her: that this wasn't the first time she'd woken and wandered in the middle of the night. The thought lingered as she wrapped a blanket around her shoulders and tiptoed outside.

Her breath misted before her, its hazy tendrils dancing in the chilly breeze. The sky was clear, with no clouds in sight. The majestic Silver River gleamed fiercely upon the world below. Seven stars shone the brightest. The sight seemed familiar—intimate—a tapestry of stars that had welcomed her each night—

Pain suddenly stabbed her side, sharp enough to take her breath away. Her knees buckled as she fell onto the cool grass. Fingers dug into the earth. The heat inside her grew fierce, hungry. She squeezed her eyes shut, praying for it to ebb.

When she opened her eyes, dark rings of scorched grass lay beneath her hands. She tore her palms from the ground and rushed to her feet, staring at what she'd done.

Overcome by the urge to get away from it, she followed the trail.

Pebbles bit into her bare feet as she climbed, step after step, until she reached the summit. Mist clung to the forested valley below. Above, the stars blinked in a silver-strewn sky. Moonlight bathed the landscape, and the night pulsed with the restless chirr of crickets. She let her eyes drift, immersing herself in the sight.

A sudden pressure popped in her ears. She winced, a fleeting vertigo sweeping through her.

Then—silence. The night seemed to fold in on itself. No crickets. No rustling leaves. Even the wind had ceased its dance. In its place, a low hum stirred in her bones.

"I'm glad you came," said a voice—too close, too far, every word echoing from everywhere and nowhere at once.

The air shattered like splintering glass, and what she saw tore the breath from her lungs.

The entire world was burning.

10

WHEN ALL THE
WRITINGS END

We do not walk our paths—we are written into them.
Even our rebellions are part of the verse. When all
the writings end, the divine quill shall rest, and the
final name shall be etched in starlight upon the
parchment of the heavens. - Poliormos

Smoke coiled across the land in thick, writhing ribbons. Violent flares erupted skyward, stabbing the heavens. In the distance, mountains split open, belching fire and smoke. The winds screamed, blasting streams of scorched air as a terrifying blaze devoured everything in its path.

The metallic tang of wild magic enveloped the landscape, prickling Kharis's skin as if she were standing in a field of thistles. Ash drifted like sinister snow, flakes clinging to her sweaty skin.

Bodies clashed. Metal clanged against metal. Screams echoed in every direction. Loosed arrows whistled past, the fletching of one grazing her cheek as it zipped past her. In the distance, great stones fell from the sky, their collisions cratering the ground and sending plumes of debris high into the heavens.

A horrific landscape filled her vision.

The pristine meadows of her childhood and the ancient forests where she played and hunted were ablaze. The quaint villages, with their welcoming people and smiling children, lay in ruins, destroyed by the monstrous fire before her. It raged on like an endless beast, consuming the horizon.

Kharis shielded her face from the burning winds. "This is a nightmare." Prayer and command folded together: "Wake up, Kharis. Wake up. You're dreaming."

"Is it?" someone said. "A dream?"

She flinched and stumbled back. A young man now stood beside her. His face—her face—beautiful and terrible in its familiarity, every line and curve the same except for two. His long silver hair lifted in the heat, rippling like moonlight. His glowing silver eyes locked on the ghastly inferno, his face revealing no emotion.

She retreated a step. "Who are you?"

His brows knitted, as though he carried centuries of sorrow. "You must remember—"

"But I don't." Her voice cracked as the words ripped from her. The void in her mind throbbed like an open wound.

"You must, Ori," he said again, softly. "The final threads are drawing taut, weaving into the last rows of an epic saga— but only if you remember. Only you can guide its end." He gestured to the burning world.

"No." She shook her head. "This is a nightmare." She swallowed the scream clawing its way up her throat—then froze. Her fingertips glowed like embers, crimson flames climbing her hands. She tore her gaze from her hands to the inferno devouring the world.

"Did… Did I do this?" The words scraped from her throat, half-broken. She dreaded the answer.

"You must end it, sister," the man said at last, turning fully toward her. "Only you can mend the wounds and thread what was torn apart. Head north, Ori, and save this world."

His voice held the weight of prophecy.

"If you don't, the curse will fester," he went on. "The loom will tangle, and you'll be forced to unmake this world and begin again." His fingers tenderly brushed the line of her jaw. "It's time to end all the writings, sister. Time to come home."

Something deep inside her stirred, as if it had been sleeping for a long time and was finally awakening.

Magic.

Barriers splintered. Claws broke through, groping for release.

Blessed Mother.

Her panic rose. She forced her breath small and even— one, two, three—counting desperately to find a quieter channel. Her black markings flared, pulsing violently. Like chains, they tightened across her body to hold the monster at bay, but her magic roared, thrashing against its cage.

Iridescent scales bloomed across her skin—petal-like and glinting like tempered steel. Enveloped in stardust, she burned as brightly as the North Star.

The stranger turned, his form equally haloed in silver light. "Ori—"

"Kharis," she cut him off. "My name is Kharis."

And yet... that name—Ori—had struck a chord, as if it had belonged to her once.

"Who are you?" she demanded again.

His silver eyes glowed. "You've made it to Hegra." He held her gaze, a slow smile creasing the corners of his eyes. "Go north." His voice no longer sounded human but vast and resonant, echoing through earth and sky. A voice that could sunder the world. "End all the writings, sister. Tie the last threads in the tapestry firm and true. Only then shall you be free."

The air rent in two, and he vanished, sucked into the crack.

"No, wait!" Her hands came out to grab him. "Come back! What is that supposed to mean?"

The fracture sealed with a shudder. But the air still hummed with the echo of his power. She wanted to scream, to drag him back, to make him explain. Anger coiled tight beneath her ribs, hot and rising.

She had no answers. Only this rage clawing at her ribs.

End them all? A bitter laugh broke from her throat.

"I've had enough!" If no one would tell her how, she'd decide the ending herself. Her limbs moved without thought, guided by an ancient ritual etched into her bones, each step an act of defiance. The words rose unbidden, as if she'd recited them ten thousand times before.

"I call upon the Eternal Winds," she cried, and they answered, howling into the night.

"I call upon the Earth, pillar of all things."

The ground shuddered beneath her, and like some great monster disturbed from slumber, the valley split open, jagged cracks racing outward to swallow flame and ash.

"I call upon the Fires of Creation."

A flash tore through the heavens. Lightning veined the sky in arcs of molten silver.

"I summon the key to open the Door—"

"Kharis!"

Arms seized her from behind.

The world shattered. Sound crashed back in: the wind hissing through the trees, the shrill chorus of crickets, her own ragged breath. Her silver furnace guttered out, and suddenly, she was standing at the cliff's edge. Gravel shifted beneath her toes, and pebbles skittered into the black maw below.

"Thank the Fires, I found you." Leógham's arms crushed her to him, his voice shaking as he whispered in her ear.

Nausea rose in her throat. She pressed her back against him, desperate for distance from the drop. "What... what happened?"

"Sleepwalking." Leógham gently pulled her away from the cliff.

Déjà vu crashed over her. A different night, another pair of arms dragging her from the brink, another tender voice whispering the same fear. Her heart beat wildly, frantic, unmoored.

Her mind then caught up with her eyes, and her lips parted. "Everything... was burning." Her gaze whipped from hill to horizon. "Everything."

"You were dreaming. Nothing more."

His words seemed to confirm it. Sharan's ivory light bathed the forested valley. Crickets sang their endless song. Wisps of fog lazily curled around trees. The world slept in a languid rhythm.

Had it been a nightmare?

She wondered if she was losing her mind. But if her visions were nothing but madness, then the summons to go north was nothing but a phantom born of it. Could she ignore the call to go north? And what would happen if she did?

The choice split her open: go north, chasing a summons she didn't understand, or stay, surrendering to the possibility that nothing had ever been real. She didn't know which fate was worse: that the world would burn again, or that it never had.

"Come." Leógham kept his arms firm around her. "Let's get you back to bed. You need your rest."

She heard the worry, the veiled fear, threading through his voice.

"Not yet." She drew in a shuddering breath, summoning her courage. "Hold me a little longer... Please?"

"Kharis—"

"I'm falling apart." Her body shook. "I think I'm going mad."

The admission terrified her. That emptiness inside her

widened, as though half her soul had already been torn away and lost forever.

Her world, stripped of memory, was collapsing piece by piece. And the more it crumbled, the more she clung to the only thing left that felt real: Leógham. She turned and buried her face against his chest, desperate for an anchor before she was swept away.

Her sobs broke loose. The strength to pretend she was brave and capable vanished. She couldn't remember much, but somewhere deep inside her pulsed a terrible knowing— that she'd forgotten something so vital, so sacred, that if left unfulfilled, it would destroy everything.

11

THE TRUTHS WE CANNOT FACE

> *Some truths do not break us all at once—they wait, quietly and patiently, until we are soft enough to shatter. - Poliormos*

When Leógham opened his eyes, Kharis slept quietly in his arms.

He'd woken in the middle of the night to find the bed empty. The blanket and the burned marks on the grass had sent him spinning. He'd spotted her on the hilltop —her silhouette black against Sharan—and had run to her, thinking the worst: that she meant to end her life.

The ground had scorched beneath her feet. What had done this? Her? He'd carried her home and cleaned her feet. He wasn't sure why he'd lain beside her, only that he'd held her until she stopped trembling and drifted into sleep. Soon after, he'd followed.

This morning, he pressed the length of her body snugly against him, her back to his chest. Their curves fit as if they were perfect for each other. Her captivating scent, like crisp summer citrus and salty like a wild ocean, quieted the noise in his head. His heart reveled in her warmth. It swam in that pleasure…

His eyes flew open.

An icy surge flooded his chest. He should've left the bed when she'd finally fallen asleep. She was going home, and he wasn't getting involved. He ran through his herb inventory to drown the rising urges, but those little embers refused to die. *Fires burn me eternally*. He had to get up, but having her in his arms was so intoxicating.

When Kharis turned and nestled into him, a hush swept through his thoughts, vast and absolute, as if the world itself had stilled with him. His arousal was swift. He swallowed hard, silently reciting the steps to make tinctures.

A soft sigh escaped her, fragile as mist. "Thank you."

Her gratitude washed over him, and with it a fierce need to protect her.

"What happened?" he asked quietly. "Ever since the lake… I can't help you if I don't know how to. If you won't talk to me."

She exhaled softly. "I let go." A pause. "I was dangling from a branch above a waterfall. People were rushing to rescue me… and I let go." A sob broke from her. "I chose to die."

His heart clenched. That was the wound at her core.

What drove her to such a choice? Fear? Despair? His eyes followed motes of dust as they drifted through the soft beams of morning light streaming in from the window. Was life so fragile?

He chose his words with care. "Were you escaping them?"

She stiffened as if searching for the answer in some hidden room in her mind. "Perhaps, because why would I let go?"

He tightened his hold, breathing her in. Why did it soothe him? Why did she conjure all these whys?

"Kharis…" He swallowed hard. "I'm sorry about yesterday."

"Why?"

There were so many ways to answer her question, but which would he choose?

"I can tell your nightmares weigh you down. I don't know how to earn your trust so you can share it with me." His words came slower, gentler. "I want to help you as you helped me... with Elinor." A beat. "So it hurts less."

She remained quiet for a long moment. With a slow exhale, the tightening in her shoulders eased.

"Fire is the most terrifying of my nightmares," she started. "So vivid I can't think it's merely a dream. I fear it's my fault." She clutched his tunic like she'd done last night.

"What if it isn't a nightmare but a memory?" he asked. "Your memories aren't gone, only blocked. Maybe your nightmares are cracks through which some slip. Perhaps you escaped this fire?"

She didn't say anything, but he knew she was listening.

"Why don't you tell me about this nightmare?" he asked. "It may help."

Her heart beat faster against his chest. "It doesn't change much. I stand on a summit, watching the world burn. I hear screaming. I hear fighting. The heat peels my skin. The wind's full of ash and embers. Someone speaks to me, tells me I must end it, but never explains how. And the world burns and burns because I'm useless."

Another quiet sob tore from her.

"This... man. He looks like me, calls me sister, but I don't know whether I have a brother. Everything is so confusing."

He rubbed his chin against her hair. "You're safe here." *In my arms*, he almost added. Then he remembered why they'd jumped into the lake in the first place. "Well... except for the mathan."

She laughed, brushing the shades of gray away. "Blessed Mother, we ran so fast. Will it come again?"

"No. Probably tending to its wounds far away from us."

She lifted her eyes, a soft smile curving her lips, and the urge to kiss her overtook him.

"Thank you," she said, "for everything."

His heart nearly jumped out of his chest. He wanted nothing more than for his mouth to meld with hers—to taste and devour her.

"Um. Yes." He released her and sat up, scratching his head. "Don't mention it."

He got up and kept his back to her, hoping the pressure against his trousers would fade, yet the sensation of holding her in his arms refused to fade. His mind reminded him it was time to make breakfast.

"I—I better get the fire going."

"Let me help." Kharis sat up on the bed. "Please."

He glanced over his shoulder. Her need to find purpose spoke to him. "What about cleaning the ash while I get more logs?"

"Consider it done." She jumped out of bed, and her bare thighs came into view before the oversized tunic settled over her legs as she crouched by the fireplace.

Aroused again, Leógham walked out swiftly, rubbing his beard to rid himself of this stupor.

Fires take me.

He plunged his hands into the water tub, the cold biting deep, and splashed his face to smother the heat clawing at him.

Have I fallen for her?

He sat on the grass, flicked wet hair off his face, and cupped his mouth with a shaky hand. *She's leaving. I can't get involved.* But another thought rose above the din in his head. If others were looking for her... If she thought death was better... *I'll keep her safe, whatever the cost.*

He got up, letting the cold morning air bring him clarity, and grabbed an armful of wood, the bark biting into his palms.

A lesser pain, he thought. *A reasonable one.*

12

THE HEGRAN PROMISE

To vow in Hegra is to summon ancient magic. Once forged, the land will hold you to your word. There is no escape. No counter spell. Do not take it lightly. Even if mountains fall and oceans rise, your promise echoes endlessly through every leaf, every sunset, every drop of rain. - Poliormos

Leógham finished his breakfast, but Kharis, unusually quiet, pushed her porridge around her bowl. Typically, a bottomless pit, she was lost in thought with nary a spoonful to her name.

He pursed his lips, hating to see her like this—even more determined to coax a smile from her. The thought struck him like sunlight breaking through clouds. *The meadow.* She'd loved it there. It would surely lift her spirits.

He'd frame it as a simple, practical suggestion, something ordinary. Leógham leaned back in his chair, keeping his tone casual. "The weather's nice today. Warm and sunny. We can wash our clothes." He let the words hang for a moment.

"And bathe," he added with a small, encouraging smile. "A proper scrubbing all around. What do you think?"

Kharis nearly sniffed her sleeve. "That would be nice."

Without a pause to let her reconsider, he packed for their outing.

Leógham led the way, keeping the pace steady and unhurried. The bellflowers were still in bloom. Lavender and ivory petals swayed in the breeze, their sweet scent drifting lazily over the meadow.

They found a spot and settled. Leógham stole a glance, catching her smile as her eyes wandered over the blooms. It was a small victory, but one that warmed his heart.

A gust swept through, catching her long hair and flinging it across her face. She trapped a handful behind her ear, while the rest lashed and shimmered around her.

Judging by its length, it had been years since she'd cut it—perhaps she'd never planned to. It cascaded in black waves, long enough to brush the small of her back.

"I have some leather if you wish to tie it." She nodded, and he reached into his knapsack. "Here. Let me."

He gathered her hair, his fingers threading through the dark strands to plait them. When he tucked a few loose wisps behind her ear, his knuckles grazed her temple—light, almost accidental, but it stole his breath all the same. The urge to kiss her awakened in him again. He waited, hoping she'd look at him, but her gaze remained on the horizon, her mind somewhere else. His hand dropped, the moment slipping away like water through his fingers.

"Leógham?" Her voice was soft, her sapphire eyes overly bright. "I don't think anyone's coming for me."

He tilted his head, slightly confused by her comment.

She took a deep breath. "That day, at the lake, I remembered the waterfall. People were trying to reach me, begging me to hold on. And yet, I let go of the branch."

He remained quiet, sitting beside a woman exhausted by the few memories she had—the painful ones.

"No one's coming for me." Her words sank into him like stones cast into deep water. She hugged her knees on a quiet exhale. "If I survived the fall, others would've found me, unless..." Her teeth snagged her bottom lip. "Unless I'm dead, and this is the afterlife."

"You aren't dead."

"I can't dispute it since I feel very much alive." Dappled sunlight danced on her face. "Not dead. Not dreaming. Not where I should be."

Leógham found himself at a loss, unable to argue against any of it.

She lay in the grass, her eyes fixed on the expanse of blue above.

His memories burned like a scorching fire, always stoked and fed. Kharis stared at cold ashes, wondering about the embers long gone that had once ignited her fire. He settled beside her, arms folded under his head, and gave her a pensive glance.

"Some people remember every detail of their memories—the scents, the sounds, the grief in them. The void of missing memories haunts others."

She turned to him. "Which one are you?"

"I belong to the first. I remember everything."

Kharis heaved a slow breath. "Leógham, I..."

He waited for her to finish, giving her the time to gather her thoughts, but the silence stretched. His head turned, and his heart clenched at the sight. Tears rolled down her face, glistening in the sunlight, her expression caught between heartbreak and resignation.

"Kharis...?" He sat up. "Are you all right?"

"You're the only one I can trust." She drew a sharp breath. "I know I'm asking a lot of you, but could I stay with you until I find my way home?" A nervous pressing of lips. "I don't want to be a burden or cause you any trouble. I..." Her chin quivered. "I don't know what else to do."

He saw it then, with a clarity that left no room for doubt. Hers wasn't a request meant to be weighed, nor a problem to be solved. She was asking not to be left alone while the world rearranged itself around her. Sending her away—or waiting for someone else to claim her—felt wrong in a way he couldn't explain.

This was not pity. It was his choice.

"You wouldn't be a burden," he said. "Trouble and mischief? Perhaps." He chuckled at the idea, pondering what else this bewildering woman would put him through. He clasped her hand, steadying her fingers with his own.

"Look at me." When she did, he held her gaze. "I'll never leave you. Please, don't worry about it—"

A flash flickered in the air. The air hummed, soft at first, then sharpened. An invisible hook attached to his chest, yanking taut. A shimmer rippled outward before sinking into his skin like ink into cloth.

Leógham inhaled sharply, knowing what it meant: He'd made a vow, and irrevocable magic had sealed it. A quiet burn spread through his bones with the unmistakable weight of a Hegran promise. The ringing in his ears became insistent, then faded. There was no turning back now. As a permanent contract lacking a counterspell, it bound. These took root. These changed the course of lives.

What have I done?

His pulse stuttered. He'd tethered himself for life. Wherever she went, he'd follow. Into danger. Even death. *Flaming gods.* He'd bound himself to a foreigner.

But then she smiled at him—grateful, luminous with trust—and it cut cleanly through his rising dread. The panic loosened its grip. His breath returned, slow and steady. His heart no longer bolted like a startled horse. His mind, instead of spiraling, stilled.

He would stay with her—protect her. It felt right. And so he held her hand a little tighter.

"Thank you." Her voice came smaller, steadier. "I have little to offer, but I'll work hard and not get in your way. Please, continue to light my path."

Another expression he'd never heard, but it resonated

with him. "I'll light your path, but only if you light mine. Do we have a deal?"

She gave him an eager nod and dried her tears.

"Are you ready to head out? The lake isn't far." He dusted the back of his trousers and extended his hand to her. She took it, and this time, his heart jolted with such joy that an internal lightness overwhelmed him. He set aside his worries, allowing this emotion to lead.

After a steady hike through the woods and up the pass, they reached the top, where the lake came into view. It was a near-perfect circular depression nestled among mountains and forest. Its striking turquoise waters gleamed in the sunlight, contrasting beautifully with the dark green bordering its shores. The lake's surface mirrored the snow-dusted peaks with flawless clarity. Large boulders ringed the shoreline like scattered pearls.

Her expression lit up, and his thoughts bounced all over.

Once they reached the lake, Kharis removed her boots, walked toward a boulder along the water's edge, and sat with a contented look, toes skimming the water's surface.

"I'll drop our things," Leógham said. "Stay here."

She grinned, throwing him a quick, rascal-like look.

"You don't know how to swim." He glared at her, fists on his hips, but she stared back with blissful cluelessness. He hung his head, accepting defeat. "It's deep over here. Be careful."

He wasn't sure she'd listen to his advice. Her stubbornness irked him some days. *The way she is and the things she says.* He shook his head. *People will know she isn't from Hegra.* That worried him the most.

With the promise made, leaving her behind was no longer an option. If found, she'd die. He would, too, and his family would be punished. He let that thought sink in. A beat. Then another.

Burning gods. He raked his hand through his curls. "How do I do this?"

He dropped everything, tugged his boots off, and shrugged off his tunic, then his chemise. When he turned toward Kharis to suggest a bathing location, he stopped mid-thought. She'd already discarded her tunic, trousers cuffed to her thighs, tattooed legs dangling over the boulder's edge.

Leógham blinked, stuck somewhere between shock and propriety. The serpentine markings on her back slithered beneath the binding across her chest in a hypnotic fashion, their pull impossible to resist.

Flames above.

The line he didn't dare cross was inching toward him, testing his restraint. His mother's every lesson on consent screamed at him. He turned away, aware he'd been staring at her for too long. His heart was beating faster, its rhythm joyously wild. His mind wasn't faring much better, tangled in a whirlwind of thoughts buzzing like bees irresistibly drawn to flowers.

Get it together.

The soap's scent stirred unwelcome memories of Hegra. Duty versus desire. Freedom versus conformity. He clenched the bar of soap so tightly that his fingers left deep indentations.

How will I do this?

The indecision tore him apart.

1 3

THE WELCOMING

Water is ancient and wise. It remembers all things and moves toward its end with quiet certainty. When the earth bars its path, water does not resist—it bends, carves, or finds another way. - Poliormos

After bathing, Kharis caught glimpses of Leógham through the bushes. His sense of modesty ran deep, keeping a considerable distance until they were dressed.

Her black snakes shifted subtly beneath her skin, tightening and loosening in a slow, steady pulse.

"Maybe they frighten him?"

The way he averted his gaze whenever they were exposed made it the most plausible answer. She traced the patterns on her arm, taken by their intricate design. Still, the thought lodged in her mind like a thorn, refusing to loosen.

Quietly, she crept toward the bushes and peered through the leaves. Dappled light framed Leógham's silhouette, his bare back corded with muscle. His skin bore the scars of battles—but no markings like hers. It seemed Hegrans didn't ink their flesh the way hers was.

She returned to her washing, dipping the bar of soap into the water, rubbing it over the trousers, and—as Leógham had taught her—pressing the fabric against a smooth rock. The rhythm distracted her. *Scrub, turn. Scrub, turn. Rinse, rinse. Repeat.* The steady motion soon gave rise to humming, and before long, it grew into singing. Verses rose from a place beyond memory.

> "A thousand years ago, our world was broken.
> A thousand years ago, they came.
> They burned our forests.
> They razed our land.
> A thousand years ago, our hope was stolen.
> But a thousand years ago
> Four warriors came with their armies.
> They fought his darkness.
> They brought the sun.
> Four warriors came with their armies,
> And the battle was won.
> We mourned our losses.
> We gave them our son,
> And from that turmoil,
> A weapon was born.
> The lands we reclaimed,
> And life was golden."

Leógham stilled when he heard her sing.

She often hummed while absorbed in her tasks, unaware she was humming. This was different. She was singing, and the words caught him off guard. Soft and unexpectedly sweet, her voice drifted through the trees like sunlight through mist.

His hands paused, and he closed his eyes to listen more closely.

"We rose from our ashes,
Like the phoenix of old.
And a thousand years ago,
We feasted and sang,
Under a brilliant Zahari sun.
But while our land recovered,
And hope was once woven,
The gods imprisoned the four.
And a thousand years ago,
While we feasted and sang,
Their lands were frozen."

The gentle cadence unspooled the tension within him. He found himself spellbound, turning toward where she was washing her clothes. Through gaps in the foliage, he caught glimpses of her body as she sang.

Every nerve snapped taut, his eyes locked on the mesmerizing blur of skin. The pull was unbearable. He wanted to leap over the thicket, wrap her in his arms, kiss every inch of her—claim her.

Magic suddenly flared beneath his skin. Heat surged down his arms, arcs sparking at his fingertips, scarlet flames flaring first... then streaking darker. In a blink, black bled into red, the kind of magic he'd sworn never to summon again.

Blessed Fires. His breath faltered.

The last time these flames had risen—during the civil war —death had flanked him. Back then, he'd crushed enemies with inhuman ease, with impunity, with never-ending rage. With a ragged curse, Leógham stumbled to the water's edge and thrust his hands—and his head—beneath the surface, forcing the heat to gutter out.

One heartbeat.

Two.

Three.

"Kharasdir..."

Kharis stopped mid-motion.

A soft, melodic male voice drifted across the lake's surface like a charm. It sounded so familiar. Slowly, she turned toward the lake. Sunlight had scattered into a kaleidoscope of rainbow shimmers as though the lake had heard her song and now answered with its own.

Her brows drew together as unease and curiosity tangled within her. A lazy fish drifted near a rock, undisturbed. Nothing else moved at the bottom.

She bit her lip, caught between instinct and yearning. Fear pricked her stomach, but curiosity tugged just as hard. Deeper still, recognition sang—she'd heard this voice before. Did she know who he was?

She edged toward the shore, but an echo pierced her mind, and she was back beneath the water: lungs burning, limbs flailing for a surface that never came. She stumbled back, aware she'd nearly drowned, but was the danger real, or imagined?

Before, she'd fallen into the water. This time, she'd choose. Boulders lined the deep end, offering enough holds to pull herself out if needed.

Bracing herself on one, she pushed her fear aside and eased into the water. Her heart fluttered when her feet found no purchase, the depth deceiving. She clung to the ledge, water lapping at her collarbones. The moment stretched endlessly, every muscle primed to pull herself out at the first sign of danger.

But nothing happened.

The intriguing weightlessness coaxed curiosity where fear had existed. After a few deep breaths, her heartbeat slowed. Summoning her courage, she drew in one long breath and let go.

Her body drifted, slowly descending.

Her feet touched the bottom, a wispy cloud of silt settling beneath them. Some ten marks above her, sunlight filtered down, casting shifting halos through the water. The sky above rippled. The sun smeared into gold.

"*Kharasdir...*" The voice curled around her, resonant and joyful. "*You came.*"

A gentle current lifted her hair in slow, drifting waves. From the depths, a diaphanous tendril reached for her, its touch featherlight—a whisper rippling against her skin.

Then came another.

And another.

They moved like silk ribbons in a slow, reverent dance, winding around her limbs and tracing the pulse at her wrists and throat. Her snake tattoos stirred, shimmering to life in a luminous blue. One by one, they peeled from her skin like bands of light caught in the current, drifting outward to meet the tendrils.

A warm current wrapped around her like an embrace. With it came a sense of belonging. Pressure swelled in her ears, and the silence fractured into a melodious thrum, as though the lake itself wanted to sing with her. If she yielded to its call, would she surface again? If she climbed out, what truth might she lose?

Leógham... The thought of him cut through the tempting haze. She bent her knees and pressed her feet into the silty floor, preparing to thrust herself upward.

And just as quickly, the water *moved*.

14

THE WATER GODS

How swiftly resolve crumbles when faced with simple, yet undeniable truths. - Poliormos

Leógham held his head underwater until his lungs burned.

When he flung it back, water streamed from his hair in a silver arc. He dragged air into his chest, weighing whether to plunge his head under again. He'd do anything to quiet the heat roaring through him, because the images refused to fade: the curves on her body, the sway of her movements. Desire gripped him like a fever.

Then he became aware of it.

The silence.

Her singing, which moments ago had ensorcelled him, had vanished. Frowning, he turned toward her spot behind the bushes. He saw no movement. No sounds from her, either. Only birdsong and the rustle of wind through the trees.

Where did she—?

Leógham sprang to his feet, tugging on his trousers, and scanned the shoreline for her.

"Kharis?" he called.

No answer.

He spotted her clothes, her boots, the bar of soap. But not her. The lake shimmered, a thousand tiny suns dancing across its surface, indifferent to the terror rising in his gut.

"Kharis?" he shouted again. "Where are you?"

A sudden flash of cobalt tore through the water. The lake convulsed. Waves surged from the center, battering the shore and scattering liquid shards. Then, as swiftly as it began, the lake fell still, its surface smooth as glass.

The wards have been triggered. Someone, or something, had tried to break through.

Leógham vaulted over brush and rock and dove headfirst into the lake. The cold slammed into him like a blow. He powered through it, arms cutting through the depths with desperate force. A shadow hovered below. Limbs floating. Hair spreading like dark smoke.

Kharis!

His arms locked around her, and he kicked hard, pushing upward. His lungs screamed, muscles burning as he fought for the surface.

Water parted above him, and cool air hit his face.

"Kharis," he rasped. "Talk to me."

She gurgled. A fragile breath broke from her lips, followed by a weak gasp.

Relief slammed into him.

He swam for the shore, dragging her with him. When his feet finally touched the bottom, he barely restrained himself from gripping her arms too hard.

"Are you all right?"

She coughed again, then whispered hoarsely, "I'm fine."

Fine...?

He'd told her to be careful. He'd warned her. And then he'd found her at the bottom of the lake...

"Fine?" His heart hammered in his throat. "You could've

drowned." He tightened his grip on her without thinking, pressing her to his chest to anchor her to the world of the living. "You could've died." And he couldn't bear the thought. Not again.

"Leógham...?" She shivered, words broken.

He took a jagged breath to calm the storm brewing in his chest and forced calm into his voice. "What happened?"

"I wanted to try it."

"You don't even know how to swim!" His nostrils flared, heat pulsing through him like a fever—angry at her, yes, but angrier at himself.

Then, it hit him like a hammer to his head.

She was nearly naked. In *his* arms. Pressed to his bare chest.

Instinct took over. He let go and jerked her back, putting space between them. She slipped beneath the surface with a startled gasp.

The fires can burn me now. And forever.

He caught her arm and dragged her toward the shore, water sloshing around them. Kharis coughed and gasped, muttering her peculiar curse, "Blasted!"

He released her, keeping his back to her. He meant to walk away, build some distance, but his legs refused to obey.

"Leógham...?"

He cast a backward glance. Her chemise clung wet and translucent, outlining more than it concealed. He cursed silently, looking up and debating whether a second plunge into the lake might restore his sanity.

Silence stretched between them, long and taut as a drawn bowstring.

"I'm truly sorry," she said. "I think..." She paused. "I think I belong to water."

A chill slid through him. He turned around, scowling. "What did you say?"

"Um..." She grimaced. "That I should ally with water.

Forge some kind of connection." She glanced away. "I have much to thank it for."

A muscle jumped along his jaw as he turned her words over. "What do you mean?"

She took a step back, a heated flush rising on her cheeks. "I mean... I should thank the water gods who have protected me." She fiddled with her sleeve. "I should've died when I fell down the waterfall. Maybe they led you to the lake where you found me. I don't know how to explain it, but I can't ignore it, either."

Leógham didn't answer immediately. She had a right to her beliefs, even if they roused every warning bell in his head. He took a deep breath to let his anger recede. He'd shouted at her, but was he truly protecting her—or silencing his own fear?

"I shouldn't be afraid." She picked at a thread before finally looking at him. "If the water gods look after me, maybe I should stop running and start listening."

Water gods. The phrase made his skin crawl. "Assuming such things exist, how do you forge this"—his lips twitched— "alliance?"

Kharis shrugged. "When I entered the lake, it felt like..." Her eyes narrowed as she searched for a word. "A welcome."

His voice dropped an octave, all softness stripped away. "A welcome?"

She offered an uncertain nod.

A cold prickle slid down his spine. He believed her amnesia was genuine. But what if this—*all* of this—wasn't chance?

The answer stalled on his tongue.

She wasn't Hegran. She moved like a trained assassin. And she hid secrets in her skin, magic unknown to him. And he—fool that he was—had bound himself to her via a Hegran promise. Were these moments with her fleeting? An idyllic illusion that would shatter the instant her memories returned? He swallowed the ache and steeled himself to keep a calm demeanor.

Leógham, the healer, stepped back.

Leógham, the steadfast, duty-bound Hegran warrior, emerged. His tone was steady. Cold, even.

"If I'm to light your path," he said, "I must know what I'm walking into."

She wrung her hands, biting her lip, yet nodded. "When I stepped in, my snakes changed. Not black anymore—they glowed blue, as if the water had called to them."

He dragged a hand through his hair to hide the unease knotting his gut. The inscribed magic in those tattoos had reacted to... the water? The notion had him cracking his knuckles. "What happened next?"

She glanced up, then lowered her head, as if suddenly afraid of the man now facing her. "Tendrils came out of nowhere, but something held them back."

Leógham knew what had stopped them.

"Sit," he commanded.

She obeyed without question, settling onto the sandy shore.

"There's something I've been meaning to tell you," he started. "And now's the right time. This place—what you see —isn't what it seems. It's a contained sphere, magically sealed and heavily warded. No one enters this realm without my explicit invitation."

She looked up, eyes wide, lips parted in surprise. "You... created it?"

A bitter smile flickered across his face. "The Elatharim did, a long time ago. This was my uncle's realm. He offered it to me after Elinor died."

"Your sanctuary," she said quietly.

He inclined his head. "Magic sought you, no doubt. But my realm repelled it."

Her face paled. "What would it want with me?"

He had no answer to that. "Has it happened before?"

She shook her head hard. Her fingers caressed her forearm, as if to calm the serpents inked there. Through the wet fabric, he could see them glide over her skin, slow and graceful. It took effort not to touch them, let alone watch them.

He hesitated, the question weighing heavily, then tilted his head toward her arm. "Does it mean anything that I can see your markings move?"

Her breath caught. "You see them... move?" Her gaze dropped to the arm, and her hand stilled. "Is this—?" Her voice faltered. "Is this why you avoid looking at my body?"

His pulse jumped. "I—no—I don't *avoid*—" He coughed, eyes flicking toward the woods. "It's not appropriate to..." He rubbed the back of his neck, back to fumbling like a fool.

"Anyway." He cleared his throat. "I don't... avoid it." He tilted his head, focusing on the wispy clouds. "Why would I?"

Her face said everything. She didn't believe a word.

He dropped to one knee and gently tilted her chin up. A glorious silver starburst radiated into her lovely sapphire irises... Blue eyes, a known trait of the Water Kin clan. His chest hollowed. *Hegra's oldest enemies.* Every child was taught to fear and hate them. Had he dragged one into his home? Into his heart?

And if she were one of them... what would he do?

"Do you know who the Water Kin are?" he asked, the words clipped.

She paused on a blink, then shook her head. "No." Her brow furrowed. "Should I?"

Her confusion was genuine. Blessedly, gloriously genuine. His hand dropped from her chin. He rose and crossed his arms, pivoting clumsily.

"No need to know," he said, forcing a light tone. "Just curious."

"Are they your water gods?" Her eyes sparkled with innocent wonder.

Leógham let out a soft laugh, the sound loosening some of the knots in his chest. "It's not like that. In Hegra..." He hesitated about what to say or how to correct her, then shrugged.

"No. We don't have water gods."

15

POLIORMOS

A promise made from the heart does not heed the turning of stars nor the ruin of empires—such a promise walks beside the soul until time itself forgets to count. - Poliormos

When Kharis and Leógham reached the cabin, the last light had faded. Violet dusk brought the first scatter of stars.

Leógham lingered, leaning on the veranda, looking at Sharan. In three more weeks, the moon would be full again, and Tung would give Sharan its peculiar red eye for three nights.

His nephew would return by then.

A knot settled in his stomach. *Flaming gods, three weeks is all I have.*

Hrag's arrival would drag everything into the light, and Kharis would no longer be a secret. How would he explain her to him? To anyone?

Through the window, he glimpsed Kharis, oblivious to the storm raging in his mind. How would he protect her from them? From the world? One of his hands fisted. He still had no plan, loathing how truly and utterly powerless he felt.

Inside, Kharis stacked logs into the hearth as he'd taught her, her movements unhurried, as if she belonged here. And fires help him; it *felt* like she did.

"I'll get water for tea." She lifted the ewer and stepped away. Her scent lingered.

Leógham crouched by the hearth, casting a wary glance toward the door. With a flick of his fingers, a thread of fire spun into being and jumped from his palm to the logs. The fire caught instantly, crackling to life. A flame licked across his skin, scarlet at first... then darker. Clenching his hand, the sparks died before they betrayed him.

He rolled his shoulders, loosened his neck, and stepped back to stretch his back. Her scent was everywhere, and he wondered how to make it last forever. Even without a Hegran promise, Leógham knew.

He could never walk away from her.

❧

When Kharis returned, Leógham was suspending the pot above the hearth. The sight of him tending to their little space stirred an unexpected warmth in her chest. She lingered by the table, her fingers brushing the worn wood surface.

"I thought you were still angry at me." He'd spoken little on their hike back.

He glanced at her. "Angry? No. Concerned? Absolutely."

Outside, crickets serenaded the night.

"I didn't mean to worry you," she said.

"I know." He massaged the back of his neck, his nervous tic. "And I didn't mean to yell at you. I just..." He trailed off, shaking his head. "I'm glad you're safe." He said nothing more, instead walking toward the shelves, fingers tracing book spines until he selected two.

"Here." He handed her one. "Dinner won't take long."

He pulled out a chair and sat, heaving a long sigh. The book he'd chosen opened in his hands, and the reading soon absorbed him. He twirled a lock of his hair as he read, unaware he was doing it.

Kharis sat across from him, the book he'd given her untouched on her lap.

What made him happy? Not content, not at peace, but truly, deeply happy? She owed him that much—and now was the time to learn.

"Leógham?"

He hummed in acknowledgment, his attention never leaving the page.

"What's your book about?"

His eyes lit with surprise. "It's from an ancient Hegran philosopher."

Before he could retreat into the text, she pressed, "But what is it about?"

His fingers tapped on the page. "It's hard to summarize. This volume explores the concepts of time, reality, and illusion. Some scholars say it's about love, but I think it's a metaphor."

That piqued her curiosity. "Tell me more. Please?"

Leógham pursed his lips in thought. "Maybe I should start at the beginning and give you context." He marked the page he'd been reading and closed the book. "This philosopher was a prominent member of the Elatharim, an ancient race that birthed elemental magic."

Her lips parted slightly, her mind already spinning with possibilities. Leógham let out a short laugh.

Her eyes narrowed. "What's so funny?"

"Your curiosity is… endearing." His smile got her heart fluttering. "The author mentions a few individuals. Lord Vinashtagha gave rise to fire magic. Lady Sora, water. Lord Haizal, air. And so forth. Their actions reshaped the world. One of them, for example, created this realm."

She couldn't help her, "Ooh!"

"Because of them, every clan member today is tied to elemental forces—fire, water, wind, and such. At some point," Leógham leaned back in his chair, "they returned to Andaheimur."

The word rolled through her mind like thunder. Light shattered the fog, enough to shift her into a vast, otherworldly realm of gleaming ivory. Endless and still. A place in a constant state of creation, yet eternally empty.

And just as quickly, that fragment of memory vanished.

The fog rushed back in, but a honeyed taste lingered in her mouth. "Tell me more about your book."

Their eyes met—and held—until he glanced away, running a hand through his hair. "Yes, of course."

He wetted his lips, fingers brushing the book's edge. "The author often mentions one in his writings. He called her the other half of his soul, a missing piece of himself. He wrote that, until they were reunited, the universe itself would remain incomplete."

"The other half of his soul..." The words clung to her. "They must've loved each other deeply."

Leógham shifted in his chair. "Not in the literal sense." He sounded cautious. "Yes, he longed for her, but as a philosophical ideal. He was exploring what that yearning *meant*, not pursuing a person so much as seeking truth across time and space."

The warmth drained from her smile. "Oh. I see."

"You look disappointed."

She waved it off with a nervous laugh. "It's not romantic, but still interesting."

One of his brows lifted, but she stubbornly kept her grin.

He went on. "This philosopher believed the universe evolved from chaos to order, emptiness to wholeness. He wrote of elemental balance and the fusion of opposites. His beloved was symbolic. A metaphor for harmony. Some scholars say he spoke of a woman. Others believe he spoke of the soul. Or the world. Or the Infinite itself."

"The Infinite?" Kharis echoed, curious.

"The Infinite is the source of all creation." He gestured to the window. "The force that sustains all that you see."

A spark lit in her mind. "Ah! Like the Blessed Mother."

His lips twitched, not quite a smile. "Yes," he said. "But we don't use that title in Hegra."

A gentle correction. Leógham was always courteous when she used her terms, apparently foreign to him, but for the first time, there was a thread of unease she hadn't seen before.

"What's your interpretation?" She steered him back.

Leógham crossed his arms. "I don't know yet. Maybe that's what I like most. The meaning changes each time I read it."

"So... if he's searching for her, how did he lose her?"

A quick snort escaped him, followed by a smirk. "You're full of questions tonight."

"When am I not?"

He rested his head in his hand, elbow perched on the armrest. His eyes held her, and the world seemed to thrum around him until a hint of red brightened his cheeks, and his gaze dipped. "Your curiosity knows no bounds."

"If I'm interrupting—"

"You're not." His fingers traced circles on the cover. His eyes kept their glow, as if he wanted to know what else stirred her curiosity. "Poliormos is best discussed like this—as conversation."

The name came with a sudden tremor.

It echoed in her mind, reverberating through the hollow spaces where her memories should've been. She didn't know how or why, but the moment Leógham uttered the name, it had somehow belonged to her.

"The author is... Poliormos?" The name rolled across her tongue, wrapped in centuries of forgotten truths. A relic that belonged to her, even though she couldn't explain why.

Leógham nodded. "Yes, and this book's called *The North Star*."

And like that, a long-dormant spark flickered awake, pulsing with quiet insistence as though reaching for her, calling her toward something vital—something she'd forgotten.

Leaning into the pull of this strange current, she asked, "Would you mind reading aloud?"

Leógham blinked slowly. Then his smile widened—slow, warm, and dazzling. He reached for the book, flipped it to the page he'd marked, cleared his throat, and began to read:

"My love for you is a whisper on the wind, a call as
soft as the hush of summer leaves. I do not command
it, nor chase it, but it always finds you. I follow,
though the path may be steep and the way uncertain,
for your love does not deceive, nor does it seek to
bind. It asks for nothing, yet it gives all. It lifts me on
wings unseen, steadying my hand when doubt lingers.
Your love does not demand. It simply is, and in its
truth, it endures in me."

"That..." Her breath slipped out slowly. "That was beautiful."

He looked up from the page, gently biting his lip. "Shall I continue?"

She nodded once. "Please."

He read on, his voice steady.

"My beloved has wandered into the garden, where
lilies and peonies bloom in splendor. As I look upon
the one I love, my sorrow is appeased, and my heart is
calmed, never concealed. As I gaze upon my beloved,
my thirst is quenched; my soul is tempered and—"

"I know this!" She straightened, nearly bouncing in her seat. "I've heard this before."

He paused, brow furrowed. "You have?"

She leaned forward, nodding, feet tapping the floor. "Please, keep reading."

He resumed. Kharis recited as he read, the words spilling from her lips in perfect rhythm with his.

"I am my beloved's, and my beloved is mine. We walk together, hand in hand. Never ahead, and never behind."

When the last line fell into silence, she lingered in it— eyes closed, lips curved in wonder. The passage felt right. Intimate. Familiar. As though the message wasn't in her mind but in her soul.

"How do you know this passage?" Leógham asked, his voice strained.

The magic of the moment dimmed.

"This book's not widely known," he said. "Poliormos was an alchemist, an astronomer, and a healer, well versed in the workings of the natural world. His treatises shaped generations and became part of the canon. *The North Star* is... obscure. And yet, I believe it to be his most pivotal work."

She sat back, and something dark inside her stirred. "Why do you believe Poliormos is a *he*?"

His words faltered. "Shouldn't it be obvious? He's on a quest to find his beloved."

Her head tilted, fingers curled around the armrests. "And that makes the author... a man?"

Leógham's posture stiffened. "It's implied in the tone, the focus, the subjects covered... He yearns for the woman he loves."

"Or it could be the other way around," she said. "A woman writing of the man—*or woman*—she loves."

Leógham closed the book with a snap, biting the inside of his cheek. A gust of wind rattled the window panes.

When he spoke again, his voice had cooled. "In Hegra, it's men who seek. Men protect. Men provide." A beat passed, then his tone hardened. "As for your other suggestion... that kind of relationship isn't accepted in Hegra."

A small ember popped and landed on the floor, glowing for a breath before fading to black.

"Men face danger, take risks." His words came sharper now, more rigid—a recitation ingrained in him. "Why would a woman do any of that?"

Kharis drew in a deep breath, shoulders rising, then stiffening. "Are you joking?"

She rose. Slowly. Menacingly.

Her eyes narrowed with icy precision. "I would traverse the Netherworlds of Ifran to find the one I love. I would fight ten of those monstrous mathanim to save him."

The air around her shimmered with heat.

"And if he were lost to me," she struck her chest, breath heaving, "I would plunge through every timeline and world, through every universe. I would *not* stop, Leógham. Because if he were worthy of my love, my devotion for him would be boundless."

She stepped in close, bracing her hands on the chair's arms. Her face hovered a breath from his, the fire in her chest unrelenting.

"Why do you assume women feel or do less?" she asked. "That love, when woven into a woman's heart, is weak and inconsequential? That we're soft or small? That we should sit idle while fate unfolds?"

Leógham's lips parted, cheeks reddened, but no sound followed. She straightened and crossed her arms. "What proof do you have that Poliormos was a man?"

His gaze dropped to the book. "Well... the writing—"

"Set aside your *assumptions*," she cut in. "What if I told you I wrote that book?"

He raised his hands in a calming gesture. "Kharis, please. There's no need to get upset."

"Oh, don't." Her voice flared. "Do *not* tell me how I should feel."

"Fine," he snapped. "No one knows for sure."

The air between them sizzled with tension.

Leógham exhaled sharply. "Little is known about Poliormos, who lived during the Third Hegran Period, a thousand years ago. Many volumes survived the Shattering, but they were written in a language that lacked gender. Later translations supplied it—"

He sniffed the air. Froze.

"Flames above—the stew!"

16

BURNT STEW AND BITTER TRUTHS

Bitter truths, like burnt food, are easier to swallow when you have no choice. - Poliormos

Kharis and Leógham sat in tense silence, their spoons navigating the charred remnants in the stew. The occasional crackle from the fireplace interrupted the uneasy lull. Kharis didn't look at him, scraping her spoon along the bowl, nudging blackened bits aside. He could've sworn red sparks snapped across her fingers, as if, at any moment, she might ignite and leave him as scorched as the stew.

He set his spoon down, his appetite long gone. There was no easy way to broach the subject except to say it outright.

"Kharis?"

Her grip tightened around the spoon. "What is it?"

"My nephew will arrive in three weeks. He already suspects something, so I can't hide you any longer."

Her jaw worked once; the spoon tapped the bowl. "Understood."

"Thus, we must tell the same story to keep you safe."

Her gaze shot to him, sapphire orbs locking onto him. "Same story? What do you mean?"

Leógham massaged his temples, a headache already forming. "I must hide that you're a woman."

Her lips twitched; her jaw set. "And how, exactly, do you plan to do that?"

The headache slammed onto him.

Leógham set his bowl down. "You spoke of becoming a man. The thing is, given your build, you can pass for a young lad. With the right clothes, and..." He hesitated as if the following words might seal his doom. "A tighter binding for your chest, it would work."

Kharis hugged herself, hiding her chest, and stared at him as though he'd lost his mind. "You want me to pretend to be a boy?"

"Yes." Leógham didn't know what to do with his arms. "You're rather lean of form, and if we dress you in loose enough clothing, it could work."

"Lean... of form?" Her cheeks flushed. "Are you saying I already look like a boy?"

"No!" Leógham put his hands up. "That's not what I'm saying." He pinched the bridge of his nose. This was already spiraling out of control. "Look," he tried again. "Hrag will ask questions. Hence, we must have the same story: I found you badly hurt, unconscious, and have cared for you since. A young mathan mauled you—he'll believe that."

"Leógham." He froze at her sharp tone. "Why must you hide that I'm a woman?"

He knew it was coming. "Well, I must hide more than that."

Her stare pierced him like daggers. "What else?"

He wavered. "That you're not from Hegra." Her frown deepened, but he went on. "To begin, you don't speak like one. You must avoid your expressions—"

"Which ones?"

He scratched his head, looking for ways to make this

more palatable to her. "Blasted. Blessed Mother. Blessed be the earth and sun. Spear me—"

"Then teach me Hegran cursing."

That flustered him. "I'm *not* doing that."

"Fine," she spat. "I won't curse, then. I won't even speak. How about that?"

His lips twitched as he swallowed her remark and began pacing. "We must hide"—his eyes flicked briefly to her arms—"your markings. No one can see them, but that shouldn't be a problem. We wear a lot of clothing—"

"Why?"

He grimaced. "Because we can't walk around half-naked—"

"No, Leógham. Why must I hide my markings? I haven't until now."

"Because they scream you're not from Hegra," he said through gritted teeth.

She lifted her chin and crossed her arms, settling back in the chair. "So what if Hrag sees them?"

He paused, trying to suppress thoughts of the dark consequences. "He'll see you as a threat to Hegra."

Kharis stared at him for a moment too long before she said, "So your brilliant solution is to dress me as a boy and lie about everything? That's your plan?"

It sounded absurd when she put it like that. "Yes."

She huffed. "Do you honestly think he won't see through it?"

"He won't if we're careful. Hegrans won't question what they expect. A young lad recovering from a mathan attack? Plausible. An unmarried woman with mysterious markings and no clear origin? Unacceptable."

Her lips pursed. "What if I don't want to hide who I am?"

Leógham balked at the challenge in her voice. "Then you'll be putting *us* at risk."

She glared at him. He rubbed his chin, aware she needed a

better explanation, so he pulled his chair closer to her and sat.

"I don't know where you came from." He softened his voice. "That alone will raise suspicion. Your markings are unique—a practice unknown to us. According to Hegran Law, your father's household claims you until marriage. Yet, no one would question your presence in my household if you were my fostered student."

He could almost hear her brain clicking and whirring as he explained.

"Many of our laws are outdated," he continued. "Eight years ago, a civil war engulfed Hegra. The side seeking progress won, but barely. The effects of that war still linger, and Hegra remains divided between those who seek change and those who stubbornly cling to the old ways. The effort to abolish these laws continues, but tension remains high even after eight years."

A crease formed between her brows.

"Before the Civil War, some twenty years past, Hegra was embroiled in a conflict with a foreign kingdom. That war was equally bloody, resulting in a stalemate that left deep wounds on both sides. The thirst for revenge runs deep among Hegrans. Combine that with our internal struggles, and you have a kingdom on the edge of chaos—a tinderbox waiting for a spark."

Her hands balled into fists.

He rubbed his forehead. "If I couldn't explain your presence, Hegrans will see you as an enemy. They will imprison and execute you."

Her eyebrows arched, mouth agape. "But I just want to go home."

"And you will," he reassured her.

Kharis didn't answer at once, tracing the edge of the table with her thumb. "So if they look closely enough," she said, "All I have to do is disappear."

His jaw tightened. "If they're looking closely enough," he said, "you won't survive it."

She pressed her lips into a slight grimace. "What kind of place is Hegra?"

"A cursed land." What else could he say? "You could stay here, but I promised never to leave you, and that promise is binding. So, if I were to go to Hegra, you must come with me."

"And if I don't?"

There it was. The tone of defiance that he dreaded most. "Then we can't find out how to return you home."

She looked away, fingers flexing once.

He exhaled quietly. "Everything rests on hiding you in plain sight. It wouldn't be hard to—"

"What name should I use?" Her gaze turned sharp. "You said mine's the name for a flower. Could a Hegran man have a flower's name?"

Her angry edge was back, accompanied by a sprinkling of sarcasm to complete this tasty dish.

"Let me think." He paced the cabin, anxious about what lay ahead for them. *Names, names...* He ran through every male name he could think of, but when he stared at the fireplace, inspiration struck like a spark.

"Benkhi." He turned sharply. "It means 'fire' in the old tongue. Oh, and it fits you." It so fitted her.

"Benkhi," Kharis repeated, testing the name as if it were a garment she wasn't sure would fit her.

Leógham crossed his arms, fingers tapping his bicep.

After her long pause, "Fine."

A small victory, so he allowed himself a small smile. "Good. It's best to start using it now before my nephew arrives. If we fool him, we can fool anyone."

Fooling Hrag. His head began throbbing again.

"Back to the story." He clapped his hands once, already sounding like a tutor. "You got lost while hunting, and a young mathan attacked you. I found you severely injured and took care of you. Now you remember nothing, which isn't a lie." He paced back and forth, wringing his hands. "Our stories must be identical because, otherwise—"

"Yes," she hissed. "It will put *you* in danger."

Leógham stopped, hands falling to his sides, and faced her. "It will endanger *anyone* who knows."

She went completely still. "For helping... me?"

He nodded once. "Your identity as a non-Hegran or a woman must remain hidden. If you're caught, they won't come for you. They'll come for me, my family, and anyone who's shown you the slightest gesture of kindness."

Her shoulders slumped, mouth slackening.

His pulse throbbed in his throat. He rolled his neck and shoulders to calm down. *Can I pull this off?* From the corner of his eye, he saw Kharis studying him with a deep crease on her forehead.

She should stay here. I'll go to Hegra, look for what we need, and—

A sharp sting flared across his skin, halting the thought. The binding magic from the Hegran promise pulsed once, a gentle warning that carried the assurance of agony should he defy it. His hands curled into fists. He couldn't leave her behind now.

Fires burn it all.

Leógham forced a smile and settled into the chair. Their real test would come in three weeks. If they could fool Hrag, they could deceive Hegra. He rubbed a hand over his bearded face, then let it drop into his lap.

"Let's continue this conversation tomorrow," he said. "It's been a long day, and dinner was less than satisfying." He offered her a rueful smile. "With some rest, we might see things in a new light—"

"Give me your dagger."

He stilled, glancing from his belt to her face. "What?"

"Give. Me. Your. Dagger."

He blinked, confused.

"Fine," she spat. "Then you do it."

A pause.

"Do what?"

Kharis yanked her braid from under her shoulder and flung it forward. "Cut it."

"Why?"

"You keep your hair short, even out in this wilderness. I assume that's the Hegran custom for men." She followed his lack of response with a sharp, "Cut it off."

His lips parted. Her reasoning became obvious. *We're doing this.*

"Leógham?" Her voice sharpened. "Now."

He rose slowly and drew his hunting blade. His heart was pounding. Hair was a woman's pride. *What in the fires am I doing...?* And yet, for his plan to work, there was no other option. She held out the braid, and he took it. Her hair was so black, the indigo glimmering so alluring. He was the worst person in the world, forcing her to do this. *Her lovely hair...*

Kharis leaned forward, eyes shut.

A beat of silence.

"I'm sorry." In a single, clean slice, the braid fell away. The blue glimmering stopped as if the braid had been cut off from what fed its beauty.

For a moment, neither of them moved.

Uncertainty flickered across her face, and whatever he'd meant to say withered in the silence between them. He turned to the hearth, tossing the braid into the fire. The flames seized it greedily, dark strands crackling as they twisted and burned. The reek curled through the cabin.

When he glanced over his shoulder, her fingers were tracing the uneven ends of her hair, ghosting over what remained—quietly lamenting her loss. It had been long, dancing past her waist. Now, it barely touched her shoulders.

And still, she lifted her chin. A quiet steadiness settled in her features, the look of someone counting the cost and choosing to pay it. He hated himself for this. Was this the cost of surviving Hegra? To give and sacrifice and hope not to die?

Searching for anything to mend the rift, his gaze landed on the book.

"What if we read more of Poliormos's writings?" A sliver of hope stirred in his heart. "You enjoyed it." He wanted to forget this conversation, the bitter taste of it, the burden it brought. But more than anything, he wanted her to smile again. "Maybe there's a clue about who he—"

Kharis's glare cut through him, fire sparking in her blue-gray eyes.

By the burning gods... Her eye color.

His throat dried at the thought. *What can I use to conceal it?* He needed an answer quickly... and then, he'd have to tell her.

Fires turn me to ash now.

"There's one more thing," he said, his voice small.

She arched a questioning brow.

"Your eyes," he began. "We must conceal the color."

"Anything else?" she asked coolly. "Shall we rid me of my nose? My mouth, perhaps?"

He drew a slow breath. "Do you remember the war, twenty years past? The clan we fought—their people have blue eyes."

Her face drained of color. "And you think I'm one of them?"

"I don't," Leógham said truthfully. "But others will."

Her eyes flicked away, likely calculating how quickly such an assumption could lead to her death. "How do we change it —the color?"

The shelves stored powders in stoppered jars, bundles of dried herbs dangling from strings. He crossed to a cupboard and hesitated for a beat before withdrawing a small glass jar. Inside, a reddish-orange powder caught the light, drawn from flowers once prized for their potent magic—an invaluable prize, the last of it.

"With this." He held the jar between his thumb and finger. "Ground kharisot."

She sagged against her chair. "Good. We'll get more—"

"We can't. The flowers have been extinct for twenty years. No one has seen them since." He returned the jar to its shelf. "I'll make a tincture. A few drops should shift your eye color, though the change will be temporary. We'll have to time how long it lasts."

Her eyes focused on the cupboard. "And when I finish the tincture?"

His breath left him in a sharp exhale. "I'll find another way. Perhaps by then, you'll be on your way home." He picked up the Poliormos book and offered it to her. "Here."

"You want me… to read," her head canted, "when my life hangs in the balance?"

He lifted a shoulder. "Nothing to be done now. Tomorrow, you'll help me gather the rest of the ingredients for the tincture."

She stared at him, eyes wide. His mouth tightened. *What did I just say?* He looked away. He'd never meant to sound dismissive, brushing her fear aside like that.

"Kharis—"

"Fine." She rose and picked the book from the table.

As she settled, her gaze drifted toward the northern window. The fire crackled, bringing her back. Kharis then fixed her attention on the page and began to read. Her questions soon followed, piercing holes in Hegran customs until the ache behind his eyes deepened and the knot in his chest tightened.

Leógham closed his eyes for a moment, forcing calm.

Three weeks. That was all the time before Hegra swallowed them whole.

PART II

MIST AND LOSS

17

HRAG

The loudest hate we hurl at others often echoes the disdain we feel for ourselves. - Poliormos

Leógham moved through the cabin in quiet rhythm, his fingers stained with crushed herbs and resin. Hours passed in slow alchemy as the blend boiled, then simmered, until it yielded a dark orange liquid: the kharisot tincture.

Kharis leaned closer and frowned. "That doesn't look like enough."

His gaze stayed on the vial, thoughtful. *What if she's right?*

"A single drop in each eye should do the trick," he said. "The effect may last days… or months. We won't know until we try it."

Leógham handed her a small mirror and raised the vial to let one drop fall into each eye. She hissed with each. "It stings." Her breath wavered as she blinked a few times.

Wave after wave of orange devoured the sapphire in her eyes, leaving behind a dull gray. The stubborn silver starburst still gleamed, defiant like she was.

The eyes from his dreams vanished. He winced before he

could stop himself, but masked it quickly with a tepid smile. Kharis pursed her lips and glanced away.

Oddly enough, her magic didn't fight the kharisot's effect, apparently ignoring magical deception.

Four days later, blue gathered at the edges. By dusk, sapphire and silver stared back at him.

Now they knew the tincture's limit.

ঙ

Three weeks later, Sharan rose—full and glorious against the night sky, her red eye glaring. As Kharis and Leógham finished breakfast, a horse's neigh split the quiet.

Leógham jolted in his chair, his heart beating a rapid staccato. "I'll greet him first, then bring him inside. Once he's in, it must be as we practiced. And Kharis—"

"Benkhi," she hissed.

"Fires burn me." He rubbed his forehead. One slip, and everything would unravel.

He drew a slow breath and stepped outside.

Hrag was securing two horses to a tree. At eighteen, he was tall, with short brown hair, chiseled features, and forest-green eyes. He wore a black leather jerkin over a gambeson. His riding cloak displayed the Hegran bloodred dragon against a black background.

He greeted Leógham with a half-smile. "Am I here to stay or just passing through?" His tone was wry. He arched a judgmental brow.

The question stung. "You're here to stay."

His nephew's shoulders loosened. "Good. This time, the journey was rough. Lord Saigham dispatched a few Shadowmen to track me."

Leógham's nostrils flared, and he wished to run his sword through that man. "Do *not* use an honorific with that name."

Hrag smirked. "Easy. I lost them."

Leógham's jaw unclenched, though his anger lingered. "If

anyone could, it's you. Yet, I can't ignore that he sent mercenaries after you. Wretched Saigham. May the fires take him."

Hrag chuckled. "Say it louder. No one will hear."

Leógham snorted, finally allowing himself a smile. "It's great to see you."

Hrag flicked his cloak over his shoulder. "That wasn't the case last time..."

Leógham ignored the jab and tousled Hrag's hair with a grin.

"Uncle!" Hrag jerked his head away. "Must you?"

"It's tradition."

Hrag rolled his eyes. "Not a kid anymore."

Leógham smiled quietly, remembering sunlit days chasing after a happy little boy. "I forgot."

Hrag groaned. "You forget a lot of things, old man."

Leógham cocked his head, his smile lingering. "Careful now. I'm only seven years older."

"Since I'm staying, help me get these off the horses." Hrag began unbuckling the saddlebags. "I brought what you asked for." He shoved a bag into Leógham's arms. "It's what you wanted, right?" He squinted at him. "And why'd you ask Ama for clothes?"

That snapped Leógham out of his amusement, the problem now rising to the surface. He clutched the bag tighter, his insides coiling. It was now or never, and "never" wasn't an option. "Hrag... We must talk."

Hrag froze mid-motion, hand still on a buckle. "You're sending me back, aren't you?"

"No." The dialogue he'd practiced... gone. Every word, forgotten. *Flames take me now.* "It's best if I show you." He slung the bag over his shoulders. "Wait here."

Before Hrag could protest, Leógham strode to the cabin and shut the door behind him. "Clothes. Change quickly." He handed the bag to Kharis.

Kharis took it, frowning. "Um..."

"Now." He faced the door, palms pressed flat against it to bar Hrag in case he'd followed. "Please."

Silence stretched behind him. He anticipated her usual protest, or at least a snarky question, and braced himself, gritting his teeth at the notion that this would be an irritating morning. Instead, he heard the soft rustling of fabric behind him.

She was undressing.

The thought struck him hard, stealing the rhythm from his breath. Heat gathered low in his chest before he snuffed it, grinding his jaw until the image broke apart. Hrag waited outside. That alone snapped him back to purpose.

The disguise depended on it. His tunic had hung loose on her, slipping enough to bare the curve of her shoulder or her collarbones. Any glimpse of the markings beneath could unravel everything. The new garments would cover her fully, hiding her tattoos.

It has to work. Because if it didn't—

"Done."

He turned, and the transformation stunned him. A striking boy looked at him. One that would draw plenty of attention. He cursed his luck.

"Let me do the talking."

She frowned. "Bad?"

"Could be."

Outside, Hrag wrestled with the saddles, muttering. When the veranda's flooring creaked, he glanced over his shoulder. His stare honed in on the dark-haired boy, wearing the clothes he'd brought.

Leógham saw the moment a dark, ugly emotion twisted Hrag's expression.

"Who is this?" Hrag hissed.

Kharis's smile faltered. Leógham stepped in front of her. His voice dropped. "Benkhi, could you wait inside?"

Without a word, she slipped back into the cabin.

Hrag's eyes tracked her until the door shut. "Is he why you sent me back?"

"I found him injured after a mathan attack—"

"You're five days out of the only portal to enter your realm and without a horse. Don't insult me." Hrag's glare cut sharply. "You found him here. So tell me—how did he get in when no one can enter your realm?"

Heat flared behind Leógham's eyes. The air around him rippled, warping the woods behind Hrag.

Hrag's glare faltered.

"Who are *you* to question me?" Leógham straightened to his full height, his voice carrying, resonant, and controlled.

Color drained from Hrag's face. He swiftly retreated a step and bowed. "My apologies."

Leógham clicked his tongue. He hadn't meant to frighten him. Yet, if he couldn't convince Hrag, a change of plans would be necessary—a tedious prospect.

"Hrag, you've always trusted me." He softened his tone, though the pulse in his throat betrayed his nerves. "I ask for that trust again."

Hrag's eyes darted from him to the cabin. The silence stretched on. The wind stirred, tugging at the edge of Hrag's cloak. Leógham caught himself clenching his hands.

"Hrag?" He hated the pleading note in his voice. "Do I have it?"

"Yes," he muttered at last.

Thank the Fires.

Hrag's gaze lingered on the woods. His brows knit for a heartbeat before his mouth settled into a hard line. "I have every intention of keeping my eyes on him."

He turned to get the rest of the bags, but Leógham saw the tiny falter in his step despite the squared shoulders. For all his bluster, Hrag's anger was armor—concern and loyalty hammered into steel.

The second horse neighed, breaking the tense silence.

"You brought Balyus." Leógham moved to stroke his muzzle.

"Of course." Hrag crossed his arms. "Ama insisted."

Leógham smiled despite himself. Balyus was another one of Sahrit's attempts to get him to return. Always wise, in her quiet way.

"I owe you the rest," he said. "And a good hunt."

The lack of response confirmed what he already knew: Hrag was sulking. He reminded himself that Hrag, swept by Hegra's relentless cruelty, was only looking out for him.

"Why don't you get to know him first?"

Hrag's response was a sharp, "Why?"

Leógham paused, breath held for a beat. "Because not everyone is trying to stab you in the back."

Hrag's shoulders dipped. "You're too trusting."

"And you trust no one," Leógham said. "We make a fine pair." The tension crackled between them, volatile like a spark near tinders.

Nothing would be easy now.

THE COST OF OBEDIENCE

Power, unchecked by compassion, becomes its own god, demanding sacrifice. Be warned that the cost may be more than you can bear. - Poliormos

Far south, beyond Leógham's forests, the crack of a switch cut through the chamber like lightning.

The Shadowman grunted but didn't cry out. He dropped to one knee, blood glinting at the corner of his mouth, his fists pressed to the floor.

"You're my best," Saigham said. "Sharp as blades, deadly as poison, so how did you lose him?" The next strike landed across the man's shoulder.

The cloaked figure winced and rasped, "Prince Hrag hides behind magic."

"Excuses." Another blow cut the air, cracking against leather and flesh.

The Shadowman's jaw tightened. "We searched through the night, My Lord."

"Then you searched poorly," Saigham's voice rose. "You let a stupid boy slip from under your nose." His boot slammed into the man's chest, sending him sprawling. "Useless fool."

The Shadowman's only answer was a slow exhale through clenched teeth as he curled inward to ease the sting in his ribs.

"Father," came Cuileagh's voice from the archway, smooth and measured. "I'll handle it." His maroon eyes, a mirror to Saigham's, caught the torchlight. "Please, don't lose sleep over this."

Saigham exhaled sharply, saying nothing as his rage drained to icy contempt. Without a word, he stormed out.

The corridors of Teinthir Keep swallowed his footsteps. Servants scattered before him like startled birds. The clack of boots and the rustle of skirts followed his passing. Those not fast enough bowed or curtsied, limbs trembling.

Cuileagh caught up with him and kept pace. "We'll find him," he said. "Rest easy."

Saigham clenched his hand, wishing he were crushing someone's throat instead. "We're the true descendants of Prince Vinashtagha. Aghavor sits on a stolen throne while his son parades as heir. But kill his son, the last of Aghavor's line, and the Houses will fracture. Soon, they'll beg for *me*."

He breathed in, savoring that future, feeling the weight of a crown that had haunted his family for generations.

"I've waited forty years," he whispered. "I won't die watching another thief rule my kingdom." A tremor passed through him in anticipation. "The throne calls to us. I can hear it."

Cuileagh nodded, his smile wide, his red eyes burning with a feverish light.

Children's laughter drifted from the solar ahead. Saigham halted, his fury softened. He paused at the threshold, and the tension in his face eased. Two small boys—his grandsons— were building towers of wooden blocks under their aunt's vigilant eye. They were beautiful, their lineage pure and exalted, the pride of House Teinthir: glossy black hair and bright red eyes.

"Daeroth. Einar," Saigham called, and the boys turned.

"Grandfather!"

He crouched, ignoring the ache in his knees. "My fine little soldiers." From his coat, he drew wrapped sweets—honeyed walnuts—and pressed them into their small hands. "Warriors must keep their strength."

The wide-eyed boys bowed before scampering off in a flurry of giggles. A rare smile ghosted over Saigham's lips as he straightened and squeezed Cuileagh's shoulder. "Yours are good boys. Fine breeding, indeed."

Then his eyes slid to their aunt. Eilidh lingered by the alcove, half hidden, a shadow of fear flickering across her dull, uninspiring features. She bent into a clumsy curtsy. "Father."

The warmth drained from his eyes. She bore Deàrsadh's face, but where his eldest daughter had been fire and defiance, Eilidh was bland and meek—exemplary of graceless mediocrity.

"Tell me," he said coldly, "are the suitors lining up yet?"

Her lips parted, but no sound came.

He snorted. "Useless girl."

With a dismissive wave, he swept out of the room, his cloak flaring behind him.

19

THE STRANGER AMONGST US

Hasty judgments are the blindfolds we tie over our eyes. - Poliormos

K haris sat by the window rather than at the table, keeping to herself. A smoldering tension filled the cabin, waiting for the first spark to ignite.

Hrag had commandeered the conversation, scowling whenever Leógham tried to include her by asking for her opinion. His veiled insults, shrouded in thick layers of sarcasm, nettled her. The pauses between words and syllables sealed his intent in case she'd missed it.

"Oh... really?"

"Delight...ful."

"What...ever."

Each word burned like a poisonous thorn.

"Hrag," Leógham warned. "Enough."

"Oh, come now, Uncle." He wore a fake expression of innocence as his eyes flicked to Kharis. "I'm making conversation."

"I said, *enough*." Leógham's fingers drummed the table in an uneven rhythm.

"Fine." Hrag waved a hand as if heeding the warning, but when Leógham wasn't looking, he sneered at her.

I should fling my spoon at his smug face. She balanced it in her fingers, testing its weight and measuring the distance. *Right between his annoying eyes.*

Sparks pricked her fingertips. Magic bled into the metal, and a faint sizzle rose where sweat met steel. The handle darkened. A bitter metallic reek filled her room.

Leógham looked around, puzzled by the scent. She nearly dropped the utensil. *I must be easy to miss, harmless.* But her restraint was fraying, and Hrag only fanned the fire.

Leógham shifted toward her. He blinked at the spoon, then at her.

"Uncle." Hrag tapped the table. "The hunt?"

Leógham clicked his tongue. "I heard you."

Kharis gripped the spoon, the handle biting into her palm. *Strangling him will be so satisfying—*

The flames in the hearth flared, licking the air with sudden intensity before shrinking back into their subtle crackle.

Hrag flinched, head snapping toward the fireplace. "What was that?"

"Not sure." Leógham rose and crouched by the hearth, tilting his head back to peer up the flue. "It might've been a draft."

For a breath, Hrag's stare sharpened on her.

The vision of a massive blaze devouring the land served as a harsh reminder that if she ever lost control of her power, she'd burn everything. That knowledge cooled her temper.

I must get out. Now.

Spotting the empty bowls, she seized the excuse they offered. Crossing the space, she reached across the table to gather them. Leógham's hand shot out to stop her. "What are you doing?"

She clutched the bowls, tugging against his hold. "You have things to discuss. I'll wash these."

"You don't have to—"

"Let him," Hrag cut in. "The bowls won't wash themselves."

"He needs to know what we're planning for the hunt," Leógham snapped.

"And what can the boy do besides wash dishes and carry our weapons?" He reclined in his chair, arms crossed, giving Kharis a cold, scrutinizing look. "Look at him. Barely half your size. Rabbits are all he can hunt. A hindrance, I say." He glared at her. "You should stay."

It would be so easy to yield and show Hrag what she could do beyond hunting rabbits. Instead, she snatched the bowls from Leógham and counted her breaths.

"Perhaps we can discuss Poliormos later?" Leógham said —his attempt to smooth out the tension.

"What about it?" Hrag asked, a cold stare still on Kharis.

"We've been discussing passages from one of my books—"

"Why?" Hrag lifted his chin with a sneer. "He can't read?"

"Benkhi asks good questions." Leógham's voice now carried an edge.

Hrag huffed with a flick of his hand. "Not interested."

Having had enough, Kharis stormed out, rushed toward the water tub, and splashed her face a few times. But the water did little to ease her anger. It burned hot beneath her skin. Her fingertips were already glowing like embers. To tamp it, she plunged her hands into the water, the cold biting into her skin.

The hiss of steam broke the quiet.

The smoldering heat faded. Lowering herself onto the grass, she leaned against the tub. Her task wasn't to stay inconsequential—a shadow posing as a boy in a place she knew nothing about. She had to master her magic, head north, and somehow "end it all"—though what *that* meant still eluded her.

Water trickled from her damp hair. A drop hit her skin and hissed to steam. Another drop. Another wisp of steam.

The night was silent. Even the crickets had stopped chirping as if they'd sensed what she was. Kharis exhaled, closing her eyes to steady herself.

No one must ever know I'm a monster.

20

THE BURDEN OF MEMORIES

> *Some burdens we carry not on the shoulders but in the heart, where no one can see the scars they leave behind. - Poliormos*

That night, long after the cabin had gone silent, sleep refused to claim her.

The flames had long surrendered to the night's quiet, the glowing embers painting larger shadows across the walls. She closed her eyes, willing herself to fall asleep, but soon gave up. Hrag's voice echoed in her mind. His taunts and glares—every venom-laced word—replayed relentlessly.

Heat crawled over her palms, embers threatening to bloom. She clenched her hands, willing the fire to die.

Turning slightly, she made out Leógham's form stretched out on the cot. Not far from him, Hrag lay sprawled on a bedroll, his chest rising and falling with each breath. She lay in Leógham's bed, a location that generated a new set of arguments before the evening was over.

"He takes the bed," Leógham had said.

Hrag had scoffed, bitter. "Why? Let him sleep on the floor. I bet he's used to it."

Kharis had clenched her jaw so tightly her back teeth ached. She'd bitten back a dozen retorts, letting Leógham handle it.

"He was injured," Leógham had countered. "My decision is final."

"Injured or not, he shouldn't—"

"*Enough*, Hrag." The authority in Leógham's voice had silenced the boy, though his scowl remained etched on his face for the rest of the evening.

Hrag didn't like her.

He's a risk I can't ignore. A thorn in my side. A potential enemy. If he ever uncovered her secret, he'd celebrate its exposure with a vindictive glee, seizing the chance to blame her for dragging Leógham into this dangerous ruse.

She tiptoed out of the cabin, quietly closing the door behind her. Her warm breath curled up against the pre-dawn darkness. That northward tug pulled on her, always there, even in the quiet of night. But... which way was north?

She sat on the cool grass, mesmerized. This place was a sphere of contained magic. She couldn't imagine such a feat.

Sharan, midway in the sky, shone on the world below. Tung had caught up with its sister moon and gave Sharan her red eye, but what would Sharan see? The majestic Silver River was Kharis's one constant in a world that didn't feel her own. It stretched across the sky, a luminous, translucent band of light formed by countless stars that swept from horizon to horizon.

"Please guide me home," she whispered. "What about you?" Fiddling with her bracelet, she tapped on the jade stone. "Will you ever light my path home?" She reached for her braid, but it was long gone. Now, Benkhi, not Kharis, lived in these clothes, so she closed her eyes and listened to the crickets and frogs.

"Why are you outside?" a deep voice whispered.

She started, not expecting Leógham to be up.

"It's cold." He draped a blanket over her before settling down beside her. "What are you doing up?"

"Well...?" She scratched her cheek, feeling caught. "Why are you up?"

He studied the night sky. "I couldn't sleep."

"That makes two." Kharis hugged her knees and wrapped the blanket tighter around herself. "I hope it's not over the same thing."

His weary sigh misted into a billowing cloud. "I expected it to be difficult, but I didn't think it would be this bad." A pause. "Are you warm enough?"

Kharis nodded, glad Leógham sat beside her. He'd become her other constant, as reliable as the Silver River overhead. "We can share the blanket."

"It wouldn't be—"

She scooted closer before he could finish his sentence with "proper," closing the gap between them. "There, now we can share it."

Leógham stiffened like a log. This man was shy to a fault.

"I owe you my life," she said. "Sharing the blanket is the least I could do." She'd hoped for an arm to wrap around her shoulders, but Leógham remained as rigid as a stone pillar. Warm but stiff. "What are we going to do?"

He glanced at the vastness of the night sky, hands flat on the ground, fingers fanned across the clover. "It's not going well, is it?"

"It's... awful," she confessed.

"Let's give it a few days. The journey here is tiring—five days one way. Hrag also encountered a few challenges along the way. However, with some rest and a few days focused on something he enjoys, perhaps he'll be less... difficult."

Kharis frowned. "He dislikes me. I don't think that will change soon." Leógham's silence confirmed her suspicion. "Why do I sense there's more to him?"

He exhaled, the rush of air heavy. "Because there is. You already know why I'm here. Hrag... his pain runs as deep."

"How so?"

Leógham's gaze dropped to the mossy ground, lost in a memory. "Eight years ago, assassins invaded our home. That day, my father and I were away, tending to business. My mother had stayed, playing with Hrag and his sister when the attack began.

"When Mother heard the commotion, she locked Hrag in an armoire and ran out to find my niece, putting distance between him and the assailants. That decision saved him. My father and I rushed back when the alert was sounded, but we were too late."

A slow, uneven breath escaped his lips. His fingers curled into a fist against his thigh, his knuckles whitening. "I found Hrag in the armoire hours later. He was terrified, barely able to speak. No one else survived." A breathless lull. "It's why I fought in the civil war."

The story struck her like an arrow, piercing straight through her heart. Painful. Unexpected. Kharis lowered her chin, waiting for the shock to abate. What could she even say to something like that?

"I'm sorry." Her voice was unsteady. "I shouldn't have asked—"

"Don't." He softly interrupted her apology. "Hrag has his reasons for putting up a wall. Please give him some time. He'll come around."

"And if he doesn't?"

Leógham let out a sigh that misted into the chilly night air. "I'd rather not think about it until I must."

An owl hooted in the night. Another responded before the flutter of wings wove through the trees.

"He's wary of strangers, isn't he?" she asked.

"He finds it... quite difficult," he said at last. A pause. "Pain has cursed us."

"Then break it."

He turned to her, eyebrows lifting.

"Pain marks every life," she continued. "Nothing can be

done about it. When it lingers too long, it may stem from our inability to forgive ourselves. We endure it because it's all we've known—no one has ever shown us there's another way to live. We must light the darkness so those around us can envision happiness and believe it's possible."

After a pause, a small smile tugged at his lips. "Poliormos has impressed you."

Kharis shrugged. "I suppose."

Leógham returned to watching the stars. "It sounds as if you've suffered a lot."

She prayed for a memory that could deny it, but her mind remained a stubborn void. "If that's the case, my loss of memory is a blessing." She glanced at him. "Perhaps fate brought us together so we can help each other weather the storm and break our curses." She tugged at her sleeve. "We're here to ease each other's pain."

Leógham shifted his weight, some unreadable emotion softening his expression. "I like the idea." His eyes brightened, moonlight catching in them when he smiled. "I like it—a lot."

When their eyes met, the world fell away, and Kharis saw an unshakable truth: that if they faced the storm together, they could navigate their fury and reach the shore.

Even the fiercest tempest could be weathered, so long as one had an anchor.

Was Leógham hers?

The thought caught her off guard. Heat bloomed across her cheeks, her pulse quickening as she looked away. "I like the idea, too."

Silence settled easily between them.

Above, the Silver River flowed across the heavens, a radiant current she wished would never fade.

21

THE HUNT BEGINS

Every step sows a thread; some weave bonds, others snares. With every twist, a story unfolds; with each thread, a choice, a call to action—a new fate. - Poliormos

Two days later, the trio devoured breakfast before heading out. Hrag buzzed with excitement, itching to start. Kharis requested seconds to annoy him, eating each bite slowly. Leógham rolled his eyes, covering for her by serving himself another helping. When Hrag wasn't looking, she flashed Leógham a grin. He shook his head at her, but the corner of his mouth betrayed a smile.

The small victory made breakfast that much better for her. If she could, she'd sing aloud.

Leógham and Hrag gathered their belongings. The expedition, conducted on foot, would require camping in the wilderness for at least one night while tracking deer. Sensing she was in their way, she stepped outside to examine the Hegran horses—muscular, towering, with feathery hooves. She kept a respectful distance; one kick could send her flying like dandelion seeds.

The cabin door creaked open, and she turned. Leógham stepped out, an easy smile on his face, and handed her a bag.

"Is one of the horses yours?" she asked.

He tilted his head in their direction. "Balyus, the black one."

She slung the bag over her shoulders, testing its weight. "Both are beautiful animals."

"Heavy?" Leógham asked.

"Not at all. I can carry more—"

"Great." Hrag stepped out of the cabin and, having heard her comment, tossed her a bag that she nearly missed—his payback for breakfast.

Leógham, reaching the same conclusion, glared at him.

"What?" Hrag feigned confusion. "He said he could carry more."

Leógham frowned. "I thought *you* were going to carry it."

"And he said he could carry more—"

"I'll do it!" Kharis had had enough of their bickering. She grabbed the second knapsack and slung it over her shoulder, adjusting its weight while pointedly ignoring Hrag's sneer. Leógham patted her back, a quiet counter to Hrag's pettiness.

"Let's head out." Leógham started down the trail, and both followed him. Hrag, however, turned to Kharis with a smirk that signaled he wasn't finished with her and quickened his pace to catch up with his uncle.

As expected, he monopolized the conversation to exclude her, so she ignored the men.

Kharis walked behind them, losing herself in the forest's rhythm. The path wound on, the men's voices dwindling to murmurs. Leaves whispered in the breeze. Her fingers trailed along rough bark. Time stretched, unhurried, her thoughts drifting with it—

A branch snapped behind her.

She turned, scanning the trees. Nothing moved—only light and shadow trading places. A breeze brushed the back of her neck like an icy finger, the touch raising gooseflesh along her arms. A hint of heat flared inside her but vanished just as fast. The woods remained still.

Probably nothing.

She pursed her lips, took one last glance, and picked up her pace.

22

THE STAG

What we do in this life is but echoes of what we wrote before—the exact words, drawn again and again, until the gods, satisfied, complete the final verse, and a new saga begins. - Poliormos

L eógham walked beside Hrag while keeping an ear to Kharis, who trailed behind. This couldn't be easy for her.

Despite the tension, the cool air carried the promise of autumn, light flickering through the canopy. He was about to call for a water break when a series of loud, guttural roars tore through the forest, reverberating between the trees.

"A stag," Hrag said.

Another deep bawl echoed through the woods. With Leógham's nod, they left the bags and climbed a rocky knoll. At the crest, they crawled to the rim, peering over into the meadow below.

The stag's bellow rolled through the trees as it stepped into the clearing—a young male, its reddish-brown coat gleaming in the sunlight. Heavy, well-formed antlers crowned its head, giving it the presence of a forest prince.

"It must stand twelve hands at the shoulder," Hrag whispered. His whole body hummed with anticipation, fingers twitching around the curve of the bow.

"Take the first shot," Leógham offered, hoping this would improve Hrag's dark demeanor.

Hrag crawled back and, in a smooth motion, bent the wood and slipped the string into place. Slow steps carried him to the knoll's rim. He nocked an arrow, waited, and when the opportunity arose, he released. The arrow flew, zipping through the air. A heartbeat later, it struck its mark, entering behind the shoulder and exiting in front of the opposite leg. The stag gave a sharp grunt. It staggered a few paces before it toppled onto its side.

Leógham squeezed Hrag's shoulder. "Well done. A fine shot."

Hrag returned the smile, easy and pleased. His eyes slid to Kharis and lingered there, cold and deliberate, the threat clear in his expression: that he could do the same to her.

Kharis held his stare for a heartbeat, then glanced away, neither startled nor impressed.

Leógham's chest tightened, unease stirring hard and fast.

Kharis let their voices fade to a distant murmur. The arrow's whistle and thud as it struck the stag echoed in her mind with uncanny familiarity. She couldn't place the memory, but she'd heard those sounds before. Many times before.

"I'm off to check on it," Hrag announced, his glare slipping toward her once more.

Leógham gave him a quick nod. "We'll fetch the bags and catch up. And Hrag—be careful."

"Whatever." He waved an unconcerned hand, bow slung across his back.

Kharis followed Leógham, her thoughts churning: a roaring waterfall; the burning land; arrows thudding again,

121

and again. Fragments of a life, drifting in a vast, dark ocean, and getting further from her reach.

"Is everything all right?" Leógham asked. "You've been quiet."

She sighed, her breath shaky, her emotions too tangled. She couldn't even explain them to herself.

"Outside rabbits for your stew, I don't think I've ever hunted."

Leógham stopped mid-stride. "Ever?" His brow lifted. "My first shot killed a tree." A crooked grin pulled at his mouth—an attempt to ease the moment. "One of your arrows kept that mathan from tearing me apart. I've seen enough. You're exceptional with the bow."

She drew in a slow breath, his praise drowning the echoes of shouted commands in her skull. "I don't think I was trained to hunt," she said. "The mathan... My body moved before my mind ever understood what was happening." Her fingers curled. "I get flashes of drills. Never allowed to falter, never allowed to rest. The same motions, over and over, until they were carved into me."

A metallic clang rang in her ears, marking the rhythm along with a word that haunted her.

Useless.

Leógham tilted his head. "You're remembering—"

"I want it to stop." Her hands clenched at her sides. "I can't take it anymore. I—" Her shoulders sagged, her head dipping as a weary sigh slipped out of her.

"I was trained from a young age—bow and sword." He tilted his head as if he could see it. "My training was harsh, the expectations always high. There were days when, as a boy, I hid... and cried."

She searched his eyes for the white lie—the pity—but instead saw deep sorrow, as if he, too, had been forced to do something he would've never chosen.

"I'm sorry. Truly."

He shook his head, his smile soft, and gestured to the

path. Soon, they reached the spot where they'd left the bags. Leógham bent to pick them up.

"Wait." She caught his arm. "Let me be of use. Please?"

Leógham straightened, studying her for a moment before stepping aside. "Of course."

She grabbed the two bags she'd carried from the start, and Leógham gathered the rest. As soon as Hrag spotted them, he waved his arms at them. He'd crouched over the now lifeless beast, struggling to roll it onto its side. His breath came in short, frustrated bursts. "It's too heavy to hang."

Leógham took one look and nodded. "We'll skin it on the ground. Not ideal, but it'll do."

Once they'd positioned the stag, Leógham pulled a knife from his bag and offered it to Hrag. "Tradition," he told Kharis. "First cut goes to the one who killed it."

"Sounds like an honor," she said.

Hrag shot her a look. "Are you helping or what?"

She blinked. "Um… Help?"

He frowned. "What are you, a prince now? Gonna stand there while we do all the work?"

Her lips parted, caught between apology and biting remark, before Leógham said, "Gather stones and dry wood. We'll smoke the meat." He gave a brief nod toward the trees. "Go."

Kharis nodded, grateful to step away from Hrag's glare.

As she bent to pick up firewood, a breeze slipped through the trees, brushing her face with an odd chill. It tugged at her cloak in teasing little pulls. It whispered through the grass, circled her ankles, and brushed the back of her neck with a touch too intimate to be chance.

She spun, turning to the trees. Why did she feel something out there was breathing with the wind?

23

THE PLACES WHERE NIGHTMARES LIVE

You have never been lost. You are unbound, yet blind to your freedom, unwilling to see that the chains you curse already lie shattered at your feet. - Poliormos

Leógham and Hrag worked in silence, taking turns to work the carcass. It was clear they'd done this before. The gutting went quickly. They removed the organs and set them aside for burial. Then they moved to skinning. They loosened the hide with short, sure cuts, slipping their fingers beneath to free it from the muscle.

Nearly three hours later, they hoisted the quartered meat high into the branches of a sturdy oak.

Leógham rummaged through his pack and drew out a large blanket with tiny bells sewn along its edge. At Kharis's puzzled look, he said, "The jingling keeps scavengers away."

As Hrag climbed the tree to secure the ropes, Leógham suddenly called out, "Benkhi! Here!" He tossed her the waterskins.

Kharis caught two, but the third slipped through her hands and thudded to the ground. She shot him a glare.

"Fill them." His tone was brisk. "Now, please."

Her frown deepened, but she bent to retrieve the fallen skin and stomped toward the brook. "We could've done it later," she muttered. Kneeling by the water, she plunged the skins into the stream. "Why the rush?"

Movement in the corner of her eye made her glance back. Immediately, she looked away, face hot, as Leógham and Hrag relieved themselves around the tree and nearby shrubs, marking the area to keep predators at bay.

Heart racing, she watched the brook's steady flow as she waited for Leógham's signal that it was safe to return.

The sudden crunch of pine needles and twigs some twenty marks from the brook snapped her out of her rumination. She turned to the bushes, expecting a furry face to emerge at any moment. Birds burst from the canopy in alarm, shattering the stillness, but didn't settle nearby, vanishing deeper into the forest.

She strained to listen. No branches wavered under an unseen weight. No paw scuffed the earth. Only the brook gurgled.

A breath of wind stroked her cheek like a curious finger, cool at first, then tinged with a metallic tang that lingered on her tongue. Every instinct screamed that something was lurking beyond her sight. She searched past the shadows—expecting the twitch of an ear, the shift of a silhouette, a mathan—but the woods remained unsettlingly quiet.

"Benkhi!" Leógham's shout broke the moment. "We're done."

Kharis waved an arm in response, but as she pulled on the waterskins' straps, she faced the shadows beyond the brook once more. Nothing moved. She blew a worried huff, shaking off the concern, and walked toward the men.

"We're heading back," Leógham said. "Hrag can use the horses to pick the meat up tomorrow."

Hrag bent to gather his things. The strap of his pack caught on his finger, and the metal clasp cut the skin.

"Fires!" He yanked his hand back. Blood swiftly welled on his fingers.

"You all right?" Leógham asked.

"Nicked myself." Hrag lifted the finger, crimson trickling down the hand. "All's well."

Just then, a gust of wind curled around him, as if tugged by the bright smear of blood. It rustled leaves and sent a frenzied scattering of dust through the air. Hrag flinched and swatted at the space beside him.

"What was that?" He frowned, shaking out his sleeves as if expecting something to crawl free.

Kharis turned sharply toward the creek. The far bank was still, shadows undisturbed—but her snake markings prickled. Her gaze lingered on the forest before she forced herself to look away.

They packed their gear, scattered dirt over the firepit, and started down the winding trail, the forest closing in behind them.

Hrag strode ahead with Leógham, keeping her out of the conversation as expected. He'd launched into hunting stories —game hunted, close calls, mishaps in the wild—peppering them with self-congratulation. Leógham offered occasional comments, but more often he let his nephew dominate the discussion.

Kharis trailed behind, glad to tune out while Hrag took center stage. It gave her space to think—

"Benkhi!"

She jerked her head up. "What?"

Hrag half-turned, walking backward with a smirk. "How old are you, anyway? Thirteen?"

"Hrag," Leógham warned, his voice carrying a subtle edge.

Hrag's eyes swept her from head to toe before he scoffed. "Whatever. Wouldn't want to offend *the prince*."

Leógham groaned, dragging a hand down his face. "Blessed Fires, Hrag." A flicker of red suddenly flashed through his emerald eyes. "Can you... not talk for a while?"

Kharis stiffened, unsure if the light was playing tricks. Hrag stilled, pressing his elbows against his sides. Leógham took a step back, lips tight, lowered his gaze, and whirled away.

"Keep walking." His voice was hoarse, harsher now. Without another glance, he strode ahead, long and fast, as if fleeing the moment.

Kharis started after him, worried, but Hrag grabbed her arm, nostrils flaring. "Leave him alone."

She snatched her arm, having had it with him. "Why?"

His eyes narrowed, mouth twisting into a cruel smirk. "I don't like you. You're a scrawny whelp with nothing worth stealing. And yet here you are," he glowered, "in a place where you shouldn't be. You're hiding something. I know it."

Her pulse spiked. "You know nothing about me." She shouldered past him, but he clamped her arm, wrenching her back. The grip was rough—bruising—feeding the terror clawing up her throat. And with it, her magic swelled, pushing against her skin.

"Let me go." She tore her arm free and shoved him.

A flare leaped with her touch. Hrag staggered as he looked down. Smoke curled from his jerkin where her hand had struck, a scorched mark seared into the leather.

"What did you do?" he hissed.

But she was already running to catch up with Leógham—desperate to escape Hrag.

"I'll get you for this!" His voice chased her through the trees.

She didn't look back.

Leógham moved at a blistering pace, carving a path through the forest as if waging a silent war.

Then, without warning, the forest stilled. The sudden silence crushed the air flat. Pressure popped in her ears. Her snake markings constricted her. A sharp, ragged breath tore from her. The world tilted, and she hit the dirt.

Leógham was beside her in an instant, his hands gripping her arms firmly.

"What is it?" His eyes searched hers. "What's going on?"

Her markings pulsed wildly. She couldn't explain how she knew this, but her body was on high alert.

"Something's coming," she whispered hoarsely.

Leógham furrowed his brow as his eyes darted between the dense trees and the shadowy underbrush. "I don't hear or see anything unusual."

"What's going on?" Hrag had caught up with them.

"Stay alert." Leógham unfastened a dagger from his lower leg and handed it to her. "Take this."

But she didn't. Her gaze fixed on a dark patch of woods where the air rippled.

"Leógham..." Her heartbeats throbbed in her throat. "It's coming toward us—"

A violent gust tore through the trees, slamming into them with brutal force. The ground vanished beneath her, and the world became a blur of color and strident sound.

24

THE DJINNSHIRUKH

Power does not ask for permission; it demands surrender. - Poliormos

The blow flung Kharis skyward.

Her markings flared hot as she spun past trees and sky, then crashed to the forest floor, tumbling through grass and leaves. Her body skidded until a tree stopped her short. Still dazed, she scrambled to all fours, spitting grit, swiping dirt from her face, and crouched low, her back pressed against rough bark. Whatever had struck them hadn't come to kill at once. It had scattered them on purpose.

The forest had fallen unnaturally silent, the eerie quiet amplifying the pounding of her heart. She strained for a sound—Leógham's voice, Hrag's shout—proof they still lived, but nothing came. The air crackled with magic—pungent and cloying, like hawthorn in bloom, clouding her senses. It clung to everything, masking its source. She swallowed her ball of panic. Survival mattered now.

Sweat traced a line down her temple. Her eyes darted from tree to tree, nerves strung taut, hunting for a flicker of motion—anything that betrayed what stalked them because something was out there. Hunting.

"Tsk, tsk," said a resonant voice, close to her ear.

She jolted, every muscle snapping tight. Her head whipped around. The forest loomed silent and still.

"All those lessons—wasted on you."

Her entire body stiffened.

The voice threaded through her mind. Male, deep, mocking. Its restraint was terrifying, as though the barest rise in volume might tear the world apart.

"Who are you?" she rasped, wondering if she was losing her grip on reality.

"Ah." He chuckled wickedly. *"I see Farrádh took your memories, then."*

Was she going mad? Her mind spun with questions, but she bit them back. If she wanted to survive, she had to keep her eyes sharp and her mind sharper. Then a dark thought struck her. Was this voice... the attacker?

"Don't let fear control you," he said. *"It's natural to be frightened. The emotion does have a purpose, after all. The paradox is that fear is not to be feared."*

What was this: a lecture before dying? "Are you making fun of me?"

"Hmm. Am I?"

A rustle in the underbrush drew her attention. A tendril of air floated past her before moving on. An icy shiver settled in her chest. "Blessed Mother. It's choosing one of us."

The voice cackled, cutting through her thoughts. *"You've figured it out."*

She gritted her teeth. "Go ahead. Laugh while I stare at death."

"Did you forget you're the Djinnshirukh, the one who decides who lives and dies?"

Déjà vu slammed into her, rooting her to the spot. Those words—she'd heard them before. His laughter followed—low, needling. He prowled through her mind like a cruel cat among fragile glass, toppling pieces to relish the shatter.

"I... know you."

He tittered. *"Do you, now?"*

A screech tore through the silence. Kharis jerked back against the tree, every nerve on edge. Whatever was out there, it was selecting its first target.

"Are we done with the questions, Djinnshirukh?"

"Why are you calling me that?" Her lips tightened on a hard swallow. "Are you here to kill me?"

"An interesting turn," the entity mused. *"To look at you is to look at death. Have you forgotten?"*

"Yes," she hissed. "And I'm running out of time."

"Fascinating." It halted its billowing movement. *"Remember my name, and I shall help you."*

Had there been a face, she would've punched it.

She squeezed her eyes shut and plunged inward, into the void of her mind. She moved cautiously through the fog— then faster, slicing the haze with desperate arms.

A small crimson flame flickered in the dark. *"Here, here."*

When she moved to catch it, it darted out of reach, flaring somewhere else. He laughed, enjoying her desperation. Kharis sprinted after the flame, getting angrier by the moment.

"I don't have time for this!" She dove—missed again. "Ragha, please. Stop."

"Ah, yes!" There was a note of approval in his voice as his name rippled into existence. *"You remembered."* A dark chuckle followed.

"Ah, little sister." Ragha released a long, theatrical yawn. *"A deal is a deal,"* he drawled, his words smooth and serpentine. *"You remembered my name, so I shall help you as agreed."*

She rose slowly, her back scraping against the rough bark.

"Leaving?" Ragha said.

"I don't have time for this. People I care about are in danger—"

"And that is precisely why you shall listen to me." His voice brushed her ear, as if he were disturbingly close. *"Everything alive exudes heat. Still your mind, and no one will ever hide from you."*

His presence flooded every corner of her mind, building pressure behind her eyes, stretching from his world to hers like an endless tether. Through this bridge between worlds, power poured into her like a swollen river. Kharis swallowed a scream, her fingers clawing into the dirt. This power tore her open, breaking past every barrier to reach her core— magic buried so deep she hadn't known it was there. A blast of fire seared through her mind.

His voice slammed into her like a raging storm, pounding through her skull. *"Now, show me how formidable you are."*

When she opened her eyes, the forest had vanished.

No more greens or browns—only a shifting kaleidoscope of red, orange, and gold, flickering across a backdrop of dark purple. Everything moving pulsed with heat.

Blessed. Mother.

Her gaze flitted across the glowing forms—each was a life. A fawn hid in the bushes, not far from her, its outline a radiant halo of warmth, its breath a plume of molten gold. Birds flapped on branches, mice scurried under roots. Even the tiniest creatures cowering in the underbrush lay exposed, their fragile sparks laid bare before her sight.

"I…" She couldn't believe her eyes. "I can see them?"

Ragha laughed. *"I told you, Djinnshirukh. No one can hide from you."*

Some eighty marks from her, she spotted three figures, the halos of heat unmistakable. Her eyes locked onto the biggest—her target. Her fear dissolved beneath the need to protect Leógham and Hrag. Her breathing slowed. Her pulse locked into rhythm. The tremor left her hands.

Power thrummed through her veins. The ancient beast inside her had finally awakened, and in that breathless pause, she understood that this power was hers to command.

"I think I feared this magic once." She drew a breath, her heart racing. "I don't know what I was before, but now, I'll be the monster that hunts monsters."

"*Good.*" A low, silken hum curled through her mind, heavy with destiny. *"Let's play. Shall we?"*

Scales shimmered to life across her skin like armor. Iridescent and intricate, they gleamed like stars, casting a silver haze that lit the forest gloom like Sharan at midnight. Onyx claws slid from her fingers. Her sight sharpened further, her periphery stretching wider. Shadows snapped into razor clarity, every shape and movement laid bare.

The monster's breathing, once barely a whisper, now thundered in her ears. Its foul stench twisted through the air, and her nose caught it instantly as if it were a ribbon. Even if this creature hid from her, she'd find it.

Kharis grinned.

Thirty marks to the monster's left, Leógham stood alert, back pressed to a tree.

Fifteen marks to its right, Hrag lay still. Too still.

His body heat was waning. His heartbeats faltered.

Her nostrils flared, and she picked up the coppery scent of blood.

The beast padded toward Hrag—its first victim.

She shot forward, a silver bolt through the dark woods, and drove the creature into a tree. The blow rattled her teeth; the canopy quaked, leaves and pinecones tumbling through the air.

25

THE SHAPE
NIGHTMARES TAKE

> *Nightmares wear no fixed shape, for they are clay in the hands of dread—ever molded into a mirror that reflects its maker. - Poliormos*

Leógham gripped his hunting knife, every nerve thrumming.

A gust tore past him, whipping his hair and dragging a stench that didn't belong to the living. Another followed—colder, sharper—scraping his skin like ice. He spun, trying to track it, but whatever circled him moved like a shadow: soundless, toying with its prey.

Some thirty marks from him, a bolt of silver sliced through the trees. He snapped his head toward it just as a thunderous crash shook the forest. The canopy shuddered; a piercing screech split the air.

"Benkhi? Hrag?" he shouted, fear rising. "Where are you?"

No answer.

His grip tightened on the dagger. He remembered the signs—the strange wind, the shifting shadow, the eerie silence before the strike...

"Flames above," he whispered, sweating. "It's a winged nightmare."

26

THE TWO MONSTERS

> *A shield never asks if the battle is fair. It simply stands between the blade and the one it must protect.*
> *- Poliormos*

The world spun for a heartbeat. Kharis staggered back, head ringing, vision blurred. Before she could find her footing, a low, resonant growl crawled out of the dark. The beast was staking its claim. This was its territory, and Hrag, its meal.

It stepped from the shadows like an avenging wraith, towering over her, twice her height. A black body, golden eyes burning above a muzzle lined with knife-edged fangs. Long claws raked the ground; torn wings unfurled, scattering a frigid gust through the trees. Scars webbed its hide, ribs jutting through matted fur—a creature now ruined and furious.

Kharis steadied herself, tracking every twitch as they circled. The beast snarled, fangs flashing. It roared, then lunged.

Her body moved, reflex taking over.

She vaulted off a tree and flipped midair—gravity a

suggestion, not a rule. The monster's claws missed her by a breath. Hers raked the creature's back in a single, fluid arc. Blood spattered her hands. She landed and sprinted to draw the beast away from Hrag.

The forest closed around her in a frenzy of trunks and roots as she wove between narrow gaps. The wind shifted, and the creature suddenly appeared before her.

Blasted!

Kharis twisted past its claws, hers meeting flesh. The creature shrieked, reeling beneath her assault. Magic surged, roaring in her blood, begging to be unleashed.

"*Now,*" Ragha urged. "*Kill it now.*"

"There's no need to k—"

The world flashed white.

A lightning bolt split the ground beside her. The shock hurled her into a tree, and stars burst behind her eyes. She gasped, dragging breath back in shallow, ragged pulls, one hand curling over her ribs.

A groan tore from her throat as pain flared through every nerve. The air stank of ozone—sharp, metallic—burning her lungs, the side of her jerkin smoldering from the near-miss, heat biting deep into her shoulder.

A crackle.

Her eyes snapped open.

The tail sparked like a cursed lightning rod.

Another bolt split the dark, screaming past as she threw herself into a roll.

The tree behind her exploded in a deafening crack. Wood and dirt pelted her. She spat grit, ribs aching with each inhale. Her ears rang from the blast. Her eyes stung with her sweat.

Blinking through the haze of blood blurring her vision, she saw a mass of black fur and muscle hurtling straight for her.

Driven by the heat of battle, Kharis bolted forward, dropping low and sliding beneath its belly as dirt pelted her face. The monster soared inches above her. As its hindquarters thundered past, she slashed upward, claws tearing into the thick root of its tail. Flesh split. Blood sprayed hot across her cheek.

The beast shrieked, its landing ruined. It staggered, one hind leg dragging, wings twitching unevenly. The tail hung limp, dragging uselessly behind it. Enraged, it wheeled toward her, growl rumbling deep, jaws snapping.

Kharis turned to run, only to slam into a trunk that barred her escape. The monster dove for her, jaws yawning.

She threw herself aside as its teeth sank into the wood with a sickening crunch. Heart hammering, she scrambled for the nearest tree, her boots finding purchase as she climbed it.

The creature writhed, muscles bulging as it fought to free its jaw. With a ferocious wrench, it tore loose, wood exploding. A shriek ripped from its throat. Its sides heaved as it faltered on unsteady limbs. Blackened blood oozed from its gashes, hissing where it struck grass.

From her perch high among the branches, Kharis studied the broken creature. Had it always been a monster, or had someone made it one?

"End it," Ragha begged her now. *"Killing ends its suffering."*

Her fingers twitched, magic prickling under her skin. It would be so easy.

But then... what of her? Had she always been a monster, or had someone made her one?

The beast shifted, its golden eyes snapping up at the sound of her on the canopy. It opened its wings, and the wind tore through the trees. Branches splintered, dirt blasted upward. With a soul-rattling shriek, the monster launched like a tempest loosed from chains.

27

FIRE AND FURY

Love fuels the fire, and righteous fury shapes the flames. Fear cannot endure this pyre. - Poliormos

The blow knocked her off. Kharis tumbled, clipping branches like a wayward pinecone as she fell. Heat flared along her markings. When she hit the ground, the impact rang through her right wrist. Scales hardened along her skin, taking the worst of the impact— enough to leave her shaken, but whole.

She scrambled to her feet, one leg stiff. Magic sparked at her fingertips.

The monster circled her, chest heaving between growls, as if aware of the power she hadn't used yet.

"Just end it," Ragha urged. *"Grant it mercy, Djinnshirukh."*

A dark memory tore open inside her. In it, she'd heard herself saying, "It's a mercy if I kill them." Images unreeled: the air thick and choking, the copper stink of blood, the sour tang of urine, faces blurring in an endless procession of mercy killings.

This recollection stole her focus.

The monster struck.

A claw raked her thigh. Pain burst white-hot, stealing her balance. She went down hard, the air ripped from her lungs.

The beast slammed its weight into her, a massive paw crushing her chest until breath came in thin, useless pulls. Its foul breath washed over her face, fangs bared in triumph. The sky vanished behind the monster's bulk.

She clenched her jaw. One hand locked around the monster's paw, pushing it back, while the other shoved its jaws away from her face. Pain screamed through her arm, muscles burning.

Darkness crept at the edges of her sight, closing in with every failed gasp.

She wouldn't go quietly into the night, not this way. With the last of her breath, magic answered her summons.

Heat roared through her hands. Fire flooded her palms, blazing outward in a violent surge. The monster shrieked, rearing back. The weight lifted from Kharis's chest.

§

The harrowing screech froze Leógham. Sweat trickled down his spine, cold as melted ice. He swallowed hard, hating the not-knowing—the uselessness, the powerlessness.

Silver light had slashed through the trees, fifty marks away from him. The forest strobbed in violent bursts. The brilliance had grown, flare upon flare, splitting the dark. Sharp cracks of sound had followed, like the sky splitting.

Abruptly, the forest plunged into gloom.

A wail not of this world shattered the stillness. Everything was unraveling too fast. Every instinct screamed the same command: *Run.*

But he wouldn't while Kharis and Hrag were still out there.

He straightened and squared his shoulders, as he'd done during war. His jaw set. Anger snapped him into focus. Black flames answered his call—old companions he'd sworn never to summon again—and coiled alive and willing in his hands.

"Hrag, Benkhi!" he shouted. "Answer me!"

A faint reply drifted through the trees—barely a breath.

"Uncle..."

His heart lurched.

"Hrag!" His legs moved before common sense could catch up. Leógham tore through the underbrush, branches whipping his face, lungs burning—driven toward his nephew.

Kharis's head snapped toward the shout.

The monster twitched, ears flicking toward the sound, golden eyes weighing the odds. It snarled at her, then darted off, loping toward Leógham.

Her heart kicked hard—flint striking a spark. Her stardust ignited into a storm of crimson fire. Wings of flame unfurled as she launched herself, flew past the creature, and slammed down between it and the men with the force of a falling star.

A wall of heat struck the beast's face. Its nose blistered. Whiskers curled. The monster reared back, claws gouging deep trenches in the earth.

A torrent of black fire roared past Kharis and swallowed the creature whole. It screeched and thrashed until its body exploded into a cloud of ash. For a breath, nothing existed but the drifting ash and stench of scorched fur. The ringing in her ears faded. The woods fell silent again. Only the faint hiss of cooling embers remained.

They were safe once more, but triumph didn't sing in her heart. Scales shimmered beneath her flames, claws still drawn. She'd revealed she was a monster.

She turned around slowly, dreading this moment.

Leógham had lowered his hands, black fire guttering out

between his fingers. His chest heaved, the remnants of his power rippling through the air. He stared—eyes wide, mouth parted, caught between awe and fear.

"Kharis...?" His voice broke on her name, half question, half plea.

She rushed past him and knelt beside Hrag. Blood soaked her hands as she gathered the boy close. The monster's claws had raked through his chest, leaving a brutal pattern of deep gashes. The wounds gaped—bone exposed, breath faint, his warmth slipping away. His hold on the world was unraveling, its fragile threads about to snap.

Her magic surged without a summons. Silver fire burst from her hands, instinct given shape, and with her touch, the flames sank beneath his skin.

Leógham called her name again, but his voice faded into nothing.

THE SIBLINGS

I have lost you ten thousand times, yet in every shadow, in every echo, you remain. - Poliormos

A black shore greeted her, bathed in the Silver River's ethereal glow. Obsidian sand glittered beneath her feet, the breeze carrying the lull of waves and the sting of marine brine. Despite her fractured memory, Kharis knew this place: the dark oceans of Välissa, the bridge between worlds. And she knew what must be done, as if she'd walked this strand countless times.

Atop the far dunes, a tall, slender figure waited. Long silver hair streamed in the salty wind, moonlight catching in its strands. His silver eyes tore from Tung to fix on her. Shadows veiled his face, yet she sensed the ghost of a smile.

The man who'd called her Ori.

There, cast on the black sand, she found a rope of golden kelp torn from the forests of the deep, adrift as though a storm had hurled it to land. Its glow was as faint as the sun's last breath.

She wasn't sure how she knew, only that she did. The kelp

frond was a soul tether, torn from the kelp forests. Its fading glow could only mean one thing. Hrag was dying.

An incantation flowed from her. Fragments of memory once broken became whole. A skein of crimson yarn shimmered into being. She drew a thread and wove it into Hrag's tether. When it fused, red bled into gold, then silver, the tether pulsing with renewed life. Like a sigh into the wind, it vanished, drawn back into the ocean's depths. A flicker of moonlight now danced among the golden kelp below.

Sobs and laughter tangled in her throat as tears spilled, warm against the chill marine breeze.

The stranger had settled before her, silver eyes burning. Sharan's glow outlined him in moonlight, his hair floating weightless in the current of his power. His face emerged—a face too much like her own.

"You did well, Djinnshirukh."

Kharis recognized the resonant voice. "Ragha?"

"Hello, little sister." His smile brimmed with both affection and mischief.

Brother? The word tasted strange in her tongue, yet it warmed her, unsettlingly so.

Ragha tilted his head toward the sea, toward the kelp forest shimmering beneath the waves. "Yours is a tether that shall not break, not even in death. Now he is bound to you, as it should be."

"Why?"

He chuckled, amused. "Why not?" His eyes held hers. "Over millennia, we have worn many faces, taken many avatars." His smile faded. "I have failed you ten thousand times, yet your sacrifice remains as a promise that every end comes with a new beginning." Thunder gathered beneath his words. "Head north, Ori. If you fail to end all the writings, the curse will not die with you. It will unmake the world again."

She forgot to breathe, a familiar fear rising. "Am I... the Endbringer?"

But mist unfurled, blurring the sea and stars alike. The waves ebbed into silence. Before the final hush, Ragha's tender whisper reached her.

"I am proud of you, little sister."

The fog thickened, pushing her back.

29

THE FIRE DWELLERS

Leógham watched, breath locked in his chest.

Wreathed in flames, her hair streamed in a phantom wind. Incandescent waves of power rippled outward, shaping the fiery aura engulfing her. Claws jutted from ash-blackened fingers. Her exposed skin, scaled, shimmered like diamonds in sunlight—brilliant, otherworldly.

Silver light spread from her arms into Hrag's wounds, pulsing beneath her touch. In Hegra, touch drew magic away from others. Here, it flowed the other way.

His lungs forgot their rhythm. Every belief he held strained against what he was seeing.

Hrag's bleeding slowed, then stopped. Deep slashes drew together as silvery light threaded through torn flesh, stitching and threading, leaving soft pink skin in its wake. He'd seen healing before. Nothing like this.

Hrag's chest rose suddenly. Under Leógham's palm, his heart beat strong and steady, warmth returning to his skin.

Kharis straightened slowly, wincing. Fire clung to her, obscuring more than it revealed. Through a thinning veil of flame, he caught the sleeve's torn fabric, then a glimpse of blood soaking it—before the fire surged again. She didn't look at it.

When she lifted her crimson gaze to him, a faint crease formed between her brows. "I'm sorry I hid this from you."

"You..." The word left him on a breath. "You're a Fire Dweller?"

Her lips parted, then pressed together.

The glow within Hrag dimmed. The last ghostly threads of silver unraveled beneath his skin and went dark. She withdrew her hands and rose on soundless steps, clutching her arm.

Hrag stirred, his body shifting as he returned to consciousness. His eyes darted, unfocused, before fixing on Leógham. "What... What happened?"

"A winged nightmare attacked us." Leógham steadied Hrag. "Benkhi saved you."

Hrag squinted, eyes narrowing on Kharis, her form wrapped in flames. "That's not a nightmare... Wait." He blinked rapidly as if trying to clear his vision. "Blessed fires! Benkhi's a Fire Dweller?" He turned sharply to Leógham.

Kharis's firestorm collapsed inward, shrinking until the flames melted away, revealing her form. Her magic lingered in the air like a sweet perfume. Leógham filled his lungs with it, the sensation dizzying. He stepped toward her without realizing he'd moved.

"Benkhi." Wonder threaded her name. "I'm also a Fire Dweller."

Her eyebrows shot up.

"Eh?"

30

DANGEROUS QUESTIONS

> *Some questions are gates. Once opened, their answers will change everything, and the worlds behind them cannot be undone. - Poliormos*

When Leógham tapped two fingers beneath his eyes, Kharis understood right away, turning around to search for the eye tincture in her knapsack. Behind her, Leógham and Hrag argued, voices sharp. Hrag railed over the torn clothes and bloodstains—proof of the wounds he'd received: His skin bore no scars.

"Is this what you were hiding when you sent me back? Look at this." Hrag gestured sharply at his torn clothes, at the dark stains marring the fabric. "A mathan nearly kills him, but a winged nightmare was child's play?"

"You nearly died, Hrag," Leógham shot back, looking in his bag for a tunic to give Hrag. "Be grateful Benkhi kept you alive—"

"Why?" Hrag stabbed the air with a finger, words spilling over each other. "So that I owe him? That healing—" He broke off, then surged forward again. "Why are you hiding him? Where did he come from? Why is he here—?"

"Enough!"

Leógham rose to his full height, the motion forcing Hrag back a step. There was a weight in Leógham's stance that made Hrag's fingers twitch. He hesitated, then snatched the tunic from Leógham's hand.

"After everything you said and did to him," Leógham said, "is this how you repay Benkhi's kindness? I saw what he did. Do you want him to show you more? Perhaps undo his work?"

Hrag's jaw clenched. His glare flicked to Kharis. "I still think—"

Leógham groaned loudly, his hands on his hips. He shook his head before he seized Hrag by the arm and dragged him away, out of sight.

Kharis found a clean tunic and slipped toward the creek. The eye drops burned as she blinked them in, and through the sting, fragments of their voices carried to her.

"Why are you doing this?" Hrag barked.

"What do you want, Hrag?" Leógham nearly shouted. "For Saigham to learn of this? Perhaps even kill him?"

If Hrag answered, she missed it.

Who is Saigham...?

When they returned, Hrag kept his head down. His shoulders were tight, his mouth set hard.

They started for the cabin without another word. Each step pulled at her thigh until heat flared, and the snakes tightened their grip on her leg.

Leógham's stride beside her was steady, unbroken. A faint smile lingered at the corner of his mouth.

Hrag trailed several paces back, his glare burning a brand between her shoulders. She risked a glance back. If he spoke of what he'd seen, who would listen? Who would come looking? Her disguise felt thinner with each breath.

Leógham walked on as if there were nothing to fear.

Hrag was the storm at her back; in stark contrast, Leógham was sunlight breaking through.

And so she walked, caught between what pressed at her back and what waited ahead.

THE THINGS WE
DENY OURSELVES

If the day needs the night; flowers, the rain; and the falcon, the wind, why would I deny myself... you? - Poliormos

The tension carried throughout the evening and into the morning. Kharis had hoped for a quiet breakfast, but the arguing felt endless.

"You're *not* going back," Leógham said firmly, arms crossed. "Forget the meat."

Hrag scowled. "You can't be serious. I'm not leaving perfectly good meat behind."

"The winged nightmare—"

"—is long gone, Uncle." Hrag shot a thumb at Kharis to emphasize the point. "You're so overly cautious." He stormed out of the cabin, marching toward a nearby tree.

Leógham followed, tense with purpose, ready to stop him. Hrag pressed his palm flat against the tree. A faint, golden light stirred beneath his skin. The glow spread outward until soft threads of light unfurled from his hand, and like spun silk, the strands wound through the forest, tracing branches, slipping into roots, and curling around moss-covered trunks. Leaves fluttered without wind. The undergrowth hummed softly.

Kharis's mouth parted. Was that... Hrag's magic?

It didn't blaze. It didn't pack a powerful punch. His magic *sang.*

Hrag pulled his hand away, a smirk tugging at his lips.

"There," he said. "Nothing but *rabbits* in my future."

At the word, he shot Kharis a pointed glance before swinging onto Kantha's back. Her shoulders tightened.

"Don't look so smug, Benkhi. They aren't the only things I can track." He nudged Kantha forward, Balyus in tow. "I'll be back before you can say 'overreacting.'"

Leógham muttered something under his breath and stalked back inside.

Kharis let out a long, weary sigh.

At least, with Hrag gone, there was peace again. She knelt by the water tub, scrubbing pots, bowls, and utensils, yet her mind was far from the task. Now that she knew she was one, the urge to learn more about Fire Dwellers sparked a restless energy she couldn't shake. Questions tumbled through her mind, multiplying like wildflowers after a spring rain. Most pressing of all: What did it mean to be a Fire Dweller?

She realized she was smiling. "Maybe I'm not a monster after all."

A hummingbird hovered near, its jewel-toned wings a beating blur. Kharis watched it, amused by its curiosity, as though it understood her.

"What do you think, little one?"

The tiny bird floated by her face as if agreeing with her comment and darted away in a flash of iridescent green and magenta.

Inside, Leógham gathered ashes from the hearth. Now and then, his gaze drifted to her, and when he looked away, a faint smile lingered.

When their eyes finally met again, heat rushed to her face, and her grip faltered, a bowl nearly slipping from her fingers.

With renewed determination and a traitorous flutter in her chest, she plunged her hands into the soapy water and scrubbed the pots harder than necessary.

&.

Leógham stepped out of the cabin. The fresh air cooled the lingering heat on his skin. He stood on the veranda, watching her, the flutter in his chest strangely pleasant.

"I'm done on my end," he said. "What about you?"

Kharis raised the last bowl, water dripping from its edge. "Everything's clean, but we'll need more of your soap soon."

"Already working on it. Just finished boiling the ashes. Now they'll cool and settle." He scratched his bearded cheek, suddenly jittery. "It'll be some time before the liquid cools or Hrag returns. Would you like to go for a walk?" He gestured toward the path behind him.

Kharis smiled with her nod.

At first, they strolled in amiable silence, the occasional hum of insects coloring the quiet around them. Leógham cast her glances, his lips quirking into timid smiles whenever her gaze flitted his way. She returned his, and his chest ached pleasantly.

The silence stretched clumsily between them, urging him to say something—anything.

"The weather's nice," he ventured awkwardly, rubbing the back of his neck.

Kharis nodded.

Leógham swallowed hard, searching for the right words to begin a conversation about her power and his feelings for her. She was a Fire Dweller; courting her would be acceptable; his father might even approve if she turned out to be Hegran. With her fire magic and black hair pointing to an ancient Mórad Lahm lineage, marriage was possible, too. But did she feel the same? He turned the question over and over, looking for a way to ask—

She darted in front of him. He almost lost his footing.

"Is Hrag a Fire Dweller?" she asked. "His magic is different."

Leógham slowed, the question catching him off guard. "His father is Forest Kin. That's the magic he displays."

"Ah." She brightened. "So much to learn." She fell back into step, then drifted ahead of him, walking backward now, light on her feet, her gaze fixed on his face. "Tell me, is your power like mine? I've been dying to ask since yesterday. Your flames..." She tilted her head. "They're black, right?"

He glanced away, stumbling over his answer. "...Yes. Sort of." He tipped his chin toward the path. "It's uneven ground. Careful, or you'll trip."

With a chuckle, she spun around, clasping her hands behind her back.

"Ours is similar." He raised a hand, summoning a small scarlet flame in his palm. It flickered and danced as he made it jump from finger to finger. "We're grouped into clans based on our elemental magic. Ours allows us to control fire."

"Lord Vinashtagha's gift."

He inclined his head, and at the bend in the trail, they stopped.

"And who created Forest Kin magic? It was beautiful to watch."

"It existed long before the arrival of the Elatharim." His gaze dropped to the trail as he weighed his words. The cabin came into view through the trees. "Forest Kin magic is the oldest in Tír."

Her eyes widened. "Are they the most powerful?"

"Not necessarily." He let the flame shrink. "Fire Dweller magic is the most sought after because it touches the Fires of Creation."

"The fires from the Netherworlds of Ifran." Kharis bubbled with enthusiasm.

"Fires of... Ifran?" His shoulders tensed again at yet another one of her odd expressions.

She tapped her lips as if chasing a memory. "One of two creation elements—"

"Two?" His eyes darted toward the trees, trained to expect unseen ears. "Don't say that out loud, or the clan will brand you a heretic. Better yet, never mention it."

"Huh? Why?" Kharis cocked her head.

"To the Fire Dweller clan, fire is all that matters."

Kharis laughed.

Leógham scowled at her. "This isn't a joke. As a Fire Dweller, you should know this—live it."

Her lips twitched, threatening to lift, as she sat on the grass.

"Every element is vital," she said, "playing a role in the world. To believe otherwise is like trying to cover the sun with one hand and pretend it's not there."

He sat beside her and threw her another glare. "A thousand years ago, a king made a similar comment. In the battle that ensued, he lost his crown and head."

Kharis blinked slowly. "Over it?"

"Hegra *is* the Fire Dweller's realm. Fire is all that matters to us." The small scarlet flame he'd summoned flickered on his fingers like a ribbon caught in the wind. "Be careful about what you say, or like that king of old, you're bound to lose your head." The flame shifted through shades of red as it danced on his palm. "Ours is the first to arise after creation, but as the magic in Hegra dissipates, so is our ability to call upon it."

The tiny tongue of fire hopped from finger to finger. Kharis smiled, her gaze lingering on it. A swell of heat rose in him. The way she watched him...

He swallowed hard.

"Kharis—?"

"It's Benkhi!" she said. "You can't forget."

His hand clenched instinctively, extinguishing the flame.

A pink butterfly drifted past. Leógham followed its weightless dance until it came to rest atop a flower, its wings pulsing like a breath. He took a deep breath, summoning his courage.

"When you transformed—" He searched the sky, buying himself a moment. "You were splendid. Exquisite."

Her eyes widened. "You thought so?"

"I still do," he said quietly.

Her smile crinkled the corners of her eyes. "I was exquisite." She tapped her feet against the ground in a playful rhythm. "I was splendid!"

His smile slipped free before he could stop it. The moment opened, warm and dangerous, and he wondered if this was it—if he dared push further and confess his feelings for her.

His pulse jumped.

"Benkhi…" Suddenly, facing a winged nightmare seemed simpler than this. How hard could it be to say, *I wish to court you?*

Kharis tilted her head, waiting. His thoughts only tangled further.

"I like…" He hesitated. "I like… your ability." He groaned inwardly, fingers curling.

She laughed softly, the sound bright and unguarded. "I haven't seen your transformation." She leaned forward, face alight. "Is it like mine?"

Leógham considered it. "Probably." After a beat, "Our transformations affect other Fire Dwellers."

"Oh?"

"The magic beckons others," he said. "Fire always calls on fire."

"Hmm." She pursed her lips. "Then why didn't you transform when I did, if that's the rule?"

His breathing faltered; he hadn't expected that question. "Yours was…" He searched for a word. "Compelling." It had clung to him: magnetic, wrapping around him even after she'd shifted back.

He scratched his cheek. "It took everything I had not to. I had to keep my focus on Hrag."

"I see." Her eyes narrowed slightly. "If you transformed now, would your fire magic awaken mine?"

A slow smile curved his lips. "Would you like to see?"

Kharis gave him a crisp nod.

"Very well."

He rose, closed his eyes, and drew a slow, steadying breath. The trick was balance—too much air and the fire would devour him; too little only gave him embers. He pictured its shape and the memory of heat beneath his skin, feeling the pulse answer from deep within. With a thought, he summoned it.

Flames bloomed, engulfing him in a radiant scarlet blaze.

FIRE MAGIC

> *Behold the sight of a soul on fire, crowned in glory,*
> *sublime and sacred, forged for the eyes of eternity,*
> *lighting the darkness for all to see. - Poliormos*

It started with a soft, involuntary inhale.

Crimson flashed across Kharis's vision, her magic announcing itself before it rose. The world fell away, leaving only the scarlet flames dancing along Leógham's body. He was formidable, as if fire itself had taken his shape and claimed it as its own.

Heat bloomed beneath her skin, her blood surging like molten rubies. The little flame that lived within her—her core—stirred without a ritual or words. It was her curse and her gift: fire that roused to emotion, not to commands. It soon flared wildly as if it had waited its whole life for this. Embers lifted from her skin, swirling like butterflies caught in an updraft.

Leógham opened his eyes, blazing scarlet, and locked onto hers.

Kharis felt it—the call.

His magic crashed into hers like a horde of dragons. It

carried the weight of conquest, yet it curved toward her power instead of overwhelming it. Hers opened in answer. The collision was wild, exuberant, and disorienting.

Her muscles locked and strained. Her nostrils flared as heat tore through her veins. Unlike his magic, hers rewrote flesh. The snake markings on her skin blazed to life, melting into liquid fire that raced along their coils. One by one, they slipped beneath her skin, and in their wake, iridescent, petal-like scales unfurled, draping her in a luminous silver haze.

She drew a sharp breath and let it take her.

Her aura ignited.

Crimson, amber, and gold burst outward in a crown of flame, and she rose, the force of his presence begging for her own.

The ground fell away. The world narrowed to heat, light, and him.

DUSK AND DAWN

In the hush of dusk and the breath of dawn—when neither day nor night holds sway—the gods awaken and watch, unbound by time. - Poliormos

Leógham extended his hand. The moment his fingers closed around hers, the world fell away. Her touch overwhelmed him—stars colliding, breaking, and reshaping into new constellations. Power surged through him, prying him open as his scarlet flames deepened toward black.

Fire magic was never gentle. It didn't obey balance. One flame moved to master another, to devour what it touched. Yet his power didn't seek to claim her. It circled, yielded, and pressed where she yielded in turn. Where she drew, he gave. Where he pushed, she answered. The currents braided together, brightening as they wove, until he could no longer tell where one ended and the other began.

Then, wings emerged from nothingness.

His breath caught.

Fire Dwellers couldn't summon wings. The crimson in her eyes rippled, silver flooding them instead. Her flames turned into argent fire. She was luminous—the North Star herself, descended from the heavens to take his hand.

His magic bent without command. It did not resist. It yielded, aligning itself to hers, moving to an ancient rhythm —tide and moon, fire and wind. His scarlet flames shifted, darkening, deepening, reshaping themselves in response.

It shook Leógham to his core.

Black flames conjured the ghosts of the Hegran civil war: bodies reduced to ash, light and sound crushed flat. Back then, he had been Death, incarnate, his black fire consuming souls. He couldn't lose the control he'd spent eight years mastering.

Like a veil falling over the world, a void swallowed them.

He gasped to control his breath.

Tiny silver embers drifted through the void like fireflies, spilling their glow across the nothingness. It was haunting. Beautiful. Against this obsidian expanse, her flames blazed defiantly, bringing light.

Her magic sensed the fear coursing through him and sang in reply. Leógham yielded. He felt the fracture, the breaking, the slow unraveling of every barrier he'd built to cage the dark magic within, and he was powerless to stop it.

And yet...

Their joining was formidable—incandescent.

Night and day. Dusk and dawn. Bound together.

For one impossible moment, they created beauty brighter than stars. Black flames poured from him, roaring with a ravenous heat that pushed the void outward.

It was exhilarating.

And it was terrifying.

Leógham gritted his teeth. The abyss beckoned, ever so sweetly, and he was slipping toward it. A groan escaped him as he forced his walls to rise again. With sheer, punishing effort, he tore his hand from her. The moment their skin parted, the bridge fractured.

His black flames vanished, ash-dark veins fading beneath his skin.

Her silver ones faltered and dimmed.

The void collapsed. Trees returned. Then earth. Sky. Sound.

Leógham staggered, breath coming in ragged gasps. He drank in the air, grounding himself, fighting the tremor in his limbs and the ache in his chest.

A reckless part of him wished the moment had never ended.

Their mingled magic had been exuberant, powerful, intimate beyond words. The image of that onyx void lit with silvery starlight clung to him; how he longed to bask in all that beauty again.

Kharis stood still for a heartbeat longer, her head tipped back. She released a slow, steady breath and lowered herself onto the grass.

"I have goose bumps," she whispered.

Leógham's eyebrows lifted. Did she not realize what had happened?

Quietly—cautiously—he sat beside her.

The glow in her eyes had faded, but not the intensity. They had also returned to being sapphire and silver. The same eyes as the woman in his dreams. His heart jolted, breath stolen in a single beat. The urge to pull her into his arms surged again.

Wait. Her eyes…

Before he could fetch the tincture, Kharis lay on the grass, gazing at the sky. Her smile was radiant like the sun at dawn. A tremor rose in him.

What have you done to me?

"Leógham," she said, smoothing her tunic. "Could you transform again?"

He blinked. "Are you asking me to do it again?"

It was painfully tempting. His heart ached to obey. His

mind rebelled, screaming in every dialect he'd mastered: Nej. Nez. Nei.

Her teasing chuckle brought him back. "I mean, is there a Hegran prohibition I should keep in mind?"

He laughed, shoulders easing. "No prohibition against transforming. Fire Dwellers live to be Fire Dwellers."

"Good." A hint of amusement colored the word.

He rose to fetch the vial of kharisot liquid.

"Where is north?" she asked, halting him.

Odd question. He gazed at the clouds above them. "This realm is a bubble of magic—a fold in the fabric of existence. Directions don't hold meaning here. No matter where you walk, you'll circle back to the cabin, the only point this magic remembers. So," he shrugged, "no north."

She hummed. "I can't fathom that much power."

A lone cloud wandered across the sky, its edges dissolving in the soft wind currents. A cry split the air—a falcon, high above, soaring through the sunlit blue.

Kharis raised her hand to shield her eyes from the sun, then sat up, squinting at the sky. "What's that?"

"A falcon...?" When she didn't remark, Leógham followed her line of sight.

"Oh, that?" It was barely visible, a faint shadow low on the horizon. "It's Lirun, the blue moon. Sharan and Tung rule the night, but Lirun's a day moon. You can barely see it, though sometimes it shows itself at twilight or after a storm."

She went still. "A blue... moon?"

He chuckled. "Of course. Everyone knows that."

"Your sky has three moons." Her face paled. "I don't remember three moons... I don't remember this sky."

Leógham cocked his head. "What do you mean, you don't—"

"Uncle!"

The shout ripped through the woods. Leógham turned sharply, heart thudding hard.

Fires. Hrag had returned.

MIST AND MOSS

Even Sharan, so distant from the sun, waits for the moment when dawn might turn its gaze upon her. - Poliormos

"Your eyes. The color's back," Leógham whispered before rushing to Hrag, who lifted a triumphant arm, pointing at the deer meat strapped to Balyus.

As they unpacked it, Hrag launched into a breathless account about fending off a flock of curious birds to retrieve it. Leógham nodded occasionally, arms full, humming in acknowledgment. His gaze kept drifting toward the cabin. *Has she used the drops?* She hadn't shown up to help, perhaps staying away from Hrag.

While Hrag set to work dressing the meat, Leógham stacked wood and coaxed the fire in the smoker to life. Together, they hung the racks of meat to smoke, then shared bread and hard cheese and sipped tea.

"Where's *the prince?*" Hrag drawled.

Leógham tipped his chin toward the smoker. "Don't mind him and check the meat."

Hrag sniffed and opened the metal door. A puff of savory smoke curled out. He inspected the meat and nodded.

Then, bluntly, "What's going on with Benkhi? He never misses food."

Leógham frowned, looking past the corner. Kharis sat on the grass, her knees drawn to her chest as she stared at the sky. Besides keeping an eye on Lirun, she hadn't said much else.

"Let him be." He rose. "Here, help me bring the meat inside."

A short while later, the heavy tray landed on the table with a loud thud.

"All right, time to try it." Hrag sliced a piece, his enthusiasm unabated, and savored its flavor.

Leógham took a piece for himself and chewed slowly, yet his thoughts circled Kharis. "I'll take Benkhi a slice."

Hrag's eyes narrowed slightly. "Is everything all right with him?"

Leógham sighed. "Sometimes, the memory loss overwhelms him. I can't imagine living like that." His thoughts dipped into his grief. "Imagine knowing you had a mother, but you couldn't remember her face or name. Instead, there's an empty place where someone precious used to be. That's where Benkhi is, wondering which shadows are real."

"Will he ever snap out of it?"

Leógham shrugged. "Hard to say. His injuries were severe, and yet, there he is, sitting with the horses."

Hrag scratched his temple and walked to the window. "He's odd, isn't he?"

"Let me hit you in the head with this pan."

"Huh?" Hrag blinked, completely thrown.

"I'd like to test your theory." Leógham picked up a pan and held it. "Let's see if you're odd after taking a blow to the head."

Hrag waved his hands in surrender. "Forget I said anything."

Leógham grinned. "Smart."

Hrag's tone shifted. "Uncle?" A pause. "What's Benkhi's eye color?"

Leógham's pulse quickened. "Gray," he answered quickly.

Hrag let out a thoughtful hum. "I could've sworn they looked blue—"

"Gray, Hrag," Leógham said, firmer now. "Don't let the light fool you. Fire Dwellers have gray eyes that turn red—ash to embers. Never blue." He clenched his jaw. Why had the tincture failed? It had always lasted four days.

Hrag stared out, fingers drumming the windowsill. "I'm unaware of any Fire Dweller House announcing a search for a missing member."

A cold prickle slid down Leógham's spine. "Maybe they're keeping it a secret," he said evenly, masking the sudden chill settling in his gut.

"But why? Benkhi can transform at will. That alone makes him powerful. Any House would be proud. So why hide it?"

Leógham had to think of something. "Get over here," he snapped.

Hrag turned around. "What for?"

"I still want to test the theory." Leógham hefted the iron pan again with mock menace and lunged.

"Uncle!" Hrag yelped, but laughter exploded through the cabin as he scrambled away, dodging swipes like a seasoned fighter.

"Old man!" he taunted, weaving through furniture to skillfully evade Leógham's swings.

※

After stuffing himself, Hrag snored contentedly. Leógham stepped out with a plate of smoked venison and settled beside Kharis. The late-afternoon light gilded the sky, gold melting across the heavens as the sun dipped lower, streaking the clouds with deep shades of rose and pink. And yet, it was her stillness that held his attention.

She turned to him with a wistful smile that tugged at his heart. The kind of smile shaped by things left undone, by dreams out of reach, by memories that refused to return. He pulled the eye tincture from his pocket and handed it to her.

"It appears your magic burns through the kharisot effect."

She grimaced, then let a drop fall into each eye, blinking with the sting. "How do they look?" She leaned in so he could see.

Leógham swallowed hard at her nearness, fighting the sudden urge to kiss her. "Back to gray." He forced a casual tone.

Kharis sighed in relief, and Leógham took the moment to probe. "Is everything all right?" He leaned slightly. "You've been keeping an eye on Lirun for a while."

She exhaled softly. "I remember very little, often blurred. Sharan and Tung have always felt familiar, known. But Lirun..." Her brow furrowed, shaking her head. "There's nothing. I can't remember a blue moon at all."

"Give yourself the time to mend fully." He tried to sound reassuring. "Rest, and the memories will find you again."

She nodded, though her eyes held doubt.

He studied her, unsettled by the thought that her sky might truly lack a third moon, and by what it implied. He pushed the notion aside at once. *It's a ridiculous impossibility.*

"I..." The words tangled on his tongue. "I would love..." Cheeks warming, he thrust the plate of venison toward her. "Your opinion." *Gah!*

Kharis accepted it, picking up a slice and chewing it thoughtfully. Around them, the forest began to shift toward twilight. An owl called in the distance, its low hoot welcoming the coming evening. The soft flutter of bat wings drifted overhead. Birds rustled above as they settled into their roosts.

Kharis didn't pick another slice, and she wasn't one to leave food behind; her appetite often rivaled Hrag's. She was, after all, *his* bottomless pit.

Nervous about her silence, he gestured toward the plate with his chin. "What do you think?"

"Delicious. I like it."

A brow arched. "But?"

She shook her head softly. "No 'but.' I love it. I bet Hrag stuffed himself."

Leógham snorted, leaning back slightly. "The snores are proof of it. He took the bed, by the way."

She laughed, and his heart fluttered at the way it lit the evening. He bit his cheek, summoning his courage. "If you need to talk... Just know I'm here for you."

"Leógham...?" She faced him. "Does your offer still stand? To stay with you?"

He offered an easy nod. "My promise to you is binding. Of course, you can stay with me." *Forever, if you wish.* "I won't back down."

Her smile unraveled him. He couldn't help the fierce sense of protectiveness that flared beneath it. Possessiveness, too, though he kept that buried.

"Eat." He gestured to her plate. "There's plenty more inside."

She held the plate toward him. "Have some."

His heart nearly leaped out of his chest, the jolt so sharp it stole his breath. A Hegran gesture of courtship. Was she—? The thought hit like lightning. Was she inviting him to court her?

Blessed Fires.

This was everything, the world wrapped in a pretty bow. Hope, so foolish and bright, flickered again. He carefully reached for the plate, one hand brushing the back of hers as he plucked a slice of venison. Heat sparked at the contact, his touch charged with meaning.

"I'll eat whatever you feed me." His eyes held hers as he chewed slowly to seal the intent. "Anything you give me." His answer to her was yes. Always yes.

Kharis only smiled, returning to the darkening sky as if nothing monumental had happened at all.

And just like that, the moment passed.

He studied the space between them, the hush brimming with possibility. *Should I move closer?* He imagined her nestled against him, her breath steady against his chest. He nearly scooted closer, but the fear of Hrag catching them froze him. *Fires burn me.* He couldn't let the moment slip away.

"Would you like to go for a stroll?" He posed the question before he could second-guess himself.

She turned to him, her smile chasing the sadness away from her eyes. "Yes."

Her reply made him grin. "The hilltop?"

"Yes!" That single word sent his heart bouncing like a wild creature.

They climbed the narrow trail. The last light of the setting sun washed the earth in molten amber and rose-gold, shadows lengthening around them. Silence stretched between them, full of promises neither dared to speak.

3 5

THE DECISION

> *A wise person remembers that their smallest turning*
> *may be the crossroad of another's fate. - Poliormos*

That evening, Kharis held onto her wooden bowl,
ready to eat outside where she wouldn't have to deal
with Hrag.

"Sit with us." Leógham pulled out a chair for her. "Please,"
he added softly. "Join us."

Hrag rolled his eyes with a tsk. However, since the
winged nightmare attack, something in him had shifted. The
cutting contempt was gone, and the rudeness tempered. His
suspicion still lingered. Yet now, whenever his gaze met hers,
a strange flicker of awe stirred behind it.

Kharis lingered by the door, unsure. Leógham met her
gaze in a silent plea, and inclined his head toward the chair.
She accepted the invitation and sank slowly into the seat.

The fire crackled softly while they ate, spoons scraping
against bowls filled with venison stew steeped in juniper and
thyme. Outside, crickets sang. And for once, Hrag seemed
content, hunched over, chewing noisily.

Leógham finished first, turning the spoon in his hands,

tracing its edge with his thumb. Was he thinking of serving himself seconds? His jaw worked as if he were weighing it. Then, with a quiet breath, he set the spoon aside.

"I've decided," he said. "I'm returning to Hegra."

Her spoon froze mid-motion, stew trembling on its edge.

"I've been away far too long," he added, as if to soften the blow.

"Truly?" Hrag straightened, eyes wide. "You are?" His face split into a grin a moment later, the gesture boyish and unguarded. "At last!" He shoveled another mouthful of stew, a smirk spreading across his face as if he'd been waiting months for this news.

Kharis forced her spoon to her lips, swallowing hard against the sudden tightness in her throat. Fooling Hrag was one thing. Fooling the world was another.

Dangerous, every step of it.

In Hegra, she would be Benkhi, not Kharis. With so many eyes on her, maintaining the disguise would be far more difficult. She knew nothing of Hegra, its customs, its history, the countless rules that governed its people. The books on the shelves, all plants and healing, offered no answers.

A chill coursed through her. She was truly an outsider. Worse, what would she do once she finished the eye tincture? Her skin bore the ink of magic unknown in Hegra. How would she handle baths or the privy? If anyone saw through her disguise, the verdict would be swift: execution.

And not hers alone. Leógham and Hrag, too. Traitors, both of them, for having helped her. She could almost hear the jeers of a faceless crowd. The rope cracked taut as soldiers dragged Leógham to the block. Hrag's face blanched as the blade fell, knowing he'd be next.

She almost choked on the stew.

And yet... Deeper and insistent like a heartbeat: the pull northward. A journey she didn't understand yet had to fulfill, and to do this, she had to leave this magical realm.

Hrag, oblivious, slurped the last of his stew, humming contentedly to himself.

She set her spoon down, willing her fingers not to tremble. She'd learn to navigate Hegra. And Leógham would be by her side. He'd have answers when the questions came, because they would—questions from her and everyone else.

When she dared a glance, Leógham's grin had faded. He sat rigid, eyes fixed on his empty bowl, his fear a mirror of her own.

Blessed Mother. We're done for.

THE CHINK IN THE GLASS

> *The imperfections in the glass reflect the trials it has weathered and the journey still to come. - Poliormos*

The days slipped by in a blur of preparation. Leógham moved through his rituals—sorting, folding, mending—until, on the eve of their departure, his belongings lay in orderly rows, ready for what awaited them. Early the next day, as Leógham packed the horses, Hrag lingered inside, going over every corner because he didn't know when they would return to this place.

Benkhi had stacked the bowls on the table, rather than on the shelf. *Typical.* One caught his eye, though: the one Benkhi always used. A single word had been carved on it: *kharis*.

He frowned. *Shouldn't it read 'kharisot'?*

His uncle wasn't one to misspell words. Hrag turned the bowl in his hands, his thumb brushing the carved letters again.

"The name for a flower," he mused.

Outside, Benkhi adjusted a strap on one of the horses, following Leógham's instructions. Aside from his uncle, no other Fire Dweller had ever undergone a complete transformation until Benkhi.

That jet-black hair... Only the Mórad Lahm bloodline bore it, descended from King Gairashtagha through his son, Prince Vinashtagha. Of all Hegra's noble Houses, only three still traced their lineage to that line: Teinthir, Seidith, and Luádthir. So which one claimed Benkhi? And why had no word come if he'd gone missing?

He couldn't be House Teinthir. Of that, Hrag was certain. Saigham would've called foul long ago and demanded his immediate return.

The eyes, though... Fire Dwellers sported gray, but those with black hair bore Prince Vinashtagha's eyes, red as flame. Benkhi's were gray, yet sometimes, Hrag swore he saw blue. *Water Kin?* His shoulders shuddered. *Impossible. Benkhi summons fire.*

Someone with Benkhi's ability could upend everything in Hegra: challenge King Aghavor's claim to the throne, split the Houses, plunge Hegra into another civil war. He'd fought a winged nightmare and survived unscathed. Who would dare stand against him?

Something's amiss.

Healing magic was rare, even among the Forest Kin. Hrag clutched his chest instinctively, aware that a creature forged by wind magic had easily ripped his body apart. No one came back from that. Yet Benkhi had healed him, as if the damage had never happened.

Possessing it placed Benkhi with the Forest Kin clan, but if Benkhi summoned fire, his father was undeniably a Fire Dweller. A woman, however, could carry her father's *and* her mother's magic... *No. Not possible. Benkhi's a boy.* He rubbed his forehead. In Hegra, bloodlines were neat and predictable. *An anomaly? Is this why Uncle hides you?* Hegra branded anything that strayed from the pattern an aberration. And aberrations were eliminated.

His uncle and Benkhi stood close, shoulders almost

touching. That lack of space between them gave Hrag pause. That first night after he'd arrived, they had sat outside, displaying that same degree of intimacy, sharing a blanket. Leógham hadn't moved away nor chastised the boy over it. And now, they were talking near the horses, not observing the minimum required Hegran distance of five steps.

Such physical closeness was not the Hegran way. If he hadn't known better, he might have thought his uncle was in love with Benkhi.

The idea stirred, then stalled. *They wouldn't be, would they? Not in Hegra—*

A whinny halted his thoughts. Outside, Kantha stomped and shook his mane. Laughter rose with it.

Hrag placed the bowls back on the shelf, questions unanswered, and walked out.

FAREWELL

> *As I walk the path toward my fate, I shall press on,*
> *steadfast as the river that cleaves the land—patient,*
> *unyielding, and eager for the sea. - Poliormos*

Leógham traced the contours of the cabin he loved. The familiar walls, worn and weathered, echoed their farewell.

"Leógham?" Kharis drew him back. "Are you all right?"

The bittersweet ache coiled tighter. "I came here after Elinor died, and this place became my sanctuary from the pain, the sorrow, the world." A flicker of warmth broke through his grief. "It was here that I found you one moonless night, and fate showed me a different path."

This magnificent realm, born of unfathomable magic, had been his uncle's gift, a rare treasure in a world slowly losing its wonders. "As magic fades, this place will vanish too. This might be the last time I ever see it."

And if that were the case, he knew, with a certainty that ached, that it would never shelter them again.

He took in every detail to preserve it in his memory: how sunlight filtered through the trees, casting shifting mosaics on the mossy ground, or how melodic chirps echoed in the morning air. He filled his lungs with aromas that had become familiar: the sharp, clean scent of pine; the earthy tang of tall grasses; the lingering fragrance of meadowsweet.

Hrag stepped out with a wide grin. "I'm ready."

Leógham forced a small smile. "Same. Everything's packed. Horses are ready." Then he turned to Kharis. "You're riding with me." He mounted, took her wrist, and lifted her as she stepped into the stirrup, sitting her in front of him.

Her brow quirked. "I could've sat behind you."

"My height would block your view."

Her laughter came out softly, but when she glanced down, she quieted quickly. "I'd better not fall."

"You won't. Not on my account."

As he adjusted the reins, his arms brushed hers, a brief touch that sent a jolt through him. Their knees fit together, and her back pressed against his chest. Sparks fired in his veins.

Mighty fires.

He gripped the reins, his body framing hers, and took a deep breath. *Having her this close to me...* He feared he'd be the one falling off the horse.

"How long will it take to reach Hegra?" she asked, breaking the tension only Leógham felt.

"Five days," Hrag answered. "Then a few hours more."

Leógham chuckled, grateful for the distraction. "Hrag knows this path like the back of his hand."

Hrag smirked. "Even Kantha could find his way here blindfolded."

Leógham smiled at that. He'd come to cherish Hrag's steady companionship. "Thank you for coming, even when your mother pushed you to."

Hrag shrugged it off. "I'd have come even if she hadn't." He clucked, shifted his weight, and Kantha moved forward at once.

Leógham glanced back at the cabin one last time, his eyes

suddenly wet. Blinking hard, he wiped his eyes. Hegra waited beyond the horizon. Its capital, Ashtalon, brimmed with secrets and intrigue. He'd face it all. There was no more running away.

Leógham clicked his tongue and flicked Balyus's reins; the stallion surged forward, and the forest closed behind them.

38

WELCOME TO HEGRA

*To arrive is not to end a journey—it begins another. -
Poliormos*

F ive days slipped by in a quiet rhythm of day-long
rides through ancient forests, and nights spent
trading stories and songs beneath the stars.

On the last leg of their journey, Leógham stirred awake
before the others. Wisps of mist drifted through, the air rich
with loam. Golden beams glittered off the morning dew.
Stretching out the stiffness from riding, he sighed. Today
marked the end of this enchanted realm. The thought settled
in his chest like a weight.

He was leaving a place he loved and entering one he
loathed.

Resigned, he padded into the woods to tend to nature's
call. The forest was different this morning—quieter. The
scent of damp moss hung around the faint hum of a waking
world. When he returned to camp, Hrag was already packing
with his usual efficiency, humming one of Benkhi's songs.
Leógham's smile broadened. Hrag could be stubborn,
prickly, and sharp-tongued when it suited him, but beneath

that thorny exterior lay a heart far larger than he'd ever admit.

Kharis returned to camp and packed her belongings with a strip of smoked venison dangling from her mouth—a practical, unceremonious breakfast.

"Here's mine." She tossed her bag into Leógham's hands.

Leógham strapped it on. "Perfect. Yours was the last one. Let's get moving."

They rode in silence, all three tired after four long riding days, followed by nights of storytelling, singing, and laughter until late. Kharis swayed in the saddle, her body battling sleep. Her head would loll forward, only for the jerk to wake her, coaxing a grin from Leógham. Within heartbeats, the swaying would start again.

Until she felt it.

Sure enough, she perked up, gripping the saddle horn tightly. "Um... there's something ahead."

Leógham suppressed a chuckle. "Is that so? Tell me what you feel."

Her breathing was a gentle movement against his chest. When she spoke, her voice had softened. "There's an intense surge of magic ahead."

He leaned forward slightly, intrigued. "Show me its direction."

Kharis's head tilted slightly as though she were following an invisible thread. Her hand wavered in the air before finally pointing firmly ahead. "That way."

Leógham's lips curled. "Look again."

Two towering trees shimmered faintly, their trunks leaning toward each other to form a natural archway.

She went completely still. "Those weren't there before."

"Because only I can summon them," he said.

She shifted in the saddle, glancing first at him, then at Hrag.

"He can find them because I've granted him access to this realm," Leógham said. "My invitation marks him, and lets the portal recognize him." He gestured to the faintly glowing sigil between Hrag's eyes. "Without it, even he'd see nothing but trees."

Her brows lifted, a multitude of questions likely swirling in her mind, before she faced the trees again. "So... what are they?"

"Those two trees form a bhal."

"Bhal?"

He nodded. "Offshoots of the ancient Mahabhal. They draw from the Great Tree's roots. Once, bhalim connected every realm, channels through which the Mahabhal's magic flowed freely. But that was long ago, before the Shattering."

He gestured ahead. "The space between them is the portal we cross into Hegra. Look closely."

The shimmer between the two trees stilled, condensing into a circular gateway whose surface was as smooth as liquid glass. Light rippled outward, scattering across the forest floor like spilled stars.

The bhal had responded to his call. But today it did something else, too.

Tendrils of light drifted from the portal toward Kharis, brushing her skin with playful curiosity. She stilled, then raised a tentative hand. They curled around her fingers and spiraled up her arm, light and teasing, until a giggle slipped free from her.

"If butterflies could kiss," she murmured, "it would feel like this: soft, fleeting, unreal."

Hrag had once described the light, the rippling air, and the sudden pull that drew him in, but nothing like this. She never ceased to astonish him.

The bhal had never behaved like this before, as though it knew her.

"Is this how I came through?" she asked.

"Perhaps." The thought both chilled and fascinated him. "Or perhaps, something far greater is at work here. Magic is weakening, bending he rules to survie a little longer. This bhal is one of the few left in Hegra. The rest have withered. Magic hides the surviving ones, like this one."

"It saddens me to hear this." Her gaze lingered on the glowing trees. "This bhal is magnificent. May it outlast us all."

Her wish brought him a little hope. "May it be the Infinite's will."

Hrag's loud throat-clearing ended the moment. "Anytime now."

Sniffing, Leógham closed his eyes and pressed his ring and middle fingers to his lips, murmuring an incantation. The bhal's glow surged, swelling into a brilliance so intense that Kharis raised an arm to shield her eyes. The space between the twin trunks rippled like liquid glass, light bending inward until it formed a trembling veil.

Leógham and Hrag spurred their horses forward, and all three vanished into the light.

The familiar tug came first—a pull at the chest, twisting the world inside out. It felt endless and brief all at once, the space between worlds folding behind them. Sunlight fractured into gold. Pine and meadowsweet lingered in the air. For one suspended moment, it was beautiful.

"I can hear their whispers," Kharis murmured, her form nearly lost in the light.

Leógham frowned. He hadn't heard anything but the rush of wind. "Whose?"

"I don't know. They sound... ancient."

Then the light shattered, gray bleeding into gold.

A frigid wind struck his face, clawing at his cheeks. The world steadied, but he didn't.

The crossing had taken more from him than he'd expected. His grip tightened on the reins; his vision swam. He forced his breathing to slow, waiting for the weakness to pass. He drew his cloak tighter, but it was of little comfort against the biting cold. The sky overhead was ashen, heavy with drizzle and fog, swallowing the distant peaks.

Kharis gasped audibly.

He couldn't blame her.

The vibrant forest they'd left behind had given way to a landscape drained of life. The trees were skeletal, their bare branches reaching skyward like desperate hands. Snow lay thick across the ground, each step of the horses' hooves breaking it with a crisp crunch. The wind's mournful howl broke the eerie silence.

"How...?" Kharis's voice trembled. "How is it winter?"

The wind lashed at him again, sharp as icy needles, making his eyes water. Nothing had changed in a year: neither the suffocating bleakness nor his hatred for this place.

His breath misted in the cold air.

"Welcome to Hegra," he said flatly.

PART III

THE REALM OF HEGRA

39

THE SHADOWS OF WHAT WAS

There is no curse as wicked and dark as being forced to wear a mask that is not yours. - Poliormos

The stark landscape demanded Kharis's attention, an insistent voice pressing against her senses. Before, it was a barely-there whisper. Now the call was clear, sharp, the pull stronger. Her body leaned forward in the saddle despite her will, muscles tightening, breath held, as if pausing were a kind of pain.

North, it urged. *Go north.*

A haunting silence cloaked this world, the wind sometimes intruding in it with its chilling gusts. No birdsong. No curious furry faces rustling the underbrush. Only the desolate hush of a dying land.

Her gaze lifted. The sky was a lid of iron-gray clouds, sealing out all trace of blue. Sounds had dulled behind her, while the air seemed to hum with quiet insistence. The wind cut across her face, drawing tears that clung to the corners of her eyes. But something else unsettled her: this world... It was eerily familiar.

A frigid gust blew past her, the sting sharp as needles. She rubbed her arms, tucking her hands beneath them for warmth. The cold still found her, lingering on her skin. Noting her gesture, Leógham shrugged off his cloak and draped it across her lap.

"Are we headed north?" she asked.

"No," he said. "West."

"Will we? In time?"

"No," he repeated with a slight bite. "West."

She pinched her lips at that, but as surely as gravity pulled all things to earth, the north drew Kharis's gaze.

Leógham exhaled when the clearing finally came into view, glad for the reprieve it announced.

Hrag, who had slumped in his saddle, straightened. "Finally," he breathed. "I need a nap."

"We'll rest here for a bit." Leógham rubbed his eyes. "I could use one as well."

He dismounted with a low groan, joints stiff from the ride, then helped Kharis down. She took a few limping steps, rubbing her hips.

"The *prince*, as graceful as a chicken," Hrag muttered.

She turned a glare on him that shut him up mid-breath. Riding for five straight days had been tough. Leógham, who hadn't ridden in a year, felt it in the burn along the insides of his thighs and the dull, unrelenting ache of his sitting bones. He feared Kharis fared no better, and the thought tightened a knot in his chest.

Leógham said nothing, watching as she slowly adjusted her stance. The horses wandered, tails flicking as they pawed the snow, looking for something to graze. Hrag sauntered to the base of a tree, leaned back against its trunk, arms crossed, and closed his eyes. Within moments, his breathing deepened, and a snore escaped his lips.

Kharis moved stiffly, as if every muscle begged for mercy. He tipped his chin toward her legs. "Sore?"

A grunt. "I'm fine."

He studied her a moment longer, then tilted his head toward the edge of the clearing. "Come." As they walked, he said, "I've missed your torrent of questions. What's on your mind?"

Kharis shot him a funny look, her lips twitching as if she couldn't decide whether to laugh or grumble.

"You've been quiet since we entered Hegra." He was curious yet gentle with his probing.

She glanced around. "It was startling to leave summer and enter winter"—she snapped her fingers—"like that."

Leógham studied the dense cloud cover. It had stripped the sky of its blue. The world had lost its horizon.

"The weather can't be helped," he said. "This land had once been as green as the forest we left behind: sunlight threading through a lush canopy, the air alive with color and scents." His hand curled. "We've lost the northern territory, buried beneath ice. Each year, that frost creeps closer."

The trees swayed under the weight of snow, creaking and groaning.

"I don't hear birds," Kharis said. "It's the first thing I noticed. That silence throws me off, as if the land has given up on life."

Leógham hated how this endless winter had cursed a once-thriving kingdom. He rolled his shoulders before gripping the back of his neck, stretching it side to side to ease the tension.

"I felt you shiver," he said, eager to change the subject. "Are you warm enough?"

Kharis clutched her arms tighter, leaning toward him. His body moved, and he wrapped his arms around her before he could even think. A natural, instinctive gesture. The cold disappeared, and the comfort of her presence pressed against him. He swam in it, and for a quiet moment, all the ugliness vanished.

Then he froze, the ruthless laws of Hegra rising like a wall. He yanked her back abruptly. Her head snapped back, hair whipping across her face.

"We're in Hegra." His voice was low yet sharp, holding her at arm's length. "Remember: Here, you don't touch anyone, and you don't let *anyone*, not even me, touch you. You cannot forget this."

Her eyes widened behind the curtain of black hair, her body still, her shoulders slumped. She stilled, looking at him as if he'd slapped her. Her expression pierced his heart like a dagger.

"I'm sorry." She took a step back, head lowered. "I forgot."

Leógham breathed out shakily, glancing at Hrag, who was still snoring against the tree and conveniently unaware. When he turned to Kharis, hoping to apologize, she was already by the horses, busying herself with a saddlebag.

He stared at the hands that had pushed her away. They suddenly felt foreign to him, like strangers attached to him.

He silently cursed this wretched place. Hegra had begun its work.

THE PLACE WHERE
GRIEF LINGERS

When sorrow meets sorrow, lost souls find solace, and
hope blooms quietly. - Poliormos

Hrag woke from his nap with a loud yawn and stretched his arms high overhead, joints popping in protest. He swished a mouthful of water to clear the stale taste, then tipped the skin back for a long drink.

His uncle sat against a nearby tree, eyes closed, arms crossed, looking as though he'd managed a nap. Across from them, Balyus nudged Benkhi, eliciting a burst of laughter from the boy. Kantha nickered, his ears flicking as though eavesdropping on the moment.

Hrag lingered on Benkhi, who seemed to fit in and stand apart all at once. His suspicions lingered, but for now, he'd have to bide his time. "Even Kantha likes him."

Leógham stirred, one eye cracking open. "What was that?"

Hrag glanced over. "I thought you were napping."

"I tried, but you're a noisy sleeper."

Hrag shrugged, unbothered. "You aren't far behind me."

Leógham's brow furrowed. "I don't snore."

"Ha! Only when no one's around."

With a grunt, Leógham stretched his neck and chest, regarding Benkhi and the horses before his gaze wandered off.

"Tired?" Hrag asked.

Leógham sighed, rubbing at his eyes. "I could sleep more."

Hrag had picked up on the subtle shift in his uncle's demeanor: tense, already brooding, nothing amused him anymore. He bent forward, knees straight, to touch his toes, easing the stiffness in his back, and glanced at Benkhi, ensuring the boy wouldn't hear. "I can tell everyone I failed."

The hard line of Leógham's jaw relaxed, and the furrow between his brows smoothed out. For a moment, he resembled his old self. "I'm returning. I can't stay in the cabin forever, and you know this. Besides," he gestured to the boy, "there's Benkhi now. I promised I'd help him."

Hrag snapped up straight. "Promised?" A sudden cold overtook him. "As in a *Hegran* promise?"

"Yes."

"Uncle..." He swallowed the protest rising in his throat. Leógham, bound to a stranger without a way to undo the magical contract. He shook his head, refusing to believe his uncle had made such a fool's bargain.

"Nothing can be done now," Leógham said. "Just... keep it to yourself." He exhaled, done with whatever thoughts haunted him, and pushed himself to his feet, rolling his shoulders as he stretched.

Something was off about the boy, but Hrag couldn't ascertain exactly what. "I've never seen Kantha and Balyus get close to anyone. It's almost as if they've known him forever."

Leógham smiled at the thought. "Horses are intelligent, sometimes even more than people." He turned to Hrag. "Still going ahead?"

Hrag hesitated, pursing his lips. "I'll take Benkhi—"

"No," Leógham interjected. "Hegran promise, remember? Go ahead or continue with us. I'm fine either way."

Hrag frowned. "But Uncle, if you intend to visit—"

Leógham raised a hand, eyes shuttering, and took a deep breath until it restored his composure.

Hrag decided not to push. "I'll take my leave."

"Safe travels, Hrag." Leógham offered a soft smile.

Hrag knew he'd forced it.

&.

Kharis fidgeted with her belt, nails digging into the leather grooves, as Hrag mounted Kantha, waved them off, and cantered away. Gone was the chatty young man who filled the silence. Now, she stood beside a man who worried her. Leógham was tense. Withdrawn. Angry, even. The easy camaraderie they'd shared at the cabin had vanished.

She'd learned the signs: the way Leógham's gaze drifted toward the horizon, the furrow between his brows when his thoughts bothered him. Respectful of his need for space, she pushed her questions aside for now.

Soon, they mounted Balyus and trotted down the snow-packed trail. It widened into a well-trodden road that climbed and curved through the rolling hills. From the crest of one rise, Kharis spotted broad fields, orderly orchards, and a village veiled in valley mist. Wisps of smoke curled from chimneys—signs of life against the stark winter landscape.

As they reached the final ridge, the view opened before them, revealing a castle perched on a hill, its stone walls gripping the slope like a vigilant guardian. The two tiers of ramparts followed the land's contours, rising one above the other. The lower enclosed the bailey and the gate, while the upper protected the main hall and its towering keep.

Leógham dismounted and led Balyus to the ridge's edge, where the valley spread out beneath them. He paused there, brooding as his gaze swept the castle and the lands below. Questions crowded Kharis's mind: Where were they? Who ruled this place? Leógham's silence warned her to keep to her own.

He guided Balyus up a narrow, shrub-choked trail to a gnarled oak at the summit, its branches clawing at the gray sky. A solitary stone marker lay at its roots, its face worn smooth by the weather. After securing the horse, Leógham knelt before it and bowed his head.

"I've returned." His voice broke, shoulders quivering.

Understanding clicked into place.

Kharis slid from Balyus, scanning the frozen ground.

The land offered little in this desolate winter, but near a tree, she found a small cluster of white flowers pushing through the snow. Kneeling, she loosened the frozen soil with a dagger and gathered a few. The cold bit, and her ungloved hands turned raw and red. She pondered whether interrupting his orison was acceptable. The walls Leógham had built since crossing into Hegra felt higher than ever.

She approached him on hesitant steps.

"I don't intend to offend you." She held out the flowers. "I wanted to offer these as a sign of my respect. If this isn't proper in Hegra, please forgive me. Say the word, and I'll leave."

Leógham considered them, his expression unreadable. A long silence stretched between them before he gave a slight nod. Letting out a breath, Kharis knelt and dug a small hole beside the marker. The frozen earth bit at her skin, but she planted the flowers with care.

Leógham had turned away, squeezing his eyes shut, trying to send his grief back into its cage.

Kharis rose, brushing snow off her trousers. "I'll be with Balyus—"

His hand shot out, closing around her wrist. "You don't have gloves." His thumb lingered on her reddened skin, over every scrape and cut as they slowly healed. His lips pinched into a thin line, and he glanced away.

"Please..." he said, his voice shaky. "Don't... go."

The words fractured as they left him, sounding nothing like a plea, but as loss made into sound. His gaze slid past her, as if meeting her eyes might break him outright. What could she do to alleviate his pain when her own sense of loss remained imprisoned in the fog that held her memories hostage? The ache in his voice, in his face, asked something of her now.

There was only one answer she understood as right.

Kharis lowered herself before him and cradled his cheek in her palm, her thumb brushing the damp heat of his skin.

"Look at me."

His eyes lifted.

The words surfaced with sudden certainty, echoing a vow he'd once made to her. "I promise I'll never leave you. Please, don't worry about it."

The air between them shimmered. Ripples of warmth danced along her skin, wrapping her like a comforting cloak before sinking into her flesh. A heady scent enveloped her, and for a breathless moment, the world was brighter, better —and then it was gone.

Leógham's restraint broke. He folded into her, his face buried in the crook of her neck, his body shaking as grief poured out of him.

Kharis wrapped herself around him and said nothing. Staying was enough.

DRÍEADH MANOR

A home isn't its walls but the people who welcome you within. - Poliormos

Kharis and Leógham rode the steep incline toward the castle. The gravel road gave way to an uneven cobblestone path. Balyus' hooves echoed in a steady *cloppity-clop*. The urge to head north asserted itself louder here.

As they neared the gates, the portcullis creaked open. Artisans had carved an emblem into the keystone: a dragon displayed, jaws agape, fire spilling from its mouth. Beneath it ran a carved motto, the words darkened by age: *There is only fire*. It reminded Kharis of her nightmare: the terrifying blaze devouring the world.

Balyus crossed beneath the portcullis, and, like a beast's maw, the gates clamped shut behind them.

Beyond the gate, a black banner bearing the same dragon hung above the courtyard, its edges snapping in the wind. Along the walls, rows of narrow black and red pennons marked with the dragon's head fluttered. Guards bore the same device, embossed on leather armor or stitched across their cloaks. The dragon, crimson upon black, blazed from every guidon crowning the battlements.

A fanfare split the air, the three notes carrying across the courtyard. Atop the keep, a standard *per fess gules and sable* began its ascent. The guards along the walls turned as one, backs straightening, hands pressed to their breasts. It unfurled with a sharp crack, the fabric snapping high against the gray sky, visible for leagues.

Leógham dismounted first, then her boots hit the cobblestones with a soft *tap*. She quickly stepped aside to keep her distance.

At least two dozen guards stood across the lower bailey and ramparts, their eyes sharp, their stance precise and disciplined. Leógham ignored them, his fingers curling so tightly around the reins that she feared his gloves would tear.

Questions pounded in her mind like a siege battering the walls of her self-control. Leógham gave no indication he planned to answer any. Pulling on Balyus, they crossed the length of the lower bailey, his silence absolute.

The plaza quickly filled with soldiers clad in black armor, their faces stern. Kharis counted thirty of them. More guarded the parapets. These were his soldiers. Moving like a single body, trained to respond to his presence. Not a whisper of challenge or surprise. Just readiness. Deference.

Who commanded this kind of power? And why hadn't Leógham said anything?

Men and women dressed in black—civilians, judging by their lack of armor or weapons—hurried down the broad staircase and assembled in orderly rows at the bottom: men at the front, women at the back.

Kharis followed Leógham, her eyes flicking toward the soldiers and their cold, unfriendly stares. She gave a small, nervous smile, hoping it might soften some gazes, but no one looked at her or returned the gesture.

"It appears they've missed you." She hoped for an explanation.

His response was a flat, "I've been away for a long time."

That was it? The warning to remain invisible and inconsequential throbbed like a drumbeat in her skull, so she swallowed her remarks—for now—and fell in step behind him. The questioning murmurs among the staff hung in the air, some tracking her with wary eyes.

When Leógham reached the stairs leading to the upper bailey, soldiers saluted, boots aligned with precision, their postures impossibly straighter, their arms stiffened at their sides. Attendants bowed or curtsied, but none met his gaze, hands rigidly still at their sides.

A groom shouldered past the crown, bowed, swiftly took possession of Balyus, and led the horse away.

Hrag, the only familiar face atop the stairs, stood beside a striking woman clad in a heavy black-and-red brocade dress, its subtle shimmer catching the light. A high collar framed her neck, her amber hair drawn back into a neat, elegant bun.

Without a word, Leógham ascended the stairs to meet them, his strides swift. Kharis remained at the bottom, uncertain what to do next and aware that a few watched her intently. Leógham exchanged words with the woman, who dipped into a graceful curtsy. Hrag bowed low, his expression unexpectedly serious and deferential.

Kharis blinked. *Since when does Hrag bow to anyone?*

A hush had fallen over the courtyard. Fidgeting, she glanced at the men and women now standing still, their attention fixed on the exchange. *Who* was Leógham?

Not wanting to be left alone among strangers, she stepped forward, intending to join him, only for a soldier to bar her path with his spear.

"Where do you think you're going?" He shoved her back with a firm hand.

The sudden force knocked her off balance. Her boot skidded on ice, and she hit the ground with a thud. Before she could move, the cold kiss of steel pressed against her throat. Ragha's voice burned in her mind. *"There is only fire, little sister. Go north."*

Leógham spun at the shout, and his face twisted. Scarlet fire burst to life in his fists.

A gasp rippled through the crowd.

"He's with me!" His voice rolled like thunder across the bailey.

He descended, snarling like a beast. The soldier who'd shoved her stiffened, posture faltering, eyes darting. The crowd recoiled, clearing a path for Leógham, who was at her side in an instant. The flames vanished from his hands as he dropped to a crouch beside her.

"Are you hurt?" His voice was eerily soft.

Her cheeks heated. "No." She kept her eyes down, avoiding the faces now watching her, and brushed dirt from her clothes as she rose.

"I'm sorry," he murmured to her, then turned sharply to the soldier. "Apologize. *Now.*"

The soldier, pale-faced, swiftly bowed to Kharis. "Forgive me, My Lord." He stepped back into position, joining the others, but the look of fright on his face remained.

Leógham held her shoulder like a claim. She stared at the cobblestones, biting her lip. Measured footsteps drew her attention. The woman from the stairs descended, skirts lifted in haste. Her eyes, emerald-bright like Leógham's, framed her graceful smile.

"Please forgive us." Her voice was pleasant, melodic. The sweet scent of primroses clung to her. "My son tells me he owes you his life." She curtsied low, and her gesture fueled more whispers in the bailey.

Kharis offered a quick, awkward bow, breath tight, keenly aware that each person watching became a threat that could lead to her ruin.

Hrag swaggered, grinning and waggling his eyebrows. "Ama, this is the one I told you about: the Fire Dweller who can transform fully."

The woman turned to Leógham, her brows rising in question. He confirmed it with a crisp nod.

"Benkhi." Leógham motioned toward the woman. "This is my sister, Lady Sahrit."

Kharis dipped into a second bow to mask her surprise. *A noble line?* Questions rioted beneath her calm, but she kept her composure—barely.

"You must be exhausted," Sahrit said, her eyes always on Kharis's face, never her dirty clothes. She took a step closer, her voice soft. "Please, come." She gestured Kharis along, her smile beaming.

"Welcome to Dríeadh Manor."

THE LIBRARY

*Truth is the deep water beneath all things. Lie, and its
swift currents shall not spare you. - Poliormos*

When Kharis stepped inside the residence, joyful
chaos pulsed through the grand foyer. Scores of
servants wove around her, their arms full.
Chatter spilled from doorways, mingling with the thud of
hurried footsteps and the occasional burst of laughter. Not
far, servants unfurled a banner of the crimson dragon, gold
thread flickering against the light as they hoisted it toward
the rafters. Beneath the beast's talons ran a single line of
script: *There is only fire.*

Her steps slowed. The words snagged her gaze, burning
in her mind, echoing her nightmare.

She glanced away, brushing her hands against her
trousers for the third time, trying to wipe away the dirt still
clinging to her. No one looked at her. Not directly. But she
sensed their side glances, half-paused steps, or the subtle
shift in tone as she passed. Never had she felt so out of place.

A man dressed in a black uniform approached Lady
Sahrit discreetly. Stout, with graying temples, and carrying a

formal, dignified demeanor, he bowed to Leógham, then smiled at Kharis, the gesture warm, almost fatherly.

"Your Ladyship, Lord Leógham's chamber is ready," the man said, "but I wanted to confirm the room his guest is to use—"

"Neagh," Leógham said, his tone clipped. "Lord Benkhi will use the Blue Room." He reached for Kharis's elbow and pulled her forward.

"Where are you going?" Sahrit called, frowning as they started down the hall.

"Library," he replied, not slowing nor looking back.

Kharis stumbled after him, half dragged, her protest swallowed by the speed of his stride. She glanced over her shoulder at Sahrit, who looked as confused as she was.

§∙

Leógham shut the library doors with more force than he'd intended, the sharp sound echoing through the space. He leaned back against the carved wood, breath ragged, as if he'd run rather than walked.

Hegra pressed on him like a vise. Here, the air felt heavy, poisoned by expectation: his father's demands to serve and obey, the endless scrutiny, the choking memories.

He hated Hegra.

Worse, he hated how easily it drew resentment from him.

He thought he'd buried it at the cabin. There, among the trees, he'd learned to breathe again. But here, it stirred again, hot and sharp beneath his skin. The same emotion that made him dangerous.

Calm yourself, Leógham. Breathe.

He closed his eyes, rubbing his forehead as if he could erase the image of Kharis sprawled in the dirt, with the soldier looming over her, spear raised. Fire clawed up his throat again—

"Are you all right?" Her voice dampened it.

Leógham opened his eyes. She stood not far from him, her brow creased. When she stepped closer, he raised a hand.

"Don't. Please."

She held herself, fiddling with her cloak. "Right, distance." Her brows drew together, her teeth catching her lower lip. "Leógham...?" A beat. "Are you well?"

"I just need a moment." He drew a long, deliberate breath, forcing the heat to sink deep where it couldn't harm. "It's... It's been an overwhelming day."

She nodded, knowing, and backed away further, clearly fighting the urge to close the distance and check on him. Questions glinted in her eyes.

He dropped his hand at last, his pulse still pounding, the calm he'd worked so hard to earn trembling like a fragile flame in the wind. He tipped his head toward the room, a silent invitation for her to explore. She glanced around, then nodded in agreement. With her quiet smile, the knot in his chest loosened.

Here, Hegra's demands couldn't reach him. Bookshelves brimming with leather-bound spines formed a mosaic of stories and knowledge that asked for neither his strength nor courage—only his time.

Soft light streamed through the upper windows, landing on a spiral staircase that led to the second floor. The scents of parchment, ink, and polished oak carried him back to boyhood, when he hid with a book whenever the world felt too sharp.

Kharis roamed the library, scanning every corner with the look of someone discovering a hidden realm. He didn't move, afraid to break the spell. Fingers traced the titles on the book spines, her eyes bright, curious. There was a bounce to her step as she moved, betraying her enthusiasm. But it was her smile that captivated him. The smile of someone facing an invaluable treasure.

She's... so lovely.

His pulse stumbled.

Reality clawed its way back.

This fluttering in his heart was dangerous. *She's a man here.* His mind took over, reminding him of the rules that governed this land and the dangers they would face if she were caught. Yet, when she spun around, beaming at him, his heart drummed faster, refusing to obey the logic his mind imposed.

"Lord Benkhi?" she teased, laughter dancing beneath her words.

His shoulders eased.

"I had to think fast," he said. "Honorifics are routine in Hegra." He rolled his neck to ease the knot of tension in his muscles. "I didn't expect my sister to overplay everything."

Sinking into a plush seat, she gave him a sharp look, her voice suddenly edged with something other than curiosity.

"It seems you forgot to tell me a few things."

His blood turned to ice. Of course, she would ask this. He glanced away, scrubbing his hand over his face. There was no escaping this reckoning. He rubbed the back of his neck, the old habit, and pushed away from the door, taking hesitant steps toward the chair beside hers.

"This is my house—"

"Yes." The word came out sharp. "I can see that, but why?"

His eyes dropped to the floor. The answer clawed at his throat.

Her eyes narrowed, expecting an answer.

A tense quiet stretched out between them. His chest rose and fell with effort.

He met her gaze at last.

"Because I'm the crown prince of Hegra."

43

THE SHADOWS BETWEEN US

> *It is not grand betrayals that shatter trust, but the shadows of secrets left unspoken. Those unravel the soul. - Poliormos*

"Crown... prince?"

Kharis's breathing faltered. Her tongue numbed as the truth sank like a blade into her back. Her anger swelled fast to fill in the hollow his omission had carved open.

She opened her mouth to unleash her rage when the world split.

The room faded. Cold rushed in.

The vision crashed into her like a lightning bolt—blinding, cruel. She reeled inward, falling into a deep, dark well, its walls slick with forgotten memories. The surface rippled, black waves disturbing the glassy surface.

A half-remembered fragment stirred at the bottom.

She'd met a crown prince before. She had trusted one. Had been close to him. Loved him, too.

And he had lied to her.

Everything he'd done for her—his care and affection—

205

had been for his benefit alone. The memory burned the back of her throat like a poison. No name or face emerged from the watery maw except the pain from his betrayal. What promises had he made and broken? The ache told her it mattered. Omissions. Half-truths. Years of them.

The details had vanished like smoke, but the scars had remained. *Lies.* She was so tired of them.

"Kharis...?"

Leógham's voice seemed to come from a different world —from lifetimes away. She couldn't answer. If she moved, if a single muscle twitched, this fragile thread of memory would snap, and the images would vanish like the steam in a cooling cup of tea.

She had to remember. She needed to.

The voices in the well swelled beneath the water's surface, tangled and writhing, each clamoring to be heard— voices that had belonged to another world, another time. The churn grew violent. Shapes twisted, some laughing, some weeping.

She waded through the chaos, hands plunging into the water, hoping to catch something—anything—and make it reveal its truth. Then, beneath the maddening turmoil, she saw a glimmer of gold, flickering far below.

Warm. Familiar.

Kharis dove for it, desperate to understand why it shone so fiercely. Was it the sun? And why did it fill her with such joy... and unbearable grief? It came with flashes of vibrant colors, fiery spices, and glorious scents. Sweet jasmine. Crisp orange blossoms. And gold, gold, gold everywhere she looked.

Yet this memory, this solitary voice, lingered at the bottom of a well in her mind, out of reach. No matter how deep Kharis dove to grasp it, it slipped through her fingers each time.

44

THE ART OF MASKS

*A mask, worn long enough, soon becomes a face. -
Poliormos*

Leógham had braced himself for her anger. He had
kept his identity a secret. What had he been
thinking, hiding something that defined him, even if
he loathed it? What had he imagined would happen once
they reached Hegra? There had been chances—too many to
count—to tell her the truth. After Hrag's arrival, most of all.
And yet, he had chosen silence.

He expected the storm to break. Questions. Accusations.
Repercussions. None came.

The silence was worse than any harsh words she might
have hurled at him.

The light in her eyes faltered with his admission. She
stared as though seeing him for the first time; as if the title
had rendered him unrecognizable. Then her gaze hardened,
turning sharp and dangerous. Her hands clenched, sparks
arcing across her skin. Her lips parted, and he steadied
himself for the judgment he deserved—because if their roles
were reversed, he wouldn't have been kind.

But her expression fractured. The rage that moments ago had surged through over her—tightening her jaw, twisting her lips into a snarl—collapsed. Emotions flickered on her face, too quickly to name.

Something else broke through, seizing her completely. Now she looked at him without truly seeing him.

An uneasy stillness settled in the widening chasm between them.

Slowly, he lowered himself into the chair beside her. *Fires. Why didn't I tell her?* The weight of that *why* crushed his chest, robbing him of air.

"Kharis...?" He tiptoed around the ruins he'd caused.

No scolding followed. No sharp correction for speaking her real name. Not even a glance.

All he got was icy silence.

A knock broke the library's heavy lull.

Leógham's jaw tightened. *Of all the times to interrupt.* His temper flared, and he hated how easily it came.

He turned toward the door, forcing the evenness in his voice. "Enter."

The door creaked open. Sahrit stood at the threshold, never crossing it, her hand gripping the doorknob.

"What is it?" he asked.

Before Sahrit could reply, Kharis rose from her chair, offering her full attention. Leógham shot her a questioning look. When she didn't meet his eyes, he sighed again, quieter this time, and stood.

"What do you need?" he asked more evenly.

Sahrit turned a ring between her fingers. "I... I wanted to confirm Lord Benkhi's use of the Blue Room."

He chuckled softly. Sahrit, addressing Kharis as "Lord Benkhi," tickled him, but when Kharis glowered, his amusement dissolved. *You laughed at the title before.* Except she didn't seem to think it was funny anymore.

Kharis strode toward Sahrit and opened the door fully.

"Please, Your Highness. Join us."

Sahrit blushed and looked to him for permission. He offered a curt nod, an unspoken *Get on with it*.

Kharis guided her inside. Leógham silently groaned. *Stay calm. Control your anger.* He knew his sister was doing her job, her interruption expected, but his irritation was rising fast.

"What's your concern?" he asked, the words now clipped.

Sahrit shifted her weight, her fingers twisting together. "It's the choice of room."

"I place my trust in your judgment," Kharis said. "Any room will—"

"The Blue Room," Leógham cut in unkindly. "Lord Benkhi is the only other Fire Dweller who can transform fully. I want him close to my quarters."

He paused—too long. "As for the Blue Room..." His hand curled into a fist. "The room can have other uses now."

Sahrit's lips pressed into a thin line before she inclined her head, the gesture taut, her silence cold.

Kharis met his gaze with a disapproving glare, and his fire suddenly banked.

"Your Highness," Kharis said. "Please—sit."

"No need for formalities. You may address me as Lady Sahrit, please."

"As sister to the crown prince"—her glare slid back to Leógham, the silent reprimand sharp enough to draw blood —"I'm grateful for the honor. Our journey was long, and we're both exhausted."

Kharis had reclaimed the moment to save his face. He bit the inside of his cheek and, silently sulking, dropped into a chair opposite them.

"I'd be honored if you'd join us for tea," Kharis went on. "Your company would make it better."

Sahrit covered her small, flustered gasp. "I didn't offer you anything. Please accept my heartfelt apologies."

He lowered his chin as a hard knot formed in his throat.

She would've offered, had he not dragged Kharis through the hall like a storm.

"I'll order tea and have it brought here," Sahrit said.

"I've learned that your son, Lord Hrag, is quite the engaging storyteller. You must be proud of him," Kharis said.

The comment eased Sahrit's posture, her chest rising with a deep breath. Kharis kept the conversation flowing, her neutral voice pitch straddling the line between masculine and feminine. Leógham fell into silent scheming. With proper clothing and precautions, her disguise would hold until he figured out how to return her safely to her homeland. If she kept to the background, no one would notice her presence or ask impertinent questions.

"Thank you," Kharis said. "I look forward to it."

His thoughts snapped back to the moment, aware he'd missed part of the conversation. "Come again?"

"Lady Sahrit has invited me to a tour of Dríeadh Manor."

His stomach dropped. "I see," he muttered, forcing the words past a throat gone tight.

Sahrit rose, smoothing her skirt. "I'll ensure the Blue Room is ready for Lord Benkhi."

Leógham gave her a brief nod, relieved that this ordeal was over. The conversation had taken more effort than expected, but it had unfolded smoothly enough. Kharis's disguise held, and he was glad for that. She walked Sahrit to the door with the same polished grace, exchanging pleasantries.

As the door clicked shut behind Sahrit, Kharis lingered, her hand resting on the handle.

She then turned slowly, dangerously, as a queen about to pass judgment. Leógham's stomach clenched. The polite smile she'd worn for Sahrit was gone, replaced by a smoldering glare that made him swallow hard.

Fires take me now.

45

THE UNBEARABLE
WEIGHT OF LOSS

Loss is the weight of an empty heart. - Poliormos

"What is wrong with you?" Kharis's gaze burned into him. "Your sister was trying—*trying*—to welcome you home." Her voice cracked, her words sharper. "I understand why you're mad at the world, but it doesn't give you the right to hurt the people who love you."

"Benkhi, I—"

"Sit," she commanded.

His body moved before his brain caught up, dropping into the chair with a solid thud, facing her like a prisoner awaiting his sentence.

"We haven't finished our conversation." There was fire in her voice. "And the time it takes your sister to bring us tea ensures we do."

He stiffened like a cornered hare while Kharis paced the room like a restless, growling dragon.

"I can accept why you would withhold your identity from me—"

He rose, palms up. "Benkhi, please—"

"I'm *not* finished."

Leógham sank back down.

"If you ever lie or withhold the truth from me again," she said, a snarl at the end of it, "our arrangement is null and void. I won't work with someone I cannot trust."

Leógham raised his palms in a conciliatory gesture. "I should've told you. My intention was never to deceive you." He meant it from his heart. "Please accept my apologies." He reached out for her without thought, only to pull his hand away, and lowered his head. "Allow me to make this up to you."

Kharis gazed at him, chin high. Her silence lasted long enough for his unease to settle deep. Then, "What's with the Blue Room?"

His body went rigid, pulse hammering his ears.

Fires burn me forever.

Explaining himself meant revealing his feelings for her. And given how furious she was right now, that truth would only make things worse.

"Leógham?"

He breathed slowly, unevenly. "It was my wife's chamber."

"What?"

She halted mid-step and turned slowly as though she hadn't heard him correctly.

"Elinor's room," he said, his voice lower still.

Kharis's mouth thinned into a hard line. Her eyes narrowed into slits of steel. Leógham swore more growls rumbled in her throat.

"So that's why your instructions flustered your sister." She groaned, raising a fisted hand as though she were imagining throttling someone—maybe him. "You want me to be invisible, yet you force everyone to ignore the fact that you're putting a stranger in your deceased wife's bedchamber?"

Leógham avoided her piercing stare.

"Can't you see how dangerous this is?" she asked.

"Kharis—"

She snarled at him, the warning clear. No more "Kharis."

Apparently, his veiled confession—why he'd chosen a room meant only for his spouse—had gone unnoticed. She paced the room with a hand pressed to her forehead. "This is bad," she kept saying. "So bad."

Intense eyes shot daggers at him. "You cannot put me in her room. That," she snapped, head tilted, "places me at the center of all attention, *crown prince*." Her lips curled into a cold, little smile.

"Do not—" The words ripped from him before he could temper them. His fingers curled tightly, knuckles aching. Her sarcasm had stung worse than he cared to admit. He forced his mouth shut, swallowing whatever he'd almost hurled back at her.

Kharis collapsed into a chair. "Put me in a different room. I don't care if I sleep in the stables with the horses." She drew in a breath, a sob hidden beneath it. "I have nothing to call my own, not even the clothes I wear." A sharp breath followed. "Had it not been for you, that soldier would've thrown me out."

The memory surfaced, and the truth in it hollowed him. His anger flickered.

She closed her eyes, fingers rubbing the deep lines between her brows. "The only thing that keeps me moving forward is the hope that tomorrow might be better. That I might find an answer or remember something useful *tomorrow*."

Tears finally spilled. She slumped forward, elbows on her knees, head in her hands. She looked so small. So exhausted.

"I miss my loved ones," she said. "Yet I can't remember anything about them. Shadows are all I have now." She straightened with a shuddering breath, meeting his gaze. "I'm lost, Leógham. I... I don't know how to navigate your world."

He heard what lay beneath the words—the

uncomfortable vulnerability of having to rely on someone else. That honesty, spoken so plainly, unraveled him. His anger shrank, his pride dulled and bruised.

I'm a fool. A petty, selfish fool.

He drew a long breath, ashamed of having lost his temper. He'd sworn to keep it under control, yet here he was, a year later, allowing it to rule him again. Worse still, he'd turned it on her, who, hours ago, had held him in his grief.

This time, he couldn't blame Hegra's suffocating rules.

This failure was his alone. "I'm truly sorry."

The silence stretched, each heartbeat painful in his chest.

Kharis had buried her face in her hands, her silent weeping tearing his heart apart. He'd built this wall. Now, he had to tear it down.

This woman—this strange, stubborn woman—had appeared out of nowhere and filled the quiet spaces in his life. Slowly, without realizing it, the ache of losing Elinor had softened until his memories of her became summer sunbeams, not a blistering winter wind.

With Kharis beside him, he could face Hegra. Even the broken pieces inside him found their place, as if she alone held the pattern of who he ought to be while her presence shaped the missing half of his soul.

"I... I can't imagine not having you near." This was his truth. "I thought only of myself, never considering what you needed or how you felt." He dropped a knee before her. "Please forgive me. Allow me to make it up to you."

Glistening eyes gazed at him. "Leógham, when I asked for your help, I didn't know you were the crown prince. Given your laws, aiding me comes with an even higher cost. Everyone's in danger now." Her eyes shuttered with her grimace. "You must give me another room. Perhaps"—she bit her lip—"send me away."

He would never do that, Hegran promise or not.

His brows drew together briefly. "The Blue Room has a

hidden door that connects to my chamber. It gives us privacy so we can discuss without prying ears." He took her hands and gave them a steady, grounding squeeze. "Come. Let me show you something."

At a tall cabinet fitted with narrow drawers, he pulled one open and withdrew several rolled parchments.

"Maps." He spread one across the table, smoothing a crease. "I promised to help you find this Zahar-Ghak, and the promise stands."

She watched him a moment, then nodded.

"Bhalim are nearly impossible to find in Hegra," he said. "Without a bhal, there's no portal. But if we find one, we might reach your homeland."

"Not a road?" she asked.

He drew a slow breath, weighing how far back he needed to go. The "no lies or omissions" rule flickered in his mind.

"Long ago," he said at last, "Tír was one land. Kingdoms stretched in every direction. Magic flowed from the Mahabhal like a great river."

His thumb traced a faded line on the parchment.

"Then came the war, and Tír shattered. The realms broke apart along the ley lines, sealing the kingdoms from one another, save for a few narrow gaps where bhalim grew. Roads were lost. Portals became the only way through." He looked at her. "With access to a bhal, we can reach your kingdom."

Kharis scratched her cheek. "Why is it hard to find them?"

His shoulders drew tight, fingers brushing his bracer's worn leather.

"After the Shattering, the ice flowers appeared," he said. "A blight that feeds on magic. Their hunger weakened portals, so most kingdoms sealed theirs to keep them at bay. No one leaves. No one comes."

"Except Skógarjód," she said.

"Our last ally," he replied. "Bound by a fragile accord."

Her lips pursed. "Fragile...?"

A tired breath slipped from him. " Not everyone in Hegra accepts the price of it."

She studied the map again. "So finding a bhal..."

"Will not be easy." His gaze lifted to hers. "Perhaps not even possible." A pause. "But if you are willing to try," he said, resolve kindling beneath the fatigue, "then so am I."

He glanced at her, lip caught between his teeth, waiting for an answer.

Kharis said nothing, her brow furrowed as her fingertips glided over the inked lines on the map.

"What if, instead of chasing bhalim," her eyes never left the map, "we destroyed the ice flowers?"

Leógham sucked in a breath. "Tried and failed. It only made things worse. The source of the blight lies north, and no one goes there anymore."

Her head snapped up. "North...?"

Leógham leaned forward, eyes narrowing on her. "Yes, north. The one realm without a portal." His eyes held hers. "And listen well: those who went there never returned."

Kharis didn't respond. Instead, she bent over the map again, tracing a line northward as though charting a path in her mind. A glint sparked in her eyes. "Why?"

"We don't know." Those words scraped his throat. The not knowing. The powerlessness implied in it. "If you value your life, never set foot there. *Ever.*"

Silver flashed in her eyes. He forced a smile, trying to mask the unease squeezing his chest. "Shall we focus on the bhalim?"

A pause. Then, finally, she nodded.

The tension in his shoulders eased. "Let's rest. Ours was a long journey, and Sahrit will bring us tea soon." He stepped away from the table. "Come."

When she didn't follow, he turned—and frowned.

She was still staring at the map. Her fingers drifted north

again, tracing a slow, deliberate path toward the jagged edge of the uncharted lands.

They hovered there, at the brink.

And in the pit of Leógham's stomach, dread coiled, its grip tight and cold.

46

TEA, TARTLETS, AND TRUTHS

> *The cleverest lies are the ones wrapped in fragments of truth. - Poliormos*

K haris heard the scuffing of shoes before the knock on the library doors.

Sahrit entered, followed by a line of servants carrying trays laden with tea and food. The clink of porcelain and silverware sharpened Kharis's hunger.

One servant drew her eye, moving with the poise of someone who'd spent decades mastering these corridors. Silver threaded her dark hair. Subtle embroidery adorned her cuffs, setting her apart. Her manner carried graceful authority, and the others moved in time with her. When Sahrit spoke, she addressed her directly.

"Ailene, please let Lord Hrag know we're here."

Ailene bowed in answer, and the others followed her lead before filing out.

"The servants are setting up the baths upstairs," Sahrit said. "Lord Darragh should arrive in time to join us for dinner."

A smile finally broke across Leógham's face. "It'll be nice to see him."

Kharis's curiosity piqued. *Lord Darragh.* She tucked the name away for later, filing it among the growing list of things she needed to learn about this place.

"Lord Benkhi," Sahrit said. "Hrag told me about the mathan attack, that it mauled and nearly killed you." She skillfully poured tea and handed Kharis the cup. "It must've been terrifying."

"It was," Kharis said, thinking of the one who'd claimed their pig. "Your brother is the true hero."

Sahrit smiled and gestured toward the food. "I hope these are to your liking."

There were tartlets, meatballs, and savory pasties, all small enough to be eaten in a single bite. She took a tentative bite of a tartlet. The flavor was... different, lacking the spicing Leógham had used back at the cabin. Too hungry to care about bland food, a few more made it to her mouth. Leógham cast her a sidelong glance, an all-too-familiar smirk tugging at the corner of his mouth.

Yes, yes, I'm a bottomless pit.

Sahrit assembled her brother's plate with sisterly determination, adding generous portions—an act of welcome that revealed how deeply she'd missed him.

Leógham's eyebrows drew together. "Sahrit, there's no need to—"

She handed him the plate with a proud smile. Leógham grabbed it carefully, tiny meatballs wobbling precariously near the edge.

"Hrag mentioned your encounter with the winged nightmare." Her brow creased. "How is it you ran into one of those?"

Kharis's plate almost slipped from her hands.

A muscle worked in Leógham's jaw. "The ice flowers," he said at last. "I fear that as they drain the land, the wards protecting my realm have weakened." His gaze darkened. "And if that's true, nothing in Hegra is truly safe anymore."

A series of loud knocks drew everyone's attention, and the door swung open. Hrag walked in with a toothy grin on his face. "Look who I ran into."

"Darragh!" Leógham stood, a broad grin on his face.

Leógham extended his arm, and Darragh grabbed the forearm firmly, pulling him into a quick, hearty embrace. Their shoulders and chests touched briefly as they patted each other's backs in a gesture of camaraderie.

Touching? Kharis frowned. *Wasn't it forbidden?*

Yet here, Leógham had initiated contact without hesitation. So, was it allowed after all? Maybe it depended on trust. Or rank? Or something else entirely? Her thoughts tangled, so she tucked the moment away, with a mental note to ask Leógham later.

His wavy hair, neatly trimmed beard, and understated demeanor were a stark contrast to Lord Darragh, who was older than Leógham, clean-shaven, and charismatic. He effortlessly took command of the room, his laughter infusing it with a jovial warmth.

Hrag bore an uncanny resemblance to Lord Darragh, sharing the same cheekbones, defined jawline, and gracefully long nose, not to mention the striking forest-green eyes. *His father?* The only significant difference between the two was the hair. Hrag had inherited his mother's rich amber locks. Lord Darragh's silver hair fell at least a hand below his shoulders, tied neatly at the nape with a black leather strip.

"And who's this?" Darragh's attention snapped to Kharis.

"Apa," Hrag said, piling meatballs onto his plate, "this is Lord Benkhi."

Darragh slowed his approach, facing Hrag. "The lad who fought the winged nightmare and healed you?"

Leógham groaned audibly, grabbing Hrag by the elbow and pulling him away from the group. Darragh's grin widened, green eyes glowing. He approached Kharis with the assurance of a dangerous predator.

> ❦

Darragh paused when the boy extended his hand, puzzled by the gesture. Only males of the same household acknowledged each other like that.

Doesn't he know this?

Darragh kept his smile, willing to play along. As he reached for the offered hand, something else caught his eye. The boy, with a face a touch too pretty to belong on any battlefield, much less fight a winged nightmare, hadn't looped the sleeves over the backs of his hands, leaving the skin exposed.

Now, now, why didn't he? Quite careless. He barely stifled his sneer.

"Nice to meet you, Lord Benkhi. Allow me to offer my gratitude." Darragh's tone betrayed none of the suspicion flickering beneath. He clasped the boy's hand, and his magic sank its fangs. The lad winced and attempted to pull away, but Darragh tightened his grip. When the boy lifted his gaze, Darragh met it. His focus narrowed as he pressed inward, probing Lord Benkhi's mind.

It was like a void. Empty. *Wards?* But as he probed further, he discovered a tantalizing secret.

Ah!

Lord Benkhi tugged on his hand once more, and Darragh, satisfied with the answers he had, let go. The boy flinched, rubbing the reddened skin. Darragh watched the motion with a quiet curl of his mouth. *Serves him right.*

"May your stay be pleasant, Lord Benkhi."

His attention shifted to his lovely Sahrit. Their eyes met, and his smile deepened. *Ridiculous Hegra. Why can't I kiss my wife?* With effort, he curbed the urge.

"I'm glad to be back," he purred as he took a cup of tea from her.

Sahrit blushed.

Darragh chuckled softly, her shyness only fueling her charm. *She's so beautiful.* He stifled the temptation to scoop her up in his arms and take her away. Leógham, who'd pinned Hrag for a pointed lecture, let out a long breath and joined him.

"So, what news would you share with us?" Darragh asked.

"My news will be well met, but yours, I'm afraid, will not," Leógham said.

"Ah, brother." Darragh's voice took on a wistful tone. "Such is the truth in all things, more so in Hegra."

The conversation flowed easily, Darragh and Leógham falling into a familiar banter until the library doors opened quietly.

Master Neagh, the castle's seneschal, approached Sahrit. She listened intently, nodded, and with the same efficiency that defined him, he exited.

"The baths are ready," Sahrit said. "Lord Benkhi, I've asked one of the male servants to assist you—"

"No!"

The word rang out, loud and in perfect unison, from both Leógham and Benkhi.

Sahrit blinked, startled.

Hrag stopped chewing.

Darragh leaned back, pondering how Leógham would get out of this one.

The moments passed in loaded silence until Benkhi scratched his cheek, glancing nervously at Leógham before speaking. "I won't need any help," the boy stammered. "I prefer to handle these... um... issues alone."

Darragh arched a silver brow.

Leógham cleared his throat. "Same for me." He rubbed the back of his neck, such a tell of his unease. "I've been on my own for some time, and... uh... would like to adjust gradually. We can both manage... ah... without servants."

The room dimmed into an awkward silence.

Darragh broke it. "I see you haven't changed your wild ways, brother. Lord Benkhi," he said, "when the crown prince was a child, he'd often run to the lake and bathe there, to the nannies' dismay."

The tension eased slightly from Leógham's jaw. "I recall a different version—one where you dragged me to the lake by my arm."

Darragh leaned forward. "To slow you, of course. Never had a Hegran crown prince been as obsessed with water as you."

"Lord Benkhi," Sahrit asked, "are you certain about not needing help?"

The young man smiled with an enchanting sense of confidence. "Lady Sahrit, there's an indescribable joy when one does something on their own, even if mundane."

Sahrit's mouth curved into a faint smile. Darragh's grin dimmed. The young man had won her over.

Leógham moved toward the door, waiting. Lord Benkhi turned to the group and bowed. "Thank you for your hospitality," he said. "Until dinner." The two of them disappeared past the door.

Darragh pursed his lips, amusement turning into calculation, intending to pry loose Leógham's secrets one way or another.

Because... why would he take such a risk hiding a girl?

47

THE STRANGER AT THE GATE

Each decision is a thread woven not into one's life but into the fabric of many lives. Thus, a careless choice may become the burden of a family, a kingdom, or the world. - Poliormos

She had finished dressing when Leógham entered her chambers. His gaze swept over her, pausing at her exposed neck before a frown darkened his expression. The stern lecture came next.

"You must cover your neck always."

Before she could protest, he tugged her collar up, the stiff fabric scraping her jaw. His fingers brushed her throat—warm, brief—and her breath caught despite herself, before he fastened the buttons.

"It scratches my skin," she muttered.

He answered with a glower, a silent *deal with it*. Her pulse quickened, equal parts irritation and... the dark urge to punch him in the face.

"These," he pointed to the leather loops sewn into her sleeves, "are for the fingers." He slid her fingers through the loops, tightening the fabric across her knuckles.

"So that's what they are for." Kharis flexed her fingers experimentally.

"In Hegra, protocol disallows exposed skin, save for the face and fingers."

"Why?" The question slipped out, half complaint, half curiosity.

"Because that's how it is," he snapped, sharper than she'd ever heard.

"That's not an answer," she mumbled.

Oh, that he heard. Leógham's voice dropped low, tight with strain. "If you like your head where it is, do *not* question protocol."

"Is that so?" Kharis pushed her shoulders back. The crown prince didn't command her.

He clenched his jaw, glaring at her, then fussed with her clothes—a sharp tug here, a rough pull there, smoothing folds—every movement edged with tension. When he stepped back for a final inspection, he crossed his arms, chin high, as if daring her to complain again. She narrowed her eyes, considering it. The high collar itched incessantly, and the finger loops bit into her skin between her fingers as reminders of what was at stake if her disguise failed. Since their lives were at stake, she swallowed her remarks and glanced away with an angry huff.

"Deterrents," he suddenly said. The glare was there, but his tone had gentled a little. "Fabric protects against unwanted or conniving touches. The more clothing, the better."

She still didn't meet his eyes. "Thank you."

Leógham didn't respond. He only gestured for her to follow him.

⁂

Darragh swirled the amber liquid in his glass, watching the light dance across its surface before taking a slow sip.

While they waited for the dinner announcement, Hrag had recounted how the winged nightmare had attacked, and Lord Benkhi had healed him.

Darragh traced the rim of his glass as he listened. *A Fire Dweller with a healing ability?* He'd need confirmation from Leógham. Since Benkhi was a girl, it was plausible. The secrecy, though. *Is he hiding her because of her healing gift?* The gift was rare enough to start a war. Some people would kill to possess it. *Is that what Leógham wants: her skill?*

"I wasn't aware a Fire Dweller was missing," he said. "And, as far as I know, no Mórad Lahm House has requested aid for a search."

Hrag shrugged, thoughtful. "What if he belongs to a House far from the capital?"

"Away from Ashtalon?" Darragh arched a brow. "Do you honestly believe that's likely?"

Hrag hesitated. "Well... It's possible, isn't it?"

Darragh set his glass down with a soft clink. "Not anymore. The Houses are now bound to Ashtalon, thanks to the ice flowers. No one leaves to start a House elsewhere." He tilted his head slightly. "This Lord Benkhi poses an interesting question, wouldn't you say?"

Hrag shifted in his seat, half agreeing. "He's peculiar."

Darragh tapped a finger against the table before serving himself more, mind working out the puzzle. "Lord Benkhi's appearance should be as unexpected as the winged nightmare's." He lifted the glass, turning it slowly between his fingers. "The magic shaping Leógham's realm is faltering, and through those cracks, the impossible slips in."

He took a hard sip, trying to erase the images conjured by such an impossibility: strangers, monsters, assassins.

"The ice flowers creep toward Hegra, siphoning magic," he added, "and the world splinters further. Saigham. The Water Kin. All distractions." His eyes scanned the room before his voice dropped to a grave murmur. "If our attention shifts to war, we'll freeze where we stand in no time. This is the truth many in Hegra deny." He pursed his lips, resting the glass on his knee. "It won't happen today, or tomorrow, but it will happen, and when everyone realizes this, it will be too late to stop it."

His gaze lingered on his beloved Sahrit, who sat on a cushioned settee across the drawing room, a book open in her hands.

"This denial is what troubles me the most."

Darragh took a slow swallow, the taste grounding him.

"Saigham has been waiting for Leógham to return. Now that he is here..." He sighed, the rush of air audible. "To Saigham, Leógham's temper is proof that purity laws should rule again. Without an heir, if Leógham dies, Aghavor's bloodline ends. Saigham will seize the throne, and the oath with Skógarjód dies."

The hearth flames licked the logs, an ember popping.

"Hegra needs Skógarjód's timber, its resin, its medicines," he added. "Skógarjód needs Hegran iron and wool. Without a peace agreement, Hegra will turn its forges toward war, and the purity faction's first conquest will be the eastern forests... after they've enslaved those of mixed heritage."

His thoughts guttered at the idea of Sahrit and Hrag in chains, forced to a life of servitude under Saigham's boots for his enjoyment. He thought of the servants and soldiers past these walls, so many of mixed blood, loyal to Leógham's house. What would happen to them under Saigham's rule?

Darragh knocked back the rest of his drink in one quick motion, the liquid burning a path down his throat. "That's why we must protect Leógham. If he falls, so do we."

He set the glass down, the sound sharp against the quiet, and glanced toward the door, expecting it to open any moment. "When's dinner? This delay is longer than usual."

"We're waiting for Uncle and Benkhi." Hrag turned toward the doors. "This place is so big, I bet Benkhi got lost again, and Uncle had to go find him."

A low chuckle escaped Darragh, though it held no humor. He still needed to determine that girl's purpose.

"Let's hope that's all it is." His concerns lingered in his mind like the scent of dianthus.

48

THE GAMES OF
MEN AND GODS

The gods invented fate; men invented rules. Both call it a game. And no arena is more treacherous, balanced between chaos and divine consequence. - Poliormos

Kharis sat ramrod straight at the dinner table, resisting the urge to scratch at her neck. The collar rasped against her skin, her fingers itching to claw at it, so she pressed her hands beneath her thighs to keep them still. The pull north tugged at her without pause, a quiet insistence that frayed her concentration and made every moment stretch thin.

She fixed her gaze on the cornices, anywhere but the men in the portraits glaring down at her. This would be a long night.

As she'd suspected, dinner was a formal affair—rigid, polished. Servants glided with precision, pouring wine and replacing candles. Four people sat at the table, and yet it became a performance staged for a hundred eyes.

Leógham presided over this meal, his posture stiff. Hrag

sat at his left, always chatty. Darragh occupied the seat to Leógham's right, missing nothing.

Sitting to Darragh's left, Sahrit's presence was subtle enough to be invisible. *Hegra will be proud, no doubt.* She wore a stunning black-and-silver brocade gown. A gem-encrusted hair brooch secured her long, glossy hair in an intricate twist.

Kharis sighed, fingers discreetly ghosting over the ends of her own hair, so short it barely grazed her shoulders. She'd do anything to shed her men's clothes and wear something beautiful like Sahrit. Instead, she forced herself to eat, every mouthful bitter. She missed Leógham's cooking. She missed the cabin, the forest, and their quiet evenings.

Hrag, no surprise there, dominated the conversation while Lord Darragh filled any lulls with comments on the state of Hegra, his eyes on occasion lingering on her. Kharis glanced away every time. Leógham offered the occasional chuckle, but she caught the hollowness in it. His thoughts were elsewhere.

Darragh set his goblet down. The soft click carried through the dining hall.

"Lord Benkhi," he said, smiling as though he were about to praise the wine, "as you may know, our Houses pay close attention to the crown prince's favor."

Kharis's fork paused halfway to her mouth.

Darragh leaned back, fingers steepled. "When he chooses to foster a boy, it is understood the child comes from a loyal House." His gaze never wavered. "Yours, for instance."

Darragh's gaze held hers, mild and expectant. Waiting.

Hrag snorted, already waving a hand. "Apa, it's a miracle Benkhi remembers his own name."

Leógham's chair shifted.

"Speaking of loyalties," Leógham said, lifting his cup. A servant stepped at once, the pour smooth and practiced. "Will Skógarjód question Hegra's motives at this juncture? The monarchs have been quiet since the last council. Too quiet, some would say. Are we to expect goodwill or disfavor?"

Silence stretched, fragile as thin ice.

Darragh swirled the wine in his goblet and drank. When he set it down, his smile widened, reshaping itself. His eyes slid from Kharis to Leógham, the question neatly folded away.

"Goodwill," Darragh said. "Always."

Kharis exhaled quietly and kept her gaze down the rest of the evening.

When the servants cleared the last dish, pears poached in sweet wine, they adjourned to the Drawing Room. Its vast fireplace, carved into the snarling maw of a dragon, washed the hunting trophies and ancestral portraits in flickering firelight.

She found herself seated at a small round table where Hrag was shuffling a deck of cards. "Baraxas," he announced. "Hopefully, you remember how to play this game."

Across from him, Sahrit sat, her presence calm and unassuming while the cards flashed between Hrag's fingers like blades.

"Four each."

It sounded like a question, a silent test. Kharis ignored him, and he dealt the cards with deft.

Kharis studied her hand, feigning calm though all she wanted was to flee to her chambers and tear off her garments. The vest pinched her ribs. The collar scraped her throat. Yet, here she was, trapped at a table with annoying Hrag, playing a game she didn't understand.

The cards trembled in her hands. One displayed five suns etched in gilt. Another, three staves crossed like an X, the third, four chalices overflowing with silver; and the last one —a king wielding a flaming blade.

"Let's begin," he said.

"A general never rushes into battle." She stalled for time

with a forced smile, hoping to make sense of her hand. "One must plan carefully."

Hrag smirked, leaning back. "Let's see if you survive."

He laid down his first card: a knight holding a coin. Sahrit tilted her head, a faint curving of her lips betraying a good hand, before she played her own: a king holding one of those lavish goblets. Hrag's eyes narrowed, a low hum rumbling in his throat.

"*You waste time with games, little sister.*" Ragha's voice slid into her mind, moving as if he wanted to see the cards she'd been dealt. "*The north calls.*"

Her hold faltered, and the cards nearly slipped from her fingers. Ice flowers unfurled in her thoughts—delicate, deadly blossoms choking the veins of Hegra's magic. She saw the map again, the place she must go, except no one ever returned from there—

"Are you playing or yielding?" Hrag smirked.

She refocused on the game and chose to gamble. Strategy. Deception. Survival. These were the principles that would keep her alive in Hegra. Kharis stared at her hand and chose her king, tapping the card against the table to mask her uncertainty with bravado.

Hrag's smile faltered. "The fire king?" Then he groaned—loudly. "Of all the luck."

Sahrit offered a faint nod of approval.

"Beginner's luck," Hrag grumbled. "Let's see if you can keep it, *prince*."

Kharis had won the round, but Ragha's whispers tugged her thoughts northward.

The game went on. The cards lay between them like soldiers, but in her mind, the actual battlefield waited at the edge of the world.

GRIEF AND DUTY

Grief may leave scars, but duty binds the heart. -
Poliormos

D arragh released a sigh, scrubbing a hand over his
mouth. He'd planned to join the card game, hoping
to engage "Lord" Benkhi and perhaps draw *her* into
a proper conversation. Those plans dissolved when he saw
Leógham.

The crown prince moped, slumped in a high-backed
chair near the fireplace. His apple brandy remained
untouched. His eyes, half-lidded, gazed at the card table now
and then, and more importantly, lingered on Benkhi longer
than they should have. Darragh's interest sharpened. There
was something there, and he meant to uncover it. His mind
filed it away for now. He'd test the girl later. Quietly.
Thoroughly.

Darragh strode with his glass in hand and sat beside him.

"Sahrit and Hrag seem to be enjoying themselves with
Lord Benkhi," he said. "Why not join them?"

Leógham pressed his lips together, an awkward twitch of

the corners hinting at what Darragh could only assume was an attempt to smile. He took a sip to mask his disappointment. Hrag's booming laugh rang out at the table, and Sahrit's quiet chuckle followed. Their guest, Benkhi, looked at ease, her smile bright, as if she belonged here more than Leógham did.

"Have you lost your fondness for brandy?"

The question startled Leógham. "No. Um… Just feel out of sorts."

"How so, brother?"

Leógham's fingers tightened around his glass. "It's odd to be back, that's all."

Darragh angled his head, studying him. "Well, it's to be expected. You were away for a long time." He put his hand up as Leógham opened his mouth to defend himself. "However, it's good to have you back." He raised his glass. "Let's drink to that."

Leógham's shoulders eased, and he returned the gesture, lifting his glass with a nod before taking a sip.

Another burst of laughter erupted from the card table. "The dragon card!" Hrag groaned dramatically, his voice carrying across the room.

Sahrit laughed while Lord Benkhi grinned in victory.

"Seems lively over there." Darragh glanced at the group. "Let's join them."

Leógham tugged at his sleeve. "I'd rather sit here."

Brooding, as usual. Darragh sipped, watching the group. His curiosity burned quietly. If he couldn't join the group, he'd get answers from Leógham.

"What will you do with Lord Benkhi?" He kept his tone casual, still thinking about the strange emptiness he'd sensed in her mind. Had she walled her thoughts?

Leógham's silence stretched.

"Eventually," Darragh mused, "he'll return to his family—"

"That's the goal," Leógham finished his drink in a single, abrupt gulp, the harsh burn making him grimace.

The subject was closed. Darragh forced a smile, disappointed that his first attempt at getting information about Benkhi had fallen flat. His curiosity simmered, but he knew better than to push Leógham now. There would be other opportunities to pry.

He looked at his glass and swirled its contents, light glinting off the amber liquid. He knew it was a dangerous question, but he had to ask.

"When will you return to the capital?"

Leógham groaned and poured himself another glass. "I just arrived. I must settle affairs here before I head out."

His expression softened asSahrit laughed at Hrag's theatrical moan over another lost hand. "She has done a wonderful job handling the estate on my behalf, but now that I'm back, it's time for me to retake the reins."

Few women in Hegra commanded such authority. Leógham had been shrewd in his decision to name her steward. She was sharp, more than capable, and loyal. This position also kept her far from Ashtalon's political vipers. For all his temper, Leógham had done right by her. Whether he admitted it or not, it was protection disguised as trust.

And defiance, too. In a kingdom ruled by men, giving Sahrit such power was Leógham's quiet rebellion—a glimpse of the reformer he'd become once Hegra allowed him the chance.

Leógham took a sip, then paused, looking at the contents of his glass. "Besides, what's in Ashtalon for me?"

The question didn't surprise Darragh, but duty was duty, and the capital didn't wait for anyone, not even a crown prince. "If you don't take the reins there, someone else will."

Leógham let out a dry, humorless laugh. "Who?" His scoff carried a bitter edge. "Saigham?"

"He won't hesitate," Darragh said. "And then he'll twist everything until he chokes us all, like it used to be before your father took the reins of Hegra. Stay here, and you'll watch Hegra burn from your window."

Leógham scowled.

Darragh's patience had run its course. Leógham's apparent indifference grated on him, appalling in its complacency. "Contemplate your situation carefully. Saigham speaks of the stolen throne and reviving purity laws behind closed doors, and he's not alone in this. If you don't stand in the capital, he'll crown himself king in all but name. Your sister has a son, which is good, but she can't rule, which isn't good. I'm not a member of the Fire Dweller clan, even if married to one, and thus, Hrag nor I will be recognized as kings in Hegra—"

"I know," Leógham cut him off.

Darragh cringed, then schooled his face into neutral. "Then you understand that without a plan now, when your father dies, things will unravel fast." His jaw clenched as he suppressed the dark thought of yet another civil war. "And don't forget the Water Kin, because they haven't forgotten—"

"*I know,*" Leógham snarled.

Darragh leaned closer, his voice lower. "You *must* have a son—"

"Enough."

Leógham's shout cut through the hum of conversation. The room fell silent, all eyes on him. He scratched his temple, the gesture tense, his face flushed.

"My apologies," he muttered, setting his glass on the low table and storming out of the room without a glance at anyone.

Darragh let out a slow breath. The silence in the room stretched thin until Hrag got up. Darragh raised his hand.

"I'll handle it," he said. With that, he straightened his doublet and followed Leógham.

Leógham stormed down the hall. His breath came fast, his heart pounding as though something feral chased him. The heavy doors yielded to his shove, and the cold night air bit at his skin, snuffing the fire about to spill.

Why did I return?

Hegra was already suffocating him.

Behind him, hurried footsteps broke the silence.

"Leógham, please, listen to me," Darragh called.

Leógham's nostrils flared. "Give me one good reason."

"To honor my sister's memory."

Elinor…

Leógham's anger drained from him in a rush of air. His hands fell to his sides, fingers uncurling as the tension bled from his frame.

"I…" He paused, drawing another deep breath to steady himself. "I'm sorry, Darragh. I spoke in anger. Returning to Hegra…" His boot scuffed the frosted cobblestones. "Returning is harder than I imagined."

"I know." Darragh stepped closer and cupped Leógham's shoulder. "But knowing this doesn't lessen what awaits if you turn away from the capital."

Leógham stared out into the dark. Frost silvered the stones. Clouds covered the sky. And unbidden, an image surfaced of Kharis at the table, hands pinned beneath her thighs to stay still. Watching. Quietly enduring. Trapped. It wold be worse in Ashtalon.

He lowered his gaze and huffed, rubbing the back of his neck. "A son? I wish I could adopt Hrag and call it done."

Darragh exhaled slowly. "You can't adopt him while his father is alive."

"Then I say we kill him." Leógham winked at him. "He deserves it."

Darragh raised his eyebrows, though a faint half-smile tugged at his mouth. Then his tone grew serious. "Look, I can arrange a marriage and—"

"How does that resolve the issue?" Leógham's anger clawed at his chest again. "The civil war started because of me, Darragh. The day after my father named me his Heir Apparent, in case you forgot."

"Leógham—"

"Bloody purity laws." His hands clenched again. "Nothing will ever change the fact that I'm of mixed blood—"

"Do *not* start that argument," Darragh warned. "Your silence and detachment are why Saigham gathers power in the capital. Nothing else. If you won't speak, he'll speak for you, and he'll crown himself with your birthright."

Leógham tsked. "Hegra is divided because of me. Roísín and Mother are dead because of me. The world is holding its breath because of me. So tell me, how does having a son end it?" He ground his teeth. "I had one, remember? And he died with his mother."

He drew a deep breath, swallowing the scream building in his chest. Memories clawed at him, sharp-edged and merciless. They always lurked, ready to rise and torment him.

Marriage...?

There was only one woman he'd ever consider. Instead, he had to face Hegra's fastidious concepts of duty, responsibility, and unyielding law.

Leógham looked up, fists trembling, wishing for an answer and a sliver of hope.

"Besides," he said, half a laugh, half a curse. "Where would I even find someone like your sister?" Like Elinor. Like Kharis.

Darragh studied him, his eyes sharp now, the warmth in his voice banked. "Then we must offer a different answer to the succession question. And soon, because Saigham won't wait." He gestured toward the dark path circling the grounds. "Walk with me."

Leógham hesitated, then fell into step beside him, their strides not quite matching. Darragh said nothing more, hands clasped behind his back, body slightly forward-leaning

—already formulating a course of action. And as they walked, Leógham felt it with cold certainty.

Regardless of whatever Darragh planned next, fate was already in motion.

THE DRIFT OF DAYS

> *Time drifts in silence, like dust in sunlight—no footprints, no whispers, only echoes that haunt us in the dark. - Poliormos*

Six days blurred together, each slipping through Kharis's fingers like fine sand.

She trailed behind Lady Sahrit, who gave her a tour of the kitchens, bustling with activity, the various rooms in the castle, the armory, the gardens, and more. Kharis nodded in all the right places, but her thoughts wandered: heading north, ending all the writings.

She spent her days in Leógham's library, poring over books to learn about Hegra's culture and memorize its tangled web of roads, rivers, and names. When not reading, she wandered the gardens, pacing among dormant bushes. The sun remained imprisoned behind ashen clouds. Evenings brought customary meals, polite conversation, and baraxas.

But Leógham...

He and Darragh spent long hours sequestered in the Keep, the fortress within the fortress. There, councils met, and state matters unfolded behind walls thicker than a man's height. The heart of Hegra's power beat there, far removed from the residence's warmer, messier pulse.

When not in council, Leógham trained hard, the clang of swords and shouted orders carrying from the secluded courtyard. He even took his meals at the Keep. Whatever the councils debated, he returned with shadows under his eyes. She saw the strain in the tight set of his jaw and the heaviness he tried—and failed—to conceal. As if the battle he fought behind those walls had to do with her... and the danger of keeping her here.

And still, every night, he entered her bedchamber through the secret panel.

"You're in Hegra," he'd warn her—always the same refrain, and the same guarded tone. "Everyone believes you're a man. You must lock that door every night."

But after the warning, softer things followed. He'd ask about her day: what books she'd found in the library, whether the soup had been tolerable. Sometimes, he laughed quietly at the things she shared.

The moments were never long. The silence would stretch, and duty would reclaim him. His hand would hover over the hidden latch, reluctant to leave. "Remember"—and she was almost tempted to recite the words with him— "you're in Hegra now. No one must find out."

Last night, he didn't come.

She had heard raised voices beyond the panel—his, sharp with anger; the others, apologetic. Soldiers? Servants? Lord Darragh? Then the muffled sounds of movement: boots, armor, the rustle of hands readying him for rest.

After that, silence.

৯৯

This morning, she walked to the window, her eyes drawn to the northern range, its pull a whisper calling her name.

When she stepped into the hallway, the sun hadn't yet risen, but the faintest streaks of dawn teased the edges of the tall windows, illuminating the dust motes dancing in the corridor.

She turned toward Leógham's door. The man she'd known in the cabin—quiet, steady, kind—had faded. In his place stood someone quick to anger. She still wondered what made him smile now that he did it less and less.

She sighed. Free to do as she pleased, the invisible Lord Benkhi took a deep, satisfying breath and headed for the kitchens.

The scents were the best clue to its location, its layout obvious: a central space where the four residential wings intersected, so servants could easily distribute food. She peeked in, observing the many faces working to feed everyone. The clatter of knives, the rhythmic pounding of dough, and the bubbling pots made up the organized chaos.

Lady Sahrit stood at the far end, speaking with the castle steward and head cook.

Kharis slipped inside, careful to stay out of everyone's way. A few cooks and bakers looked up from their work, offering smiles and quick bows as she wove between tables cluttered with ingredients and utensils.

Sahrit greeted her with a smile. "I'm surprised to see a Lord awake this early."

The comment gave Kharis pause. Leógham, Darragh, and Hrag were still abed. In fact, none of them had stirred before midday in the past six days. Was that a custom among men of their rank? Another mystery for her growing list.

"I didn't mean to interfere," she said. "I came to grab something to eat while taking a walk outside. Perhaps some fruit?"

"Fruit?" Sahrit grimaced. "I'll have Neagh bring you something more substantial."

"No need," Kharis protested. "You're busy."

"We're only finalizing tonight's menu," Sahrit said.

Kharis perked up. "May I ask what's planned?"

"I was hoping for pheasant as tonight's main course, but according to Ondriagh, we don't have any. Therefore, we're settling for a different option."

A wide grin crossed Kharis's face. "I could hunt for those." The idea of going out and putting her skills to use excited her.

"Lord Benkhi, how could I impose—?"

"Not an imposition." Kharis leaned forward, her tone earnest. "If Master Neagh shows me to the weapons room, I can be on my way and, with luck, bring what's needed before midday."

Sahrit pursed her lips. "You're a guest in this house, and I wouldn't want—"

"Please?" Kharis batted her eyelashes. "It would be an honor to repay your kindness." Then, she turned to Neagh. "Would you point me in the right direction?"

Ondriagh, the head cook, cleared his throat. "Your Ladyship, if the young Lord is successful, your request becomes a reality. If not, we still have time to explore other options that His Lordship will surely enjoy."

Sahrit exchanged a glance with Neagh and sighed. "Very well. Master Neagh will take you to the weaponry, but on one condition. You must eat something before heading out." Her tone carried motherly firmness.

Kharis flashed a big, splashy grin. "Deal."

The scent of leather and metal teased Kharis with its familiarity. She moved through the room, her fingers brushing the hilts of swords with unfulfilled longing as she headed for the bows. She tested their weight and flexibility, and chose one that felt right in her hands. Setting it aside, she turned to the arrows, sorting and selecting tips with small heads. One by one, she slid them into a leather quiver slung over her shoulder.

From behind her, Neagh said, "You have a discerning eye, My Lord."

"Thank you." Kharis glanced over her shoulder with a polite smile. "I'll also need a dagger."

Neagh selected a belt and dagger from a peg. Kharis fastened them before returning to the armory wall. Her gaze swept the array of swords hung in precise order.

"May I?" she asked.

"Of course," Master Neagh said. "No man of the House should go unarmed."

Kharis stepped closer, running her fingers along the scabbards, tracing the etched leather. She tested the swords' balance, feeling for a weight and length that matched her well. At last, she settled on one bound in deep red leather.

"This one." She drew the blade free, and it sang against the scabbard's steel throat with a clear, bright *shing*. A dragon's face adorned the handguard, the grip wrapped in bloodred leather to match the sheath. A wide fuller caught the light like a streak of silver water.

"An interesting choice." Neagh's eyebrows lifted. "No one has ever unsheathed this sword. Lord Leógham found it in the forest as a child. No matter how many times he gifted it, it always returned to this wall."

Kharis examined the faint markings along the steel. "Sigils..." She lifted her eyes. "An incantation?"

"Perhaps," Neagh said.

She returned the blade to its sheath, the satisfying click sending a small thrill through her. "May this blade agree with my hand."

She buckled it to her belt, the weight settling easily at her hip.

"Thank you. Now, if you'll give me directions, I'll be on my way. I intend to surprise Lady Sahrit with the finest catch these lands offer."

51

THE LAKE BENEATH THE SKY

> *There are times when fate beckons like an insistent whisper to reclaim those who have forsaken their purpose. - Poliormos*

K haris shielded her eyes, looking at the slate sky hiding the sun. The dawn scattered into light, but given the dense cloud cover, determining the time of day would be challenging. The chilly air stung the tip of her nose. Her breath misted, creating whimsical little wisps.

The high-collared gambeson and leather brigandine, bearing Leógham's colors, offered both insulation and protection. A woolen cloak completed the ensemble. With these, Neagh had explained, soldiers would know she was a member of the House with permission to hunt in the crown prince's demesne.

Master Neagh had thought of everything.

Warm against the chilled air, she forged ahead. The snow crunched under her boots as she hiked through the woods. A flicker of movement darted between the trees. She spun, heart jolting. A flock of birds burst skyward, wings thrumming against the silence.

She scanned the trees, expecting someone to emerge from behind them, but the forest stilled again. Pursing her lips, she tapped the dagger and sword at her sides and resumed her pace.

Leógham's estate was quite large, and his hunting grounds were no exception. It made her wonder where his land ended.

Using Neagh's instructions, she eventually spotted blue peeking through the trees.

On this windless morning, the lake reflected the snowy peaks and forest like a flawless mirror, and the landscape felt eerily familiar, the déjà vu arising like a half-forgotten dream. She'd been here before, water reaching her ankles on a warm day, the breeze dimpling her wet skin.

Do I know this place?

A chill breeze wound through the trees. Leaves quaked and quivered.

She felt that magnetic force, pulling at her with the susurrus of a promise. Her body moved, pivoting until her focus landed on the mountains, their icy peaks rising against the morning light.

"North," she exhaled softly.

A sudden croak shattered her focus. Kharis turned sharply toward the sound. A raven perched on a gnarled branch nearby. It watched her, its beady eyes gleaming with an inquisitive glint.

"Hunting. Right."

She strode toward the lakeshore and settled onto her haunches, surveying the terrain as she formulated a plan. She caught herself fidgeting with the leather loops, the strips chafing the skin between her fingers. Leógham had warned her about this, but perhaps...? She unfastened them and rolled her sleeves up to her wrists, careful not to reveal her black markings.

Much better. She wiggled her fingers, testing her range of motion, then blew hair off her face.

She still had to figure out how to hunt pheasants.

52

THE DASHING LORD DARRAGH

> *Do not assume shape is a measure for strength, for even the humblest form may carry the exceptional weight of the divine. - Poliormos*

The hours slipped by in a steady rhythm of tracking, aiming, and striking true to earn her catch: six plump pheasant roosters and a wild turkey of considerable size. She tied the birds with a sturdy cord, slinging them over her shoulders. The weight was substantial, evidence of a morning well-spent.

The thought of Lady Sahrit's approval lightened her steps.

Kharis glanced skyward. Dense, dark clouds stretched endlessly, blanketing the sky in an unbroken expanse of gray. She hadn't seen the sun, not even a fleeting glimpse of blue sky, since entering Hegra.

Her breath vanished into the chill as the frigid air nipped at her cheeks.

Ice flowers, Leógham had called them; strange plants feeding on the land's magic. A thought stirred: how much colder would it be in the north?

She spun around, facing north again, and took a step, the underbrush crackling beneath her feet. Then another, and another. The tang of frosted earth sharpened in her nostrils, the rough bark grazing her fingertips as she walked past.

She moved through the woods, pace quickening, parting shrubs along the way, until her fingers closed around a thorny gorse bush. The pain jolted her back. She flicked her hand, realizing she'd walked away from the castle.

What am I doing?

She picked at her skin, pulling out a thorn. After another shake of her hand to ease the sting, Kharis turned toward Dríeadh Manor when a bright shimmer caught her eye.

Through the shrubbery, she spotted Lord Darragh, pressing his hands against a tree. A shimmering haze clung to his skin, leaving a sparkling residue on the bark. She'd seen Hrag do the same. She moved soundlessly, slipping behind a tree to watch.

Lord Darragh brought his hands down.

The glimmer faded.

His eyes honed in on her location.

"You can come closer." An inviting tone.

Kharis frowned, for she'd done a decent job hiding. With a sheepish smile, she stepped out. "Good morning, Lord Darragh."

Those piercing forest-green eyes stared at her. "Good morning... Lord Benkhi."

The intentional pause and the probing eyes unnerved her. She readjusted the weight she carried as her excuse to look away and keep her distance.

Darragh took notice of the catch right away. "Ah! Impressive. It appears we have dinner assured." He swiftly closed the distance between them, getting too close to her. His smile—a little too wide, a little too knowing—set her on edge.

She collected herself and took a casual step back. "It's the least I could do to repay the hospitality. Lady Sahrit was looking forward to pheasant for dinner, but the kitchen was out."

Darragh narrowed his eyes. "That kitchen never runs out. She wanted to surprise Leógham since pheasant is his favorite."

Kharis forced a grin, hoping to disarm him. "Then I repay Lady Sahrit's welcoming gestures and Lord Leógham's hospitality."

He pursed his lips, his gaze sharpening. "I know Leógham rescued you after a mathan attack. But if my son's account is accurate, you paid your debt in full. Battling a winged nightmare tends to even the scales."

Kharis looked away.

"Which means," he went on, a dark smile tugging at his lips, "you're free to go home. I could even arrange an escort—"

"I'm under a fostered arrangement with His Highness," she interrupted.

"What a coveted honor." He didn't sound genuine. Then, a corner of his mouth lifted. "And how are you finding it here?" His question was far from innocent.

She bristled. "It's comfortable."

"Ah!" His expression grew sharper. "Then you stand in complete opposition to Leógham."

She narrowed her eyes, aware he was fishing for information. Thus, with the sweetest smile she could muster, she asked, "Lord Darragh, what brings you to the forest this morning?" *Shouldn't you be sleeping?*

He turned to the trees, fingers tracing the bark of one as though inspecting a precious object. "My clan. Our magic stems from nature, giving us a sense of balance."

"How so?" She regretted the question the moment it left her lips.

He raised an eyebrow and gave her a long, assessing stare. "A refresher, then." His tone made it clear this was more of a test than a review.

She stiffened but kept her expression polite while itching to escape Darragh's peculiar inquisition.

"As Forest Kin, I'm bound to the woods and everything living within them. Through my magic, I slip into that web, listening and learning."

Blasted. If she were from Hegra, she'd know this. A dull throb built at her temples. "I see. Practical magic."

"Indeed." His eyes betrayed a flicker of amusement. "Very... *practical* magic. And because of it, I could sense you nearby."

He was circling her now, using words as a subtle prod, each glance a calculated move in his game. Kharis took another step back.

"What do you mean?"

"Nature is complex." His voice was dangerously smooth. "Tapping into the bhalim lets me see what eyes cannot. Every living thing exudes an aura." He got closer to her. "And yours is rather... vigorous."

His eyes glowed with an unsettling power. Her instincts screamed louder now, urging her to run away and put as much distance as possible.

"I must leave if I'm to deliver these." She threw a glance toward the castle.

Darragh's gaze slid to her free hand. A chill washed over her. She'd forgotten to put the loops back on—a costly oversight.

"The ground around here is uneven," Darragh said, overly polite. "Allow me to help."

Kharis stepped back and tucked her free hand behind her back. "You know full well that's not appropriate."

Darragh's expression darkened. His voice turned icy and unnervingly calm. "That isn't my concern." He closed the distance again. "I'm far more interested in what you so cleverly hide."

Kharis's throat tightened.

Darragh tilted his head, his stare like that of a predator

closing in on its prey. "Tell me." His voice was soft, almost taunting. "Is Benkhi your real name, or do you have a prettier one?"

Her breath hitched, balance faltering. *How?* Every thought collided in her mind. *How did he find out?* The trees twisted into a whirlwind of indistinct shapes.

Get a hold of yourself, Kharis. She swallowed her panic and locked her glare onto Darragh like steel meeting steel.

"How dare you address me with such liberty?" she snapped.

But Darragh's lips curved into a slow, menacing smile, his eyes glinting with something dark and unspoken.

53

THE GEM AND THE THORN I

To assume is to miss an opportunity, for it closes your eyes to what you should see. - Poliormos

Darragh didn't answer; he smirked, victorious. His magic stirred, and he lunged for her, his fingers clamping around the hand gripping her prized catch before she could react.

But the instant he touched her skin, the world fractured.

A blast of light hit him with the force of a laden wagon going downhill. Breath ripped from his lungs. His stomach heaved. Up became down. His body twisted, organs shifting beneath his skin as the world overturned and reeled around him.

Then, as abruptly as the chaos had come, it ceased.

With a sharp snap, everything stopped, and an otherworldly realm unfolded before him. Black voids collided with endless radiance. Time held its breath, teetering between creation and destruction. Potent magic pulsed wildly in this space, answering no law he knew.

Darragh staggered, now inside a cavern of impossible

size, its vaulted ceiling disappearing into an infinite darkness. At its center, a massive tree stretched upward, its branches spiraling outward like rivers of light.

Recognition dawned on him.

The Mahabhal.

Darragh stared, breath faltering, the marrow in his bones nearly melting. "How?"

The colossal tree rose like the axis of the universe, and at the heart stood Benkhi.

Her figure blazed with silver radiance as if she'd transcended flesh. Threads flowed through her fingers, commanding the loom that shaped the worlds into being. Her hands moved the warp and weft in perfect harmony, weaving a tapestry so intricate it defied comprehension.

Her silver gaze found him, pinning him where he stood.

The Mahabhal only recognized an intruder. The air thrummed in warning before the Tree unleashed its wrath: a massive burst erupted from its core, striking Darragh. It hurled him backward as if he were no more than a speck of dust caught in the universe.

The cavern dissolved, and he found himself floating in a black void for an agonizingly slow moment until a crushing force slammed his soul back into his body.

Darragh gasped, his eyes snapping open. One hand braced against the tree. The other remained clamped around Benkhi's, his fingers locked and unwilling to release it. His senses cleared in time to see a scarlet aura blaze into view.

"What are you doing?"

Leógham's resonant voice struck like lightning. He wasn't asking a question, but offering a warning, dark as prophecy. Scarlet flames curled around his clenched fists, licking the air. Darkening.

I'm dying today.

His pulse kicked hard in his throat. He tore his hand from Benkhi's and stumbled back, heart pounding.

Leógham loomed, ready to burn trees and shatter stone,

but when Darragh glanced at Benkhi, he cursed beneath his breath.

May the Infinite save us. She's one of them.

A being touched by the Mahabhal could retaliate without lifting a finger, and he'd just forced his will on hers. Darragh steeled himself to fight her, confident that death awaited him. His fists trembled as magic gathered, biting into his hands.

"Who are you playing with, Leógham?" Darragh asked.

The accusation only sharpened Leógham's expression. "I'm expecting an answer, Darragh. Now!"

His voice reverberated through the tall beech trees, shattering the last threads of Darragh's spell on Benkhi. She blinked rapidly, her senses snapping back into place. She turned on him, her gaze narrowing. A faint, otherworldly shimmer lit her sapphire eyes, and whatever courage Darragh had gathered hollowed out in an instant.

"You saw it, didn't you?" Her voice dropped low.

"I... yes." Darragh stepped back, taken by the blue in her eyes. "Yes, I did."

Leógham's nostrils flared. "Lord Darragh. Lord Benkhi. What's going on?"

Benkhi clicked her tongue. "He knows."

"What?" Leógham snarled.

The girl, bless her courage, didn't flinch. Her eyes widened suddenly, then they sharpened next.

Darragh's stomach dropped.

"When we met at the library," she said at last, her voice eerily calm.

Darragh's throat tightened. He forced himself to swallow. Dragging down a breath, he met Leógham's gaze, but the trust had shifted, a fine crack running through it, faint yet final. *What have I done?*

Benkhi groaned, hands fisted. "I knew something was off. You wouldn't let go of my hand." Her glare hardened. "You were searching for me this morning, weren't you? You were using your magic to locate me."

Darragh pressed his lips together, unwilling to confirm it.

Leógham's frown deepened. He took a deliberate step toward Darragh, his height and bulk adding to the threat. "What does this mean?"

Darragh raised his hands in surrender. "It's not what you think—"

"Explain yourself," Leógham's tone dropped into a sinister register, "before my patience wears off."

Darragh's shoulders sagged. "Saigham's spies were searching for you. He even had his Shadowmen follow Hrag. When I saw Benkhi, I had to ensure he wasn't one of them. That's when I discovered he is a she."

He took a deep breath, pondering his mortality. "I don't know why you're hiding this, brother. Touching her was all I needed to find out."

Leógham's jaw flexed. His hands curled into fists at his sides. Slowly, he turned to Benkhi. "I told you to keep to yourself, didn't I?" Arcs of scarlet flame danced between his fingers.

"Leógham, please." Darragh stepped between them, his palms raised in surrender, his voice low and steady. "Calm down. I'm the only one—"

Leógham pushed him aside, the vein at his temple pulsing. His breath came sharp through his nose. He towered over Benkhi, his frame tense and rigid as scarlet bled into the green of his eyes.

"I told you to stay invisible. To not touch anyone or let anyone touch you, because *touch* is a weapon to unlock secrets."

Her aura shivered silver. Leaves whispered, though no wind moved. Roots shifted beneath Darragh's boots.

"Leógham," Darragh warned, sensing the shift.

The air hummed like a beast stirring from sleep, but Leógham didn't stop, jabbing a finger toward her, his words sharper still. "Darragh didn't just grab your hand. He now knows our secret, and *you* let him."

Heat shimmered off Benkhi like vapor rising from scorched stone. Static crackled in the dry air. The wind changed direction.

Darragh gulped. *Too late.*

54

THE GEM AND THE THORN II

He who builds his judgment upon the shadows of his fears shall find his house collapses when the sun reveals the truth. - Poliormos

Heat flared beneath Kharis's skin, the tiny flame in her core awakening. A crimson flash swallowed her vision; her eyes had changed color.

"That was the wrong thing to say," she said through clenched teeth, "and the wrong way to say it."

Fire flowed through her veins now, burning hotter with every heartbeat. She tilted her head, slow and deliberate, her teeth bared in warning. Her voice dropped an octave, rough and thick with menace.

"*Who* do you think you are to speak to me like that?"

Shock tightened both men's faces.

"How dare you suggest this is my fault?" Her voice dropped as the beast clawed its way up from the bottom of her deep, dark well. She held it back by sheer will, breath by breath, her knuckles whitening as her stare forced Leógham to step back behind the line he'd crossed, doubt flickering in his eyes.

She lifted her chin, fury blazing through every word. "Confront your own failings, *crown prince*, before you dare lay them at my feet."

Kharis struggled to leash her magic. Stardust slipped free from her, flaring into bright silver sparks that lashed the men. They jerked back and winced at the stings.

Without another word, she spun on a heel, her cloak billowing in a wide arc. A curse slipped from her lips—vivid, violent: a vow to spear and gut them, too.

She didn't look back, marching toward the castle. Her magic crackled like a storm, leaving two stunned Hegran men rooted in her wake.

⸙

Darragh braced himself, certain Leógham would erupt into a tower of scarlet flame. No one had ever spoken to the crown prince as Benkhi had and lived to tell the tale.

But to his astonishment, the outburst never came.

Instead, Leógham gripped the back of his neck as he watched her retreat, his gaze raw with desperation. He raised an arm, half-reaching for her as if to call her back, but his words faltered. His hand hovered in the air, then dropped uselessly to his side as she vanished into the trees.

Darragh said nothing, taking a moment to compose himself.

Memories of Leógham came to him: a boy of sixteen, seeking survivors when his house was attacked; his howl when he found his mother's body; his eyes glazing with something wild during the civil war; the nights he woke gasping in the tent; the night Elinor died...

Leógham's temper, born of fear and trauma, had always been a volatile force, flaring without restraint. A year away hadn't softened it much. It still simmered within, waiting to surge like a beast held back for too long. But Darragh had also witnessed something unmistakable beneath Leógham's anger. He'd seen that look before: with Elinor. And emotions could be Leógham's undoing.

The Mahabhal's power still throbbed in Darragh's veins, lingering like a divine echo—part awe, part warning. Benkhi was no mere wielder of fire magic. The force that had shaped worlds flowed in her blood, and that was worse.

Darragh thought of everyone she'd touched, and how their fates had been pulled into her orbit. His breath slowed. Why now? Why Leógham? Was fate simply lying in wait...?

If the girl leaves, we die. If she stays, we might die anyway.

"I yelled at her," Leógham muttered, hands limp by his sides now.

Darragh steadied himself. "Go after her."

Leógham's gaze snapped to him, eyes blazing so brightly the forest itself might ignite.

Darragh swallowed hard and forced himself to hold his ground. "Do you understand what she is, or the power she holds?" *Elatharim.* His throat burned.

Leógham's back suddenly straightened, breath held. His voice quieted. "Yes. I know."

Is this why he was guarding her? A chill swept over Darragh at the thought of Benkhi's power wielded by Saigham.

"She cannot become our enemy. Apologize, Leógham, for she can't leave us. Do whatever it takes to keep her with us. For all our sakes." A beat passed. "After that, you and I must talk. I... have questions."

Leógham froze. His expression shifted as understanding dawned.

"Darragh, I—"

The words caught. There was so much behind the things he didn't utter.

"You have my trust," Darragh said. "My lips are sealed." The silence stretched as he rubbed his chin. "There are a few problems, and none is small."

Leógham frowned. "And those are?"

Darragh leaned in slightly. "We must hide the color of her

eyes. It appears her magic burns through whatever you used—"

"She's not a shapeshifter."

"Thank the Infinite," Darragh said dryly. "If she were, I'd kill her myself. Still—what did you use?"

"A tincture with ground kharisot."

Darragh's brow rose. "Clever, but the flowers have been extinct for years." He pursed his lips. "And when she runs out?"

When Leógham didn't answer, Darragh pinched the bridge of his nose. "You've placed her in Elinor's chambers, and although keeping her close is a good idea, you've effectively announced her status to everyone."

Leógham crossed his arms. "Which is…?"

Darragh exhaled. "She's supposed to be a man, Leógham. Treat her as such—distance, discretion."

A muscle feathered in Leógham's jaw.

"I get the disguise," Darragh said, "but she's dead if found." *Or maybe we will?* "You must be extremely careful with your… gestures of affection," he said. "She's not the only one at risk now. Hegra has never been generous to those who defy convention. Everyone believes Benkhi's a pretty boy. Let's ensure she doesn't become *your* pretty boy."

Leógham glanced away. "Fine. So I move her." His fingers drummed against his bicep. "Where?"

"Let me think about it. It should be done quietly, without inciting gossip. Whispers spread fast, brother, and this isn't a kingdom known for its tolerance. If I figured your secret out," Darragh said, "Saigham will, too."

55

A LESSON IN JUSTICE

The law is not blind, though it claims to be. It sees bloodlines and power, and it strikes hardest at those who dare defy its shape. Mercy is rare where fear writes justice. - Poliormos

K haris stormed through the forest, cursing with each step.

"Blasted fool," she hissed. "The Fires can burn him for all I care."

She dragged in a breath. Then another. By the time the castle loomed ahead, her stride was steady again. Her vision, however, remained sharp, and the enhanced clarity confirmed her eyes were still crimson.

A twig snapped, and she turned, half-expecting Leógham to gingerly step out. Instead, a lone figure lurked behind the treeline, some fifty marks away. Their heat aura flared orange and yellow in the dark woods. Not Leógham or Darragh, of that she was certain.

Who followed me?

Her eyes narrowed, her hand going for her hilt. Whoever

they were, they bolted at her gesture, vanishing into the forest.

Her stomach knotted. Her magic had burned through the eye drops' effect, revealing her true eye color—a danger she couldn't risk. She let the magic flow to maintain the crimson color until she reached her chambers. A mild pressure began to build behind her eyes.

She entered the castle and made her way to the kitchens.

Magic thrummed beneath her skin, heightening everything. The faintest glare pierced her eyes like a blade; the heat from the ovens pressed in. Every scent struck at once: the sweetness of fresh bread tangled with the sour reek of spoiled milk; burnt sugar warred with the acrid scent of old oil. The rasp of knives on a whetstone—*shrk, shrk*—clashed with the clanging of pans and bursts of laughter.

Life had been honed to its sharpest edge.

When her magic flowed like this, without the outlet of battle, the world became unbearable. Forcing the flood to quiet was the trick, but she couldn't stop the flow just yet, because the moment she did, everyone would see her eyes were blue.

With a steady breath, she schooled her face into calm.

By the far wall, Ondriagh and Neagh sat, having tea. Ondriagh's face lit when he spotted the fowl slung over her shoulder. He rose quickly, hands already reaching for her catch.

"These are great, Lord Benkhi. Phenomenal!" His voice rang out, drawing approving nods from the kitchen staff and a teeth-grinding smile from her. "Lady Sahrit will be thrilled. We're serving Lord Leógham's favorite dish."

At the mention of his name, Kharis bit back another curse, inwardly wishing the fires of Ifran would claim him.

Ondriagh, catching her mood, added with a playful gleam, "Hungry?"

"Starving." Her nails bit into her palms.

He shared a knowing glance with Neagh. "I'll have the servants bring her a plate."

Neagh bowed, all brisk formality. "Lord Benkhi, this way."

She followed him through the corridor, but at the grand staircase, she halted. "Allow me a moment. I must wash and change first."

"Of course, My Lord. I shall await."

She climbed the steps two at a time, the pounding in her skull unbearable now. The magic scorched her veins; her vision shimmered at the edges. *I can't take this any longer.* She had to stop the flow or lose control.

Frantic, she pushed the doors open—and froze.

A female servant was rifling through the drawers, fingers quick and guilty.

"What are you doing?" Kharis stepped into the room, exuding a wild storm of magic. Red sparks arced through her body.

The servant gasped, stumbling back. A small leather journal slipped from her hands—the one filled with Kharis's notes on Hegra. It hit the floor with a dull thud.

"My Lord—"

Crimson fire engulfed her fists, flames licking her knuckles. Kharis struggled to keep it from exploding. "I'll ask once more. What are you doing *here?*"

Ghostly pale, the servant whimpered and collapsed to her knees, wide-eyed and trembling. Her lips moved soundlessly, breath coming in sharp bursts. The woman's frantic heartbeats pounded against Kharis's skull. The air reeked of spoiled eggs: the servant's fear, manifested. The recognition struck her like a splash of icy water.

Her magic guttered instantly, drawing a gasp from her.

"Get out!" Kharis shouted, keeping her eyes closed. "Get. Out."

The woman bolted, skirts snapping against the floor as

she fled, shouldering past the servants who'd gathered in the corridor.

Kharis rubbed a palm against her chest, trying to ease the ache behind her ribs. She picked up the journal from the floor, breath still ragged, and flipped through the pages. *Only notes on Hegran customs.* Sketches of mountain paths. Lists of supplies she might need for a long journey. Nothing that could betray who she truly was.

She pulled it close, aware of how close she'd been, and strode straight to the vanity. The drawers gaped open, their contents shoved and scattered. Her bracelet with the jade stone was where she'd left it.

What was she after?

A cold thought slid down her spine. If she'd left the wrong page exposed, if a single clue had slipped free… One careless moment, one forgotten corner of herself, and everything she'd built here would have collapsed like wet paper.

"My Lord?" Neagh's voice rasped from the doorway, breathless.

Braced against the vanity, Kharis gave him the bare facts, keeping her back to him. He listened without interruption.

"On behalf of the House of Hegra," he said after she'd finished. "I apologize for this intrusion, My Lord. A grave breach. I will see it dealt with. Lady Sahrit shall be informed."

"Thank you." Her pulse still pounded, but she forced a steadier tone. "What becomes of servants in these cases?"

Neagh's pause unsettled her. "The law is harsh."

Kharis grimaced. Her first taste of Hegran justice soured on the tongue. If this was the fate of a servant… what awaited her? What of Leógham? What of all who had helped her, once discovery came?

I must leave this place.

Her heart pounded anew. "Master Neagh, could you grant me a moment? I have yet to change, much less wash."

"Of course, My Lord. Take as long as you need." He bowed himself out, closing the door softly behind him.

Only then did she kneel beside the bed, easing up a loose plank under it to uncover the hidden space beneath where she'd concealed the small jar of tincture. She poured water into the basin, scrubbed her hands, then tilted her head back. A sting of liquid fire touched her eyes. She stared into the mirror as the orange drops devoured the rich blue of her eyes, turning them a dull gray.

After a moment, Kharis sat on the edge of her bed and exhaled, long and uneven.

Followed in the woods.

Spied on in her chambers.

And her disguise fraying, thread by thread.

Her heart stumbled with a sudden lurch. The chill that swept through her had nothing to do with Hegra's winter.

❧

Wearing clean clothes, a clean face, and gray eyes once more, Kharis met Master Neagh at the bottom of the staircase. His expression betrayed nothing, but the brief flick of his eyes toward hers made her ponder. Had he noticed her actual eye color?

The worst of her headache had passed, but a dull throb still pulsed behind her temples.

She followed him into the dining room, the vaulted ceiling soaring above the long table set with polished silverware and fine china.

Lady Sahrit spotted her at once. "Lord Benkhi," she greeted her, a hand pressed against her chest. "Neagh told me what happened. I offer you my utmost apology for the intrusion."

Kharis bowed, though a part of her still felt the sting of prying eyes. Tonight, she'd have to tell Leógham what had happened. And if he raised his voice at her again, she wouldn't hold this time. Sitting farther down the table, Hrag paused only long enough to throw her a narrowed glance before shoveling roasted potatoes and a slice of meat into his mouth.

"I brought pheasants." Kharis hoped to steer the conversation away from the matter with the servant.

Neagh offered a quick nod, confirming it. Sahrit's face brightened.

Kharis took a seat, and a servant appeared almost instantly, setting a plate before her. She dove in, eating with the focus of someone who hadn't tasted food in days. Using magic always left her ravenous, yet no matter how much she ate, the hunger never eased. It gnawed at her, hollow and unrelenting, as if the wrong food fed her body.

"May I be of further service?" she asked in between bites.

"I wouldn't impose on you further," Sahrit said.

Kharis shook her head, offering a sincere smile. "I enjoyed the task and was glad to be useful." She glanced at Hrag. "Others might want to join me next time."

Hrag remained blissfully unaware, too focused on his food to catch the barb.

Sahrit clutched her hands to her chest. "Such a young man and already showing much promise."

"Ha!"

Kharis turned to find Hrag smirking at her. "Lord Benkhi swears he's sixteen. If it were up to me, I'd say he's no older than thirteen. Just look at him, Ama. He doesn't even have hair on his face."

Kharis scrunched her nose at him. "Well, I don't see any on yours."

"Of course, you don't." He brushed a hand over his jaw. "I shave it off. What excuse do you have?"

Kharis bit back a retort. His jest was harmless, but beneath it lay a daunting challenge. *How long can I keep up this disguise?*

"Lord Benkhi is a guest in this house," Sahrit said sharply. "It would be best not to forget that."

"Fine. No more talk of hair." Hrag didn't sound like he was taking his mother's warning seriously.

Kharis ate her meal while her mind whirled. Since the winged nightmare incident, Hrag had been warming to her cautiously. A joke here, a teasing remark there, constantly testing the edges of an unspoken boundary.

Sometimes, like today, companionship laced their bickering.

And strangely, Kharis was glad for it.

"So, you went hunting this morning," Hrag said, twirling his fork. "Are you up for archery practice?"

Kharis swallowed her last bite. "And miss an opportunity to beat you? Never. I plan to win every round."

Hrag smirked blandly. "And that's how you express your gratitude?"

Kharis leaned back, crossing her arms. "I'm thankful to Lady Sahrit for her generous hospitality; if she asks for my help, I give it willingly." A sly grin spread slowly across her face. "And when you're done choking on your potatoes, let's go. I can't wait to collect on my bet."

"Collect on your bet," Hrag muttered with a sour chuckle. He stuffed another slice of meat and the rest of his potatoes into his mouth, cheeks puffed out, and mumbled, "I hope you can keep up."

He walked out, gesturing for Kharis to follow him. Sahrit watched him leave, eyes sparkling. "Lord Benkhi," she said softly. "You're the brother Hrag needed."

Kharis paused. The term warmed her, and yet, the bitter lesson she'd learned upstairs reminded her that in Hegra, he could quickly turn against her. She masked the worry with a playful wink.

Spotting the apples in the fruit bowl, she picked one up and pocketed another. She dipped into a sweeping, elegant bow that drew a soft laugh from Lady Sahrit, then followed Hrag out the door, a small voice urging caution in her ear.

THE DANGERS OF
ASSUMPTIONS

An assumption may feel like certainty, but it can rob you of seeing someone for who they truly are. - Poliormos

Leógham had searched for Kharis without success. *Not in the gardens. Not in the library. Not in the drawing room.* He was running out of space in the castle. *Did she leave?* That thought tormented him.

He entered Sahrit's study and found her focused on the household and estate ledgers.

"Have you seen Lord Benkhi?"

Sahrit lifted her eyes, her focus lost. She tapped her quill against her chin, thinking. "They left together after the midday meal... Archery practice, but Leógham, since you're here, you must know—"

"Later," he grunted, then left the room before Sahrit could finish.

Where is she?

As Sahrit had suggested, he approached the archery garden, where a few servants were picking up the arrows from the ground and putting the targets away.

"Have you seen Lord Benkhi?" he asked, his words clipped.

Everyone halted, offering timid bows and curtsies. "No, Your Lordship," one said.

The servants glanced at each other, their eyes wide, their faces pale. Leógham realized he was scaring them and turned away.

"Never mind. If you run into him, tell him I'm looking for him."

⚜

Hrag stepped into the fencing room and heaved a heavy sigh. After archery, Benkhi had convinced him to spar with him.

Why am I here?

He stole a glance at Benkhi, whose broad grin was answer enough for him.

The space was as he remembered: ample and open, with tall windows lining the southern wall. Warm light flooded in, giving it an airy, almost grandiose feel. Dust motes floated lazily in the dim sunlight.

"Who do you practice with?" Benkhi, endlessly curious and annoying, asked.

Hrag resisted the urge to roll his eyes. "Uncle. He's superb. And my Apa's quite good, too."

Benkhi's brow furrowed slightly. "Lord Darragh? I wouldn't take him for one."

"Oh, he's skilled with the sword," Hrag said with pride. "If I were you, I'd be careful around him when he's wielding one."

"Duly noted." Benkhi raised his hands in mock surrender. "Now, where do you keep the wooden swords?"

Hrag touched his sword, still strapped to his belt. "Don't we use these?"

Benkhi shook his head, looking scandalized. "You said the Dragon's Bane is magicked, forged from dragon bones. This is a sword for battle. Practice will only dull the blade. Besides, wooden ones ensure our safety since these," he tapped his sword, "can cause major damage. You know—cut, slash."

Hrag frowned. "The wooden ones can still leave nasty bruises."

Benkhi shrugged playfully. "I'll go easy on you."

"Ha! We'll see about that."

Benkhi unfastened his belt, then searched the racks, hollering from across the room. "Found them!" He walked back with two.

Hrag sighed, reluctantly taking one.

Benkhi immediately swung his, testing its weight. He moved fluidly, whipping the blade left and right as though facing an invisible opponent. His stance was solid, shifting his weight smoothly as he jumped, pivoted, flipped, and thrust the sword forward.

What in the Fires...? Hrag hadn't expected this—not even close. *I'm way over my head.* He glanced at the door—

"Aren't you warming up?"

Hrag froze. "Um, what...?"

"You must move and stretch your body first," Benkhi explained.

Hrag furrowed his brow. "If I do, I'll get tired before I start."

Benkhi gave him a bland look, shaking his head like a disappointed tutor. "If you don't, you'll get injured faster. Come, stand beside me."

Hrag's shoulders sagged. "I'm not getting out of this, am I?"

The corners of Benkhi's eyes crinkled with his broad grin. "No, you're not."

৯৯

Leógham stalked through the castle halls, cursing Darragh under his breath. Yet he had been right. Leógham should've apologized before she had stormed off.

Upon seeing him, a few servants scampered off. The ones caught unaware paused in their tasks and bowed low, a few fidgeting with the objects in their hands. Leógham huffed and kept moving. Even after a year away, fear still clung to people. It had become a shadow that trailed him, refusing to fade.

Furious at himself, at his temper, and his foolish mouth, he slammed his fist into the wall. Pain radiated up his arm, but it didn't replace the ache in his heart. He didn't know where Kharis was, and the not knowing made it worse.

He struggled to gather his thoughts and form a plan. A nearby window overlooked the forest. The idea of searching the woods tugged at him, but as he turned toward the nearest exit, muffled voices reached his ears.

The familiar timbre of her voice—sharp, commanding— caught him like a hook to the chest. His anxiety melted in an instant.

But another voice accompanied hers, a deeper one.

Male.

A flicker of jealousy flared within him.

Instinct urged him to storm in and confront whoever dared to be with her. But he forced himself into icy composure and padded down the hall, pausing outside the door to peer in.

Inside, Kharis and Hrag swung wooden swords, moving in unison through a series of strikes and blocks, legs switching, blades sweeping across their bodies. Even more surprisingly, Hrag mirrored her with surprising competence.

Doesn't he dislike fencing?

"Again," Kharis called.

It snapped Leógham out of his daze.

They struck again, right then left, rhythm sharpening.

Leógham decided not to interrupt yet. He'd found her,

and the churning in his stomach eased. She moved with agility and grace, twisting and turning with precision. Her display of strength and elegance enthralled him.

Hrag followed her lead, and a pang of possessiveness surged through Leógham, wanting to shove Hrag aside, take his place, and spar with her himself.

"Ready to do it faster?" Kharis asked.

"Sure." Hrag wiped sweat from his brow. As he took a moment to collect his breath, Kharis's attention shifted toward the door.

"Lord Leógham," she said curtly, dipping into a stiff bow. The gesture was polite, but the implied coldness stung him.

"Uncle." Hrag's beaming smile lessened the hurt. "You should join us. Lord Benkhi is teaching me a few steps and some interesting techniques."

Leógham smiled despite himself. Hrag's enthusiasm for the blade was a novelty. Kharis's anger was not. He took a step forward, then checked himself, teeth catching the inside of his cheek. Hrag stood close, bright and unaware. Kharis didn't look at him at all. For a breath, Leógham weighed where his gaze would do the least harm.

He turned to her at last. "Care to teach me?"

Her nostrils flared. "Is this how you apologize?"

The question landed cleanly, leaving nowhere to hide.

He drew a breath. Then another. His mouth tightened before he spoke. "No."

He went down on one knee, head bowed. "I crossed a line and hurt you. I have no excuse." His heart battered his ribs, each beat loud in his ears. "Please," he said quietly. "Forgive me."

Behind him, Hrag released a breathless gasp.

The room fell silent.

In Hegra, gestures of apology were always private. To witness the crown prince of Hegra kneel, humbling himself before anyone other than the king? Unthinkable. And yet here he was, on one knee, his pride discarded at her feet.

He'd do it before the entire kingdom if it would grant him her forgiveness, if it would prompt her to speak to him again.

The hush dragged on, each moment an eternity. He bit his lip, willing to stay put and wait, but the hope he'd carried had thinned to nothing. She wasn't going to forgive him. Worse, she would—

Footsteps sounded behind him. Leógham stiffened.

Darragh entered the room and stopped just inside the threshold. He took in the scene at a glance: Hrag and Kharis, the wooden swords, Leógham on one knee.

His expression didn't change, his eyes never leaving Leógham.

"Get up," he said mildly. "Now."

57

UNTIL THE VERY END

Wrath oft sparks the fire, but never douses the flame.
- Poliormos

"Lord Darragh," Kharis said, chin lifted. Oh, how she wanted to make him pay for the forest fiasco. "Lord Hrag warns me to be cautious around you when you wield a sword." A sweet smile graced her lips. "Care to demonstrate?"

Darragh's mouth twitched, his hands up in mock surrender. "Oh, no, no. By the looks of it, I should be prudent and remain a spectator when you wield a sword."

Kharis ignored his quip and pointed her sword squarely at Leógham, kneeling on the floor, waiting for the forgiveness she wasn't ready to give.

"I have no choice but to ask you, Lord Leógham."

Darragh's eyebrows wiggled. "It seems Lord Benkhi has challenged you."

Leógham glared at him.

"Come, son," Darragh said. "We're about to witness history. Your uncle is exceptional with the sword, but perhaps Lord Benkhi might teach him a lesson… or two?"

Leógham shot him another withering glare.

Kharis pursed her lips. Why was Darragh goading Leógham into sparring with her? Darragh's playfulness felt calculated. He wasn't just teasing. He was testing, too.

Darragh snatched Hrag's waster and handed it to Leógham. "Here you go." His grin broadened.

Leógham took it with a warning snarl and gave it a few twirls, slicing through the air in sharp, precise strokes as he moved through a cutting progression—his implied "surrender while you can" message. The tiny flame inside her flickered, hungry.

"Lord Leógham," she called sharply. "Are you ready? Or do you hope boredom will strike me first?"

Leógham stopped mid-twirl, his glare meeting hers.

Darragh stepped forward. "Allow me to referee. Two clean hits out of three decide the victor."

Kharis moved into position, sharpening her focus on Leógham, while he stood at ease, the waster at his side, its tip pointed down.

Heat flared in her chest. Leógham wasn't taking her seriously.

"Ready?" Darragh asked.

Kharis nodded in assent. So did Leógham.

"Go!" Darragh raised his arm sharply and stepped back.

Kharis moved, her body reacting on instinct. Leógham barely had time to block. She redirected his blade downward in one fluid motion, throwing him off balance.

Before he could recover, her left fist drove into his jaw. The impact snapped his head to the side, momentum twisting his neck as his footing faltered. Leógham staggered, boots scraping as he fought to stay upright.

Kharis retreated smoothly, gliding back into her spot, her weight settled, her guard restored, deeply ingrained training guiding her.

§

Darragh froze.

She had struck the instant he was open. A gauntleted blow like that would have shattered bone. Even barehanded, the timing alone had been lethal. In an actual fight, that opening would've ended things before they began.

The girl was bold enough to face Leógham. Landing the first blow hadn't been bravado or luck. It had been discipline and skill, honed through years of training.

Out of the corner of his eye, he caught a flicker of movement in the corridor. Two servants had paused mid-step, watching the match. His glare sent them scurrying.

"One hit by Lord Benkhi!" he announced.

Leógham's eyes widened, then narrowed. He worked his jaw, his pride more bruised than his face, limbered his neck, squared his shoulders, and, this time, took a proper stance.

"Ready?" Darragh checked on both before uttering, "Go!"

Leógham charged with a precise thrust. Benkhi moved faster, slipping to the side. His momentum carried him past her. She brought the flat of her waster across his back in a sharp *thwack*. Leógham arched with a startled gasp. Before he could recover, Benkhi pressed her boot against him and drove him forward, using his weight to topple him. He hit the floor hard.

Hrag's breath hitched. Darragh blinked once, hard. His gaze cut from Leógham to the girl and back again.

Three hits already? This wasn't a lesson. It was utter humiliation.

Leógham rose slowly, panting through the pain, and paced around to shake it off.

A sentry lingered too long by the doors, lips parted. Darragh cursed silently. Word of this bout wouldn't remain within these walls for long. Leógham had never lost a match. By nightfall, whispers would reach the halls of Ashtalon: a young lord had bested the invincible crown prince. Saigham would hear of it. Darragh's stomach clenched.

Time to end this.

He cleared his throat. "With clean three hits for Lord Benkhi—"

"Again," Leógham shouted. "We're going for five."

Darragh's brows arched. "Wait. Five?" He turned to Benkhi. "Do you accept?"

Her face was unreadable. Her curt nod wasn't.

Darragh wrung his hands as he glanced between them. Leógham was supposed to ask for forgiveness. Instead, he tightened his grip, both hands on the hilt now. Darragh huffed, unhappy about the direction this challenge had taken. He turned to Leógham, his eyes sharp with a silent warning. Leógham ignored him. Darragh closed his eyes for a heartbeat and settled into position. *I tried to stop you.*

"Ready?" He raised his arm reluctantly. "Go!"

Leógham attacked. Benkhi blocked. They circled. Their swords clacked in rhythm—strike, deflect, recover. She feinted low, then drew him off balance with a thump to his right thigh. He staggered back, stunned.

"Stop!" Darragh thrust out his arm, a cold prickle climbing his spine.

The girl's speed and explosive punches had surprised him, adding to his growing list of concerns. Unlike Hegran women, Benkhi was exceptionally skilled. If she were serious, Leógham would've already been dead.

She'd received no hits while striking him again and again. And while her ability was undeniable, it wasn't like the techniques drilled into every Hegran boy. Leógham had concealed one *tiny* yet vital truth: Benkhi wasn't Hegran.

Darragh's anger flared. He felt like snatching the waster from Benkhi's hands and whacking Leógham with it, because he'd damned them all.

"Time to yield—" Darragh began.

"No," Leógham bellowed with dark pride. He widened his stance, meeting Benkhi's unflinching stare. "I do *not* yield."

"Leógham!" Darragh barked, breath flaring. "Benkhi has won the match." His eyes silently pleaded: *let this go.*

"We keep going," Benkhi said from behind him. "Until the very end."

Darragh's mouth fell open in alarm. This was no longer a match. It was penance. Benkhi was teaching more than swordsmanship. She was exposing a truth and rewriting hierarchy. And in Hegra, that was... bold *and* alarming. He clicked his tongue and took to the floor, silently cursing himself for having encouraged this match.

Leógham had asked for forgiveness with words. Benkhi answered with steel.

Darragh's patience snapped. "Then go."

58

WHEN MEMORIES BLEED

> *There are moments when refusal becomes the purest form of victory. - Poliormos*

Leógham struck first, expecting to overpower her with sheer strength. To his surprise, she didn't budge. Kharis held firm, her blade locked against his. She'd braced her left hand against the flat of her waster, muscles taut, eyes steady. She was smaller, slighter—she should've yielded. And yet she held the line as if the ground anchored her.

How?

He leaned harder, testing her defenses. Nothing. *The markings on her skin—do they lend her strength?*

A wicked smile crossed her face as if she knew what he was thinking. The gesture made him falter, his weight shifting back a step.

Kharis moved. She pushed the swords to the right, and her knee struck between his legs. Leógham gasped, a rasped groan that came from deep inside him. His core ripped apart with a flash of light that blinded him. The pain shot up his stomach like a white-hot knife stabbing him repeatedly. He bent over, only for her knee to meet his face.

Leógham collapsed to the floor, curled into a ball of desperate, trembling flesh, clutching his manhood.

❦

Kharis stepped away from Leógham.

Outside the hall, a sentry straightened too quickly, his hand fumbling on his spear.

There was no rush of victory—only a sharp, sinking regret. The sight of Leógham on the floor, breath ragged, limbs unsteady, twisted deep in her gut. For a heartbeat, he wasn't Leógham, but another body brought low.

"Finish. Him."

The words scraped through her mind. Heat pressed in. The hall wavered. A different floor lay beneath her feet, scuffed and dark. A figure loomed above her, shadowed, furious.

"First rule of Djiharai," the voice barked. *"Once the enemy is down, you finish them. No prisoners."*

Kharis blinked. The fencing hall had melted into the ghost of another. Steel rang loudly, swords clanging, armor jangling. The sounds nearly pushed her past her breaking point. The staff's pounding on the floor became deafening.

"Finish—Him," the voice bellowed.

"No!" Kharis cried, and the chaos in her mind shattered. "I refuse."

She drove the sword downward with all her strength. The flooring cracked. The sword's tip shattered, flying across the room.

"Uselessss," the phantom voice hissed. *"Nothing but a monster."*

The vision receded, leaving a silence that rang in her ears. She straightened, trying to steady herself.

The fencing hall slid back into focus as the last threads of the vision dissolved and the shadows reshaped themselves into familiar forms. Hrag and Darragh stood before her, mouths parted, eyebrows lifted in stunned disbelief.

Leógham lay on the floor, his semblance twisted in pain. The wooden boards had splintered inches from his face.

Blessed Mother, what have I done?

She kept her head down, too scared to meet anyone's gaze, and approached Hrag with unsteady steps, handing him the wooden sword with utmost respect. It now had a broken tip, exposing the lead core. He took it, his eyes brimming with questions.

"Sorry," she whispered, then fled the room.

59

THE LETTER

In the game of life, the pieces fall to those bold enough to move them. - Poliormos

"Are you certain, Neagh?" Sahrit asked. "About Eram and Juell?"

She'd suspected Eram for some time; had watched him linger where he shouldn't, listening when he thought no one had noticed. Sahrit had waited, hoping he'd slip and reveal his tie to Saigham. Juell's actions, though, surprised her.

"Yes, Your Highness." Neagh's brow furrowed. "Soldiers caught Juell a while ago, hiding in the village."

Sahrit shook her head, weary of blood and punishment. "Entering Lord Benkhi's chambers... Hers was a foolish mistake. And what of Eram?"

"It seems he has vanished. No one has seen him since this morning. One servant claimed he was bound for the village, but the soldiers didn't find him."

Probably waiting for Juell. "Wasn't she close to Eram?"

"They were." Neagh's ears reddened. "Quite... close."

Another foolish mistake. "And Eram's family?" she pressed.

"Gone as well, Your Highness."

Sahrit's fingertips drummed the desk. "I assumed Juell had run off to meet with Eram, perhaps rifling through Lord Benkhi's possessions for whatever she could sell." She halted the finger drumming. *Was she spying on us as well?*

"But why would Eram's wife and children vanish, too?"

She leaned back, wondering if now that she was in trouble, Eram had fled the village with his family.

"This is indeed troubling," she said. "Thank you for sharing the details. The matter, sadly, is now out of our hands. We can manage without Eram or Juell for now, but I'd like to discuss replacements with you and Ailene tomorrow." She opened a drawer and retrieved parchment. "Ready a messenger, please."

Neagh inclined her head. "Of course."

"One more thing, Neagh. I'm sure the gossiping has been churning since it happened, but it's best not to alarm the other servants. Perhaps Eram abandoned Juell to her misfortune and slipped away."

Neagh inclined his head, lips pressed thin. "As you wish, Your Highness."

The seneschal exited the room, and Sahrit pondered her next move. Looking for paper, she readied her ink and quill and wrote a brief message to her father.

Leógham has arrived. Expect us in four days.

She studied the note with concern. "I should discuss this with Leógham and let him weigh in."

The quill hovered over the paper. Then she shook her head.

"No. If I tell him, he'll refuse, and we can't wait any longer. It's our move, or we'll spend our lives answering to Saigham."

It's time. She pushed doubt aside before she could second-guess herself. *There's no room for uncertainty now.*

She folded the parchment and took a small bar of red wax from a drawer in her desk. The color brought back that memory—the king's words, spoken with sadness and pride: "If only you had been born a man."

She swiftly pushed her father's words aside, melted the wax, and pressed her seal into the page.

This letter has to be sent.

60

WHEN LEGACIES ARE
WRITTEN IN BLOOD

History devours those who cling to its shadows. What was stolen once may be stolen again by the same hands, unless wisdom breaks the pattern. - Poliormos

Saigham could only smile this evening. His grandchildren nestled with him on the plush chair as he turned the vellum page. His voice stayed soft, almost musical, as he read the tale of King Gairashtagha, the first ruler of the Mórad Lahm. Daeroth's glossy, black hair gleamed against the firelight. Einar pressed against his grandfather's knee, red eyes wide with wonder, small fingers hooked around the fabric of Saigham's robe.

Their rapt faces warmed his heart. Pride pulsed beneath his ribs. These boys were born for a higher calling, for a legacy stolen long before they drew breath. He brushed their heads with gentle affection. One day, the crown would rest upon Daeroth's head, and Einar would sit to his right, defending it. Soon, Saigham would restore King Gairashtagha's lineage.

A scuff of boots disturbed his moment with them. Cuileagh stepped into the room, a Shadowman at his shoulder. The children, disciplined and obedient, straightened right away.

Saigham closed the book and set it on the low table beside him.

"It's late," Cuileagh told his children. "Go to your mother."

Daeroth's mouth twisted. Einar slumped. "But we were almost at the good part, when the king returns after battle." He dragged a sleeve across his nose.

Saigham's smile warmed. "A story can wait, Einar. My business with your father cannot."

Their mouths tightened for a heartbeat. Then they bowed like miniature soldiers and chorused, "Good night, Grandfather." Their slippered feet padded across the floor as the nanny ushered them out. The door closed with a gentle thud.

Silence breathed once.

Saigham exhaled slowly, and the kindly grandfather melted away. Lord Saigham of House Teinthir emerged, a man carved sharp by centuries of bitterness, his purpose hard as iron. The fire behind him cast his long shadow across the chamber like a claw.

"What is it?" He weighed the interruption's worth.

Cuileagh stepped forward, shoulders squared with quiet anticipation. "We've received a message." A slow, wicked smile curled his mouth. "Leógham has returned to Dríeadh Manor."

Saigham's pulse steadied. The rightful line to Hegra's throne would rise again. The map in his mind shifted, pathways narrowing to one single, glorious conclusion.

He drew in a measured breath. "Everything in place?"

Cuileagh's maroon eyes flickered as he leaned forward. "They won't see us coming. Leógham will not survive the day, Father."

A warm sense of triumph uncoiled in Saigham's chest. "Proceed as planned."

Cuileagh bowed and beckoned the Shadowman to follow him.

When the chamber emptied, Saigham returned to the book. The painted crown beneath the title glimmered faintly in the firelight. He traced a finger over the faded gold, the touch stirring the old ancestral wound carried through generations. His ancestors had ruled Hegra by divine right until the Shattering. In the chaos that followed, Aghavor's bloodline seized the throne. History celebrated it as the dawn of a new era.

Saigham's forebears remembered it as theft.

Restoration was justice long overdue.

His breath came slow and steady. Hegra would belong to him.

Soon, the crown would come home.

61

THE GATHERING

Rage burns brightest when fueled by bruised pride, but it doesn't heal wounded hearts. - Poliormos

Darragh stood in a corner, waiting for the dinner announcement. He wore Hegran black as tradition demanded, as did his son. His beloved Sahrit tempered the grim color with cerise brocade. Lord Benkhi, however, was conspicuously absent.

Darragh's gaze flicked to Leógham. The crown prince sat by the fireplace, brooding, shoulders hunched, one boot tapping in restless irritation. His face bore the aftermath of his defeat—blackened eye, swollen nose, split lip—all badges of ruined pride. He shifted in his chair with visible discomfort, wincing yet trying to hide it. Every time the door creaked, he looked up, only to snarl when it was a servant.

Darragh sighed. A year away hadn't tempered Leógham's anger.

Sahrit, seated across the room, pretended not to notice, though Darragh could tell by the way her fingers toyed with her ring that she was bracing for another storm.

The doors opened again, and Neagh walked in. "Dinner is served."

Before anyone could move, Leógham's voice boomed. "Where's Lord Benkhi?"

"He's indisposed and extends his apologies," Sahrit said evenly.

Leógham grunted. "Then I suppose he starves."

Darragh's jaw tightened. *By the gods, not now.*

"I've already sent food to his chambers," Sahrit replied calmly. "It's for the best, as we have family matters to discuss —two, in fact."

Leógham's glare darkened. "What are they?"

"One servant left—"

"So what?" he bellowed, lurching to his feet. "All our servants are free to find work elsewhere."

Sahrit remained composed, her hands neatly folded in her lap. "One servant was caught in Lord Benkhi's chambers and has been apprehended. The other was spying on us and remains at large."

Leógham did not answer at once. His mouth tightened. For a heartbeat, Darragh thought he might speak, but instead his gaze hardened. "You said there were two matters. What's the second one?"

"A messenger left this afternoon. The palace expects us in four days."

"What?" He slammed his fist against the mantle; metal sconces rattled; ornaments toppled with a clatter. He stormed out, shoulders rigid and fists flexing at his sides, leaving a wake of bitter indignation.

Darragh sighed. The heat in the room—Leógham's anger made manifest—lingered. "Go," he told Hrag, gesturing toward the door. "Make sure he doesn't burn the dining table or the castle."

Hrag walked out, shoulders slumped.

Darragh rubbed his brow as the old worries resurfaced.

Anger still ruled Leógham. Some Houses would march at his side into battle, but they would never trust him with Hegra's future. Releasing a long exhale, he approached Sahrit, willing to do anything to see her smile again after her brother's outburst. He would deal with Leógham later. *How dare he yell at her?*

He extended his hand, flashing his charming grin. "It would be an honor to accompany you to the dining room, Lady Sahrit." *Benkhi would've said that.*

Sahrit raised her face, eyes glistening.

He hated leaving her behind when duty dragged him to the capital. Now, they were bound for Ashtalon—a nest of vipers clothed in silk. He understood why she'd sent the letter, but peril awaited them, and the price would fall hardest upon those he loved.

And Benkhi—*is that even her name?*—was another element of danger. If her disguise unraveled at court, Sahrit's letter might as well have summoned their ruin.

Masking his unease, he said, "You look exquisite this evening. More beautiful every time I see you."

Her smile lit up her face, and his heart stumbled at its radiance. He'd kill without hesitation, wade through rivers of blood, if it meant keeping her safe.

Clearing his throat, he forced his tone back into ease. "I've heard dinner will be a wonderful affair. Unfortunately, Lord Benkhi will miss the pheasant he hunted this morning." As they walked toward the dining hall, he cast her a sidelong glance, his tone conspiratorial. "I ran into him in the forest. You should've seen him, so proud of his catch, practically glowing. He couldn't wait to surprise you."

He turned to her. "Did he make you smile?"

"He did," she said softly.

"Ah!" He pressed a hand to his chest in mock outrage. "Then he's earned my jealousy. But," he added with a playful grin, "I forgive him since he made you smile."

Her soft laugh was music to his ears. It sharpened his devotion. He'd do anything to ensure her smile never faded.

And so, as he walked, he threaded his fingers through hers—a blatant violation of Hegran law.

62

THE DINNER

> *Actions, not words, define who you are. - Poliormos*

Leógham brooded through dinner, his fork pushing food around his plate. Each motion punished him anew: the sting of his split lip when he chewed, the dull throb beneath his jaw, the deeper ache that flared with every breath. His gaze occasionally flicked toward the empty chair next to Hrag.

The forest came back in flashes: his panic twisting into anger once her secret lay bare, raising his voice at her, her expression shifting. Her trust had shattered, betrayal flaring, fury hardening her features. His grip tightened on the goblet until the metal bit his fingers.

Why would she forgive me?

Darragh spoke as if nothing had happened. Hrag had joined the discussion, yet neither of them mentioned Lord Benkhi. Sahrit had been much quieter this evening. Leógham gulped his wine, pain be damned. He'd lashed out at the two women who meant everything to him.

He hated this dinner, the thought of leaving Dríeadh

Manor, or that Kharis wasn't at the table. The idea that she could leave him filled him with a fear that froze his blood.

The urge to strangle Darragh overwhelmed him. *Why didn't he speak to me first?*

Leógham often glanced at the doors, praying Kharis would change her mind and join them. But she never came. Her chair remained empty. When servants brought the main course—roasted pheasant with wild mushrooms—Leógham drew a tight breath.

Everyone waited for him to take the first bite, but all he did was close his eyes, shutting out the weight of their stares. He never gave Kharis a chance to explain herself, jumping right in with his assumptions.

Once a fool, always a fool.

His fisted hands flanked the plate.

The servants waited, exchanging worried glances. The silence lingered.

With a loud huff, Leógham got up, his chair scratching the floor.

No one moved.

He took his plate and stormed out of the dining room.

"Keep eating," was all he said.

She'd caught these for me. Leógham couldn't think of anything else as he marched down the hallway. Each step jarred his bruised ribs. The limp in his gait deepened despite his effort to hide it. He climbed the steps with stubborn determination, each rise a small victory. Once he stood before her door, he knocked.

She didn't open it.

Leógham knocked again, holding onto the dish, careful not to spill a single item.

No sound came from inside. Not even a "Go away."

He pursed his lips. This was his doing. With a weary sigh, he pressed his forehead against the door. His body ached, but it was nothing compared to the pain in his heart.

Then, resolved to make this right, he stepped into his

chambers and locked the door behind him. His hand settled on the secret panel in his bedroom, his pulse quickening. He rapped lightly against the wood before pressing his palm to it.

The panel shifted.

With a sharp inhale, he stepped through into her chamber.

The figure beneath the mound of bedcovers had to be her. He paused, the ache in his ribs a reminder of how unwise this was. With a low breath, he lowered himself to one knee. Pain flared through his side, sharp enough to steal his breath, but he steadied the plate in his hands and forced calm into his voice.

"Please eat something."

Kharis didn't move.

The walls he had built faltered. His mother was dead. His wife and son were dead. He had been dragged back to Ashtalon, and now Kharis's hatred pressed in alongside the rest.

A hum rose in his ears. His eyes stung with unshed tears. A lump tightened his throat.

"Please," he whispered, one last attempt before accepting defeat.

The floor tilting halted when a gentle hand came to rest on his shoulder. He lifted his head, and he met her eyes—a collision, a reckoning. A universe stretched within them. He felt small, adrift—a wanderer at the edge of something infinite. All he could hope for was to become one more star in her heavens that she wouldn't cast away.

This was his only chance at making things right.

He extended the plate toward her, his hands unsteady, and braced himself, expecting her to hurl it against the wall because if their roles were reversed, he would have.

Kharis slid down the bed, took the plate from him, and set it aside. Propping herself up on her knees, she examined the injuries on his face, her fingers gently tracing the bruises to assess the damage. His breathing stopped as heat radiated from her fingertips.

"Don't heal them," he said, pulling his face away. "Please."

Kharis held a question in her gaze and lowered her hand, the silver sparks fading.

"I..." he stammered. "I want them to remind me that I must become a better person."

Kharis nodded quietly, hands resting in her lap. "Leógham—" She pinched her lips. "I... I'm so sorry I hurt you." She threw her arms around him, a sob escaping her. "Please, forgive me."

He sucked in a sharp breath, his ribs protesting—or cracking again—but he didn't pull away, torn between agony and the comfort of her touch.

"Why are you apologizing?" he whispered.

"You had no right to yell at me for something I didn't do, but I had no right to hurt you in retaliation."

"I deserved it," he said. "All of it." His chest heaved with a shaky exhale. "You... Um... I'm sorry."

Leógham pressed her against him until his breathing fell into sync with hers. The world outside faded, time stretching until there was nothing but the thrum of two hearts beating as one.

After a while, Kharis pulled away and sat back. Leógham reached out with a slight wince and pulled the plate closer, presenting it to her. She chuckled, and it was the most beautiful sound he'd ever heard.

"Did you storm out of the dining room to bring me this?" she asked.

Leógham sheepishly nodded.

"Have you ever eaten with your hands?" she asked.

"Fires, I forgot utensils."

Kharis stopped him from rising. "That's not what I asked." She tore a piece of pheasant with her fingers, dipped it in the sauce, and brought it to her mouth, humming as she chewed. "The flavor is magnificent. Did you try it?"

He shook his head, the movement small, timid. "I left before I had the chance."

She chuckled. "You're in luck because I happen to have some." She pulled another piece apart, the juices glistening on her fingertips, and lifted it toward him. "Here, open."

Heat crept up his neck at the gesture, at the implied intimacy—at the invitation hidden in that gesture.

His fingers twitched.

Should I?

He hesitated, his jaw still tender from her blow. Chewing would hurt. But the thought of refusing her would hurt more. Eager to make his intentions clear, he leaned in and gingerly opened his mouth. Her fingertips ghosted over his lips, fleeting yet electric.

"What do you think?" she asked.

He chewed slowly, the taste rich and layered, his senses blurring at the steady way she observed him. "I'll compliment Ondriagh tomorrow."

A laugh slipped from her. "That would be a good start." A pause. Then, teasing, "Would you like more?"

Leógham's chest tightened, heat pooling low. There was no jest or challenge in her tone—just an offering. His pulse stuttered.

"Yes," he murmured. *Yes, to being fed. Yes, to your hands. Yes, to all of you.*

She tore another piece. This time, he tracked her movement, unable to look away as golden droplets trickled down her fingers and clung to her skin. He parted his lips and took what she offered, but when she pulled her hand away, instinct took over.

He caught her wrist, gentle but firm.

Without thinking, he brushed his lips over her fingertips and drew the sauce from them, his tongue catching the salt and spice clinging to her skin.

§&.

Her breath fled.

His tongue brushed against her skin, sending shockwaves through her. It wasn't the act itself. It was how he did it. Slow. Unhurried. Certain. As though she was meant to be savored.

Oh, gods above and below.

She feared erupting into a firestorm. Her senses narrowed, the world drawing tight around that single point of contact. Want slammed against the fragile walls of her restraint, testing them.

More.

The thought surfaced unbidden, sharp with need. Her body drew taut, every muscle strung tight. Heat radiated from her skin, rippling the air in warning.

His mouth.

Every instinct in her reached for it, aching, insistent.

Leógham's eyes fluttered open.

For a heartbeat, he only stared at her, caught somewhere between sleep and waking. Then his body went rigid.

A shadow crossed his face, as though he had surfaced from a dream only to realize how close he stood to the edge of a cliff. The moment shattered, and all those pieces, big and small, came crashing down at once. He released her hand and drew back, color rising to his cheeks.

Kharis's hand remained suspended mid-air.

Why did he stop?

Heat shuddered outward from her in a low, invisible pulse, warping the space between them like breath over flame. Her sleeve slipped to her elbow, revealing the black markings that curled along her arm, always pulsing. Always moving. But now they flared brighter, crawling faster, drawn toward him despite her will.

She lowered her hand.

Leógham dragged his fingers through his hair, as if he needed something to do with them now that they were no longer on her. "I'm sorry," he whispered, his voice hoarse, color burning high on his face. "I didn't think."

Silence stretched between them. Hesitant. Awkward. As if the wanting had nowhere else to go. Kharis drew a slow breath and let it out carefully, willing the heat in her veins to ease. She had to say something or else he'd leave, and this fragile thing between them would fracture beyond repair.

"I was told pheasant is your favorite dish."

Leógham glanced up. "It is," he said, quieter than before.

She lifted the plate and held it out to him. "Eat more, please."

His want, his flustered expression as he retreated from his boldness, sent a jolt through her.

The man from the cabin was gazing at her.

Her heart thumped against her ribs.

She inhaled softly, searching for the clarity to untangle whatever this was between them. It slipped away the moment she took in the bruises darkening his face.

Why would he treat me as a woman after what I did to him?

Her blows had struck more than flesh. They had landed on his pride, cracking the fragile ground under them. *Hardly the way to earn trust from the man trying to help me.*

After another exhale, she clasped her hands in her lap. "We promised to help each other weather the storm as we break our curses," she said. "So rather than fight, we should aim to understand each other."

Leógham nodded.

Once, the storm had been Hrag. But in Hegra, the storms would be far more vicious and less forgiving.

"Leógham?"

He met her gaze.

She held it, searching his face. "Why are you always on the offensive, even with those who care about you?"

WHEN WE ALLOW THE
PAST TO WHISPER

When you release fear, hope begins to bloom. Do not bar the door against what frightens you—let it speak its truths, and you may yet find serenity and wholeness. - Poliormos

The question hit Leógham like a splash of icy water. Anger had been his answer for everything—his shield.

He took a deep, pained breath, memories pressing in. "I couldn't protect my friends during the civil war, nor could I protect my mother, my niece, Elinor. A mathan nearly took you. I couldn't stop the winged nightmare from almost killing Hrag."

The words left him hollow. He'd been useless then, and now. "How do I let go of this fear?"

Kharis worried her lip.

"Fear does not fade because we wish it gone," she said. "It lingers, like the scent of smoke after a fire. It always points to a hurt left untended. Until that hurt is faced, the work is never done."

"Poliormos," he said, recognizing the words.

She nodded, her lips tight. The light in her eyes dimmed, her sorrow surfacing without edges or name. With her memories gone, grief remained, but stripped of its story.

"My own hurts..." Her eyes wandered. "They exist, but I cannot reach them. Still, I can help you."

Her gaze lifted to his, tentative but earnest.

"Will you let me try?"

Her gaze lifted to his, careful, hopeful. She lingered at the threshold, yearning for a chance at redemption.

"How would you like to do this?" he asked.

She thought for a moment. "Tell me about Elinor."

The breath stilled in his lungs.

His first instinct was silence. To leave the name buried and undisturbed. He'd locked his memories of Elinor away because touching them sharpened the ache and made her absence feel like a fresh wound. For a year, he'd kept the pain hidden as if that could dull it. The tightness in his chest returned. He rubbed his forehead, wavering between staying and leaving, but the heaviness within had grown too much for him to carry alone.

He closed his eyes and let a breath go. "What would you like to know?"

She hummed, considering. "How did you meet?" She hugged her knees, open to listening, offering him the space to speak.

The quiet stretched.

His throat burned with the effort of holding it back. And yet, weary of bearing it in silence, he didn't turn away this time.

"The first time I saw her was at my sister's wedding. Our realms had arranged the marriage between Darragh and Sahrit." A quiet chuckle followed. "I sometimes wonder if Darragh pushed for it. He has loved my sister for as long as I can remember. Sahrit agreed to the arrangement, and soon, the wedding was upon us."

His gaze drifted, caught in the past.

"Elinor sat beside her mother, wearing a gown as lovely as she was. I remember thinking she looked like a gorgeous butterfly. I was seven. She was six." He swallowed hard. "I saw her again at my mother's and niece's burials."

Kharis's hand came to rest over his. "I never meant to—"

"It's fine." His fingers tightened briefly beneath hers. "We cannot speak of joy without touching sorrow. I should know this better than most."

He drew a sharp breath, steadying himself. "What I remember of her is blurred because Sahrit's cries wouldn't leave my mind, following me even into sleep. I wanted revenge. Rage filled me, burning away everything else."

His head tilted back, and a heavy sigh escaped him.

"And so, at sixteen, I joined the civil war. It had begun because of me. My hand ended it."

He felt no pride in it. His thirst for justice had not been quenched then. It was easy to punish men. Fate, on the other hand, had remained out of his reach.

"My father was against it since I was his only heir. I went anyway. Wrath stripped me of restraint and shaped me into someone ruthless, someone I barely recognized. A year later, the brutal war ground to a halt. My father reclaimed Hegra. Prison and execution awaited the guilty."

His gaze hardened. "But the anger did not die then. It lingered, simmering in the background, ready to explode. And it did—often."

His insides clenched.

"Unable to forgive, I became a cruel version that I didn't know how to stop. So my father did the only thing he felt would help me: He sent me to Skógarjód on a fostering arrangement."

Kharis tilted her head. Leógham sensed the question hanging on her lips.

"Everyone believed my uncle, Prince Foághlam, was my last hope."

Recognition lit her gaze. "The one who taught you about healing."

He nodded. "Uncle believed I might mend myself by learning to mend others. But I have none of the Forest Kin's magic. What I learned was earned by hand. Herbs. Salves. Stitches. No spells." His mouth curved faintly. "Worse, I lacked a reason to care. No purpose to anchor the work."

"You must've found one," she said softly, gesturing toward herself.

His heart kicked against his ribs. For a moment, he wondered if he could go on.

"You see," he said at last. "It was in Skógarjód that I met Elinor for the third time. She was sixteen and had grown into a beautiful young woman. Quiet as a whisper. Warm as a sunbeam. Far more delicate than a butterfly."

Elinor had brought such light to his life.

"I was seventeen," he went on. "Clumsy. Tongue-tied whenever she was near. The first time she stood close enough for me to catch the scent in her hair, every word I knew abandoned me."

He laughed, thinking of the awkward young man he'd been.

"She softened me. Slowly, the monster inside me faded away. Without realizing it, I found reasons to seek her out. Poor ones." The corners of his mouth lifted. "Asking about a book she'd returned, bringing back a cloak she hadn't lost. Anything to linger longer. Once, I offered to carry a basket for her and nearly dropped it when our hands brushed."

He smiled at the warm memories.

"Elinor was... exceptional," he continued. "Others saw only the cruelty I wore and kept their distance. She looked past it. She saw the boy beneath. She was always glad to see me, her smiles genuine, her eyes lighting up whenever I came. It was impossible not to be drawn into her joy. Little by little, the darkness loosened its hold."

He let out a quiet breath. "She was fragile, though. Pain

would seize her without warning, leaving her confined to her bed for days at a time. She bore it quietly, never once complaining. Suddenly, I wanted to heal *her*."

His gaze dropped to his hands.

"Resolved to find a cure for her illness, I returned to Foághlam with purpose. During this time, Elinor and I exchanged letters. She told me of her garden and the books she loved. I wrote about the forests and mountains my uncle took me through."

Three years, distilled into a breath.

"I trained without rest, and slowly my destructive power shifted into protection. One day, I realized I wanted Elinor in my life. Not borrowed moments, or words on parchment, but *us*, permanently. Our families approved. A match between Hegra and Skógarjód served more than the heart. I mustered the courage to ask, and she said yes. The festivities lasted for days."

Leógham pressed his lips and looked to Kharis. She held his gaze, quietly urging him on.

"The day of our wedding was one of the happiest days of my life. Elinor was radiant. I was twenty; she, nineteen. We believed the years ahead belonged to us. I brought her to Hegra. In our fourth year of marriage, she told me she was with child. I didn't know joy could be so complete. Then," he took a deep breath, "her health began to fail."

Kharis leaned forward. "Leógham—"

"I must speak of this." His fingers curled tight. "I've been running away from these memories. Elinor would've never asked that of me."

Kharis moved closer, her hand closing over his. "We stop when you stop."

Leógham drew a shuddering breath.

"Elinor didn't survive the labor. Nor did our son. I learned then how deep despair can pull a man. A single moment stained my hope black. When it dawned on me that they were truly gone, I... exploded."

Tears pricked his eyes.

"I tore through the corridors like a beast, not caring whether I lived or died. I stormed into the courtyard, screaming at the gods, at my father, at every soul in Hegra who dared breathe while my wife and son didn't. I raised my blade against my own men, screaming until my throat bled. My grief wanted fire, and I wanted the world to burn with me." A pause. "A wing of the castle burned before they stopped me."

His shoulders trembled as he pressed on.

"I live with the shame of what I did. I believed I'd mastered my rage, but that night, it devoured me. Without Elinor, nothing held meaning."

He swallowed hard. When he risked a glance, Kharis listened, her eyes warm, full of understanding as if... as if she'd done the same.

"Guards stopped me in the end," he said. "Shackles clamped around my wrists before I even knew I'd fallen. When they dragged me before my father in chains, the look he gave me told me everything. I begged for leave from Hegra—to run and hide. He granted it, not out of mercy, but fear. He believed that if I stayed, grief would shape me into something monstrous before I ever took the crown."

He gulped, his throat dry.

"'Hegra always comes first,' he told me. 'Come back when Hegra is first for you.' I hated him for that. I'd lost my wife and child, and all he could care about was Hegra."

He clenched his hands on a sharp inhale.

"Elinor and my son were cremated in Ashtalon, but I brought their ashes here. My uncle offered his realm, and Sahrit, ever wise, convinced me to allow Hrag to enter it every full moon to bring provisions. A year into my exile, you appeared out of nowhere. The rest, you know."

Kharis blinked tears, her voice barely steady. "I'm truly sorry for those you loved."

"So am I," he said quietly. "But you taught me something

one night—a truth that stayed." His gaze held hers. "I won't drown in grief. I will live in a way that honors my friends. My mother. Elinor." His breath eased. "And I'll cherish those who still stand beside me."

She recognized the words. A small, broken smile answered him.

For the first time, the weight in his chest loosened, and the night didn't feel quite so dark. Outside, the wind rose, whistling past the castle's crenellations.

He lingered on her expression, warmth stirring where sorrow had ruled. "What else would you like to know?"

She hesitated only a moment, pushing hair from her damp cheeks. Then her gaze met his. "Everything."

PART IV

THE TUG OF FATE

64

THE NORTHERN WIND BLOWS

The voice of fate is seldom loud; it waits patiently to be heard. - Poliormos

Darragh's attention lingered on Sahrit longer than on the food laid before him. He was still watching the curve of her smile when Leógham entered the dining room, favoring one leg. Benkhi trailed behind.

The room stilled.

Purple bruises marred Leógham's face. Servants lowered their gazes too late. What unsettled Darragh was the way Leógham carried his injuries. Without anger or a simmering threat in his stride. Just a strange quiet, as though something heavy had been lifted at last.

This time, Leógham didn't go straight for the food table, as was his habit.

"Good morning." He bowed to Sahrit, lowering his gaze. "Please accept my apologies for last night. I was unfair to you, and my behavior, uncalled for."

Sahrit's fingers stilled on the rim of her cup.

Hrag's fork never made it to his mouth.

Darragh stared. In all his years, he'd known two sides to Leógham's temper. One struck like lightning. The other pounced like a hunting beast. Apologies were never part of it.

Sahrit studied her brother, the pause stretching long enough to unsettle even Darragh. He wondered what he would do or say if Leógham ever sought his forgiveness.

At last, Sahrit's expression softened.

"Thank you," she said. "I appreciate the apology."

Leógham bowed once more, then strode toward the food table. He returned with two bowls of barley and mushroom pottage, setting one before Benkhi and keeping the other for himself. He broke a loaf of dense rye bread and placed it beside her bowl.

Darragh's jaw tightened. *Serving her?* Leógham had ignored his advice to keep his distance. *What next, a seat on the council?* His gaze slid to the servants. It wouldn't be long before they traded whispers about this morning.

Leógham turned to Sahrit. "Could you ensure the breakfast service includes boiled eggs?" She inclined her head, and he set his fork down, a distant thought shadowing his expression. "I believe we have matters to discuss?"

"We do," she said.

Leógham nodded once. "Preparations underway?" he asked between bites.

"Neagh is overseeing them this morning."

Darragh's mouth parted. Leógham was issuing requests and thanking people. The shift unsettled him more than the bruises did.

"Darragh." Leógham glanced his way. "Would you accompany me to the village?"

Darragh inclined his head. "A stop at the tavern would be most welcome." Perhaps a cup of ale would loosen Leógham's tongue because he had to know how deep this change ran. "Is there something in particular?"

"The issue with the servant. Juell, was it not?"

Darragh felt sorry for the girl. Whatever awaited her would not be gentle.

"I wish to speak with Chief Harrald," Leógham said. "After that, I intend to reacquaint myself with those working the estate and assess needs, concerns."

"And Juell?" Benkhi asked, tracing the edge of her bowl with the spoon. "What is to become of her?"

Leógham's gaze shifted to Darragh. The message landed cleanly: silence. Darragh shifted slightly in his chair.

Leógham lifted his cup and drank. "What the servant did was unfortunate," he said at last. "I will see to it." His fingers tapped against the table—his familiar habit when pausing on a thought. "We leave after breakfast." Another glance followed, sharper this time. "Neagh, ready the horses."

"Of course."

Benkhi said nothing, but her knuckles paled as she drank from her cup. She lowered her head, spoon trembling in her hand, and kept eating.

The men left after breakfast.

To stay busy, Kharis trailed Sahrit everywhere. Sahrit and Neagh took inventory, spoke with the kitchen staff, and met with merchants. By late afternoon, they sat at a table in her study, hunched over ledgers and stacks of parchment, poring over expenses and revenues, their quills scratching as they cross-checked every detail with meticulous precision.

"We maintain two ledgers," Sahrit had explained to Kharis. "One for our records; the other we submit to the Crown for tax levies."

Fidgeting didn't ease Kharis's worries: Juell, the journey north, or how long her disguise could hold. The longer she stayed, the greater the danger she posed to this house. She couldn't repay their kindness with misfortune. Excusing herself, she made her way toward the library.

Upon entering, she reached inside her doublet and drew out her leather-bound journal. Grabbing a quill, she bent over the maps, tracing routes across Leógham's estate, the forests, and the mountain passes leading north. A plan slowly took shape, her notes swift yet thorough. Aware of the spying, she wrote everything in code.

As it turned out, Hegra was vast, and it would take her at least two weeks to reach the northern range. Her journey ahead demanded preparation. She scribbled across the parchment, her mind racing faster than her quill. Provisions. Horses. Warm clothing. Enough weapons to fight her way through. And allies, if she could trust any.

"Ah, little sister."

She started, her quill slipping from her fingers.

Ragha leaned over her shoulder, a smile tugging at his lips. His form was as thin as gauze, light bleeding through him. Silver hair spilled like liquid moonlight. His eyes glowed with an otherworldly radiance.

"At last, you prepare to go north. No more wasted time."

She rose, the chair catching behind her knees. "Others will see you."

He laughed. "Only you can."

"Perfect!" She dropped back into the chair. "Talking to the air. Now everyone will believe I'm going mad." She rubbed an eye, her pulse still racing. "So… How is it you can appear like this?"

One of his brows lifted. "We dwell in this world, sister, but also in another."

She regarded him, masking her confusion. "Well…" Her hand twitched. She almost reached for him, wondering if her hand would pass through. Instead, she picked the quill from the floor. "Stop appearing like this, interrupting my work."

He smirked. "Shall I whisper in your ear?"

Throbing thre inkwell at him tempted her. "In all

honesty, I prefer this to you talking in my head. If I end up mad, I'd rather choose how it happens, since I can't choose my destination."

"There is always a choice, sister... but what will *you* choose?"

Her markings stirred. She set the quill down, biting the inside of her cheek. "Choice? Sure. Do nothing and watch the world burn, or go north and die." Her frown deepened. "If you're here to help, then tell me what 'ending all the writings' means."

Ragha's ghostly fingers traced the titles of the books on the table, his spectral cloak billowing in a phantom wind. "A long time ago, the Weaver added a thread that didn't belong." He moved to the shelves, lingering on a book that had caught his eye. "The gods forced the Weaver to remake the Tapestry."

She drew the chair toward the table. "Why?"

His fingers stilled on the book, then he looked at her. "Because the Weaver added that thread to save me."

She dipped her quill in the well. "From what?"

"Oh, many things," he said with a half-smile, always enigmatic.

"Bad ones?" she pressed, eyes narrowed.

"Terrible ones." For a heartbeat, she couldn't tell whether he meant it or mocked her.

Kharis sighed, turning toward the window.

North... That familiar tug pulled harder than ever, a summons she could no longer ignore. She crossed the room and parted the curtain. "Why go north?"

"Everything that matters began there."

She narrowed her eyes. "And what, exactly, am I to do once I reach the north?"

In the window's reflection, Ragha wavered, his likeness shimmering like a disturbed pool. It still amazed her how much they resembled one another. "You shall know when you arrive."

Her fingers curled into fists, tired of all these riddles. "Your details are riveting. Truly. I know *precisely* how to save the world. In fact, why wait? Let's do it now."

The glow in Ragha's eyes dimmed, as if her sarcasm had tainted something sacred. His reflection fractured into rippling shards. Kharis winced, pressing her hands to her temples at the sudden ache behind her eyes.

"Stop this."

Ragha took a step back, his form returning to being whole again. The pressure vanished, the pain fading with it.

"I need concrete answers," she said. "No more puzzles. Tell me, why did the Weaver add this thread?"

The question seemed to unravel him from the inside out. His form flickered, edges fraying like smoke in the wind as though the world now resisted his presence.

"You must remember," he said.

"Well, I can't," she snapped. "Unless you tell me how to release my memories."

He gazed at her, his presence thinning, the light in his eyes dimming once more.

"To remember is to create," he said. "Memory allows us to exist in the river of time, anchoring us against its pull." He drifted closer, weightless and terrible, silver light gathering in his eyes. "Remember, little sister, or this world dies."

He vanished in a burst of glimmering smoke.

"Remember what?" She let out a breath—part anger, part despair. She splayed her hands out wide, then curled them. "What do you think I'm trying to do?"

She returned to the table, tapping on her journal. These notes weren't enough to guide her.

"I must learn about Hegra." Her ignorance of its history would expose her. Besides, she had to find out what had happened in the north long ago. She crossed to the nearest bookshelf, scanning the rows of titles, and pulled out the volume Ragha had studied so intently—a worn history tome by a General Oriander Maximus.

"Is this a joke?" She turned the book over, brow creasing at the name. It tugged at her memory, the pulse slightly painful. With a grunt, she brought it back to the table and bent over its pages, her quill scratching the only sound in the library.

65

THE TASTE OF MEMORIES

> *Beware the power of fate. Most times, it whispers. But on occasion, it arrives like a storm, shrouding the heavens, churning all it touches, and leaving nothing unchanged. - Poliormos*

The late afternoon shadows shrouded the library. Kharis climbed the spiral staircase to the second floor, balancing a stack of books in her arms. At the top, her eyes landed on a familiar gold-colored, leather-bound book. *The one from the cabin?*

Leógham had brought little; his wistful gaze had lingered on the books he'd left behind. She pulled it from the shelf, a hand caressing the cover. *The North Star.* The thought of Leógham reading it to her again stirred a quiet warmth. It faded at once when she remembered his mention of arranged marriages—his and Sahrit's—leaving a dull ache in its wake. Leógham was a crown prince. She was a nobody in a foreign land.

And monsters don't get happy endings.

"Lord Benkhi?"

Kharis's grip on the book faltered.

Sahrit's voice rang out from below.

"Up here." Kharis waved a hand, then slid down the banister, the rush exhilarating. When her boots hit the ground, she anticipated Sahrit's disapproving glare, but the woman had focused her attention on the stack of books on the table.

"Have you read these already?" Sahrit asked. Her fingers traced the title of one. "Books about Hegra?"

Kharis tugged a strand of hair behind her ear, "Most of them." She fidgeted with her belt. "I got carried away, hoping for something to trigger my memories." *Liar.*

When Sahrit's brow furrowed, Kharis's posture faltered. "I can put them away."

"Oh, no, please." Sahrit's smile didn't quite reach her eyes. "Don't worry yourself. I brought tea."

As if on cue, Ailene entered with a tray bearing an ornate teapot, delicate cups, and an assortment of honey cakes and jams. Once placed on the table, she bowed and walked out. Sahrit was about to follow.

"Lady Sahrit," Kharis called. "Would you join me?" She gestured to the tea service. "You could use a well-deserved break. Master Neagh can manage for a little while."

Sahrit halted mid-step, the careful lines of her face softening. "I... suppose he can." She took the offered seat and reached for the teapot, but Kharis stopped her.

"Let me serve you, please. Ever since my arrival, you've been most attentive to my needs. Allow me to return the kindness."

Sahrit observed her with a curious expression. Then, "You're so courteous."

Kharis huffed a small laugh, lifting the teapot.

"I'm glad fate placed you in our path," Sahrit said. "Your presence in this household has been a gift."

Kharis stilled, a faint heat rose to her cheeks, then busied herself with the cups. "How do you like your tea?"

"Plain," Sahrit said. "Though it isn't proper for a woman of my station."

Hegra again. With a conspiratorial smile, she pressed a cup into Sahrit's hand. No cream. No honey. Sahrit tilted her head slightly but said nothing, sipping instead.

As their conversation shifted topics, Kharis heard the shuffle of servants beyond the doors, their murmurs mingling with Ailene's steady instructions. Dusk had settled over the library, and rather than summon help, Kharis lit a few candles.

"You're most attentive," Sahrit said. "As a Fire Dweller, you're baffling because our clansmen are so... so—"

"Obstinate? Temperamental?" Kharis interjected, Leógham and Hrag flashing through her mind.

"Challenging," Sahrit corrected, ever diplomatic.

"Irritating," Kharis countered.

"Burdened," Sahrit added in a hushed tone. "You're none of those things."

"Ah!" Kharis lifted a finger. "I'm on my best behavior around you."

Sahrit laughed, and the moment eased into comfortable companionship. "The men should be returning any moment now."

Kharis hummed in assent. "More tea?"

Sahrit nodded. Then, after a moment, "Hrag tells me you remember little of the mathan's attack."

Kharis froze as the tea poured in a soft, steady trickle. *I hate lying.* She set the teapot down.

"I... see flashes and images," she said, "but I can't thread them together in any way that makes sense." That much was true. Her memories had evaporated from her well of recollection—gone like rain puddles under a warm sun.

"I remember defending myself against something," Kharis said.

Fragments surfaced: scorching flames, the clash of blades. But why these? More stirred beneath them, fighting for a chance to continue existing, climbing out of the hole that had swallowed them.

"I recall being struck on the left side of my body." *But with what?* The question gnawed at her as her fingers brushed over her ribs. "The collision sent me flying. I think I hit a wall." Was that why her left side had been more bruised? "Then I grabbed onto something."

The echoes of memory rippled, always indistinct.

The coarse texture of whatever she'd clung to lingered in her palms long after she'd let go. Sharp sounds rang in her ears. Flashes of vivid color—purple fabric, brown eyes, crimson flames. And then... Silver light flooded everything. Brilliant. Blinding. Concealing a face despite being so close to her.

The jagged images surged forward like a roaring river, sweeping her into a moment when her life hung by a thread. Bursts of them flared in her mind like dots of colored chalk bleeding across a wet canvas. A broken landscape flickered to life, shifting and elusive, until one image sharpened into startling clarity.

"A tree." Kharis rose from her chair.

The picture came into focus. A hand—her hand—had grasped a weathered branch. The tree... Its gnarled trunk had reached out to catch her, halting her fall.

"Someone tried to reach me." *But who?* "The tree wouldn't hold our weight for long." Her legs had dangled over raging waters. She had tried to pull herself onto the trunk. Icy spray had soaked her through, the cold biting at her. The outline of a figure had emerged from the mist, inching toward her with slow, deliberate movements. Their golden eyes had gleamed with the sun's intensity, framing a gorgeous face touched by the Divine.

"Go back," Kharis screamed. "You must live, Saya!"

Her memories launched a violent assault.

Her vision whitened.

The world erupted into chaos.

٨

Sahrit couldn't move from her chair. Fear and awe had frozen her muscles.

Lord Benkhi looked like a star given flesh, billowing clouds of stardust enveloping him. Unseen winds lifted his black locks as if he'd summoned a cosmic storm.

Sahrit wanted to bow, to weep, to flee—all at once.

Benkhi's magic unfurled, crackling in the air, the taste metallic on Sahrit's tongue. Her own rose in reflex, rippling over her skin to shield her.

Then he called out a name, his voice ragged: Saya.

Silver sparks flared from him, dancing across his body. A deep, thrumming hum rose, as if thousands of bees had taken wing inside the library walls. The temperature spiked; the air warped. The candles melted, yet darkness never closed in. At the heart of the room, Benkhi burned silver-bright.

Sahrit shot to her feet, her pulse roaring in her ears. Panic clawed at her chest, rousing her Fire Dweller magic. Aquamarine flames burst along her hands. Pain lanced up her arms as her Forest Kin magic recoiled. Two forces, born as opposites—one devouring, one preserving—faced off. She gasped, holding herself together by sheer will as the magics within her pulled in contrary directions.

"Lord Benkhi, please, wake up," she wailed, struggling to hold herself tight. "Please!"

Her green fire swelled, and so did her pain.

The doors creaked. Leógham's silhouette filled the frame. "I heard yelling—"

He froze.

66

BETWEEN THIS
WORLD AND THE LAST

A soul does not cross the threshold of worlds by strength, but by the weight of what it cannot abandon. - Poliormos

"Fires, no!"

Leógham rushed toward Kharis. The silver light thickened around her, bowing and flexing as he attempted to push through. It snapped back hard enough to stagger him. He set his jaw and drove forward again, shoulders bowed, every muscle screaming as he fought for a way in. Stardust stretched, clinging and reluctant beneath his hands. Metallic cold bit through his sleeves as he searched for a gap, fingers jabbing and clawing.

With a final shove, the resistance buckled. He broke through, plunging into the light like diving into deep water, and wrapped his arms around her form.

"Benkhi," he gasped. "Wake up."

Silver poured from her until it swallowed them both. She was slipping fast, dragged deeper into the trance that had claimed her.

His breath came fast. *I'm losing her.*

"Benkhi, please."

Silver stardust flared to life, and flames erupted in a spiraling vortex of heat. There was only one thing left.

"Sahrit!" he roared. "Do it!"

Horror flashed across her face. "I'll hurt you."

"Now!"

Her cry tore through the chamber. "Forgive me!"

She raised her hands—and unleashed hell.

Emerald fire roared forth, slamming into Leógham and Kharis and casting a blazing cage around them. Leógham choked as Sahrit's power seized him. Thorned tendrils writhed in the inferno, raking and tearing, hunting the invasive silver magic.

His lungs locked. His muscles seized. Sahrit's power drove into him like barbed roots—fierce with Fire Dweller hunger, protective with Forest Kin instinct. The two ancient forces collided, becoming one.

And it hesitated.

Sensing Leógham wasn't its quarry, the power twisted toward Kharis, turning on her like a starving dragon scenting its prey.

No. Not her.

Leógham unleashed his magic in a burst of scarlet fury. The green beast roared and struck like a serpent. His vision blurred. Pain thundered through his bones. His fire howled for retaliation, but he forced it down, taking the brunt of the assault, every nerve alight as Sahrit's power raged through him until he could no longer tell where his magic ended, and hers began.

Kharis trembled in his arms, still trapped in her trance.

Through the agony, he held her fast.

Kharis clung to the branch, fingers screaming, skin raw. With the added weight, the tree trunk peeled away from the cliff wall in a slow, agonizing lurch. Brittle roots tore free one by one, each snap as sharp as a breaking bone.

Water spray blurred the face before her and stole the breath she needed to scream.

"Saya, *stop!*" she choked, her lungs burning as she shrieked over the waterfall's roar. "You must live!"

The trunk shuddered again, pitching them closer to the waterfall below.

Through the mist, those golden eyes held hers, overflowing with love and affection. This person had mattered more than breath, more than life itself. Kharis couldn't remember what she'd lost—only that a grief deeper than the oceans had stitched this moment into her soul.

Tears stung her eyes as she said, "I love you."

Her last words to the one with golden eyes. A final farewell. One last moment of thanks. Kharis let go of the branch, and air tore past her. The sky spun. The earth vanished. Her world tilted into darkness.

A wail tore from her, shattering whatever fragile hope had remained. What was the point of everything if she had lost what defined her? Her memories. Her sense of self. Her choices. Even the affection that had lived behind those golden eyes.

In the depths of that dark void, something reached for her.

Ethereal tendrils slipped around her, soft as silk. The scent of primroses brushed her senses, coaxing breath back into her lungs, reminding her to live, to hope again. Warmth gathered slowly, pushing the cold away. Patiently, this gentle, primrose-scented magic drew her back.

The world regained its shape. The face with golden eyes dissolved, and another emerged with an emerald gaze.

"Leógham...?" Her knees gave out beneath her.

"I have you." His grip tightened. "You're safe."

The fight drained from her. The fear, the emptiness, the weight of it all slipped away. She sank against him, trusting him to always catch her.

Yet deep inside her, Ragha whispered that safety never lasted long. Not until she went north.

CLARITY

> *There is a moment when fear dissolves, and doubt falls silent. A breath between breaking and surrendering. In that space, after the world has revealed its cruelest face, we come to know the shape of our own. - Poliormos*

Darragh, who'd entered after Leógham, swiftly ushered Sahrit out of the library. With a final nod to Leógham, he shut the heavy doors behind him.

"Are you all right?" Leógham tightened his hold on Kharis, refusing to let go of her even as pain throbbed through his body.

"Benkhi?" he whispered, his vision swimming.

"Leógham..." Her voice was faint.

He sighed with relief, even though his chest ached with every breath.

A hundred thoughts raced through his mind. Her memories were returning slowly, like an unhurried skiff, quietly gliding through the water and parting the fog to reach the shore. This episode had been an invasion, an aggressive assault that scorched everything in its path without mercy. It had seized her, plunging her into a space he could barely reach.

And losing Kharis would be like losing his entire world.

He released her, the motion drawing a hiss from him, and guided her toward a chair with a gentle nudge. "Come," he said softly. "Sit."

The tea service sat on the table, probably cold by now, but he poured some for her anyway, hoping it would bring color back to her cheeks. "Here, drink this. It'll do you good."

She took a few sips.

"Would you like anything else?" he asked. "Do you think you can eat?"

He held one of the honey cakes. His forehead wrinkled as she declined the offer. He took the cup from her, set it on the table, and knelt before her. His hands moved with unexpected tenderness, smoothing her hair back from her face and gently tucking loose strands behind her ears.

"Can I get you anything else?"

She shook her head. He bit his lip.

Leógham had craved the flutter that came with her laughter, their timid glances, and all the oddness she brought to his life. He wanted nothing more than to hold her when she slept, chasing her nightmares away. The wish was absurd. He reminded himself that her safety depended on her remaining invisible and on him staying away.

Duty. Responsibility. Hegran Law.

He'd steeped himself in it. Yet the feeling inside him screamed for all of her. Tenderly, he pressed his forehead to hers. Both grew still, sharing the same breath, immersed in an intimate moment where nothing and no one mattered anymore.

Kharis had defined perfection for him. He needed her in his life.

Clarity finally shone upon him.

"I love you," he uttered without thinking, the words as fragile as butterflies.

Her fingers stilled against his jaw. She closed her eyes and drew in a slow breath. Then, "I don't want to be a man anymore."

He pulled away. Her brow furrowed, her lashes trembling as tears gathered but didn't yet fall.

"I've lost everything." Her hands trembled as they caressed his face. "But you... I don't want to lose you." Her tears spilled at last. "I don't know that I could survive losing you."

Her words shaped a different world. A brighter, better one. A world brimming with color and summer sunlight. A world that included him.

He cradled her face, gentle thumbs caressing her cheeks. "From the moment I first saw you, I knew you were the one I'd been waiting for. Guilt consumed me. If I had loved Elinor so deeply, so fiercely, why did I feel this way about you? But you occupy every waking thought. You have become the air I breathe, the sun that warms my face, the garden where I rest my weary soul."

Her lips parted.

"I have questioned all these emotions," he went on, "but one has emerged as the flag for the rest: I want you in my life, so I'm here to tell you I will never leave you."

Fresh tears pooled in her eyes. "Leógham..."

"I want *you* in my life," he repeated. His mouth was so close to hers that it lit an even bigger fire in him. "And I want to kiss you now, tomorrow, the day after. I want to kiss you from this moment until my very last. Do you wish me to?"

"Yes, Leógham," she said through her tears. "You may kiss me from this moment until your very last." The smile shaping her glorious mouth was all he needed.

He tenderly pressed his lips to hers—a tentative gesture. A quiet, thoughtful first. The sensation was enough to undo him—gentle, sacred, impossibly real. His mind spun. His heart ignited. He lost himself in this all-consuming heat, melting into it. He was about to pull away when her arms wrapped around his neck. She drew him close and kissed him back.

The fire became a blaze.

She pressed him against her body.

He sank into her.

Her tongue brushed the seam of his mouth, and he moaned, the pleasure of it overwhelming. He parted his lips, wanting more. A sigh escaped her, his name a whisper at the end of it. He quivered at the sound, escaping her lips with such desire, and a deep, seductive sound dragged through his ragged breath.

His kissing turned ravenous. His mouth moved to taste and learn.

Flames devour me.

His heart pounded with such power that he feared his chest would explode. He pressed deeper and harder, biting her lips, getting drunk on them. His mouth greedily explored every inch of her face, biting her earlobes, dragging his teeth along the length of her jaw, sucking and licking her skin. Forgotten needs gushed from him in fast, greedy waves. His passion surged, and every breath became a gasp.

His mouth devoured her as the walls around his heart finally crumbled. The caged Hegran dragon flew at last, tasting freedom once more.

Leógham surrendered, kissing her with a more desperate pressing of lips, his tongue dancing inside her mouth while every logical thought vanished.

Duty. Responsibility. Hegran law.

Gone.

He kissed her as if nothing else existed—only her.

She wanted him, and that epiphany made his soul soar high. He struggled to control himself and pull away from her. To take it slow. But when she moaned his name—a sweet whisper that spoke of bliss—he lost it.

Burn it all.

Before he knew it, they were on the floor, his body on top

of hers, his hands unbuttoning her collar. He pulled it down to expose her neck and bite her sensual throat, dreaming of his tongue tracing her skin on a slow journey down to her sex. Enraptured, Kharis tilted her head to give him everything. Leógham drew her closer, wanting more of her; wanting to ravish *all* of her. Their bodies pressed against each other. Curves melted into curves.

Lost in her enticing scent—citrus and sea salt—his hands explored, eager and desperate.

Instinct took over, and his sanity left him.

68

BLISS

> *Bliss is the moment when longing is answered; the first breath after a kiss written in the stars; the hush that follows a long-awaited touch; the silk-red thread that binds my soul to yours beyond time, and beyond fate. - Poliormos*

Leógham held her, unwilling to let go and unable to sleep. He wanted to surrender to the pull of dreams, but how could he when she was in his arms? She'd fallen asleep with her face buried in his chest, so he buried his nose in her hair, losing himself in its fragrance.

Kharis stirred with a yawn, and he tightened his grip in response. With slow blinks, she lifted her head, searching for his face. His lips met her forehead in a tender morning kiss.

Both were quiet, Leógham basking in the moment.

"Leógham?" Her voice was groggy from sleep. "You must return to your bedroom."

"Not yet." He took a deep breath and closed his eyes. His fingers, splayed along the gentle curve of her shoulder blades, caressed her bare back, taking the time to touch every inch of her skin, tracing her black markings—memorizing them.

"This is bliss," he said. "Why would I want it to end?"

The quiet lingered like a warm sunbeam.

"Leógham?"

"Uh-huh?"

"You must leave—"

He groaned. "Not yet, Kharis."

"Benkhi!"

"No." He rolled on top of her and held her gaze. "Here, you're Kharis." He kissed her with restrained desire. "My Kharis." His bearded cheek rubbed against hers, drawing a giggle from her. He drowned in the sound, intoxicated by her happiness. "Out there, you're Benkhi, but here, with me, you're Kharis. *Mine.*"

He lingered on her lovely eyes, wishing he didn't have to hide the mesmerizing color behind old magic. His kiss was deep, long, his tongue gently stroking hers.

"Only mine," he whispered contentedly.

"Is that so?" She wore a wicked smile.

"I have you in my arms, and I'm never letting go. So yes, you're mine now."

"For now," she breathed teasingly.

He hummed, the sound resonant in his throat. "Perhaps I must convince you."

"I'm open to your arguments," she whispered before blowing on his ear.

Leógham's chest heaved. Aroused once more, he found her mouth and kissed her again.

His fingers traced a path, slowly traveling over the curve of her breasts, thumbs lingering on raspberry-colored peaks. He delighted in the valley of her waist and the arch of her hips until he found that glorious mound of nerves between her legs and drew slow circles around it. His grin blossomed when she drew in a sharp breath.

"Should I stop?" he asked.

Her cheeks blushed. "No."

Pleased with her answer, Leógham bit and sucked her neck while his fingers stroked and caressed, adjusting his pressure in an exploration of her senses. A moan escaped her lips. Her muscles tensed. Her breathing quickened as desire took over. His mouth traveled slowly down her neck, tasting and kissing every inch of skin he encountered, reveling in this woman who had surrendered to him.

His mouth found one of her hardened peaks, and he licked and sucked as she uttered his name between gasps. His fingers kept their rhythmic cadence, wringing pleasure from her with every caress, coaxing her fleshy pearl to explode in ecstasy. Every sound she made had him quivering, and his overwhelming desire to join her grew with every one of her little gasps.

Her breathing quickened, more audible now. He knew she was spiraling into an abyss where nothing mattered but the indulgent tickling of her senses. Her body arched with a moan, hips quaking with her climax, pleasure etched in her expression. Then she stilled as if letting the currents of a mighty river take her away, her skin flushed in the afterglow.

His slow, unhurried kissing pulled her back into the land of the living.

"Should I stop?" he whispered.

She frowned. "Stop asking."

He propped himself on his elbows, a teasing smirk on his lips. "So... does that mean you're mine, then?"

She caught his lower lip between her teeth. "Only if you're mine."

He met her eyes and held them, focusing on the silver starburst against the sapphire background with its tiny silver stars. He'd never understood his dreams until now. Enthralled, he gazed into the same eyes he'd seen in dreams since childhood, sharing breath at last with the girl he never thought real. With Kharis, this puzzle had finally clicked into place.

"I was always yours." And this, he meant. "You were the one I waited for."

Her smile undid him—the sparkle in it, the warmth. The scent of her skin, her hair, drove him wild. His hands ached to explore, to memorize every inch. He shoved duty, responsibility, and Hegran law aside. A flush of heat spread through him, a deep and rising hunger. He climbed over her, craving pressure, friction, release—anything to answer the fire she'd lit inside him.

Kharis wrapped her legs around his waist, eager and willing. Ready for him. Leógham entered her slowly, carefully, letting her body adjust to his length.

She closed her eyes. Her lips parted.

The sound she made, part pleasure, part awe, nearly unraveled him. All of him was inside her, and the sensation flooded his senses. When she opened her eyes, desire rimmed them. Her hands moved slowly down his back and curled around his glutes, urging him to claim her. On that silent note of consent, her permission not to stop—to never stop—he thrust into her, moans escaping him as he drove into her.

"Kharis," he chanted her name as if it were a spellbinding incantation. His rhythm, slow at first, quickened.

Leógham let go, his core exploding in sensual waves. Tension eased from him in one indulgent moan, all thoughts gone. His body felt like a fluttering leaf in a blissful summer wind. He slumped over her, burying his face in the small of her neck, letting the sounds of her heartbeat lull him back. Shifting his weight, he pulled her closer to him.

She surrendered to exhaustion. And Leógham, pleased to have her in his arms, their curves fitting into each other, closed his eyes, hoping to join her in her dreams.

At the sound of her stirring, he opened a sleepy eye. The light announced that mid-morning was upon them. Leógham pursed his lips, deep in thought. He kissed her again, never tiring of biting her bottom lip.

"Did I hurt you?" The pink stain on the sheets only meant one thing.

Wide-eyed, she gave him a puzzled look. "Whatever do you mean?"

His ears turned hot. "It appears I was your first." He found her blushing adorable.

"Is that an issue?" she asked with a concerned frown.

"Not to me." He caressed her face and pulled her close. "Never to me."

He held her, the warmth of her body seeping into him. The rhythm of her breath, the softness of her hair beneath his chin—it was more than he'd ever let himself hope for. In this moment, worries melted away, and the world receded. There was only her.

He released her, folding one arm behind his head. A familiar thought resurfaced, ready for him to voice it at last. "I want to make this permanent. To have you by my side. No one else but you."

Kharis blinked. For a breathless moment, neither of them spoke. The morning light painted blue threads across her black hair. Leógham didn't move, afraid in that moment that he might have said too much, that perhaps she didn't want the same.

He looked at her, heart caught in his throat.

She lay on top of him, her smile warm and wicked. "You must leave now." Fingers played with his beard. "Or servant rumors will become our undoing."

He pressed his lips tightly. Had she missed the gravity of his confession? Duty pressed hard against the hollow of his ribs. *Leave to keep her safe. Obey the laws that would see her dead.* Yet every instinct screamed to stay, to hold her until the world itself collapsed.

Aware of the danger, he nodded, but his heart ached at the thought of leaving her warmth in exchange for the Keep's cold walls. "I'll get dressed and come for you."

"No." She flashed her mischievous smile. "I want to sleep more." She lazily stretched, her seductive curves tempting him again. "Someone kept me awake most of the night."

A low sound caught in his throat. He drew her close, curving a hand around her hips. "Then, I'll sleep with you—"

"Leógham."

Her tone—half amused, half warning—cut through his longing. He closed his eyes, fighting the gnawing ache that tugged him toward her. "Yes," he exhaled. "I must leave."

But the truth pulsed beneath his ribs: Every step away from her felt like betrayal—of his heart, of his promise, of everything he wanted. And every step he took toward her put her life at risk.

Leaving hurt.

Staying was their ruin.

So he sat up, running a hand through his tousled hair as he looked at the mess of clothes strewn across the floor. The larger pieces were his, the smaller ones hers. Tangled remnants of the night they'd stolen for themselves. The sight stirred a quiet satisfaction, a possessive thrill.

The memory washed over him in a heated rush: how they'd crept through the corridors of Dríeadh Manor, shadows swallowing them whole. The quick retreat into an alcove, her soft laugh muffled against his chest as a pair of sentries passed by, unaware. Every sound had been a risk. The scrape of a boot or the creak of a door would end everything.

And still, they had moved like conspirators through a world that forbade their closeness. His whispered *this way* had led them past sense and consequence. Stealing kisses—teasing, urgent, intoxicating kisses—until they'd finally slipped into her chambers, hearts pounding with triumph and fear.

And then... undressing her.

His body responded instantly, a fresh wave of longing tightening his muscles. Fires, he wanted her again. Even the mere thought of her skin beneath him made his pulse hammer.

"Leógham?"

Her voice—soft, drowsy, utterly enchanting—pulled him from his lustful haze. "What is it?"

"Let's spend the day together."

Leógham craned his neck to look at her, the light enveloping her in an enchanting halo. Was this her answer? Was she saying yes to making their relationship permanent?

"Do you mean it?" he asked, hope flickering.

She nodded, a wide grin spreading across her face. "But if you don't leave, we can't get started."

He considered it, his heart a fluttering mess—a ridiculous, boyish reaction he barely recognized in himself. "What would you like to do?" He needed to hear her say it again: that she wanted to be with him.

Kharis shrugged, stretching languidly beneath the sheets, utterly at ease in a way that made his mouth go dry. "As long as it is with you, I don't care." She smirked. "Your choice."

Leógham exhaled slowly, unable to drag his eyes from the tempting sight of her. "I choose to stay in bed with you."

She arched an eyebrow, amusement dancing in her expression.

"It was worth a try," he said with a chuckle.

The sound of footsteps in the corridor froze him mid-motion. He lifted his head, listening. The rhythm was brisk, purposeful. Muffled voices grew clearer, followed by the faint clatter of a tray. Servants. Headed to his room.

Dragging himself away, he found his trousers, tugged them on, and swiftly gathered the rest of his scattered clothing. As he straightened, he glanced back at her, memorizing how she lay there: bare-shouldered, tangled in sheets, looking at him as if he were the only thing worth seeing in the world.

"What if I surprise you?" he murmured.

Kharis propped herself up on one elbow, watching him with a teasing glint in her eyes. "Challenge accepted."

He paused, drinking in the sight of her, flushed from sleep, utterly radiant, the roguish sparkle in her eyes making his heart lurch.

With one last look, so elated he could float, he slipped through the secret door to his room just as his attendants knocked on his chamber doors.

69

AFTERGLOW

> *The moment my love met yours, the stars burned just for us. - Poliormos*

Kharis had never seen Leógham so openly, unguardedly happy, and she was, too. For once, she silenced the unrelenting call urging her north and allowed herself this reprieve to live in the moment's afterglow.

Despite her lack of memories, something deep within her stirred with a sense of recognition: Leógham was the missing piece that made her whole again. When he smiled at her, the gesture bright, genuine, and brimming with affection, everything made sense. Her love for him was both new and impossibly ancient, as if she'd loved him across lifetimes.

The family was already seated for the midday meal when they entered the dining room. His joy radiated, bold and impossible to miss. Their arrival quieted the conversation. Sahrit and Darragh exchanged curious glances.

Kharis bowed in greeting, hiding her smile and the quiet thrum within her.

Leógham went to the food table. When he returned, her

offered her a bowl, their fingers brushed. The gesture was timid yet full of meaning. Ridiculous, she thought, that something so ordinary—a touch—could undo her so completely.

She looked at the bowl and nearly faltered. Inside were five perfectly peeled hard-boiled eggs, her favorite breakfast. He'd remembered from their days at the cabin. Warmth unfurled in her chest. Was this how happiness felt?

Leógham winked at her—roguish, endearing—and fetched dark bread from a plate. Then, as if he hadn't unraveled her, he took his seat across from her.

"Good morn, everyone," he said, lifting his spoon to his pottage as a chorus of greetings followed.

Reaching for a boiled egg, Kharis took a bite. Leógham watched her, exploring her face, the spoon poised at his lips, forgotten. Last night returned in a rush: his hands, his heated breath, the weight of his body.

Darragh set his cup down. "Well, we leave in three days."

Leógham rolled his shoulders as if trying to shake off old ghosts. "It'll be good to see Father," he said. "And there are duties I've long postponed."

"Finally," Darragh said, as if the gods had answered his long-awaited prayers.

Leógham fixed him with a sharp look, and a silent exchange passed between them—weighed, knowing. His voice dropped, cold and iron-hard. "I intend to punch a few faces."

"Saigham's?" Darragh's eyes narrowed, his smirk sharp.

"He's the first. His son follows."

"Yes." Darragh slammed his fist on the table. Plates rattled. Cutlery clinked. Sahrit flinched, instinctively pulling back.

"Saigham..." Hrag scowled at the pottage splattered across his bowl and mashed a piece of bread with his spoon.

A chill crept over Kharis. Who was this Saigham

everyone loathed? She'd even seen a few sentries make spitting gestures when the name was mentioned.

Leógham set his cup down and turned to Neagh. "Could you ready two horses? I'd like to show Lord Benkhi the estate before we leave for the capital."

"Of course," he said, inclining his head before leaving.

Hrag perked up. "Uncle, can I join you and Lord—?"

"Son," Darragh cut in smoothly. "You're with me today. I need your help."

Hrag grimaced. "Help with what?"

Darragh clapped his shoulder, steering him toward the door. "Whatever your Ama says." With a discreet wink toward Leógham, he added, "Come on. If we delay, her list will get longer."

As the door closed behind them, Leógham turned to Kharis. His brow creased slightly. "You've eaten little."

Out of five boiled eggs, two remained.

"I'm fine and quite full."

Leógham didn't look convinced. She could practically hear "bottomless pit" echoing in his head, his frown brief but telling. "Very well. Let's head for the stables."

Kharis sighed. Then, perhaps out of defiance or to prove a point, she reached for another egg and popped it into her mouth with stubborn finality as she followed him out.

Once they exited Dríeadh Manor, Leógham's stride lengthened, his expression smoothed into neutrality, and when he finally spoke, his voice was cold and distant. They'd reverted to being Hegran men, bound by expectations and propriety.

The castle grounds buzzed with activity, the air thick with the sounds of boots and clanging steel. Soldiers milled about the yard or sparred with one another, their presence more pronounced than usual. She recognized Leógham's sentries, with their black and red uniforms. Nearby, silver-haired warriors clad in gold and teal—Lord Darragh's men from the Forest Kin clan—spoke among themselves in their tongue.

Then, another group.

These guards marched toward the barracks with measured precision, clad in black-and-gold armor. *The royal escort.* More would arrive before the day's end, serving as another reminder of the impending journey to the capital.

Leógham would leave in days to face enemies and untold dangers. Kharis shook her head, unwilling to follow the thought any further. Though she hated the thought of Leógham leaving, she'd welcome the quiet and the opportunity to head north.

The stable doors creaked open, breaking her thoughts. A groom led two horses out, their breath rising in thick clouds against the chill.

The black one was Balyus.

But beside him strode a chestnut mare.

Towering.

Regal.

Her massive size nearly rivaled Balyus's. Power rippled beneath her sleek coat with each muscle shift. Her feathery hooves crunched on the frost-covered ground.

"Lord Benkhi," Leógham said. "This is Bada. Gentle yet possessing a fierce spirit."

Kharis drew a steady breath and took a cautious step closer, extending a hand toward the mare's muzzle. Bada snorted softly, her warm breath ghosting over Kharis's fingers. Her nostrils relaxed, releasing a soft, approving exhale.

Girl and beast formed a bond.

"I'm under your care, Bada," Kharis murmured.

Using a stool, Kharis settled into the saddle, adjusting her grip on the reins. Leógham mounted Balyus, and with a gentle command, they set off. For creatures of their size, they moved like whispers through the forest. For a time, there was only the scent of frosted leaves curling through the air. The icy air kissed her face as Bada trotted forward.

"Did you ride with Elinor?" Kharis asked.

Leógham's posture stiffened. "Do you wish me to speak of another woman after I have bedded you?"

It was an honest question. Kharis appreciated the gesture but shrugged it off. "Elinor was your wife, a significant part of your life. Why wouldn't you talk about her? I'd rather you did than not."

He glanced at her for a moment longer, considering her. "Elinor loved Dríeadh Manor. The woods reminded her of Skógarjód, so we rode often."

His voice carried a sense of nostalgia.

The grief that had once shadowed his features had softened. Now, when he spoke of Elinor, it was with fondness. Kharis let the silence linger between them, the soft rhythm of hooves on packed snow filling the quiet.

She tilted her head slightly. "You're invested in this land."

"I am."

His smile was the steady gesture of a man who'd finally chosen to honor his past.

"I was born to wealth and privilege," he said. "That makes stewardship my duty. These lands are mine to keep whole, not to bleed dry." His gaze traveled across the estate, toward the farms and the village tucked beyond the last rise of land. "I grant my people the right to work my fields, to raise families, to endure. In return, they owe me their labor and their trust."

He paused.

"That is why I wished to speak with Chief Harrald. What I gain from this is not coin or ornament, but something far rarer. Loyalty. Stability. People who stand with me because they know I will stand for them. When they render their due, they know it returns to them in walls, in stores, in safety for their children. That is how a realm survives."

Leógham paused, his chest rising and falling as if steadying himself.

"All of it... It was my vision for a better Hegra and a richer, more fulfilling future." Then, softer, "For Elinor and the future of the children we would have."

Kharis's fingers tightened slightly on the reins. She had no right to envy a woman she'd never met, a woman who had shaped Leógham's world so profoundly that even now her name carried weight in his heart.

"I'm glad she was in your life," she said. "That she gave you purpose, that she loved you, that she was everything you needed."

He met her eyes. "You're all I need now. I'm yours now, for as long as you'll have me."

A flutter ran through her chest, and she pressed her palm lightly against it. "Even if I come with headaches?"

He replied quickly, "Feverfew tea, willow bark tisane, and butterbur tinctures."

She arched an eyebrow. "What are those?"

He smirked. "Known remedies for headaches."

Laughter spilled from her.

They rode through the forest until they reached a vast meadow stretching endlessly before them.

Leógham slowed Balyus, turning to glance at her. "Are you well? Should we take a break?"

Kharis frowned. "Why?"

His cheeks flamed an unmistakable shade of red. "I thought you would be... sore."

She blinked; realization dawned a moment later. "Oh..."

His ears reddened further, and he quickly looked away.

Kharis chuckled. "My healing magic senses when I'm hurt—"

Leógham's head snapped toward her. "Did I hurt you?"

She pursed her lips, aware he was truly worried. Her hand swept over his broad chest and imposing height.

"You're big and... all that." Her face heated up. "But no, you didn't... hurt me."

A crease formed between his brows. Then, softly, "You'll tell me if I do, will you?"

His sincerity sent a shiver through her. That there would be "a next time" filled her with a swirl of wild emotions, including the possibility that "next time" could be now. She'd be fine with that.

"Where are we going?" She steered her thoughts away from this indescribable hunger.

Leógham cast her a sidelong glance. "Wherever the wind takes us. Wherever the horses choose to go. Far away, where no one can see or find us."

A tempting thought.

Kharis turned to the towering trees and shadowy underbrush. "Even the forest has eyes." The wind stirred the frosted leaves, carrying distant voices. "We must be cautious."

Leógham drew in a slow breath, fingers flexing once before falling still on the pommel.

"Leógham!"

He jerked in his saddle, startled. "What—?"

"Catch me if you can."

Kharis squeezed her legs around Bada's ribs, and the mare surged forward into an explosive gallop. Icy wind tore at Kharis's hair as they thundered across the open field.

Behind her, Leógham gave chase.

70

JAM AND JOURNEYS

Some journeys may take us to the ends of the world, while others bring us closer to the heart we have longed for. - Poliormos

Bada raced, a cloud of icy dirt swirling behind her as the world blurred into teal and ivory. Kharis leaned forward, her breath filled with joy, reveling in the indescribable freedom, the exhilaration of speed, and her connection with such a magnificent creature.

The mare rode fast, the moment endless. The gallop eventually slowed to a canter, then a trot, until Bada walked.

Leógham rode up beside her, his presence a storm all its own. He leaned over, wrapping his hands around her waist. Effortlessly, he lifted her from her saddle and onto his horse. She barely had time to gasp before his mouth claimed hers, stealing her breath as if he'd held back far too long. She melted into him. The world fell away—nothing but the steady thrum of their heartbeats and ragged breaths.

Then reality slapped her awake.

She wrenched herself free and jumped off the saddle.

"We can't kiss like this, in the open." She grabbed Bada's

reins and scanned their surroundings. There were no trees to shield them, only an ivory meadow stretching toward the horizon.

"What if someone saw us?" Her pulse hammered at the thought. And yet here she was, undone by his kiss. She turned to him, a boot tapping the ground in frustration with him, with herself, and with the absurdity of it all.

"I'm supposed to be a man." And she hated it.

Leógham's gaze fell, his thumb grazing the edge of his glove. "I regret suggesting this ruse. It pains me to hide my desire to be with you, even from my sister." He dismounted, tension running through his shoulders as he kept the mandated five steps between them—close enough to feel her presence, far enough to obey the rules.

Kharis sighed, sensing the strain in him and the heat of all that unspoken wanting. With a playful lilt and a grin to match, she said, "Weren't you going to show me around?"

Her teasing shattered the tension like glass. His shoulders eased. His lips curved. "What would you like to see?"

A slow smile spread across her face. "I'm curious about the extent of your lands. So, where do they end?"

He scanned the landscape, eyes narrowing. "Strange. I meant to take you to the village, but we've veered north."

She flashed him a sheepish smile and shrugged.

Leógham chuckled. "We might as well keep heading this way. I haven't been here in a while, and I wonder..." He stared into the distance.

"And you wonder, what?"

He smirked, a glint in his eyes hinting at mischief. "Come. I want to show you something."

They mounted their horses and resumed their ride. "I prohibit hunting and logging in the northern part of my estate," he said.

"Why is that?"

A corner of his mouth curled slowly. "You'll see."

They rode for a while. Kharis looked up at the perpetually

overcast sky. She hadn't seen a hint of blue since her arrival. According to the servants, on rare nights, the cloud cover would thin enough to reveal stars. Otherwise, it remained unyielding.

Kharis and Leógham climbed a slope so high it almost touched the clouds. From above, Kharis saw a wide crack splitting the earth, with its two sides at different heights.

"It looks like the gods lifted one side but pushed the other down."

Leógham affirmed her observation. "This is the Hegran Rift. It marks the estate's northern boundary. The forest you see ahead is as untouched as the one behind you."

She nodded politely, but her eyes were busy mapping the descent, judging which side of the Rift might offer a safer passage. How long would it take to reach the river? What would it take to cross it, assuming no bridge existed?

"How does one head down?" she asked.

"You can ride along either side until the terrain slopes. Why?"

She shrugged. "Just curious."

Below, the river roared, carrying chunks of ice that collided with each other. Beyond it, a dark forest extended into the horizon, the forested hills resembling the waves of an ivory ocean.

North...

That whisper returned, fusing with her planning. Provisions. Strong horses. Ropes. Clothing thick enough to withstand the cold. Weapons. The list grew, even as she hummed softly, feigning admiration of the view. She needed an ally, too. Someone to journey with her. She glanced over her shoulder. Would Leógham come along?

The northern peaks were visible yet distant enough to demand a fortnight's journey. "What lies beyond the mountain range?"

Leógham stiffened right away. "A place no one goes to."

Kharis frowned at his tone. *That's his answer?*

"Fine," she snapped. "So no one goes north now, but before the ice flowers, what used to be there?"

Leógham remained silent, his jaw set. "Nothing that matters anymore," he said with finality, his tone not inviting further questions. He exhaled sharply, as if to dislodge whatever thoughts had darkened his gaze.

"Come." He gestured toward the open stretch of land before them. "This is the answer to your first question— where my land ends." His voice had regained its ease. "The answer to your second is coming up."

He winked at her and swung off his horse. Taking hold of Balyus' reins, he put two fingers to his mouth and blew a sharp, high-pitched whistle. The sound pierced the air, its echo rolling down the hill.

Moments later, a chorus of distant howls answered, rolling up to them in layered echoes. She was mid-dismount when movement at the tree line caught her eye.

They emerged from the forest.

Dozens of them.

Wolves.

Their sleek forms raced across the open field, moving as one—a tide of fur and muscle, closing the distance with effortless speed.

All of them, running toward Leógham.

Without warning, Leógham's invisible aura ignited, and scarlet flames engulfed him, curling and twisting around his form. Kharis gasped, resisting the pull of his magic, and faced the wolves.

They surged forward, fire-clad shapes racing across the snow, blazing like shooting stars. Her body tensed as heat slammed into her, fire roaring through her blood. She shuddered, fighting to hold back. Her heart thundered against her ribs, each beat like a hammer striking an anvil.

When Leógham extended his hand, and their fingers touched, she erupted in gold and crimson flames.

The wolves arrived, surrounding Kharis and Leógham in

a blur of flames and shadows. Lifting their heads, their howls rang throughout the valley in welcome.

Magic receded.

Flames flickered, then died, leaving a lingering warmth. Kharis swayed as if a fine wine had gone to her head. Leógham wrapped his arm around her waist, steadying her. She gazed at him, still in awe. Then her attention shifted to the wolves.

"Leógham...?" Her voice quivered, unsure what to make of them. They stood before her, their size intimidating. Her thought slipped out: "One of those jaws could snap me in two."

Leógham's laughter didn't confirm or deny her observation.

Their thick coats varied from white to black. Intelligent amber eyes stared straight at her—creatures apparently fiercely loyal and protective of Leógham.

"These are firewolves," Leógham said. "Magical guardians entrusted to protect Hegra. This pack guards my lands, and the northern portion of my estate is theirs in return. Therefore, I don't allow hunting and logging here."

She bit her lip. Journeying through here would pose her first challenge. And yet, he'd done this to protect the trees and the wolves. How could she express the admiration stirring inside her?

"You are—" Her stomach growled loudly.

Leógham burst into laughter, shoulders shaking. "My lovely bottomless pit," he said. "Come. Let's eat."

The firewolves settled nearby. He unbuckled a saddlebag and laid a thick, woolen blanket on the snowy ground. Kharis sat on it, anticipation rising. Her eyes followed as he rummaged through the bag, eager to see what he'd packed. A moment later, he handed her a jar filled with red-colored preserves and a loaf of brown bread.

She turned the jar in her hands, curious. "What is this?"

"Bearberry jam." Then, almost sheepishly, he added,

"Darragh taught me that women have a fondness for sweet food, so I—"

"Darragh?" she muttered. "He should mind his own business. Perhaps ask Sahrit what she enjoys, for he'd learn a thing or two."

Leógham pressed his lips together, shoulders slumped, and placed the jar down. "Well, what do you enjoy?"

She lifted a fist. "Fiery food."

"Um..." He grimaced. "Never heard of it." He tilted his head. "How do you make it?"

She crossed her ankles and leaned back on her hands. "All I recall is that some spices make your tongue feel on fire, but I don't know which."

Leógham rubbed his jaw. "I could experiment. I have a large inventory of herbs in the greenhouse. I'm sure I could find something to give your food this... fiery flavor."

Her attention shifted to the jar of bearberry jam. Leógham caught the gesture, and his lips twitched. "I thought you didn't want this."

"Who said?"

He frowned. "You did."

She looked away, ears warming. "I dislike that you didn't ask me, but I never said I disliked your jam."

Leógham crossed his arms, studying her. "You're hungry, aren't you?"

She lowered her head, reluctant to admit it. "Starving."

A mischievous glint sparked in his eyes. "I'm hungry, too." He growled.

Kharis's brow furrowed. A few firewolves snapped their heads toward them, ears pricked. Leógham howled and bit her ear playfully, making her squirm and giggle as she tried to bat him away.

"Let's feed you, shall we?" Still grinning, he opened the jar, cut a few pieces of bread, and spread the preserves with his knife. He was smiling, a rare sight since their arrival in Hegra. His joy stirred her own.

"You look happy," she said.

His hand faltered, a faint tremor betraying the effort to stay composed. When he turned to her, his grin was bright, boyish. "I am." A pause. "You?"

He handed her a slice of bread and jam. She took it, his fingers brushing against hers—a fleeting yet deliberate touch, enough to burn.

Kharis looked away, a flush rising to her cheeks. She took a slow bite, the sweet, tart bearberry preserves clinging to her lips and fingers. For a moment, she let herself savor both —the taste and the quiet ache beneath it.

"Yes." She licked the jam from her fingertips, her smile soft. "I'm happy."

Leógham's gaze lingered, softening into something warm and searching. "But you miss your family."

Kharis took another bite, chewing and thinking. *If she succeeded with her task up north, would she even want to return home?* Her eyes found his, and everything clicked into place. "I miss them, but I'd miss you more."

Leógham went utterly still. His lips parted as if to say something, but instead, in one swift motion, he pinned her down, a spark dancing in his eyes as he licked the jam off her lips.

Kharis yelped, squirming beneath him, half-giggling, half-protesting. "Leógham, not here."

"Yes, here." He kissed her, then pulled back enough to murmur, "And I will kiss you there." He gestured to his right. "And over there." He gestured to his left. "And everywhere in between."

His gaze darkened, burning with something far more profound than amusement. "I shall kiss you until my very last breath."

MISERY

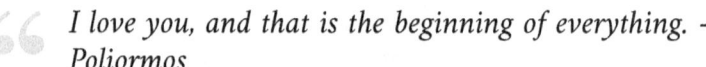

I love you, and that is the beginning of everything. - Poliormos

While Leógham packed, Kharis couldn't stop looking at the firewolves. They retreated, their paws barely making a sound as they left deep imprints in the snow. The ghost of fire magic dappled their fur.

They were majestic—otherworldly.

And terrifying.

The largest of the pack, a male with a sleek midnight blue coat, paused at the edge of the tree line. He turned his head slightly, his amber eyes flashing like molten gold as he observed her.

The moment stretched between them.

Then, seemingly satisfied, the great beast vanished behind the snow-covered trees, fading like smoke.

If Leógham weren't here, would they tear her apart if she tried to cross through here? Were they tamed, or did they only obey him? Was it devotion? Something ancient like—?

"Curious about them?" Leógham asked.

She jumped out of her thoughts. "Yes. Is it a spell—how they obey you?"

"No spell," Leógham reassured her. "More like an arrangement."

She squinted. "An arrangement?"

"Not everything needs magic." He smiled widely, not even concealing that he had no intention of revealing his secret, which cast a hitch in her plan. "Come. We should head back soon."

She scuffed the snow with her boot. "Can't we stay longer?"

He looked up, that smile still on his face. "Tempting, but we must return."

Kharis now understood why he longed for the vast meadows and his cabin. The thought of returning to the castle, with all its rules and expectations, was unappealing. It meant resuming their roles as Lord Benkhi and the crown prince—men bound by Hegran duties.

"The firewolves will be with us for a while, even if you can't see them. Don't stray too far from me."

"Or they'll shred me apart?" she asked, teasing him.

"They might do worse." He smiled, sort of. "Come, I'll help you up."

They rode for a time, their conversation rising and fading like the wind, their easy talk giving way to quiet stretches where only the horses' snorts filled it. Kharis's gaze kept straying north, drawn to the horizon. If she could, she'd have turned Bada around.

North...

The whisper curled through her thoughts like mist, threading itself into her breath and the rhythm of her pulse.

Leógham broke the quiet now and then, pointing out an ancient grove here, a bend in the path there—a hunter's habit of naming the land, but it all slid off her consciousness. Behind her, the north hummed, its pull growing stronger with every heartbeat.

Visions flashed: a mountain shrouded in mist, a vast cave lit by living fire.

Leógham spoke, his voice a steady murmur against the images invading her mind. She tried to latch onto his words, to stay with him, but the images kept coming, pulling her from this world into another. A burst of cobalt. Seven stars. Fire—endless silver fire.

Kharis pinched her thigh hard, using the pain to focus on Leógham's voice, but the world teetered between reality and dream, invisible hands clawing past her resolve. Their pull was so fierce that she was being torn in two.

Then, through the roar in her mind, a chorus emerged, haunting and achingly familiar.

> *All that was wrong will be righted,*
> *When the immortal vessel dies.*

The words tolled like bells, heavy with the weight of divine prophecy.

> *Let the world revel in fire.*
> *Tear asunder the seals that contain it.*
> *Let its flames roam with might.*
> *Let it all be destroyed,*
> *So freedom finds its light.*

Leógham's voice had become a muffled rhythm in the background. He shared something about the land or the people—she couldn't focus. His words blurred, turning into noise beneath the insistent hum in her ears.

> *Let it be consumed again,*
> *So the spirits join and transcend.*

Her muscles tensed. Her resolve cracked. She glanced

back, her breath unsteady. Beyond the trees, the silhouette of the northern range loomed, waiting.

All that was wrong will be righted,
When all the writings end.

Kharis clenched her jaw, fighting the phantom hands ghosting over her skin, coaxing her to ride north; to join the winds and gallop freely toward them.

"I want to go north," she blurted out.

Her request cut Leógham mid-sentence. He stilled. His jaw flexed. Slowly, he turned in the saddle, his expression dark, smoldering. "Why?"

Kharis forced a shrug, though her pulse thumped erratically. "I'm curious."

"Don't." His voice was sharp, like steel. "You have no business going north. No one does."

His attitude shifted; the softness from moments ago vanished.

Kharis frowned. "You're not answering my—"

"There's nothing to answer," he nearly shouted, his posture rigid, as if the mere mention of that place had soured his entire day. "The lands to the north are dead. No one goes there. End of discussion." Finality bled into his voice.

Anger flared hot in her chest. "So now you decide what I'm allowed to know?"

She was about to spur Bada into a gallop when Ragha slithered into her mind. His voice was rough, drenched in warning.

"*Watch out, Djinnshirukh,*" he said. "*You are not alone.*"

Her serpent markings stirred at the same time, sensing what he sensed. Her magic awakened, and they constricted her body protectively. Air tore from her lungs in a violent rush. She doubled forward, gasping.

A sharp tug on her arm jerked her back upright.

"What is it?" Leógham's frantic voice barely reached her.

"Talk to me." Fear twisted his face as he kept her from tumbling off Bada.

A blinding flash of red seared through her vision. The colors of the forest inverted. The muted winter ivory warped into shades of violet and black. Ahead, three crimson silhouettes pulsed in the treetops, some five hundred marks away.

"*Archers*," Ragha said, silken and knowing.

Kharis straightened in her saddle. By her estimate, they were just beyond range... barely. Her pulse steadied as she cast her senses outward—beyond the trees, beyond the archers. Shapes flickered like coals in the dark. Riders. Sixteen of them.

"*What shall you do?*" Ragha's amusement brushed her thoughts with a curious caress. "*So many possibilities. Which shall you choose today?*"

Her snakes pulsed. The call to battle thrummed in her bones. Hunger also stirred within her, sharp and ravenous. The archers' hearts beat in a steady rhythm, each thud reaching her. Their warmth bled through the air, and suddenly she could *taste* it.

Sweet. Head-spinning.

The irresistible scent of their souls teased her senses, intoxicating in its pull. Her hands trembled on the reins. Why was she so... so hungry?

Another scent cut through the haze. Feral. Musky. *Firewolves.*

Oddly enough, she couldn't spot them. It seemed their magic barred hers from seeing them. And yet, her grin was slow, dark. She and Leógham wouldn't be fighting their attackers alone. When she turned to him, the color drained from his face.

"Benkhi... Your eyes—"

"I hope you've sharpened your weapons, Leógham of Hegra," she said, "because we're about to be ambushed."

His brows lifted in shock. "What?"

Her eyes narrowed, vision sharpening as she sized up the hunt before it began.

"Three archers ahead," she said, steady and unhurried. "Three hundred marks or so. And a mounted company waiting farther on—sixteen riders, perhaps nine hundred marks beyond them."

His gaze darted between her and the trees, doubt and unease flickering across his face. "How do you know this?"

Kharis's lips curled slightly. "The same way I knew a winged nightmare was coming at us."

He stiffened, staring at her for a long moment. Then, he shifted forward, scanning the path ahead.

"Past the bend?" He rubbed his chin, jaw clenched. "Saigham wouldn't dare." A moment passed. Then, a bitter laugh burst from him. "No. This is exactly what he'd do."

Kharis's mind whirled, assessing their situation as if she'd done this hundreds of times.

"We're without an escort." Her lips tightened. "Someone must've seen us leave and sent word." The realization sparked a flame within her. "They're here because someone's been spying from within."

Leógham clicked his tongue. "Sahrit was right."

His expression hardened instantly. His shoulders squared. Frustration cooled into focus, the easy warmth replaced by calm precision.

"Let us play along," he said. "Give them the impression we haven't noticed."

Kharis offered a single, sharp nod. The fire in her veins stirred. Her hunger rose again, stronger this time, relentless. An irresistibly sweet lingered in the air. But far more potent was the fear that someone might harm Leógham. Her fingers brushed the belt at her hip, and a wicked smile tugged at her lips. The Dragon's Bane trembled in its sheath. The blade was as restless as she. Eager, even.

Without a word, she swung off her horse and landed

soundlessly. Her hand found the dagger, drawing it in one fluid motion.

"No one's hurting the ones I love," she whispered, more a vow to herself. "Not while I breathe."

"*Oh?*" Ragha clapped lightly, the rhythm playful. "*And what shall you do?*"

Her hunger roared in answer. The world sharpened—colors deepening, sounds crisp as glass.

"Leógham," she said. "Stay here."

"What—?"

But she was already moving, a blur of shadow disappearing into the forest.

THE AMBUSH

A heart unguarded is the easiest target. - Poliormos

The first archer never knew what happened. He didn't even have time to gasp before her dagger found his throat. His eyes widened, then dimmed.

Without warning, a rush slid through her veins—sharp, sweet, warm, like a sip of spiced mead after a long, cold ride through winter. Her breath hitched. Her pulse slowed.

Her hunger suddenly quieted.

She shuddered at the abrupt relief.

The lifeless body sagged, forcing her back to focus. His bow slipped from numb fingers into Kharis's hand. *A simple hunting bow. Rough-spun clothes.* These weren't trained assassins but commoners—farmers, perhaps. And that troubled her a lot. *If Leógham cares for these people, why are they betraying him?*

The thought faltered as another set of scents reached her: sweat, resin... and honey. The second archer. His soul carried the sweetness of ambrosia.

She bit down on the hunger, rising in her throat again.

Pivoting, she scanned the treetops for the third archer.

Another easy target. But they lurked lower, crouched in the underbrush, the wide riding trail cutting cleanly between them. If she killed one, the other would have enough time to alert the group hiding ahead.

She wiped the blood off her face, nocked an arrow, and drew back hard. Her arms trembled with strain, the string taut. One breath. One shot.

The arrow hissed through the air and struck true, piercing through the man's ear and pinning him to the trunk. And then it came again. That warmth. That dizzying pulse. Her hunger sated, yet her body begged for one more—

The dead man's bow clattered to the ground. *Cursed luck.*

"Marrick?" the man hiding in the bushes called out. "Marrick, what's going on?"

Her body moved. In one fluid motion, she drew and aimed. Her eyes fixed on the orange silhouette.

She released.

A sharp thunk.

The pained groan was followed by a shrill whistle that sliced through the air.

"Spear me!" Kharis cursed.

The forest exploded with the scrape of weapons being drawn, the shouts and barked orders of men hungry for blood. Hoofbeats thundered in the distance.

Kharis leaped from the tree, boots striking earth. Her eyes flicked through the chaos, measuring distance and time of arrival.

"Leógham, we're outnumbered." The Dragon's Bane sang as she unsheathed it, thrumming in her grasp. "We'll need more than the two of us. Call them. Now."

Leógham whistled, the piercing note splitting the air to summon the firewolves.

Kharis, however, didn't run for Bada. She stepped into the middle of the trail with the Dragon's Bane in her right hand and a bloodied dagger in her left.

"What are you doing?" Leógham yelled at her. "Get on your horse! Now!"

She didn't budge.

The howls came in a crescendo of lethal fury. Leógham's second whistle cut through the tension. "Benkhi," he commanded, his voice sharp, taut. "Retreat—"

"Not now!" she roared back.

"Fires burn you, you stubborn woman!"

A wall of heat slammed into her.

When she glanced over her shoulder, brilliant scarlet flames had engulfed both man and horse. Then, with a furious cry, he sent a plume of fire hurtling skyward. It exploded like a massive, bloodred flower, its glow licking at the ashen sky. The resounding boom rattled her chest.

Balyus bucked. Leógham swore a vicious string of expletives. Birds erupted from the trees, a chaotic mass of feathers, shrieking as they took to the skies.

Her world had narrowed to this instant: the riders hurtling toward her, swords gleaming, black cloaks unfurling like banners, and the threat they posed.

Her pulse thundered. Her grip on the Dragon's Bane tightened until her knuckles blanched. Each breath came quicker than the last, her restraint splintering under the force building inside her. Her magic rippled outward like a storm, bending the air, the trees, the fabric of the world.

The world lurched—and stopped.

The galloping horses slowed to a crawl, their hooves frozen inches above the ground. Eyes wide with terror now glimmered like glass, their fear trapped mid-breath. Cloaks that had snapped in the icy wind now hung suspended, each fold caught in perfect, impossible stillness. The air crystallized around her, clear and cold and utterly silent.

A shiver raced down her spine.

"Ah!" Ragha's sigh startled her. "Your power is outstanding."

She turned, and there he was, as real as she was, his body

not gauzy but solid. He had settled beside her as if he'd always been there, hands clasped behind his back, leaning close with that familiar brotherly ease.

"Did I do this?" she asked.

"We live in this world," he said, "but also in another. Right now, you stand between them, a fold in the fabric of time." A gleam lit his silver eyes as his breath ghosted against her ear. "Remember, you decide who lives and dies."

Kharis's gaze fixed on the assassins. "I won't let anyone take Leógham from me."

"And after this," his smile was a dark promise, "no one ever will."

Iridescent scales shimmered into being, and stardust flared around her. The air warped, bending to the heat that poured from her skin. The dust ignited, and crimson fire erupted from her body, licking the air in violent, dazzling arcs; the ground beneath her scorched black.

Her strength surged. Her vision sharpened.

"Show them what my sister can do." Ragha's silver eyes were alight. "For no one must stand between you and the North."

Magic roared through her.

And the Dragon's Bane awakened.

A tremor ran through the blade as if stirred from a slumber that had lasted centuries. Like a starved beast, it sank its teeth into Kharis's magic and drank, ripping it from her veins. She gritted her teeth as the sword gulped everything she poured into it, pulsing with power. Its vibrations traveled up her arm and settled into her bones.

The Dragon's Bane was ready to be wielded—to be hers.

Kharis reset her grip. Ahead, the riders stood suspended, caught in the cruel stillness of time's lapse. They had come for Leógham. If she didn't stop them, who would fall next? Assassins had already claimed Leógham's mother and niece. Now they were here, perhaps to finish what they'd begun.

I decide who lives and dies.

The thought swirled like poison. Tears welled, hot and bitter, at the cost of what she had to do. For the monster it would awaken within.

She closed her eyes. *Leógham, forgive me.*

Her cry tore from her throat—half battle, half grief. The stillness shattered, and time came roaring back like an avalanche.

And then, she moved.

In a streak of blinding speed, Kharis dashed into the oncoming charge, fearless and merciless, meeting it head-on.

Before they could even react, her blades slashed tendons and muscle.

The horrid crack of shattering legs and the startled screams of horses collapsing beneath their riders erupted the world into chaos. Bodies flew, thrown off saddles, crushed beneath fallen beasts. The earth trembled under the impact of men and animals crashing in every direction.

Panting, Kharis skidded to a stop, turning to assess the carnage she'd unleashed. A rush of warmth unfurled through her veins—wrongly pleasant, dangerously soothing. Her pulse steadied; her thoughts sharpened with unnatural clarity. She swallowed the sound rising in her throat, startled by the sudden satiation of her hunger.

She reached up to wipe the muck from her face, but it simply burned and turned to ash. The blood smeared across her body bubbled, dried, and turned into war paint.

The Djinnshirukh breathed deeply, her gaze sweeping over the survivors.

The men were rising. Staggering. Clutching blades.

Her Dragon's Bane glistened, slick with blood.

With a swift flick of her blade, red splattered across the snow. Her chest rose and fell in ragged bursts. Someone's loved one wouldn't come home tonight—that much was certain. If she struck, their blood would buy Leógham's survival. If she faltered, his head would be paraded as a trophy, his killers gloating over the coins they'd earned.

I decide who lives and dies.

To save the man she loved, she'd become the monster everyone had feared in the world she couldn't remember. Fate waited with its yellow eyes.

For the man I love...

A sense of déjà vu came to her: the notion that she'd done this before, a long, long time ago. With her decision made, a piercing war cry tore from her throat.

And she lunged.

FIRE AND RAIN, WIND AND THUNDER

> *There are moments when the world merely reveals what it has been hiding in plain sight. - Poliormos*

Leógham yanked the reins, forcing Balyus to obey. The stallion snorted, his hooves kicking up frozen earth.

He thrust a second plume of fire into the air.

The sky cracked open.

A massive explosion erupted above them, the force deafening. Bada screeched, bolting into the trees, her instinct for survival overriding training. Balyus bucked again, his wild terror barely contained. Leógham gritted his teeth, fighting to keep his mount under control, hoping—praying—that someone at the castle had seen his desperate calls for aid.

He found Kharis in the mayhem.

And his blood ran cold.

He watched, enthralled and terrified. She was a blur of blades and blood, moving at dizzying speed, slashing, cutting —unstoppable. She wove between her enemies like a phantom, fast and precise as if she'd been born for this.

It was brutal.

A bloodbath.

Leógham shuddered, a cold tremor running down his spine. This wasn't a battle with the enemy. This was a dance leading to annihilation.

Then he saw the sword she wielded.

The Dragon's Bane.

No one had ever unsheathed it, as if the blade had refused every hand touching it, constantly reappearing on the armory wall when he gave it away. Now, the blade gleamed, proud and pulsing with power in her hand. Elegant writing burned across the steel, the letters forming before his eyes.

> I am fire and rain.
> I am wind and thunder.

Leógham couldn't stop staring at it. The Dragon's Bane had never done this.

And Kharis…

She was a shadow slicing through light, a storm tearing through silence. She dodged attacks with a clarity of movement that frightened him. One moment, she faced an attack; the next, she was behind the attacker. Her blades slashed and gored without mercy, carving through the enemy. She leaped over bodies and flipped mid-air with exceptional agility, leaving destruction in her wake.

As if she were death in the shape of a woman.

Leógham's pulse spiked.

An echo from his past stirred within him. He, too, had fought like her. Unyielding. Ruthless. His heart pounded against his ribs because Kharis wasn't like any woman he'd ever met. Fierce pride swelled inside him. She was a marvel for him to cherish—his equal, his flame-blooded mate.

The thought lit something dangerous inside him.

A harrowing scream ripped through the battlefield. Leógham snapped back to reality. He unsheathed his sword.

Questions about her skills could wait. He tightened the grip on his reins and raised his sword.

"For Hegra!"

Balyus snorted, muscles coiling.

"And for her!"

Leógham spurred him forward.

AGONY

Love may be born in peace, but it is transformed in the crucible of ruin. - Poliormos

The third archer crawled toward his bow, agony flaring with movement. The arrow had pierced his gut so cleanly, so swiftly, that at first, his body hadn't registered it.

Now, it burned like fire.

Still, he moved, determined to kill the crown prince as instructed.

"Look for the fiercest Fire Dweller warrior and kill that one," he'd been told.

His fingers found the nearest arrow. He clenched his jaw, biting down on a scream, and forced his body to obey.

Then he saw not one, but two. Wrapped in flames, two Fire Dwellers tore through the men like a formidable army.

He lied to us.

He spat blood into the dirt, rage burning through the pain. The path before him ended here. He would never see his family again. Weakness crept through his limbs.

Who was the crown prince? Why were there two?

It didn't matter.

As instructed, Eram chose the fiercest as his target. He drew, aimed, and released.

And as the arrow vanished into the chaos, everything went black.

&.

"Spear me!"

It happened too fast—a sudden snap of air, then searing pain.

Something struck Kharis square in the left shoulder, below the collarbone, the impact jerking her backward. An arrow had sunk deep, searing through flesh to lodge in the scapula. Kharis staggered, breath stolen, vision white with pain.

Her enemy lunged.

She dodged. Barely.

A cry ripped from her throat, half in anger and half in pain. Her blade flashed. The man's chest split open. He stumbled, choking on his own breath. Kharis struck again. His body crashed to the ground.

Her vision blurred red, the pain white-hot. Then it vanished, overtaken by this dark sweetness.

Two men barreled toward Leógham, weapons raised. Balyus reared, his hooves slamming down. Leógham's focus locked on the first attacker. He didn't see the second one, who clenched his hands around his leg and yanked.

Leógham's balance snapped.

He crashed to the ground, landing hard. Balyus screeched, thrashing, his hooves pounding the ground dangerously close to Leógham.

Kharis dropped the Dragon's Bane and, in a blur of motion, leaped onto the attacker's back. Her injured shoulder screamed, the arrow still jutting out. With one arm, she locked his head in a brutal hold, wrenching it backward. Her dagger found his throat.

With a thrust, the blade sank into flesh—a savage twist, then a sideways slash.

Hot blood spattered her face.

The body collapsed beneath her, lifeless.

Kharis hit the ground. A faint heat slid up her arm and spread through her chest. Her pain dulled again. Some of her wounds sealed. Strength surged where exhaustion had been. She gasped, horrified by the pleasure of it.

A wet, gurgling shriek cut through the chaos. With renewed stamina, she scrambled to her feet and spun around in time to see a firewolf leap onto the other attacker.

Jaws snapped. Bone crunched.

The man screamed, then choked, his arm torn away in a spray of crimson. The wolf pinned him to the earth, its teeth sinking into his throat, and finished him.

Leógham was already moving toward her, sword in his hands. Their backs connected, their breaths ragged. Their blades remained ready.

Death reigned in the air.

The forest was silent, except for the low growls of firewolves and the moaning of the dying. No birds. Not even the rustle of wind.

Leógham's chest rose and fell against her back, his breathing heavy, but when the distant call of horns pierced the air, he blew out a sharp sigh of relief.

"Help's coming."

He'd remained transformed, his magic tingling on her skin. Another plume of fire burst from his hand, spiraling into the sky. It lit the clouds from beneath, their edges glowing like embers. Below, the battlefield stretched still, now a graveyard of men and horses.

Drenched in sweat, strands of matted black hair clung to her damp forehead. The flames that had once wreathed her body snuffed out, her magic sinking back into her. Leógham stiffened. He'd felt the shift.

Kharis kept her dagger raised, angled to slash. But her fingers began twitching.

"There might be more," Leógham said.

She struggled to steady her thoughts. "Three archers. Sixteen riders... sixteen... six."

Her focus wavered. Her count was slipping. What came after six?

She blinked. She did it again. Her sight wouldn't sharpen. Her limbs felt heavy. No. Her entire body felt heavy. Something was off.

"Count them." She pushed past the fog creeping into her mind. "Some I left alive. We must find out who planned this."

The words left her lips, but her voice sounded foreign. So distant. The ground beneath her canted like a boat on rough waters, and she dropped to her knees.

Darkness spilled across her vision.

75

DESPERATION

You fell, and with you, my world. - Poliormos

Her body slipped away from him.

"Kharis?"

Leógham turned as her knees sank to the ground and saw the arrow jutting from her left shoulder. It was buried deep, dark blood pooling around the wound. Dread sank its cold teeth into him, dousing his scarlet fire.

"You're injured!" he choked.

Kharis let out a weak laugh. "Ha! Took you long enough to—"

Her body collapsed.

"Kharis!"

Leógham dropped to his knees, his breath stalled. The firewolves encircled them, snarling, guarding. His hands—shaking, fumbling—reached for the buckles on her jerkin.

Fires. Fires. Fires.

His fingers slipped, clumsy in his desperation. He'd trained for this, but every lesson vanished beneath his rising panic. His gaze darted between the arrow and her eyes. His breath caught. He looked again. The fletching's color was a deep red, almost black at the edges. The shaft glinted with a faint, oily sheen that caught the light wrong—rainbowed and dark. A bitter almond reek curled up. An icy shudder crawled down his spine. His hands hovered over the wound, unwilling to believe it.

The arrow... Poisoned.

His mind splintered like glass. *No. No. It can't be.* His pulse pounded in his skull. Images of cold tombstones and unanswered prayers crashed into him. *Not her. Not again.* He couldn't breathe.

"I can't lose you again." The words unraveled into a plea.

A warm hand wrapped around his wrist.

He flinched.

Kharis's grip was weak, but her eyes were sharp, unwavering. "Leógham," she rasped. "Get it out."

He tried to swallow past the knot in his throat. "Help is coming—"

"No." Her command pierced through him like steel carving flesh. "They'll discover I'm a woman. You'll be in danger." Her body shuddered beneath his touch. "Get it out." Her voice sounded so weak. "I can summon my healing magic."

His mind spun, stuck between reason and emotion.

"Don't drag it out the way it came." She instructed him despite the agony twisting her features. "It's lodged in bone." Her voice weakened. "Push it through. Do you understand?"

His stomach turned.

The world narrowed to her trembling breath, and something inside him steadied. The chaos receded, leaving focus in its wake. He brushed his thumb across the oily residue. Fire obeyed his touch, blooming in a thin, disciplined arc. The poison hissed and blackened, burning away in clean smoke. The acrid tang filled his lungs, grounding him. This—this he could control.

Her fingers closed around the arrow, and she snapped the shaft. Her breath hitched, her body going rigid with pain.

"Now." Kharis bit down on the broken fletching, her eyes wide.

His body moved on instinct.

Leógham snatched Kharis's dagger and sliced through the fabric. His hands clawed at the seams of her jerkin and undershirt, tearing cloth and leather.

When he saw the damage, an icy shiver ran through him.

Blood had pooled between her breasts, the binding soaked through. The wound was blackening, veins radiating out like thin, inky filaments. The poison had seeped into her, spreading slowly.

No, no, no.

His breath quaked. "I—I can't lose you."

Kharis shuddered. Sweat rimmed her brow. "The arrow..."

Leógham squeezed his eyes shut and wiped the sweat and tears from his face. He forced himself to focus. His fingers traced the shaft jutting beneath her collarbone, following its line around her shoulder. He found the tip behind her arm. The metal snagged beneath his fingers, cruel hooks biting back when he tested it.

Barbed.

Her body went rigid as pain flared, teeth clenched hard enough to crack. Tears spilled from the corners of her eyes.

"Kharis, stay with me."

"I'm... trying."

Leógham cupped her face, his voice trembling. "Are you ready?"

A barely perceptible nod. She clamped down on the broken arrow shaft and closed her eyes, bracing herself.

Leógham seized a flat rock, engulfed the arrow in scarlet flames once more, and with a furious, gut-wrenching roar, drove it through.

Kharis screamed.

Her body convulsed as agony tore through her. Leógham lifted her torso, his hand steady despite the terror crushing his chest. In one swift motion, he yanked the arrowhead from behind her armpit. A harsh gasp tore from her lips.

Her body slumped.

Leógham shook. He wanted to snap the arrow in his hands. To thrust it into the throat of the one who had done this to her.

Her breath shallowed.

Her face paled.

"Kharis, please stay with me."

Leógham ripped off his jerkin, tearing his tunic into strips and packing the wounds to stop the bleeding. Her blinks were slow and heavy. She was beyond pain, drifting away. His thumb brushed across her cheek. His tears fell onto her skin.

"Please stay..." he pleaded.

Her lashes fluttered. Then, so faintly he almost didn't hear it, she whispered, "You found me." A weak smile appeared on her face. "I won't ever leave you again."

Her eyes drifted closed, and her body went limp in his arms.

76

RAGE AND RUIN

To take from me or harm my loved ones is to invite ruin. Behold, for when my anger rises, the stars shall flinch, and I shall burn the verses of fate to ash. - Poliormos

D arragh arrived with a cavalry of soldiers, horns blaring.

He rode into carnage: broken bodies, crumpled horses, and blood, staining the ivory world in grotesque shades of red. Its splatter added a frightening pop of color, drops glistening like tiny rubies scattered on the snow.

The dread Darragh had spent years crushing under sheer will surged back, bile rising fast.

Not now. He shook his head sharply, and his keen logic snapped into place, shoving all fears away. He swung off his horse, feet hitting the ground with force. Commands flew from his mouth, words ingrained into his bones, and burned into his mind.

"Find the crown prince. Secure the horses. Sweep the area." His hands shook. "And gather those unlucky enough to be still alive. I'll quarter them myself."

The soldiers moved in a blur of shouting, armor clanking, and boots pounding the frozen ground.

Darragh didn't care. His eyes had already found him.

Leógham.

Alive.

The surge of relief nearly buckled his knees. Then Darragh truly saw him, and his body went rigid. Leógham knelt, drenched in blood and mud, his tunic torn, his jerkin discarded. And in his arms, wrapped in his riding cloak, lay someone small. Someone terribly still.

Darragh's breath froze in his lungs.

Everything disappeared. The screams morphed, and he was somewhere else, on a different day, with a body in his arms.

His child. Roísín.

A bundle of lifeless flesh wrapped in the first fabric he could grab, because he couldn't bear to see what had been done to her. He'd held her like Leógham was holding his, rocking back and forth because he couldn't scream.

A pained cry wrenched Darragh away from the horrors of his past and back to this nightmare. Darragh rushed forward, dropping to his knees beside Leógham.

His voice wavered, afraid to ask. "Is Benkhi—?"

"No!" Leógham lashed out.

Darragh clung to this fragile shred of hope. "Are you both all right?"

Leógham barely shook his head.

Benkhi's face was too pale, her body too still, the rise and fall of her breath too shallow to count. Strangled sobs ripped through Leógham. He held her gently as if afraid she'd shatter. Or as if she already had. He rocked, back and forth, back and forth, like the night Elinor died.

Darragh reached out with a steadying hand on Leógham's arm. He didn't react at first. His eyes, glassy with despair, finally opened and met his.

"We must get you out of here." Darragh gently squeezed Leógham's shoulder. "Benkhi needs a healer."

"Lord Darragh!" A soldier shouted from behind them. "We found the crown prince's horses!"

Darragh waved without looking away. His focus remained on Leógham.

His voice gentled. "Can you stand?"

A hesitant nod. Lips trembled.

"Good. Let's get you out of here." Darragh forced himself to breathe. Right now, Leógham needed him. And Benkhi was dying.

With Darragh's help, Leógham rose to his feet, but his grip on Benkhi never loosened. In his left hand, he clutched a broken arrow shaft as if it were another weapon in his arsenal.

He lifted his head.

His eyes locked on the bodies ahead.

"Survivors?" Leógham's voice was low, eerily quiet.

"Yes." Darragh glanced at the wounded. "But barely, if you ask me."

Leógham nodded once. "Good." A pause. "Keep them alive."

His eyes never wavered from the battlefield, but the look in them wasn't human.

This wasn't Leógham, the man.

This was Leógham, the monster.

The Black Prince.

Darragh stepped back. A reflex. He'd seen this bloodlust, this darkness before. The same monster that had crushed entire battalions beneath a single night. The same creature that had set the battlefield ablaze with black flames, turning those who had dared approach him into ash.

That Leógham was back.

Darragh shuddered.

"Leógham—" He hesitated, choosing his words carefully. "Please, let me carry—"

"No!" Leógham's nostrils flared. "I'll carry Benkhi. No one else does. Only me."

Darragh put his hands up appeasingly. "Fair enough, brother. Let's get you to the castle." His voice softened, coaxing him back to reason. "You're both in a frightful state."

Some soldiers stayed behind, waiting for the wagon that would carry the dead. They would leave the horses for the firewolves. They'd earned their meat.

As for the survivors... They would be kept alive for one reason only.

To face the Black Prince's wrath.

77

ASHES AND BLOOD

> *To walk the path carved by fate is to bleed with every*
> *step—each wound a question, each scar an answer*
> *not yet understood. - Poliormos*

When the Hegran crown prince arrived at the castle, his escort at his side, the upper bailey erupted into chaos. Servants spilled into the courtyard like a sea of restless bodies. Guards and workers rushed forward, their voices blending into a muddled symphony of concern. Grooms emerged, hands reaching for reins, saddles, and horses slick with sweat.

Sahrit ran to Leógham, relief swelling in her chest when she saw her brother.

He was standing. He was alive.

But then, she stopped, and her breath vanished.

His clothing was torn and soaked in blood. He'd been wrapped in someone else's cloak. His face was pale, expressionless, and splattered with red mud. And in his arms —a body.

Shrouded in black.

Still.

Sahrit's stomach plummeted. Her gaze locked onto Leógham's, but only emptiness stared back. No denial. No reassurance. Just hollow green voids. A cruel moment of clarity dawned.

And Sahrit snapped.

"Benkhi!"

Her bellow shattered the air. The wind carried it, piercing every heart that heard it.

"Ama!" Hrag grabbed her before she ran, wrapping his arms around her waist to hold her back. Darragh leaped off his horse instantly, closing the distance, his arms locking around her.

But nothing could contain her grief.

Sahrit, the ever-composed, ever-measured, ever-regal high princess of Hegra, shattered into so many pieces that she didn't know who she was anymore. She wailed, the sound so wretched, so agonizing, that it clawed through the cold air. She was back in the bloodstained corridors of her former home.

The screams. The blood. The dead.

The day assassins slaughtered her daughter and mother.

"Benkhi!" She shrieked the name over and over, thrashing against Darragh's and Hrag's grip. She heard her name. Pleas whispered into her ear. But it didn't matter. Nothing mattered.

It had happened again.

Her magic unleashed. The moment Darragh's and Hrag's hold eased on her, Sahrit bolted toward the body in Leógham's arms.

She had to see. Had to know.

But arms caught her again.

"Sahrit!" Darragh's rasping voice broke through the storm in her mind. "Benkhi's alive."

The words rippled through her. She turned, her eyes meeting Darragh's.

"Alive?"

"Yes." His voice was gentle, his eyes begging her to remain calm.

Leógham didn't look at her. Didn't look at anyone. He walked past her, his arms locked around Benkhi's still form as if he were the only thing anchoring her brother to this world. She ripped free from Darragh and Hrag, stumbling after her brother.

"Leógham, please. Listen to me." Tears streaked down her face, warm against the icy air. "Please."

Leógham kicked the entrance doors open with a single, forceful blow. His boots clacked on the wooden floor. He climbed the stairs two at a time.

Sahrit followed, voice cracking, barely keeping up. "Leógham, please, let me help—"

"No." Fire flashed in his eyes. "No one's touching him."

The doors to his chambers swung open. Servants scrambled out of the way.

"Out," Leógham shouted. "I want everyone *out*."

And with that, the door slammed shut.

The click of the lock broke the silence. Within heartbeats, Sahrit was banging on the door. "Leógham, please! Let me in. Let me help."

Her fists struck the wood.

Again. And again.

Her voice broke. Her body broke. The past and present blurred into one indistinguishable nightmare.

"Sahrit?"

The voice was soft. Gentle. Warm hands curled around her fingers, stopping her before she could hurt herself further. Only then did she realize her knuckles were bleeding.

Her tears fell.

Darragh stood before her, always so kind, waiting for his lovely Sahrit to come back. But she couldn't. She was stuck in the past. And now this moment had trapped her, too.

"It happened again." A single, splintering sob. "They came here." She shook her head, rejecting this cursed fate.

Darragh didn't speak. Instead, he reached for her.

"Come, my love." His warmth filled the hollow inside her. "Let's bandage your hands."

Sahrit nodded at him because what else could she do?

Heartbroken, she let him lead her away. Hrag, her lovely boy—her only child now—followed behind.

❦

Tears welled in Leógham's eyes. Once more, he'd failed the one he loved.

Leógham kept his back against the door. When the banging on the door ceased, he took a deep breath, clutching Kharis. His body trembled under the stress of reining in his dread. A familiar hum fueled a hunger he hadn't experienced since the Hegran civil war.

He ground his teeth, wanting to bludgeon the one who'd hurt her, to tear his limbs apart slowly, to rip his heart out and stomp on it, to burn his body to a crisp and then char the ashes until nothing but smoke remained.

Someone had hurt her.

Someone had almost killed her.

My Kharis.

The beast inside him wanted to mangle and gouge and punch. His anger became a wild thrumming. When flames engulfed his fists, they weren't scarlet but black, dancing on his fists like old, forgotten friends.

A soft moan pulled him back, and the flames extinguished. Her body stirred, and that brought him clarity.

All that mattered was her. Only her.

He took a deep, calming breath and carried her to the bed, where he placed her limp body down. Carefully, he removed the cloak and dropped it on the floor.

Her black snakes—now shimmering rivers of molten

silver—glided over her skin. Wherever they passed, the poison hissed and vanished. Relief punched through Leógham's chest. The same magic that had saved Hrag was working through her now.

He checked her injury, unpacking the linen he'd stuffed into her wounds. The entry wound was closing fast from the inside out, with the external perimeter slowly forming a pink outline. Red, swollen tissue had replaced the blackened one. The inky filaments had disappeared, red blood now flowing through her veins.

Her healing magic continued its work, generating tiny silver sparks that mended and threaded the torn skin, burning through the poison. He turned her gently to examine the angry gash behind her armpit. The bleeding had stopped. Crusted scabs covered the wound, smaller now.

Whatever her magic was, it worked—a deliberate and accurate spell with the promise of hope.

His chest heaved and shuddered. The dread that had clamped around it eased. Leógham wailed his relief, silently thanking the Infinite. His fiercely beautiful, stubborn, and exceedingly brave Kharis would live.

All he could do now was clean her. He wiped his eyes dry with a sleeve and got to work. With scissors in hand, he cut through leather and cloth with tender care, dropping the bloodstained pieces onto the floor one by one. He was determined to burn everything and make the survivors eat the ashes.

She slipped in and out of consciousness, just as she had when he first rescued her from the lake. Back then, that woman was a stranger on the brink of death. Now she was his—his heart, his anchor—and he'd wrestle death itself to keep her by his side.

Leógham swallowed his angry tears as he brought a large basin of water to the night table and dipped a cloth into it. He cleaned the cuts and scratches that hadn't healed yet with extreme gentleness, then applied a beeswax-and-calendula salve. He washed the dried blood and dirt matted in her hair, hands, and nails until the water turned dark red.

When he finished, he dressed her in one of his sleeping shifts and tucked her beneath the covers. He perched beside her, tenderly holding her hand. When her breathing evened, he leaned down and gently pressed his forehead to hers.

"I love you," he whispered, tears still streaking down his face.

He lingered there, sharing the same breath because if she lived, so did he. Because she'd become the air he needed.

Leógham unfastened the curtains on his bedposts and closed them as his heart lit a slow fire.

Kharis would live.

The one who'd hurt her wouldn't.

Leógham opened his chamber doors. Two servants stood in the corridor, waiting—Sahrit's doing, no doubt. They stiffened at the sight of him and kept their distance from the guards. He spoke softly, though he knew from their faces that his glare was frightening.

"Take the clothes on the floor and burn them, but please save the ashes and bring them to me." He faced the other servant. "Take the washbowl and save the water. The prisoners might be thirsty."

Once they exited, Leógham gently closed the doors and turned to the two soldiers guarding it, towering over them like a blazing dragon.

"No one enters my rooms but me or Prince Darragh. Understood?"

They bowed their heads.

Then, oddly calm, Leógham walked down the hallway, holding the arrow piece.

THE COLOR OF RUIN

The cruelest fate does not kill; it binds, tests, and asks if you still remember who you were before the weight of prophecy made you kneel. - Poliormos

Darragh lingered by the entrance to the dungeons, the stone at his back cold and uneven. He wondered whether he was getting too old for Hegra.

His thoughts drifted to Benkhi, to Leógham, to the grief that had nearly shattered Sahrit only hours before. His hands curled into fists. He needed to get her out of Hegra—sooner than planned. If Saigham stood behind this brazen attack, it was only a matter of time before he came for her.

How many more losses could he endure?

How many times would fate demand the same agony?

Benkhi, please live.

The thought was a whisper, a plea, a command, because he didn't know what would happen to Leógham if she died.

Darragh understood Leógham's possessiveness because he'd allowed no one to bandage Sahrit's hands. No one else would ever be good enough, gentle enough. His fingers had trembled as he wrapped them with care—every knot in the linen a silent vow that he'd never fail her.

And yet, he'd left her behind.

Hrag and Ailene ensured she ate, drank her medicinal tea, and rested. But guilt gnawed at him, sharp as a blade. He should've stayed. *I should be at her side.*

Yet... if someone had come for Sahrit the way they'd come for Leógham today?

His hands turned into white-knuckled fists. If no one stopped him, what power would he unleash to torment the men imprisoned in this place?

Heavy footsteps broke his thoughts.

Darragh turned toward the stairs. Leógham descended, his black cloak billowing behind him. His escort followed silently, a host of shadows trailing in his wake.

He'd changed his clothes, but his face was still dirty. His eyes weren't emerald or scarlet.

Midnight-blue eyes, so dark they bordered on black, glinted with silver flecks that gave them a forbidding, star-spun depth.

The Black Prince stopped before him.

Darragh swallowed hard.

"Anything?" Leógham's voice was silvery ice.

Darragh cleared his throat, forcing himself to speak. "They have said nothing yet, but I wouldn't put it past Saigham to be the mastermind behind this attack."

Leógham's grip tightened on the arrow in his hand. That bloodied shaft was a cruel reminder of how close Leógham had come to dying.

"I'll need proof, Darragh." His voice was sharp, lethal. "*Irrefutable* proof."

Darragh exhaled slowly. "Working on it, brother. However, you may be interested to know that one of the survivors was a servant in your household, the one Sahrit mentioned."

Leógham narrowed his eyes, the expression cold and calculating. "The one who abandoned Juell?"

Darragh nodded.

Leógham's expression didn't change; his eyes still narrowed, but the darkness in them grew. He studied the arrow as if committing it to memory. "I would like to speak to him first."

Darragh looked at the arrow, then at Leógham, who stood perfectly still, stone-faced, his eyes fixed on the dungeons below.

Darragh pursed his lips. Things were about to turn ugly for Eram. "Very well. Follow me."

THE SLEEPING DRAGON

> *Others won't know how powerful you are until you choose to reveal your hidden strength in a splendid show of bravery and resolve. - Poliormos*

News of the assassination attempt on the crown prince's life spread. As the evening wore on, high captains took refuge with Leógham and Darragh in the Keep to discuss strategy and its repercussions.

With the castle on high alert, soldiers had spread across the palace grounds, posted everywhere. Captains interrogated servants, workers, and hired hands. Soldiers had descended on the village to gather and question everyone there.

Beyond the clamor, Sahrit sat in her study, staring at a blank sheet of parchment on her desk. A soft knock came at her door. Neagh entered, a satchel slung over his shoulder. "Everything is ready."

Sahrit stared at the paper once more and offered Neagh a nod. "Neagh... thank you. For your loyalty. Always."

His gray eyes softened. "I have served this house—and you—since you were small. It has been an honor, My Lady."

She let out a slow breath. "So much has happened since then." Her voice faltered. "So much." She rose, smoothing her skirts to gather herself. "Let's get started."

Outside, her breath misted in the icy air, wispy tendrils trailing behind as she drew her hood over her head. Torches limned their forms in gilded light as she and Neagh descended the steps to the lower bailey and crossed its length. Soldiers bowed to her.

The mouth of the dungeons yawned ahead.

Sahrit did not slow. Inside, she turned to the jailer only long enough to speak.

"I will see the prisoners."

The man stiffened, instinctively glancing toward Neagh. The seneschal gave a single, almost imperceptible nod.

A flicker of hesitation crossed the jailer's face. "It may be... unpleasant, Highness."

Sahrit met his gaze, her voice level. "It won't be worse than standing over my mother's mangled body after she was stabbed to death by multiple hands."

The words landed without heat or apology. The jailer lowered his head, whether in surrender or understanding, and stepped aside. "This way."

They entered the interrogation chamber. Neagh took the seat at the table and reached into his satchel, laying several sheets of parchment before him.

"Would you like more light?" the jailer asked.

"No." Sahrit glanced at him only once. "Leave us."

The jailer hesitated, casting Neagh a final, uneasy look, as though hoping the seneschal might intervene. Neagh remained still.

"As you wish." The jailer bowed and withdrew, the door closing behind him.

Neagh's ash-colored eyes glowed bright red, ready to transcribe the conversation.

"It may hurt," Sahrit warned, steadying herself.

"If it does, I'll handle it," was Neagh's stoic response.

With a grave nod, she faced the shadow slouched on the floor before her, chains drawn taut at his wrists.

A weary sigh escaped as she unwrapped the linen from her right hand. Even without light, she could feel the swelling—skin hot, joints tender, flesh mapped with faint cuts.

Taking a moment to steady herself, she braced for the pain of wielding her magic.

With a single thought, aquamarine fire blossomed across her fingers. The chamber filled with its light, but it also bit into her palm as it flared to life. Her lips twitched as she bore the pain of needles stabbing her skin.

Eram's torture had been brutal: fingers bent unnaturally, scorched marks on his arms. There wasn't much she could do except soothe his pain. Careful of his wounds, she wrapped her fingers around his arm, let her flames seep into him, and probed his mind, truth-seeking. It was a slow walk through all his memories, even the vile ones.

Words began to appear on the parchment in Neagh's hands.

With the pain removed from his body, Eram regained consciousness.

"Eram?" she asked. "You were one of our best workers. Why did you turn on us?"

He could hardly open his eyes, his entire face swollen beyond recognition. His words came out weak, a rasp in the dark. "They took them—my wife and children."

"Who?"

"Those men."

Sahrit's heart jerked. "Do you know where they are?"

"No." Eram heaved a desperate sob, slurring his words. "He said he'd kill them if I didn't do as told."

Sahrit met Eram's desperate face, keeping her voice soft and soothing. "We'll rescue them." An empty promise, since Saigham never left any witnesses.

She asked her questions and listened to him with infinite patience.

The sight of Eram, broken and chained to the wall, shattered her soul. So much blood and killing, and for what? A broken arrow stuck out of his left shoulder. Someone had driven it in repeatedly, given the several gashes on his shoulders and torso.

"Eram, do you swear by what you said?"

"All of it," he slurred through swollen lips. "I had no choice. He'd kill them."

"We'll care for them." She caressed his swollen face. "You can rest now."

Magic etched the final line onto the parchment, the letters flaring gold before cooling into ink. At the bottom, Eram's name appeared—signed by his trembling will, even when his hand had never moved.

"This letter is finished," Neagh murmured.

Sahrit nodded once.

Eram was dying. All she could do was ease his passing. She turned to the prisoner and offered a small, genuine smile. "No matter what, you were always our best worker. I understand your choice. Do not grieve. Do not let guilt make you falter. Justice will be met."

Her tone grew tender, almost maternal. "Close your eyes, Eram. You've earned your rest."

The aquamarine fire flickered on her hand, weaving an illusion in his mind.

Eram's eyes fluttered open.

He was home.

His wife stood before him, smiling, her arms outstretched. Their children ran toward him, laughter spilling through the sunlit room. He caught them all, holding them close, trembling with relief. Tears streamed down his face, cool against the hearth's heat.

"You're safe," he whispered, voice breaking. "You're *safe*."

The world glowed warm around them—they were together again.

❧

Hidden in the dim corridors of Eram's mind, Sahrit watched unseen, her heart heavy. Hers was a simple illusion to ease a burdened soul: to offer him a moment of peace, one last reprieve before death finally claimed him.

Eram's eyes closed, and his body slumped. The chains rattled in the dark. His final breath was quiet, peaceful.

Sahrit's emerald flame dissipated. Neagh's red eyes turned ash gray again. She sighed, the ferocity of the day's events troubling her.

"How are you faring?" she asked.

"I will go for as long as you do," Neagh said.

Sahrit nodded, yet waited a moment to allow Neagh some time to compose himself. Consistently stoic and loyal to a fault, his expression never showed how much it hurt him.

"Is the confession complete?" she asked.

"Yes, My Lady. Every one of his memories captured with precision."

"Thank you. Once we're done here, please take the signed confessions to my husband. He'll need them."

Neagh got up and bowed his assent.

Sahrit turned to Eram one last time, her brow taut. "Neagh, please see that Eram is cremated. He was a victim, one more pawn in this madness."

Neagh's composure faltered. "My Lady... you know the custom. Prisoners of high treason are—"

"I know." Her gaze held steady, a glimmer of heat rising

395

behind her eyes. "Let mercy break the custom. No one deserves to be left for wild beasts."

A silence stretched between them. Then Neagh bowed again, this time deeper, reverently. "It will be as you wish."

"Thank you." Sahrit rubbed her fingers, the skin even more swollen and raw, the pain creeping up her hand. "There are others, correct?"

"Yes, four more." Neagh's eyes flicked to her wounded hand with a wrinkled brow.

"Very well." The tingling in her fingers progressed from uncomfortable to painful. "Shall we continue?"

Neagh nodded and followed her out.

DUTY AND DESIRE

Duty is the altar where longing is bled dry. Those who hold power must learn to stay while their hearts run. - Poliormos

Leógham withdrew from the spectacle unfolding around him. His elbows rested on the table, his hands steepled by his face. He sat in silence, staring at the maps spread before him. Shouting and cursing surrounded him, muted and distant. All he heard was his pulse rushing through his ears.

They'd gone after him, and she'd been injured because of him.

If her disguise had slipped in the chaos, Saigham would see the throne fall neatly into his lap.

Leógham's jaw set.

All because of me.

He couldn't wait to finish this council and sit beside Kharis. He couldn't have healers, much less Sahrit, stay with her, lest her disguise be exposed. He could only trust Darragh, and he was stuck here with him.

Outside, darkness rose. Behind the thick clouds, a river of midnight stars burned, indifferent.

Around the table, the war council unraveled into open discord.

The lord marshal and his captains shouted over one another, voices sharp with anger and old rivalries. Accusations flew toward the man suspected of ordering the ambush. Some called for open war. Others demanded Lord Saigham's lands be seized, his castle put to siege and flame.

Without solid evidence against the man, it was all smoke and noise.

Yet beneath it all, a more dangerous truth pressed in. The ambush hadn't merely spilled blood. It had risked exposing secrets. What if one of Saigham's mercenaries had stayed behind to watch and report what had happened? If Saigham's spy had glimpsed Kharis's identity, the calls for war wouldn't be confined to this chamber. Saigham would wield her unmasking like a blade, cutting down Leógham and his claim to the throne at last.

King Aghavor's ravens flew in and out of an open window, delivering messages to and from the king. A large raven perched on Leógham's chair like a black sentinel, observing the chaos with its inky eyes before taking flight.

Unexpected movement caught Leógham's attention. Neagh had entered and, after a quick scan, headed straight for Darragh. Exercising discretion, Neagh whispered something and handed Darragh a bundle of parchment before sitting at the table.

Darragh flipped through the pages. His hand flew to his mouth as all color drained from his face. He stared at Leógham, who narrowed his gaze in silent command. Darragh's gaze darted, as if he were reeling from the shock. Still in a daze, he stepped forward and, with trembling hands, thrust the parchments into Leógham's hands.

"Five confession letters," Darragh croaked.

Leógham took them, scanning the first one. He didn't ask where they came from. He knew.

"I must see to my wife," Darragh whispered—pleaded.

Leógham nodded, and Darragh left, as if his only purpose in life were to be with Sahrit.

"Confessions," Leógham said, handing the letters to the lord marshall.

Voices rose as the parchment passed from hand to hand. Soon, the chamber swelled with overlapping arguments, but to Leógham it all blurred, muffled like sound beneath water. These hadn't named Saigham or his son, who knew how to keep their hands clean. Fury threatened to break Leógham. He wanted to set Hegra ablaze and watch it burn. Only one thought held him in check: to go to Kharis, as Darragh had gone to Sahrit.

As crown prince, duty and by Hegran law bound Leógham to this room. The king expected him to be a perfect rendition of a Hegran royal. A model everyone looked up to.

The irony burned him.

A warm hand clasped his shoulder. The lord marshal. "My Lord, yours has been a long day. Allow us to continue the work. You must rest." He leaned in closer. "Have healers seen to your person?"

Leógham limbered his neck.

"Gentlemen?" The room stilled at once. "See to it that the men named in these confessions are arrested and tried for high treason. I expect reports by morning." Leógham rose, and all followed, chairs scraping, cloaks whispering, armor clanging as they bowed.

Darragh had gone to the woman he loved.

Leógham shoved duty aside and strode for the door—toward her.

The world didn't need another perfect prince.

THE SHAPE OF FEAR
AND DARKNESS

> *Those who sharpen their power on the suffering of others grind down the foundation beneath their feet. - Poliormos*

Eilidh tiptoed through the corridor behind the servant, Baelynn's trembling hand tugging at Eilidh's sleeve. A single candle bobbed in the dark, its quivering flame throwing frail glimmers against the night. Every shadow seemed to stretch and breathe. Eilidh wrung her hands, certain she would be punished if anyone found her wandering at this late hour.

Cautiously, Bealynn guided her into Lady Thearith's chambers. The antechamber lay dark, curtains drawn tight, shutters latched. No lamps burned. Even the hearth had been smothered. The weight of that darkness sent Eilidh's heart racing. This wouldn't end well.

"Eilidh...?" A voice trembled from deeper within. "Is that you?"

Eilidh stepped into the bedchamber before she'd fully steeled herself. A shape lay curled in a corner, hardly moving. Her breath caught. "Thearith?"

She took the candle from Bealynn and dropped to her knees. *Blessed Infinite...* Thearith flinched at the light, covering her eyes with shaking fingers. The glow spilled over blood-matted hair, a swollen cheek, and purpling bruises spreading from temple to jaw. The candle tilted in Eilidh's grip.

Bealynn lingered behind Eilidh, fear rooting her in place.

"I asked her to fetch you," Thearith slurred through swollen lips. "I need... help." She tried to shift her weight, and a choked sound left her throat.

Eilidh reached toward her, but her hand faltered halfway, unsure where touching wouldn't hurt.

"Did Cuileagh do this?" The words slipped out quietly, a tremor crawling through her hands.

The word trembled. "Yes."

"Go," Eilidh told the servant girl. "You saw nothing. You know nothing."

Bealynn nodded, hands shaking. "Will the miss be all right?"

"Go," Eilidh insisted. "Now."

The girl backed away, nearly tripping in her haste to flee through the antechamber. Thearith's gaze followed her. When Eilidh moved to stand, Therith caught her skirt. "Please..." she said. "Don't leave me."

Eilidh bent close, brushing knuckles along the uninjured side of Thearith's face. She burned with fever. "I'm not going anywhere," Eilidh said, "but you're injured, and I must see to it."

"Don't let the children see me," Thearith breathed, clutching her ribs. Her swollen eye squeezed shut. "If they do... he'll get angry again."

Eilidh's stomach twisted. This couldn't be their lot in life. There had to be some hope somewhere, because otherwise, this household was nothing but a curse. "They won't see you. I'll tell them you're ill. Leave everything to me."

She pushed herself upright, glancing toward the door.

She didn't know where Cuileagh was, or whether he'd return, so she had to work quickly. At the washstand, she filled a basin, the pitcher shaking in her hands. Cold water splashed over her fingers. She gathered cloths and snatched a jar of calendula salve from a shelf.

Eilidh crouched and held out a folded cloth. "Bite this. If a tooth is loose, it may still be saved."

Thearith took it between ragged breaths. Tears spilled from her, the shape her despair had taken. How long would it be before she surrendered to the only escape she saw?

Cuileagh never struck the face. Eilidh had learned that much over the years. That he'd done it tonight put her nerves on edge. Her gaze lifted toward the shadowed beams overhead, imagining him prowling through the keep. If he'd started here, with Thearith, where would he have gone next? The dungeons? The training yard?

Some failure had sparked this frenzy. One of his ambitious plans had fallen apart beyond repair. And tonight, Thearith had been the first to bear the weight of Cuileagh's anger and frustration.

Please, powerful Infinite, let him stay away.

Her father wouldn't intervene, not for Thearith. His grandsons mattered; daughters-in-law didn't. *Neither do I.* The knowledge sat in her gut like a sharp stone.

"I'm using an astringent. It may sting." She dabbed at a cut behind Thearith's ear. She winced and clutched Eilidh's wrist. "He can't know you helped me."

"He won't." Eilidh dipped the cloth again, heart thrashing against her ribs. "I'll be quick and leave, I promise."

Taking a deep breath to compose herself, she continued her ministrations. A soft sound behind her froze her hand mid-motion. She stiffened at the faint scrape of wood. Candlelight trembled across the walls.

"Bealynn, I said to—"

A strangled whimper answered her.

Eilidh turned slowly. A broad-shouldered figure filled the

doorway. Her lungs locked. Cuileagh's large hand wrapped around the back of Bealynn's slender neck. Her chest shuddered with soundless gasps. Tears ran down her face, mingling with the blood trickling from her nose and spattering on the floor.

"You told her to do what, Eilidh?" Cuileagh drawled, his voice smooth as oil, his wicked smile widening.

Cold ripped through her. She rose without meaning to, instinct dragging her upright. Thearith's hand clung to Eilidh's skirt, trembling violently. The sharp tang of urine assaulted her nostrils. Eilidh swallowed hard and stayed in front of Thearith, shielding her.

Cuileagh's red eyes gleamed like coals. He cocked his head. "You know you aren't allowed to leave your room, *dear sister.*"

Her heart skipped a beat.

His smile stretched, slow and hungry, pleased by the way she stiffened. He tutted at her. "Now... what shall I do about it?"

The wick on her candle sputtered and shrank.

THE FIRST NAME

To be of two worlds is to belong to neither. Each claims us. None defines us. Yet, in this exile, truth finds its refuge. - Poliormos

Kharis sat on the shore, the black sand drinking the surf. Each wave folded itself back into the sea in a hush of tide and salt. Välissa's sea echoed the sky, mirroring the mesmerizing swath of stars. Farther out, the kelp forests breathed; their golden fronds rose with the current and fell beneath the surface. Their underwater light freckled the horizon.

The steady warmth from her snake tattoos kept the cold at bay. They glimmered, silver-threaded, busy with their craft: mending and knitting her body in the mortal world.

She'd been here for a while, lost in thought, when silver mist uncoiled and shaped itself into a man.

"I see you are well, little sister," Ragha said. "Glowing like the North Star."

His jaw, the slope of his nose, the shape of his lips—she recognized herself in him. Whether she looked like him or he looked like her, she couldn't tell. That sameness tugged at her memory.

"Hello, brother." Kharis kept her attention on the black sea and its icy breath. Her lips thinned, a question lingering there. "You *are* my brother, right?"

"Of course." Ragha's easy smile hovered. "Though the proper answer would require me to start at the beginning."

"I have time." She drew her knees up and wrapped her arms around them.

He chuckled, low and amused. "Not as much as you think. Shape your questions for shorter answers, Ori."

Her eyes narrowed. "Why the name?"

He shrugged. "Because it is yours. The first, before all the other names you've worn."

Kharis gave him a bland look. "Other names?" When he nodded in confirmation, she grunted. "You and your riddles." She dug a hand into the sand and lifted a handful, watching it slip through her fingers. "You said the wrong thread was added to the Tapestry to spare you. Why would the Weaver take such a risk?"

"Because the Weaver is my twin sister." His grin sharpened, but his eyes didn't share the mirth. "Short answer."

"The Weaver... her?" Her lips parted, her breath vanishing in the cold wind. She stared at him—truly stared— as if seeing the resemblance for the first time. Her pulse throbbed at her throat, the sea forgotten. "Your... Am I...?" She shook her head. "Speak plainly, Ragha. No more riddles."

His grin dimmed under the weight of memory. "Once, I nearly destroyed the world. The gods sent her to smite me. Instead, she saved me." His gaze turned inward. "All debts must be repaid. She helped me. I am here to help her... To help you."

She rubbed her forehead. "Wait... am I dead?"

Ragha made a face. "We, immortals, do not die."

Her jaw dropped, the breath punched out of her lungs. She jabbed a finger at her chest. "No—I—It can't be—"

"But you are, Ori. Moving through timelines with a different face and name." His features sobered. "It seems Farrádh followed through on his promise and sealed your memories. Thus, explaining this would require time you do not have."

"And who is—? Never mind." Kharis dragged a hand through her face. "So she's alive. Or I'm alive. I need ale." She exhaled sharply. "You said her punishment was to redo the Tapestry. It sounds like she's finishing it."

"The Tapestry is unending. Its cosmic strings hold the worlds together."

She frowned. "Then what exactly must she... I do?" Her voice strained against the surf.

He released a quiet, wistful breath. "Just as I was betrayed, so was my sister—twice. Drunk on revenge, I nearly unmade this world. But she?" He made a pained sound. "She cursed her traitors to protect the land, but in doing so, she cursed herself. Such is the power of a Hegran promise."

"So... a mistake?"

His brows drew together. "With my sister, nothing is ever by chance... but how I wish I were wrong, just once."

A memory flickered through her mind. "During the ambush, a hunger rose in me that nearly broke me. And yet, something eased it. The relief was glorious. Intoxicating. Was it you, helping me?"

He shook his head. "Not me, I'm afraid."

Her shoulders dropped as she swallowed her disappointment.

"That sweetness felt wrong," she added. "Still, I knew, with a kind of horror, that I wanted more."

His voice lowered. "That, dear sister, is the Djinnshirukh curse." His gaze fell to his hands. "The lives of those who rise against you sustain you in battle."

She sucked in a sharp breath. *Souls...* Warmth drained from her body. "How do I end it, Ragha?"

He brushed her cheek with a gentle touch. "As long as you delay your journey north, this curse will fester, and you will unmake the world once more." For an impossible moment, a silver tear traced his cheek. "Go north, little sister. Find your creation and burn it."

A sob lodged in her throat. "But why me? What did I do?"

His fingers brushed her temple, tenderly tucking black strands behind her ear. "In your wrath, the curse you cast upon the traitors turned against you. You birthed the ice flowers now leeching the magic of the land."

Her stomach lurched. "I—what?"

"Your judgment on those who twisted magic to betray you." He attempted a smile, lips twitching, perhaps to bring some levity. "Your questions must elicit short answers, like your hair."

This time, his humor didn't hold.

"Time to wake, Ori." He tapped her forehead once.

Light broke through in a single, sharp bloom.

THE SILENCE THAT WON'T SURRENDER

*What are we but boundaries: a mortal shell, an immortal yearning,
and silence as the sole partition between the two. - Poliormos*

Kharis opened her eyes, breath coming in quick, uneven gasps. She remembered the arrow and Leógham, bracing to drive it through. A room settled into focus: spacious, shadow-warm, smelling faintly of cedar and leather.

This wasn't her bedchamber. *Where am I? How long have I been out?*

She tried to lift herself and groaned, her body aching from crown to heel.

"Kharis...?" Leógham stirred. He'd fallen asleep in a chair beside the bed. His head lifted, his eyes bleary, but when he saw her, his face broke into relief. "You're awake." He kissed her hand, then pressed it to his face. "Truly awake."

He climbed onto the bed and gently gathered her into his arms, silent tears slipping down his face.

Once he'd composed himself, he called for food to be brought, and while they waited, he told her everything that had transpired. When the servants arrived, he took the tray himself and dismissed them. He helped Kharis sit up and fed her with quiet patience, ensuring she ate every bite.

"I must head downstairs soon," he said at last.

"What happened? Were there survivors? Did any confess?"

"Think nothing of it." He cupped her cheek. "It's over, and you're safe."

"Leógham, they came to kill you—"

"And they failed," he said, yet nothing in his tone convinced her it was over.

"The work of a crown prince never ends." Tender knuckles caressed the line of her jaw. "Darragh is helping me oversee preparations for departure so I can be with you. We leave in another day." He leaned over and kissed her. "Promise me you'll rest. I'll have Sahrit come and check on you."

"Will I see you again?"

He smiled with a certainty that stole her breath. "I wouldn't have it any other way. I'll bring dinner and feed you."

A grin tugged at her lips. "I could get used to this."

"Good." He kissed her once more. "So could I."

Kharis couldn't contain her grin. Leógham had seen the monster, and yet here he was: his smile soft, his touch tender, his eyes bright once more. Looking forward to feeding and kissing her. He'd seen what she had done and still loved her.

A tremor ran through her.

***

After tea with Sahrit and multiple promises that she'd rest, Kharis rose and dressed. When she opened the door to Leógham's chambers, silence met her first.

At the sight of "Lord Benkhi" emerging from the crown prince's private rooms, the sentries' expressions flickered before their faces shuttered. Then came the salute: spears thumped, backs straightened with ceremonial force.

Kharis lifted her chin and stepped forward. Two guards fell in behind her at once, escorting the fosterling, their footfalls quiet, but their scrutiny loud as a bell.

A dozen excuses flickered through her mind—ways to deflect, to make herself invisible again—but she doubted any would matter now.

She pushed open the dining room door but didn't step inside. The family was absent; armored men now packed the chamber. With a grimace, she turned away and headed for the kitchens, her two guards shadowing her every step.

The central kitchen buzzed with activity, a microcosm of the chaos that had overtaken Dríeadh Manor. To her surprise, she ran into Hrag, seated by one of the stone ovens, doing his best to stay out of everyone's way while he ate.

"Blessed be the—" She groaned at her near slip. "I mean, good day." She sat next to him on the bench. "Seems soldiers have claimed our usual spots."

Hrag fixed her with a steady look.

"Lord Benkhi," he drawled. "They shot you with an arrow not two days ago. Uncle wouldn't leave your side until duty finally pulled him away." He gestured toward the door—toward the mayhem outside. "We leave tomorrow. So"—his tone sharpened—"why are you here, walking as if nothing had happened?"

Kharis shrugged. "The arrow grazed me. The scrape won't even leave a scar." It bothered her to lie.

"Like the winged nightmare attack, I suppose." Hrag frowned, pensive. "I have no scars to prove it happened."

She clicked her tongue, then jerked her chin at what he ate.

He shot her a silent insult and gestured to the bustling kitchen with a cynical sheen. "It's cheese and bread." When she nudged his shoulder, he conceded. "Fine. I didn't want to eat anything else." His brow furrowed. "I thought the servants would bring you breakfast."

"They did, and your uncle ensured I ate everything, but the noon meal is upon us, and I'm starving. And why are you not eating in the dining hall?"

He tapped his lips, feigning a contemplative expression. "What was it you said? Ah, yes! Evicted from our usual places. Benkhi, could you be any denser?"

She shot him an angry stare. "I was injured. You should treat me a little nicer."

"Ha! You said it was nothing. Not even a scar, you said."

She tsked at him.

Hrag, however, tore off a piece of bread, put a thick slice of cheese on it, and gave it to her. "Here. Maybe it'll do wonders for that foul temper of yours."

She glared at him. "You started it—"

"Eat, or I'm walking away."

Kharis blew a displeased huff and bit into the bread, gobbling the whole thing, and eyeing more. Hrag exhaled, annoyed, but tore another piece, added more cheese, and passed it to her. "You're worse than the hounds."

"Hrag?" she mumbled, half chewing. "Why was Leógham attacked?"

The amusement in his expression guttered. "Come. We're in everyone's way here."

She wolfed down the rest of her food and walked into the corridor with him. "Where's your uncle?"

He shrugged. "We're on high alert because of the ambush. He could be anywhere."

She sighed, brushing crumbs off her jerkin. "So, what are you doing on this oh-so-gorgeous-and-quiet day?"

Hrag smirked. "Oh, you know… playing nursemaid to an injured fool with a reckless tendency for trouble."

One of her eyebrows arched. "Well, aren't you lucky?"

"Absolutely. It's the highlight of my day." He grinned

briefly, then gazed into the distance as if the shape of things to come were sharper in that space.

"I'm going to the archery garden." The invitation would brighten his mood. "Want to come?"

A smile finally appeared on his face. "What do we do with them?" He gestured to their escort.

She leaned in slightly, her voice dipping into a conspiratorial whisper. "We could use them as targets."

He frowned at her, pondering whether she was serious. "Wait here."

"Don't take too long, or I'll use you for target practice, too."

Hrag gave her a long, daring look before striding back to the kitchens, presumably to arm himself with more food.

Kharis walked toward the large windows lining the corridor. Their view opened to the palace's eastern garden. Lord Darragh and Lady Sahrit walked arm in arm on a path in the garden, talking and smiling at each other. Her heart yearned for the same: to walk the garden in Leógham's arm without the need to hide their love from anyone.

"What are you doing?" Hrag had returned from the kitchens.

"Your parents are in the garden."

"They are?" He walked to the window and raised his eyebrows. "And they're so... so close, and where others can see them be that close."

She almost punched his arm. "Your parents love each other deeply. Why would they want to be apart?" She thought of Leógham. "I want a love like that, Hrag. For someone to love me as fiercely as your father loves your mother."

The confession startled Hrag. He hadn't noticed it before,

but now, with the light catching just right, it was impossible to ignore.

Benkhi was handsome.

The "pretty boy" rumors were true. Long, dark lashes framed striking gray eyes with a hint of silver. His hair, cut bluntly to fall below his jaw, flowed like glossy, black silk, sometimes slipping forward to curtain his face. But now, tucked neatly behind his ears, his features were fully visible.

Fires burn me.

Heat licked at Hrag's face. He shook off whatever absurd thought had crept into his head. "Are we going or what?" he barked, louder than necessary.

Benkhi blinked out of his trance, then grinned—the kind that signaled trouble.

"Of course, Lord Prince Hrag." He gave an exaggerated bow, sweeping his arm dramatically.

Hrag scowled. "Stop teasing."

Benkhi smirked, utterly unrepentant.

As they walked down the corridor, Hrag glanced at their ever-present escort. "So... are we still using them for target practice?"

"Absolutely." Benkhi spun in front of him, walking backward. "Ten points for the ones in black and red. Twenty for those in black and gold. What do you say?"

Hrag barked a laugh. "And what does the winner get? You know, the one with the most points?"

A kiss?

The thought hit him like a slap. *Flames take me.* Heat surged up his neck.

Benkhi only grinned, that maddening glint still in his eyes. Hrag tore his gaze away, pulse hammering, and forced a scoff, rougher than he meant. "Whatever."

What in the Fires is wrong with me?

Yet, that forbidden thought smoldered all the same.

84

BENEATH THE
SHADOW OF FATE

Beneath the shadow of fate, even the strongest wings forget how to fly. Its chains do not bind the body— they shackle the will. - Poliormos

Amid archery practice, the royal guard arrived— towers of black and gold. Muscled, disciplined men sporting unfriendly stares. Their boots struck the stone in perfect rhythm. Across their chests gleamed the insignia of the Hegran king: a crowned dragon, wrought in gold, sitting in a field of black, one claw raised to clutch a burning orb.

Kharis and Hrag had barely exchanged a glance when the captain spoke.

"Lord Prince Hrag. You have been summoned."

It wasn't a request.

Hrag's expression barely flickered, sporting the look of a man who understood his fate had just been sealed. He rubbed the back of his neck before casting her a dry, knowing glance.

"This should be fun." But Hrag wasn't smiling as they escorted him out.

Tomorrow, Leógham would leave, and the thought unsettled Kharis more than she could admit. Would she return from the north? Was tomorrow the last time she'd ever see him? And if she didn't come back, would Leógham mourn her... or hate her for her decision?

Back inside, the castle hummed with movement. Servants darted past with crates or armfuls of supplies. Guards marched in tight formation. Captains whispered over sealed scrolls and orders with a justiciar, their faces tight with purpose.

Lost in her thoughts, Kharis rounded the corner and nearly collided with a cluster of servants, some of them quietly weeping. Ailene was among them, whispering comfort.

"What is it?" Kharis asked, concerned.

Ailene broke away, curtsying quickly. Her eyes darted toward the men shadowing Kharis. "It's Juell, My Lord," she said. "Today is—" A ragged sob stopped her.

Kharis didn't need Ailene to finish. The thought struck a dark spark in her heart. Perhaps it was Juell's fate—or the weight of everything that had happened since Kharis's arrival—but the truth was the same: Hegran justice knew no mercy. Today, it would claim another life, and soon enough, it would come for her and Leógham. The tiny flame inside her ignited. *Better to burn than to kneel.*

"Ready my horse," she commanded. "Now."

A servant sprinted toward the stables. Kharis's escort stiffened, exchanging wary glances.

"My Lord?" Ailene's brow furrowed. "What are you doing?"

"Enough is enough." Her decision could unravel everything she'd worked to protect: her disguise, her safety, perhaps even her life. But the time for inaction was over. Today, she'd choose justice. "There comes a time when one must decide how to move forward. For me, that time has come."

"But My Lord," Ailene insisted. "It isn't safe. You mustn't—"

She faced her escort. "I hope you know how to ride. Let's go."

One guard gestured in the opposite direction, toward wherever Leógham was. "But—"

Kharis was already moving.

85

WRATH AND RESOLVE

> *Rise from the ashes, like the phoenix of old, to reclaim what you lost. Rise to ignite a new fire fueled by hope.*
> *- Poliormos*

Kharis reached the stables and mounted Bada. Within moments, she tore through the gates on her way to the village.

A crowd had already gathered at the square, a sea of dark cloaks and heads. From atop Bada, Kharis caught sight of Juell—ragged, weeping, her knees buckling as guards dragged her toward the raised stage, where the block waited.

"Unhand her," Kharis shouted.

The people gasped, a ripple of sound sweeping the square. Slowly, the mass shifted, parting for her. Cloaks and shawls brushed against Bada's flanks. Men and women stumbled back, making way for the rider defying Hegran law.

Chief Harrald froze mid-proclamation, scroll trembling in his hand. Guards stiffened.

"Unhand her," Kharis said again, with fire in her voice. "I won't repeat myself."

417

Harrald's gaze fell on her baldric, identifying her as the crown prince's fosterling. With a reluctant nod from Harrald, the two guards released Juell, who fell to her knees. Shackles had rubbed her wrists and ankles raw, the skin red and torn. Someone had hacked her hair most savagely, sections of her scalp still bleeding.

The sight ignited Kharis's anger all over again. *How is this justice?*

"My Lord." Harrald approached gingerly, bowing low. "We are honored—"

"Honored?" Kharis could barely curb her sarcasm. "Those who accuse should always face the consequences of their accusations. They who send another to the block should wield the axe themselves."

Harrald faltered. "Are you here to—?"

"Absolutely not." Her voice carried. "Juell wronged me by entering my chambers without permission, but theft she didn't commit. Her actions do not warrant this harsh penalty."

The captain of the guard stepped forward. His beard was a wiry tangle, his uniform straining at the seams, buckles biting into a swelling gut. Yet his breastplate gleamed, polished to a mirror shine—proof of a man determined to do his duty, even if he was never quite sure what he was stepping into.

"We're here to uphold Hegran law, My Lord," he said, voice firm with practiced authority. "Men of your standing shouldn't trouble themselves with such unseemly work. Best leave it to soldiers, not to hands meant for quills rather than blades."

"Quills?" Kharis tilted her head. "Not... swords?"

The captain gave a confident nod, missing the edge in her voice entirely. "Aye. Leave the wench to us, My Lord." He bowed, pleased with his own gallantry.

She tapped the pommel of her sword, considering, then dismounted, tossing Bada's reins and her cloak to Harrald.

Facing the stout captain, she said, "I could entertain you with the fruits of my long, *long* quill."

Laughter rippled through the crowd. The captain turned to his men, confused. One of them shrugged.

"Or perhaps," she purred, "with my very, *very* sharp sword."

She unsheathed it. Alarm swept through the villagers, feet scuffing against the dirt as they stumbled back. Even the guards shifted uneasily, hands twitching toward their hilts but not daring to draw against the crown prince's protégé.

"A challenge, then. Here and now, Captain." She smiled dangerously. "What shall it be: words or blades?"

A few villagers snickered.

The captain held himself with rigid formality, though he scratched his head, slightly bewildered. He glanced at his men. One tapped his sword, encouraging a sword fight. Another slapped the soldier's head. The captain faced her, lips pinched for a moment. "B—Blades...?"

The guards stiffened. One muttered a curse. The silence shattered into murmurs.

Kharis sighed, shoulders dropping, and sheathed her sword.

"Next time," she said, "I'll demand words, Captain—over ale, perhaps?" She winked, and his face turned as red as a flycatcher's plumage.

Her voice then carried across the square. "With the entertainment over, let us see to justice." She turned to Chief Harrald. "Master of Dríeadh village, Juell wronged me, and I alone have the right to pass sentence. I call on Hegran Law."

The captain straightened with a grimace. "My Lord, that isn't—"

"But it is," came another voice from behind the crowd.

All heads turned. Eyes widened next. The villagers parted to make way for Leógham, mounted on Balyus, and his escort. Everyone bowed low.

Kharis inclined her head and faced Chief Harrald once more. "So, what say you in this matter?"

Harrald pursed his lips, glancing toward the crown prince to gauge how this should go. Leógham gave him nothing.

"Hegran Law," Harrald admitted at last.

Murmurs spread through the crowd.

"Your Highness, what say you?" Kharis called out to Leógham.

"The Crown remains impartial and meddles not where the Law has spoken, lest it forgets what justice means. Therefore, Hegran Law, of course."

Kharis smiled at him before her voice rang out. "Juell, stand and face my judgment."

Juell, still on her knees, wept openly. Two guards hauled her upright, but her legs quaked so violently she could barely stand. The crowd stirred, whispering, as the guards brought her forward.

Juell stood barefoot before Kharis, her shift little more than coarse wool scraped raw at the seams. Her youth struck like a wound. The sight hollowed the moment for Kharis. If her disguise ever failed, this would be her, too. Stripped, paraded, and judged without mercy. She loathed Hegra, yet beneath her hatred flickered a vision of what Hegra could become if properly guided.

With the weight of fate upon her, she spoke: "Juell, you shall live."

Gasps rippled through the gathering.

Someone grunted, "He spares a thief?"

The guards exchanged uneasy glances. The captain's face mottled red, but he didn't speak. Chief Harrald dipped his head, tight-lipped, looking as though a great weight had lifted from his shoulders. Leógham arched a questioning brow, but said nothing, his silence assent.

Juell sagged in the guards' grip, half-collapsing, her sobs raw and shuddering. She may not have stolen from Kharis, but by spying on the people she had come to claim as family, Juell had committed a deeper betrayal.

Kharis went on, "For the span of seven winters, you shall serve this village, repaying the wrong you have done. But let all bear witness: your servitude shall not strip you of dignity. No hand shall strike you in anger or scorn. No man nor woman shall force you in lust or degrade you in despair. You will serve with labor, not with your body; with toil, not with humiliation. So long as you uphold this penance with obedience and honor, your life is yours to keep."

Kharis lifted her chin. "Chief Harrald, do you agree to my conditions?"

Harrald exhaled softly, a faint smile breaking through the stern lines of his face. "I do."

"And you, Juell, will you fulfill the sentence set forth?"

Her lips trembled as she nodded, her voice a whisper lost in the wind. "I will."

The land's enchantment rolled over the crowd like a tide, washing away the bloodlust that had nearly claimed Juell's life to seal a Hegran promise. The guards loosened their grip on Juell. Murmurs rose. Harrald's brow furrowed with dawning respect.

Juell broke down, tears glinting in the pale light as she tried—and failed—to express her gratitude.

Kharis took her riding cloak from Harrald and draped it around Juell's thin shoulders, tightening the hood over the girl's bald head. "It's over. Serve your sentence with dignity." She turned to Chief Harrald. "Can I trust you to provide her with clothing, a bed, and meals, so that her sentencing may be fulfilled according to Hegran Law?"

Harrald bowed. "I shall. And may this mercy strengthen justice always, a balance our Law necessitates."

Guards quickly removed Juell's shackles. Around Kharis, the murmurs faded. As Harrald led Juell away, the wind that swept the square carried the faint scent of thawing earth.

⁊❧

On the ride back to Dríeadh Manor, Leógham had remained silent, a soft, unreadable smile fixed on his face. Their escort rode close, the clatter of hooves echoing against the frozen road.

"I wasn't sure what to expect," he said at last, "when the guards came to fetch me with such urgency." His curious glance lingered on her.

Kharis turned in her saddle. "I had wondered what became of them."

Leógham's stare narrowed on her. "Why did you do it?"

Why had she risked herself after the ambush? Why leave the castle's safety? Why defy expectations and pardon Juell?

"It was my first step," she said. "A step that allows Hegra to move forward, because it has been stuck for a long time."

Leógham regarded her for a long moment. "What you did back there... It was brave. I cannot meddle in affairs of Hegran Law, but you—" His gaze softened. "You did what I couldn't—"

⁊❧

The world tilted for a breath. Leógham caught himself on the saddle pommel, blinking hard. Two nights with hardly any sleep had left his body brittle, his thoughts drifting like smoke.

"Leógham?" Kharis's voice cut through the haze, tight with concern. "Are you all right?"

He managed a small smile. "Just tired."

Without a word, Kharis drew Bada closer until their knees brushed. Reaching across, she caught the near rein of Leógham's bridle and steadied his horse with her own. "Close your eyes." She kept her gaze fixed ahead. "I have you."

Leógham let the reins slacken in his hand. Trust—so simple, so complete—flowed between them like breath. He smiled with the quiet knowledge that love was also surrender.

"Your sense of justice isn't implacable," he said. "It's merciful. Wise. Capable of transforming Hegra into what it could—should—be." The fog in his mind thinned. "I, too, must ponder my first step."

Exhaustion pressed heavier. Hegra, cruel and beautiful, never let him forget that he was the crown prince of a realm still broken, its peace a fragile truce held together by oaths and fear. Some cowards would slit his throat for the crown he bore. And love—his gaze slid to Kharis—was the most fragile thing of all.

Rest would never come while those he loved were in danger.

PART V

THE JOURNEY BEGINS

THE GAMES FATE PLAYS

Beware the threads of fate. Stray from your path, and they will weave your downfall. - Poliormos

It was still dark when someone knocked on Kharis's door. She ignored it. The down covers were warm and too comfortable to leave. And today, she deserved her rest.

The knocking became more insistent.

When servants knocked and received no response, they would walk away and return later. This wasn't it. The knocking turned into a pounding, and a furious voice drifted from the other side.

"Open up," Hrag hollered as he banged on the door.

Kharis drew the covers over her head, hoping he'd go away if she ignored him.

"Benkhi," he shouted. "I know you're in there."

No. He wouldn't be going away. Kharis got up and looked for her robe.

"What's taking you so long?" Hrag kicked the door, and the thick wood wavered. "Open this door, or I swear—"

She unlocked and cracked it open slightly. Angry forest-green eyes flashed at her.

"What do you want?" she barked.

Hrag clicked his tongue and pushed on the door. Kharis pushed back harder, keeping him out.

"Whatever," he spat. "Get ready. We're leaving in an hour."

"We...?"

"Are you dense or what? We're leaving for Ashtalon." He kicked the door again. "I can't believe I had to come and get you myself." He loudly aired that and many other complaints as he made his way down the corridor.

Kharis locked the door and threw herself on the bed, wondering whether she could fall asleep again.

"Leaving? Ha!"

She sank her face into the pillows, hoping they would swallow her—

The knocking returned.

Kharis groaned. "Blasted Hrag. Can't you leave me alone?" Grumbling, she unfastened the lock and threw the door open. "What is it now?"

Leógham stared at her, bewildered, offering a timid smile and assessing whether it was safe to enter.

Kharis stilled, lips pinched. "I... I didn't know it was you."

He donned full regalia: a polished breastplate chased with gold, a sword at his side, and a black-and-red cloak embroidered with the dragon of House Hegra. Even with the bruises on his face, he looked so handsome she feared she'd melt.

"Why must you be so tall?" she asked, looking up.

Leógham walked in and quietly closed the door behind him. "Some say I have Arrani blood."

A brow arched. "Arrani?"

"Arran was the realm of the giants, the last stronghold against the Haguru conquest. Hegra takes its name from the Haguru." A quick grin flickered across his face as he

428

presented her with a few pieces of clothing. "We're leaving soon."

She turned to the window. "In the dark?"

"Yes," he said. "It's a day's ride to Ashtalon. I want to reach it before nightfall." He handed her the garments. "These are for you. Get dressed and meet us downstairs." He was about to open the door.

"Wait." She was supposed to stay—had planned for it. And while Leógham was in Ashtalon, she'd head north and fulfill her destiny. "Why am I going?"

"Because I'm not leaving you behind unguarded. What happened..." His eyes roamed the floor with a hesitant pause. "It was my fault."

Kharis frowned. "How was the ambush your fault?"

"I didn't think." His jaw clenched. "I should've brought an escort, been more careful. I thought only of what I wanted, and that decision ended up hurting you."

"Leógham—"

"That arrow could've killed you." He squeezed his eyes shut. "The arrow meant for me." His arms wrapped around her, drawing her to him. "I won't leave you here. Alone. Without my protection. I fear it could happen again."

With half her face pressed against his armored chest, she could feel how fast his heart was pounding.

The journey to Ashtalon would add days she couldn't afford. Each step in the wrong direction risked the world she was meant to protect. Yet going to the capital also meant meeting the man who'd hunted Leógham and his family: Lord Saigham. If she went north, Saigham could still strike, and if he succeeded in killing Leógham while she chased the whisper calling her north... Then what? Her fingers curled. If fate demanded a sacrifice, she wouldn't offer Leógham first.

Kharis lifted her gaze, the decision made. "Fine. I'll go with you."

She hefted the brigandine, surprised by its weight. She

traced the faint bumps of the rivets underneath. Metal plates lay hidden beneath, hundreds of them overlapping like scales. *Arrows won't be touching this.*

Leógham fiddled with his cape, then cleared his throat. "Could I check on the injuries?"

Despite herself, a smirk tugged at her lips. He'd checked her every day without fail.

With her nod, he unfastened the ties on her shift and gingerly traced the pink spot below her collarbone, pressing around it. "No infection. No tenderness. No scar." The tightness in his face eased. He turned her around and pulled on the fabric to expose the back of her shoulder. His touch was gentle, almost timid. "The healing is exceptional. Like it never happened. Any pain?"

She shook her head.

"Good." His voice deepened, sending shivers down her spine. His fingers explored, and she wondered if he wanted what she wanted. His hands grew bolder as they brushed against her back, gently guiding her to turn. The intensity of his eyes spiked her pulse.

"I wouldn't mind doing it again," he said.

She raised her eyebrows, confused. And definitely dizzy. "Do what?"

"Kiss you." He leaned in, his nose almost brushing against hers.

His hand cradled the small of her back. With a simple tug, his lips would be devouring her. Her body shuddered, wanting—waiting—to be devoured.

She closed her eyes, ever so tempted by this man, and took a deep breath. "Kneel, Crown Prince Leógham." She meant it as a joke, but to her surprise, he dropped to one knee, gazing at her while he gripped her hips. Despite everything he'd witnessed, he still wanted to kiss her.

Perhaps she was his monster.

She kissed him—a soft, sweet press of lips.

Hungry, Leógham kissed her back, his hands slowly

running up and down the back of her legs. He drew her closer, and his kiss deepened. His flood of passion crushed her, and she surrendered to him. Her knees landed on the rug, and then she was on her back, the weight of man and metal a tantalizing treat.

His breath mingled with hers, tasting of heat and longing. The rough scrape of his beard against her cheek only fed the fire, sparking a deeper hunger. His mouth claimed hers, slow, savoring, until she trembled with the sheer ache of wanting more.

The horn blew. He stopped, breathing hard.

She cursed the hornblower.

"First call," he said, panting as he sat on his knees. "The carriage is ready."

"I'd better get ready, then." Kharis rose, but Leógham wrapped his arms around her waist and pressed his head on her abdomen.

"Thank you," he breathed out.

"For the kiss?"

"Without you, I would've died that day." He inhaled deeply as if he'd finally said something that had been caught in his chest for three days. "I'll spend the rest of my life repaying your courage so that you never regret saving me."

He gazed up at her with his intense emerald eyes.

Was it love? Gratitude? Possession? Kharis no longer cared. She was his monster.

"How—?" His posture faltered. "How do I mend my mistake? How do I make you happy—utterly, completely? How do I earn your smile?"

His questions unraveled her, stealing every thought from her mind. A warmth rose beneath her ribs, and before she knew it, a quiet smile slipped free.

She stroked his hair, fingers getting lost in his curls. "When you love, you can't command or demand obedience. It's the opposite. You're commanded. You surrender. If you wish to make me happy, accept that I need the freedom to make my choices, good and bad. If you love me, let me go, and trust that I'll always return to you."

The set of his jaw loosened. "I love you, and I love it when you quote Poliormos."

She smiled at her kneeling prince.

"You mean everything to me." He hugged her again, tighter, more resolute, his cheek pressed against the warmth of her.

A surge of emotions washed over her, but also a profound sense of belonging. Was this love? Not a single emotion, but a symphony of them, making her soul dance?

Softer now, he said, "After what happened, I feared I wasn't your everything anymore." His brow creased. "I had failed you, and you were injured because of it. How could you love someone like me—?"

"Stop."

The glimpse he'd offered… The irony scorched her like a poker.

"Know this," she said. "To protect those I care about, I'll do anything. Love drives my reckless heart to guard those I hold dear, and you"—her breath hitched with emotion—"are one of them. I'll protect you with my life if needed."

His lips parted, but the words faltered. "Do you"—his voice was hoarse, uncertain—"love me?"

He remained on his knees, gazing at her, waiting for an answer that would define his life from this moment forward.

Kharis closed her eyes, sensing the threads of fate tightening around her. Her answer would also define her life from this moment forward. She couldn't explain this man's pull on her, the gravity that had drawn her toward him, nor the familiar intimacy that vibrated between them, because despite his rough edges, guarded heart, and flaws—Leógham fit.

So she met his eyes, coming to terms with her truth. "Yes. I do."

Leógham's breath caught. Then, slowly, like dawn

breaking after a long, bitter night, his face transformed. A smile, small at first, bloomed into radiance. His eyes sparkled, fiercely alive. He rose slowly, carefully. His hands trembled as he reached for her, reverent fingers brushing her face.

"I'll become worthy of you," he said.

Kharis stilled. Undone by this man once more, she kissed him. He deepened the kiss, pressing her against him. His arms held her tightly before he slowly pulled away, gazing at her. "My day is unfolding as it should."

Kharis narrowed her eyes. "I should throw you out the window."

He chuckled as he moved toward the door, fingers working the lock. But before he opened it, he turned back to her, gaze lingering. "I mean it," he said softly. "I love you."

Warmth fluttered through her chest.

"And I'm glad you're coming willingly," he added with an unmistakable glint in his eyes. "Otherwise, I'd have to fling you over my shoulder and carry you downstairs."

She crossed her arms in reflex. "You would have?"

"If you hadn't, yes." His voice held no jest now. "Hegran promise. I can't leave you behind. Ever."

She pulled at her sleeve. "How... exactly?"

"Ancient magic binds our promises as an eternal contract. I'm never leaving your side, and you're never leaving mine."

That stopped her cold. She swallowed hard. "So wherever you go, I must go?"

"Yes."

"And wherever I go, you go?"

He gave her a curious look. "Yes."

The answer hit her like an unexpected blow. She'd planned to go north, one way or another, but now...?

Her voice cracked. "What happens if we don't fulfill the contract?"

His brow furrowed in thought. His tone was matter-of-fact. "The contract is unbreakable. Not fulfilling it brings such unbearable pain that you're forced to yield to the promise made."

No, no, no. Dread curled tight in her chest. She felt dizzy, a bead of sweat tracing down her spine. *He'll never go with me. And now I can't go without him.*

Leógham grinned, his emeralds gleaming with joy. "You're stuck with me. *Forever.*"

And with that, he closed the door behind him.

Kharis couldn't move, her heart hammering so hard it lodged in her throat. If she couldn't go north...

Her breath hitched.

There would be no Leógham.

No Hegra.

Only an endless beginning again.

A STORM APPROACHES

> *To love fiercely is to become a fortress, standing tall against any storm that comes our way. - Poliormos*

Kharis wasn't sure how she managed to dress. Her hands wouldn't stop trembling. How was she supposed to go north now that she was chained to Leógham's side?

Her last piece was the baldric: a broad strap of black leather lined in crimson, its silver buckles gleaming. Artisans had tooled the dragon of House Hegra into the leather above her heart. Once she wore it, she became more than herself. This baldric marked her as the crown prince's fostered protégé. She drew it across her chest, left shoulder to right hip, as Leógham had instructed, to show his authority and protection.

After one last look in the mirror, she heaved a long sigh: gambeson with an itchy collar, brigandine with Leógham's colors, vambraces, riding cloak.

What awaits us in the capital? The thought clawed at her. She worried about her disguise, this journey, her derailed mission to the north, and whether this relentless chaos would smother her.

"Why are we even going to Ashtalon?" She clicked her tongue, stepped out, then halted in her tracks.

Flowers?

In vases, and in bundles, ribbons knotted with care. They lined her doorway as though every hand in Hegra had stopped to pluck a bloom and place it there. Flowers—so rare in this wintry land—that their abundance felt almost impossible. For a moment, Hegra's ugliness faded, replaced by color, fragrance, and kindness. A smile touched her lips.

Downstairs, Master Neagh and Mistress Ailene waited. House servants lined the base of the stairs, all bowing low as soon as she appeared, surprising her.

"Good morning, Lord Benkhi," Ailene said first, her smile bright.

Kharis hesitated, puzzled. Was this customary when Lords left the castle?

"Good morning." She bowed in return, drawing a few stifled giggles from the back. "Um… There were flowers by my door."

"Gestures of appreciation," Ailene said. "For saving Juell. The girl was too naïve to see the scheme that entrapped her. But thanks to you, she lives."

Murmurs and nods rippled through the servants.

"It means," Ailene went on, "that what you did for her, you would do for any of us."

Gratitude now shone where fear had once lingered, brimming with warmth. Her intervention had been her first step, yet already Kharis sensed that others would follow.

"Lord Benkhi." Neagh stepped forward and presented her with the Dragon's Bane.

She blinked a few times, convinced she'd lost it during the ambush. "And this?"

"Lord Hrag searched for it," Neagh replied. "He had it cleaned, resharpened, and wished for you to wear it."

Another smile broke through. That Hrag—sullen, sharp-tongued, and utterly annoying Hrag—had gone to such lengths for her was unthinkable. She sighed quietly, her heart torn between exasperation at his moods and gratitude for the affection hidden in his deeds. She strapped it to her belt and followed Neagh. The servants bowed again as she passed, lining her path with reverence.

"They're still bowing," Kharis whispered.

"As they should," Neagh answered simply.

Once out, she crossed the deserted upper bailey. Dawn was still hours away; the torches guttered in the darkness as sounds reached her first: the clanging of armor, the neighs and whinnies of horses, shouted commands, and hooves stomping on cobblestones.

The sight stunned her next.

Limned in golden light, at least a hundred and fifty strong, the royal escort stretched across the lower bailey in disciplined formation. Black-and-gold banners snapped in the wind.

She counted dozens of mounted guards, their polished breastplates catching the torchlight. Foot soldiers stood in tight ranks, flanking rows of flag bearers, supply wagons, and a heavily armed rear guard. Menacing imperial officers flanked the royal carriage bearing Sahrit and her attendants, their dark uniforms stark against the polished wood and gold filigree.

This was no simple escort. It was a public statement—a show of power.

Darragh and Hrag chatted beside their horses, waiting for the signal to mount and set out. Both wore breastplates with segmented pauldrons and vambraces.

Darragh's breastplate was ornate, bearing the arms of his clan: a single pine tree at the center, surrounded by elaborate, sinuous floral and vine designs.

Hrag's armor, like Leógham's, bore the royal emblem of House Hegra: a fiery dragon with outstretched wings, its form beautifully etched into the metal. Intricate, raised flame patterns coiled along the sides and back, catching the light as he moved.

Why isn't Hrag wearing Forest Kin armor? Paternal affiliation was the rule, and Darragh was Forest Kin. Had she overlooked something?

Hrag spotted her and waved his arm enthusiastically. Darragh caught his son's gesture, and his gaze followed the object of his attention. Kharis waved back, parting her thick cloak to show him she wore the Dragon's Bane. Hrag smiled and gave her a two-finger salute.

"There you are," Leógham greeted, his eyes bright with excitement. "Did you enjoy the flowers?" He glanced aside, almost shy. "I added a few myself."

"It was unexpected."

"A well-deserved surprise," he said warmly. "So, will you ride with Sahrit or with me?"

Kharis looked at the carriage, pondering. "What should Lord Benkhi do?"

"Ride with me."

"And what should Lady Kharis do?"

"Still ride with me." He smiled.

She stared at him, not particularly amused. "Given these options," she tapped her lips as if pondering a tricky question, "I choose to ride with you."

"Great choice," he said with a flashy grin. "And I have the perfect horse. Come."

A groom brought Bada around, decked out with royal colors.

Happy to see the mare, Kharis approached and caressed its muzzle, letting the horse take in her scent. "I'm sorry that day was a frightful one for you. I won't let anything happen to you, I swear."

Leógham stiffened at the ambush reference but didn't say anything. He helped Kharis up, mounted Balyus, then signaled to start. Horns sounded. Soldiers readied. The cavalry mounted their steeds.

Soon, the cavalcade moved.

Kharis and Leógham had cleared the gates when Hrag trotted up to Leógham.

"Uncle, a word?"

Leógham offered Kharis a tight smile, then glared at Hrag. "Could it wait?"

"No," was Hrag's curt response.

Leógham breathed out, as if already aware of Hrag's discontent, and turned to Kharis with a "Stay here." They rode ahead a short distance before Hrag's hands began slicing the air in quick, frustrated motions. Leógham answered with a rigid set to his shoulders. The tension was unmistakable.

Kharis shook her head in disbelief.

Sahrit was harder to read. Unlike her brother or son, easily flummoxed, she maintained an outward sense of stability. She wore it like a thin veneer of duty and responsibility, held in place by obligation but slowly cracking and falling apart. Kharis worried no one could see it. One day, Sahrit would explode, and Leógham's dark moods would seem like child's play in comparison.

Darragh rode up to her with a smile that suggested he was up to something.

"Yes?" Kharis kept her eyes ahead.

"What did you do?"

"About what?"

"Leógham was purring like a well-fed kitten."

That "kitten" was about to pounce on Hrag like a snowcat. "Lord Darragh, what are you insinuating?"

"Absolutely nothing." Mischief danced in the man's smile. "He seems to behave when beaten into submission."

She glared at him. "I can extend you the courtesy."

He laughed. "Remind me never to cross you."

Kharis gave him a dark smile. "You already did. Once. You won't get a reminder next time." She hadn't forgotten how he'd grabbed her hand by force in the forest, stealing her secrets.

"Hmm, it appears you're in a foul mood."

"Well, I can't see why I'm coming."

"You don't?" His gaze fell on Leógham, then returned to her. "It's clear as day that a lovely flower has captivated the crown prince."

"Well, I pity the flower." A pause. "Lord Darragh, wouldn't my presence complicate things?"

Darragh frowned. "You have a point, but the Lord Crown Prince sees it differently."

Kharis grunted. *Hegrans and their overuse of honorifics.* "Lord Darragh, would you allow me an observation?"

Intrigued, he nodded.

"Neither Lord Leógham nor Lord Hrag wishes to go to the capital. Why is this?"

Darragh was pensive for a moment. "Tension is high with an enemy kingdom, but cruel winds are fanning the flames of discord within Hegra. Leógham has no children, so my son will be Heir Apparent."

Ah! So that was why Hrag wore the Fire Dweller crest today. A public declaration. A forced one.

Darragh's tone was tight, his agreement flat, lacking conviction. Kharis didn't need him to say it. His disapproval was evident. Suddenly, the argument between Leógham and Hrag made sense. She didn't think Hrag wanted it, either.

"Since I'm not a Fire Dweller," Darragh said, "some would vehemently resist Hrag's ascension to the throne when the time came."

Leógham rode ahead with Hrag, both ill-tempered and sulking, neither talking to the other now.

"I see," she muttered.

"The Fire Dwellers have an oath with the Forest Kin, but

some Hegran Houses, especially those adhering to purity laws, don't see it with good eyes."

Purity laws?

"And why is that?" she asked.

"The conditions of the Oath of Alliance allowed King Aghavor to wed Princess Mauve, Leógham's mother, thereby opening the way for intermarriage between our kingdoms. It was that same provision that made my marriage to Sahrit possible years later."

His voice changed whenever he spoke her name—softer, quieter, carrying a deep longing.

"Some Houses," he went on, "believe such dilution of lineages is... problematic."

Her hands tightened around the reins. "Are there people against Leógham's ascension?"

"Indeed. He's not a full-blooded Fire Dweller."

Her eyes widened. "But he's Hegran, Aghavor's son. Lineage follows the paternal—"

"For some, it isn't enough," Darragh cut in. "Purity laws began as a safeguard after the Haguru conquest. Silent dissent became statute."

Her stomach churned. *So much to learn.* Her ignorance would single her out. She was riding toward Ashtalon, the proverbial wolves' den. There, those who despised Leógham would stage a different kind of ambush. Every muscle in her body tensed.

"Further," Darragh continued, "the ambush in Leógham's lands is an insult he can't ignore. That you were injured— well, let's just say it burns him deeply."

"Who wants him dead?"

"Saigham."

There was that name again.

"It makes no sense," she said. "Going to Ashtalon is like jumping into the dragon's mouth."

Darragh half-smiled. "True, but that's Leógham. He likes to stare death in the eye. I've known him since he was seven.

He binds himself to those who matter most to him. Yet what can he do when love and loathing circle the same place? How does he choose? And does he truly get to choose?" He sighed, a note of wistfulness in his voice.

Kharis tightened her grip on the reins and wondered if it was already too late—if she'd been swallowed whole by the chaos to come.

88

ANSWERS AND QUESTIONS

*Some questions are lanterns meant for the long road
—they must be lit one at a time, or their light will
blind you. - Poliormos*

The road unspooled toward Ashtalon.

When the cavalcade halted for a water break, Kharis swung a stiff leg over the saddle and dismounted, her muscles aching from hours in the saddle. Bada snorted clouds of steam into the cooling air. Muted tones of gray shaded Hegra's landscape. The woods stood eerily silent, only icy air biting at her cheeks.

Darragh, who had ridden beside her, dismounted without a word.

Ahead, Leógham and Hrag were at it again, their faces flushed as they bickered in low, clipped tones. Kharis considered walking over. Common sense tugged at her ear. Kharis would get her answers soon enough. Whether she wanted them was another matter.

Turning on a heel, she strode toward the carriage to check on Lady Sahrit. A column of the king's soldiers flanked the vehicle, their demeanor intense. Scowling faces.

Rigid postures. But when they saw her baldric, their gazes flattened and their scowls faded.

Kharis tapped lightly on the carriage window. "Lady Sahrit?"

The curtain rustled. Sahrit peeked from behind it, pressing a single finger to her lips. Behind her, her attendants slept.

She quietly climbed out with Kharis's help and smoothed her skirt. "How are you doing, Lord Benkhi?"

"Sore," was Kharis's answer.

Sahrit released a quiet sigh. "I'm sorry we dragged you into this and that you were hurt because of clan politics. I apologize for my brother, who forced you to come. I asked him to let you stay, but I couldn't convince him." She brushed strands from her face, her gaze sweeping the front of the cavalcade. "He feels responsible for what happened and hasn't forgiven himself. Worse, I see how it torments him, because you're precious to him."

A bloom of heat flushed Kharis's face.

"Would you walk with me?" Sahrit asked. "My legs could use it."

Kharis offered her arm in quiet gallantry. "Where shall we go?"

Sahrit looped her arm through Kharis's and gestured toward a stretch of trees. "When I was younger, these woods were exquisite. Hegra's lands were lush, painted in endless shades of green. Wildflowers spilled color everywhere."

She paused, eyes distant. Then, slowly, she tugged off her gloves.

"Lady Sahrit," Kharis said, voice trembling. "Your fingers —they're swollen."

Sahrit only smiled, studying them with quiet detachment. "Think nothing of it. These wounds will heal." She reached out, brushing her hand against the rough bark of a tree with a melancholy sheen. "My beloved Hegra is dying. Ice flowers are spreading, choking all roots and freezing the land. One day, they'll freeze us all."

Her foot slipped on an icy patch. Kharis reached out without thinking, fingers closing around Sahrit's hand to steady her.

"Thank you." Sahrit's gaze lifted then, tracing the height of the spindly tree, its slender branches stretching toward the sky. "A young tree, yet deserving the glory of a wide canopy and centuries beneath the turning seasons, wouldn't you say?"

Kharis gave a brisk nod.

Warmth bloomed around her cold-numbed fingers. She glanced down and found a thin mist shimmering where Sahrit's hand had closed over hers. From Sahrit's other palm, still pressed to the trunk, a soft golden light pulsed outward, rippling through the lifeless branches.

The glow was so dazzling—

A jolt ripped through her, its flash swallowing her vision.

The world dissolved.

Kharis staggered back, grasping at nothing. When she regained her footing, her boots didn't meet the frozen earth of Hegra. Scorched, sandy shores stretched before her. Ahead, a lake of fire sprawled across the landscape, magic roiling beneath the surface. Its heat pulsed, distorting the world into a feverish blur. Orange flames shot skyward in violent bursts. Embers swirled in the hot gusts, flaring and vanishing into the ether. Beneath her boots, the sand stirred as vibrations deepened into a low, rhythmic thrum. The sound swelled until it became a voice.

"*Come.*"

Sahrit's command reverberated through the air. The threads of this world drew taut, the moment suspended— waiting for Kharis's permission.

Her lips parted. "Go."

The fog and steam peeled away, revealing the lake in its terrible glory. Flame tore across the scorched basin, devouring the horizon in a tide of searing gold and crimson. Wave after wave, the fire danced—flaring, crackling, coiling —until finally, the crescendo broke. In the heated air, a whisper of gratitude drifted, then was gone.

The air shifted, and with it, this world of fire.

Kharis drew a deep, shuddering breath, touched by the clean scent of ice and snow. Deep, lush green stretched before her. The young tree from before now stood vibrant and full of life.

"That should do it." Sahrit caressed the tree's smooth bark, treasuring it like a beloved child. Her fingers were no longer raw or swollen. The magic that had restored the trees had also healed her hands. She put on her gloves and clasped her hands neatly in front of her.

Kharis's thoughts collided. Sahrit had effortlessly commanded Kharis's magic, using it to heal the trees. But if Sahrit could pull one tree back from the brink, what of a forest? What of a realm?

Just then, Leógham strode toward them, his cloak billowing with his movement. "How are you doing?"

Always calm and collected, Sahrit dipped into a graceful curtsy. "It was nice to take a brief stroll with Lord Benkhi. Sitting in the carriage for so long can be trying."

Leógham inclined his head. "Do you wish to rest a little longer?"

"No. We should resume before the night's upon us."

"Very well." He turned to Kharis, his touch unexpectedly gentle as his hand rested on her shoulder. "And you, Lord Benkhi, how are you doing?"

Kharis didn't register the question. Alluring sounds had caught her attention.

Birds?

The forest had remained stubbornly silent all day. No rustling creatures. No chattering squirrels. Not even the lonely caws of distant crows.

But these were songbirds.

Glorious, lyrical chirps. High trills and melodious whistles. Beautiful and haunting. As if perfection had been… perfected?

Wait. These can't be birds. Someone was mimicking them. Her fingers tightened around the hilt of her sword.

"We're being watched," she said. "Listen."

Leógham's expression darkened. He glanced around, his brows furrowed. "I hear nothing."

"It's there," she insisted. "Birds—except they aren't birds."

His gaze met hers, and he shook his head again. He turned to Sahrit. "We'll continue soon. You should head to the carriage."

She curtsied in agreement. Kharis's stomach twisted with unease. Unseen eyes hid in the boughs, listening and watching. Leógham squeezed her shoulder again, a silent reassurance. His eyes softened as they swept over her face, then he turned away. The haunting calls of the not-birds lingered in the air.

"Lord Benkhi," Sahrit said. "Despite being a Fire Dweller, you seem to hear the Shin. They tend the woods and their creatures from birth to death. Their power hums in harmony with the world. Their music, or how they weave their magic into everything, is what you hear, but only the Forest Kin clan hears them."

A luminous smile unfurled across Sahrit's lips as if she were listening to something sacred.

"The Shin have been retreating from this world due to the ice flowers," she said. "Without them, our forests will die. However, your ability to pick up their murmurs fills me with joy." Her gaze held a quiet intensity. "It means a few remain."

Together, they walked toward the carriage.

"You hear the Shin," Kharis said. It wasn't a question.

"As members of the Forest Kin clan, Lord Darragh, my son, and I can. Leógham, however, does not. Which is why it fascinates me that you do."

Kharis's grip on her cloak tightened. "But you're a Fire Dweller. How can you hear them?"

"My mother was Forest Kin."

Kharis frowned, the answer making little sense. Wasn't magic passed down through the father's line? "I don't understand."

Sahrit barely raised an eyebrow, a gesture Kharis didn't miss. "Men pass their magic to all their children," Sahrit said. "Women, however, pass it only to their daughters. Thus, I carry the power of the Forest Kin through my mother and the Fire Dweller's through my father."

Kharis stiffened. *That means...* A thin thread of dread wove through her thoughts.

"You're unusual, Lord Benkhi." Sahrit's smile was genuine. "Women inherit two powers, while men inherit only one. And yet you carry two distinct magics."

A cold weight settled in her gut. Kharis forced a half-smile, offered no response, and pushed the moment aside by helping Sahrit into the carriage. With a quick bow, she marched toward Bada. *This isn't good.* One slip, and her disguise had unraveled, betrayed by magic. She cast a glance over her shoulder. *Does Sahrit know now?*

Around her, the cavalry readied their mounts. Pennons were raised. When the horn sounded, Kharis willed her sore legs to climb into the saddle, and Bada strode forward with the cavalcade.

Up ahead, Hrag and Darragh rode together, speaking in hushed tones.

Kharis glanced over her shoulder, frowning at the carriage. Sahrit's touch still warmed her fingers.

That was all it took. A deliberate touch. A gentle hold.

Sahrit's gesture had been innocent, but she'd wielded Kharis's power as if it were her own. Sahrit had asked for permission, yet Kharis now knew she hadn't needed it.

What if others did the same? Would they use her power to heal the land? Or would they drain her dry?

Touch.

This is why the prohibition exists. Her gaze fixed on Leógham's back like an arrow, fury coiling inside her. *Why couldn't he tell me this?*

He'd failed to explain the most crucial aspect of Hegran culture—the very foundation of their laws, their distance, their rigid rules. Covering one's skin, keeping one's distance. None of it was about etiquette or honor. It was survival. And she'd been oblivious to this. *A willing target.*

Her gestures, those small tokens of affection she cherished, were poison in Hegra, where touch meant power, ownership, and theft.

It all makes sense now.

And that terrified her most of all.

89

THE CAPITAL OF HEGRA

> *Truth is a silent warrior that conquers falsehood with its unwavering strength. - Poliormos*

T he cavalcade pressed forward, winding its way through the forest until the trees gave way to open farmlands and scattered hamlets.

Kharis straightened in the saddle. At last, she saw people along the roadside, peering from the edges of fields or leaning against crooked fences. In the distance, soot-smudged children peeked out from doorways. Then, as if the cold had choked the wonder from them, their gazes dulled, the spark extinguished before it could take root.

The land was dying. Dríeadh Manor had concealed this well, but in these poor hamlets, the truth was laid bare.

"*What shall you do?*" Ragha moved through her thoughts like a stiff wind. "*You are going in the opposite direction.*"

"I'll come up with something." She had to.

Ragha only hummed.

The villagers barely looked up. Most toiled with the slow, mechanical rhythm of people long resigned to survival. A few paused, only to stare with hollow eyes before bowing back to their labor.

No cheers. No smiling children darting after the soldiers. No excitement at a royal procession passing by. Even the clang of the blacksmith's hammer sounded tired.

Ahead, Leógham, Darragh, and Hrag rode in silence. Their earlier arguments had faded into nothing, replaced by the steady clop of hooves on the frozen ground. Even from behind, their moods were plain to all: backs stiff, shoulders squared, reins held tight. Even the wind, sharp and cutting, carried no voices—only the occasional creak of shifting armor.

The carriage curtains remained down, sealed tight, offering no sign of anticipation from within.

The cavalry officers, the foot soldiers, even the flag bearers—none wore so much as a hint of a smile. If there had been any joy when they left Dríeadh Manor, this place had devoured it.

Then, from the crest of the last hill, Kharis finally saw Ashtalon.

The capital sprawled beneath a bruised sky, its fortress crouched atop a hill like a solitary, brooding giant, hunched under the weight of time. It didn't stand tall in defiance, like the shining cities of old. It slumped. Heavy. Dejected.

A faint haze of smoke clung to the city's heart, rising from countless hearths. Beneath it, the city sprawled like a tattered, threadbare blanket left to gather dust. A city that should've been alive. A city that should've been great.

The capital of Hegra.

Gray.

Dull.

Bleak.

Somewhere in the distance, bells tolled. The sound crawled up the hill and died on the wind. Dense clouds covered Ashtalon like calloused hands, choking the world.

They'd been present in Dríeadh Manor, but here they were even more oppressive.

Leógham now rode at the front of the procession, her eyes fixed on his back. How many others were doing the same? Measuring the precise angle for a swift, silent arrow? Some, less bold, would bide their time, waiting for a single touch or a graze of skin to steal secrets or siphon power. Greed fueled the scheming to seize the Hegran throne, spawning a thousand plots. How were Leógham and Darragh to stay ahead of them?

Kharis sighed, shaking her head.

As the sun dipped behind the distant mountain range, the temperature plummeted. The freezing air closed in like hoarfrost creeping across glass, searching for a way inside, eager to wrap itself around Kharis's heart.

Somewhere in that place, maps would take her north, then... *Home.*

Ragha stirred in her mind like a cat stretching out after a good nap. *"Do you wish to return?"* His voice caressed her mind the way fingers tested for dust on a polished table.

Kharis poked the inside of her cheek. "Why wouldn't I want to?" She had only a name, Zahar-Ghak, and not much else. Then her eyes flicked to Leógham, and doubt crept in. Could she leave him behind?

"You never will," Ragha answered as if he'd known this all along. *"Yours is a choice made before you drew breath."* She understood from that tone that he had no intention of explaining anything.

"This place." His hum rumbled inside her head, scraping like rusted iron. *"I can tell nothing has changed. Betrayal lurks in dark corners. Rapacity drapes the walls."*

"You're chipper today," she muttered.

"Trust. No one." His insistence tasted of charcoal.

"Why?"

"Because everything you do here will decide whether all the

writings end. Head north, regardless of the cost," he rasped, his
voice dark and ominous.

Her stomach knotted. *The north.* "There's the small matter
of the Hegran promise—"

"So?" he asked, low and cutting. *"Head north, and he will
have no choice but to follow."*

"It's a betrayal of trust."

"And what shall you prefer: his hatred or his death?"

Her heart lurched. How could he ask her to do this?

"I hate you."

"And I have deserved every ounce of it." His sorrowful reply
tugged at her heart before he retreated into the darkness
within her mind.

Resigned to him, Kharis pondered the sky's iron weight.
Every patch of blue lay buried beneath a vault of clouds. The
wind blew at them, but the gray refused to yield, intent on
pressing the world smaller and tighter. The chill kissed her
cheeks with frigid lips.

It whispered, *"North."*

She ignored the pull and fixed her gaze ahead. Still, the
wind persisted, its breath curling through her black hair. A
slow heat stirred beneath her skin. Tiny embers unfurled at
her fingertips as her magic roused, restless. Kharis clenched
her hands until they faded. When the warmth died, the cold
reclaimed her fingers like a jealous lover.

But the whisper remained. *North...*

Soon, Ashtalon rose before her.

Scars from past wars marred its walls: hairline fractures,
molten pockmarks, runes long since burned out. Smoke stains
streaked the stone where siege fires once raged. Atop them, a
single Hegran flag snapped in the wind, the golden dragon its
only defiance in color. A few pennons flapped below, their
edges tattered, smacking the walls with every icy gust.

Below those wounded ramparts, the slums spread like the
wreckage of a flood: a ruinous tide of tightly packed homes.

Scavenged planks and tattered sailcloth stitched the houses together. The endless maze of slate rooftops hunched together, competing for the meager sunlight that seeped through the oppressive cloud cover.

For a people who feared touch, this crushing nearness was a cruel irony.

The air reeked faintly of burnt tallow and tanned leather, of refuse and decay. Even the dry, cold air couldn't mask the stench. Groups of people in patched wool huddled in narrow lanes beside guttering braziers, warming their hands.

Distant hammers struck metal in a grim rhythm. Crows croaked overhead. A broken bell swung in the wind outside a tavern, its tongue long gone. Ice crusted the gutters and glimmered like frozen tears along the eaves.

Snow muffled the sound of hooves, thick and dirty from countless feet. The air carried a sharp, metallic bite that slipped under armor and skin.

Kharis's fingers twitched. The embers beneath her skin stirred—her fire, eager to burn.

"*Djinnshirukh*," Ragha said. "*We should burn it all again.*"

Her fire prowled. Her thoughts circled whatever she was supposed to find and burn in the north.

"We will. All in due time."

Ragha's satisfaction pulsed through her. "*Trust. No one*," he whispered once more.

"Duly noted."

She nudged Bada forward. The city rose before her— walls of ice-stained stone and shadow.

"Ashtalon." Her breath misted in the cold. "Let's see what burns first."

90

THE THREADS OF FATE

In the waiting lies the sweetest agony. - Poliormos

Cuileagh entered the spacious chamber, his fingers toying with a letter. Lingering by the door, he let his gaze sweep the room, drinking in the scene before him with slow delight.

Punishment was routine in this house, a predictable spectacle that never failed to amuse him.

"Stupid girl," his father bellowed to the servant unbuckling his boots. His heel connected with the woman's face, sending her sprawling onto the stone floor. The sickening thud punctuated the intake of breath that followed. The woman cowered, pressing her back against a wall, blood gushing out of her nose.

"Father, please, let me—"

The slap cracked through the air like a whip.

Eilidh reeled from the blow, her slender frame crumpling to the floor. Her black hair tumbled around her face, concealing the red imprint blooming across her cheek. She lay there, trembling, too dazed to move.

His father reeled—a man with a warrior's build gone to

iron and age. Gray streaked his black hair. Maroon eyes burned in a face both handsome and hardened.

His nostrils flared. "Get out of my sight," he shouted, livid. "Both of you."

The servant wiped her nose on a sleeve, crawled forward on shaking limbs, and grasped Eilidh. Keeping her head low to avoid further offense, she hoisted the woman up and nudged her toward the door. Eilidh wavered but obeyed, favoring one leg.

Cuileagh rolled his eyes. *My useless sister.* Lacking in looks and magic, Eilidh still limped from the beating she'd received from him three days ago. *Served her right.* That thought brought him a smile.

Only when the heavy doors closed behind them did he move, striding forward in measured steps like a prowling shadow.

"What news do you have for me?" Saigham growled, sinking into his chair. His anger hadn't cooled. It lingered in the fists resting on the armrests, in the flicker of fury still burning behind his red eyes. He was itching for another outlet, another body to break.

Cuileagh didn't sit. Instead, he approached the desk and dropped the letter onto it with deliberate nonchalance. "The crown prince has arrived."

Saigham scoffed. "Leógham finally shows up."

Cuileagh studied his father, savoring his barely contained frustration. He debated whether to reveal the second piece of information now or prolong the anticipation, letting his father stew in irritation. The latter was tempting. He enjoyed watching his father spiral, but this morsel was too delicious to delay.

This one would send him on a rampage.

Cuileagh could hardly wait.

"There's one more thing you should know," he mused.

Saigham cut him a glare. "Get on with it."

"My spies report the crown prince comes with a student, a Fire Dweller protégé."

Saigham waved a hand. "And?"

Cuileagh smirked. "This boy, I've been told, has black hair—"

Saigham's glare sharpened. "Get to the point, Cuileagh. I don't have time for your games."

Cuileagh feigned thoughtfulness, savoring the moment. "As I said, he sports black hair and"—he paused to add a dramatic flair—"apparently, blue eyes."

Shock cracked his father's iron composure, and the color drained from his face. Then he twisted his mouth into a snarl.

"That child was killed—"

"Yes, but now we have another," Cuileagh interjected, inspecting his nails.

The desk rattled as Saigham slammed his fist down. A porcelain figurine toppled, tumbling from its place. He seized it and flung it across the room. It shattered against the stone wall, white shards scattering like tiny, broken bones.

"A filthy *bloodmion* sporting black hair." His graying temples throbbed, his veins pulsing as he uttered the expletive. Then he froze, the words catching. "A boy, you said?"

Cuileagh's smirk deepened with wicked satisfaction. "A boy, indeed."

Saigham's eyes narrowed. He poked the inside of his cheek. Then, "How old?"

"No older than sixteen, I'm told."

Saigham scrubbed his beard in thought. "Deàrsadh's *bloodmion* would've been about twenty now, had it lived."

Cuileagh could've let him piece it together on his own, let the horror settle in slowly, but time was precious and nobody's friend. And besides, where was the fun in waiting?

"What if Deàrsadh had another child?" he dawdled, stretching the moment. "A second one?"

Saigham let the words sit. His expression twisted in revulsion. Then something else crept in, a sinister glee curling his lips.

"Well," he murmured. "We'll have to kill this one, too, won't we?"

Cuileagh smiled. "I have an idea."

"Another," Saigham said dryly. "Must I remind you that your ambush failed, despite your assurances?"

"Allow me to offer a different strategy." His chin flicked toward the door where his sister had disappeared. "A way to rid ourselves of the crown prince and the lad, not with brute force, but finesse." His smirk sharpened. "And perhaps silence Eilidh for good."

Saigham's eyes darkened, interest piqued. A slow nod followed, along with a small, lethal smile.

"Go on," he said. "I'm listening."

WANT MORE?

A Fate to Unravel. A Path that Leads to the Deadly North.
Kharis's story isn't yet over. Get ready. *A Land of Fire and Ash* is scheduled for release in May 2026. Stay tuned!

Learn more at www.asrgelpi.com

Sign up for the author's **newsletter** and be the first to learn about special offers, including promotional offers, bonus content, sneak peeks, new releases, giveaways, cover reveals, and more.

Follow me on Instagram and TikTok. My handle on all platforms is @asrgelpi_author

Curious? Scan the QR code to browse the series, grab free samplers, and even bonus chapters!

GLOSSARY OF
NAMES AND TERMS

This glossary provides a pronunciation guide and definitions for each term. Don't let these words slow you down. As before: How you sound the letters in your head will be close enough, so don't sweat it. Go forth and confidently read this book. Welcome to Hegra.

A – pronounced like the "a" in apple
E – pronounced like the first "e" in elegant
EE – pronounced like the first "e" in eve
O – pronounced like the first "o" in honor
OO – pronounced like the "u" in utensil
G – pronounced like the "g" in general or the hard "g" in get
K – pronounced like the "k" in kale
J – pronounced like the "j" in jar
Dj – pronounced like the "j" in jar

The syllable in ALL CAPS reflects where to place the stress for the word.

MAIN CHARACTERS:

Cuileagh (KOO-leh-ach, 32) - Lord Saigham's son.

Darragh (DAHR-rach, 36) - Leógham's brother-in-law; Sahrit's husband.

Hrag (HAH-rag, 18) - Leógham's nephew; son of Darragh and Sahrit.

Kharis (kah-REES, 21) - The main female character of the story; She has lost her memories. To survive Hegra, she'll disguise herself as Lord Benkhi.

Leógham (leh-oh-GAM, 25) - The main male character of the story. A Fire Dweller; Kharis's love interest.

Ragha (RAH-gah) - An immortal who lives in another world yet connects with Kharis through a mental tether. A long time ago, he almost destroyed the world, and the gods punished him for it. Now, he's trying to help Kharis head north so she can save the world.

Sahrit (SAH-hah-reet, 36) - Leógham's sister, Hrag's mother, and Darragh's wife.

Saigham (sah-EEH-gam, 63) - A pureblood member of the Fire Dweller clan; head of House Teinthir; Leógham's nemesis.

※

KINGDOMS OF TÍR:

Arran (ar-RAN) - Mythical land of the giants. Some historians claim it lies west of Hegra.

Hegra (HEH-gra) - The Fire Dweller realm. In ancient times, the vast central plains were conquered by the Haguru, and later became known as Hegra. Prior to the arrival of the Haguru, the kingdom was known as Mórad Lahm.

Heitzalurr (hay-EET-sa-loor) - Land of the Wind Walkers, east of Hegra.

Saharthan (SAH-har-tan) - Land of the Water Kin, under the sea.

Skógarjód (SKO-gar-jod) - Land of the Forest Kin, northwest of Hegra.

Tillä-Susaät (TEEH-lah soo-SAH-AT) - Land of the Tillä-Isit, north of Hegra; the Hegrans call it the Ghasmanoör Chasm.

Ysin (ee-SEEN) - Land of the Earth Dwellers, south of Hegra.

Ghasmanoör (gas-mah-NOOR) - The land to the north of Hegra; the Hegran name for Tillä-Susaät.

§&

TERMS AND OTHER CHARACTERS:

Adatari Haguru (a-dah-TA-ree ha-gooh-ROO) - A title meaning "sparkling gem." Often shortened to Adatari, it refers to a person from the mythical land of Adatar, from which the Elatharim came.

Aghavor (a-GA-vor) - King of Hegra; Leógham's father.

Aife (EE-fa) - Queen of Skórgarjód; Darragh's mother.

Andaheimur (an-HAY-moor) - Also known as the spirit world, a realm behind a veil only immortals can inhabit.

Ondriagh (an-dreeh-ACH) - The name of the head cook at Dríeadh Manor.

Bada (BA-dah) - Kharis's horse

Balyus (Ba-LEE-oos) - Leógham's horse

Baraxas (ba-RAH-has) - A Hegran card game, played with a forty-three-card deck divided into four suits—Suns, Staves, Chalices, and Blades—each bearing ten ranks: one through seven, followed by a Squire, Knight, and King. Two Jokers serve as wild cards, though their worth is fickle, changing with the hand. Above all reigns the Dragon Card, a solitary trump capable of besting any suit.

Benkhi (ben-KEE) - Kharis's Hegran nickname when she's disguised as a man; it means fire.

Bhalim (bah-LEEM) - Children of the Great Tree, these act as portals for the Forest Kin clan

Bloodmion (Blood-MEE-on) - An expletive used for half-breeds (children born of the intermarriage between members of different clans); It literally means "dirty blood." Those who adhere to purity laws see such offspring as abominations. Thus, the expletive is impactful.

Cliffmark - A measurement of altitude, based on the height of one peak. It equals three thousand marks. A mark, the basic unit, can be used to measure height or length, and is similar to a foot.

Deogh (de-OCH) - Hot spicy tea made with thick, sweet cream, ground oats, and pear liquor

Djinnshirukh (GEEN-shee-rook) - The Akumi's vessel-prison; the Keeper of the South Wind

Drieadh Manor (DREE-ad ma-nor) - Leógham's residence away from the capital.

Elatharim, The (eh-LAH-zah-reem) - An ancient race, incredibly powerful, magical beings. They arrived in peace, primarily interested in learning about the other races. They are credited with developing the elemental magic the clans now wield. Before the arrival of the Elatharim, only the Forest Kin wielded magic.

Foághlam (Fo-ACH-lam) - A Forest Kin Prince; Leógham's tutor and uncle.

Garef (GAH-ref) - A Tillä-Isit boy rescued by Foághlam; he is now Foaghlam's adopted son and heir.

Haguru, The (HAH-goo-roo) - Historians disagree on where they came from. Some argue that they accompanied the Elatharim as soldiers/warriors. Others claim that the Haguru were darker versions of the Elatharim. This race appeared on the central plains of what was once Mórad Lahm. Their conquest of the land was swift and brutal.

Ifran (ee-FRAN) - The mythical location for the Fires of Creation

Kantha (KAN-tah) - Hrag's horse

Kharasdir (kah-ras-DEER) - Kharis's Saharthani name

Khiri (KEEH-ree) - Kharis's nickname.

Lirun (LEE-roon) - A blue moon in Hegra; visible only during the day and under certain conditions.

Luádthir (loo-ad-theer) - One of the three remaining Mórad Lahm Houses. This Fire Dweller house traces its ancestry to Prince Vinashtagha, son of King Gairashtagha. Their members are known to have black hair.

Mahabhal (mah-hah-BAL) - Also known as the Great Tree, the Tree of Legends, the Dandelion Tree, and the Tree of Life; it holds the universes together; each branch sustaining a world. It was a sacred source of magic. In ancient times, its location was Hegra. After the Shattering, the Mahabhal vanished from Hegra. A symbol of Forest Kin pride. According to lore, this tree connects heaven and earth.

Mark - A measurement of height or length, similar to a foot. Three marks, for example, equals three feet.

Mathan (MAH-than) - A bear-like monster of phenomenal height and bulk that sports four eyes. Mathanim (MAH-tha-neem) is the plural.

Mórad Lahm (MO-rad lam) - The ancient name for the kingdom of Hegra before the Haguru Conquest.

Neagh (Neh-ACH) - Seneschal for Drieadh Manor.

Poliormos (po-LEEH-or-mos) - An ancient Hegran philosopher, historian, and observer of the natural world; Wrote a series of treatises still considered canon literature in Hegra. A member of the Elatharim. She's Ragha's twin sister, and when she tried to help Ragha, rather than smite him, the gods punished her as well.

Raysänen (rah-eeh-SAH-nen) - The name of the vast archipelago in the North.

Sahal (SAH-hal) - A mythical creature, far more ancient than dragons, with enormous magical power. Lore presents them as Elatharim's companions.

Sahalim (sah-hah-LEEM) - Plural of sahal

Saharthani (sah-har-TAH-nee) - That which pertains to Saharthan.

Saya (SAH-eeah) - Kharis's sister

Seidith (seh-EE-deeth) - One of the three remaining Mórad Lahm Houses. This Fire Dweller house traces its ancestry to Prince Vinashtagha, son of King Gairashtagha. Their members are known to have black hair.

Sharan (shah-RAN) - The large ivory moon

Shattering, The - A historical event. Although Hegran historians differ on how it started, they all agree that the war ended with a cataclysmic blast that split the kingdoms apart. Now, the only way to enter another's kingdom is through bhalim (magical portals). However, the ice flowers (a magical blight) have weakened the magic of the land to such an extent that finding bhalim is nearly impossible.

Shin, The - Ancient forest protectors, wielders of powerful magic. Some historians claim they are Elatharim in hiding. Others claim the Shin existed before the worlds. Only the Forest Kin can hear them or interact with them, yet no race has been able to see them. They weave magic using song/music. They favor females and children of the Forest Kin clan, and have often taken them under their protection.

When incited, they can be ruthless. This term is singular and plural.

Skógarjóshi (SKO-gar-jo-shee) - That which pertains to Skógarjód.

Teinthir (TAYN-theer) - One of the three remaining Mórad Lahm Houses. This Fire Dweller house traces its ancestry to King Gairashtagha, the first ruler of Mórad Lahm, the ancient name for Hegra. By rule of law, the head of House Teinthir is third in the line of succession to the throne of Hegra. Lord Saigham presides over this House. Their members are known to have black hair and red eyes.

Thearith (THE-ah-rith) - Wife of Cuileagh of Teinthir, sister-in-law to Eilidh.

Toirmeagh (tor-MEH-ach) - A term to refer to abominations created by defying one of the Nine Edicts, specifically the one connected to creating life through magic; a magical abomination. Shapeshifters, for example, are considered toirmeasgh. Also, any creature born of dark or unnatural magic.

Tung (toong) - The small red moon.

Välissa (bah-LEES-sah) - An in-between realm between the mortal and spiritual realms; the bridge connecting Andaheimur and all the mortal worlds. For Kharis, it always appears as a vast black ocean. From the shore, she can see the golden kelp forests sway in their currents.

Vinashtagha (beeh-nash-TAH-gah) - Son of Gairashtagha, and crown prince of Mórad Lahm.

Gairashtagha (gah-eeh-rash-TAH-gah) - First ruler of Mórad Lahm, the ancient name for Hegra before the Haguru Conquest.

Xakea (cha-KEH-ah) - A strategy board game. The goal of the game is to take over the opponent's side of a checkered board using colored disks.

Zahar-Ghak (sah-har-GAK) - Technically, the capital of the Zahari empire; also known as the Ghak.

Kharis

Lord Benkhi

PUBLISHER'S NOTE

Dear Reader,

Thank you for choosing *A Land of Mist and Loss*. We're excited to share this story with you and truly appreciate your enthusiasm and support!

If you enjoyed the book, please consider leaving a review. Your review matters, and here's why:

- **Support for Authors:** Your review helps others discover new stories, giving authors the visibility they need to keep creating.
- **Guidance for Fellow Readers:** Your guidance helps others discover stories they'll love, creating a ripple of discovery and joy.
- **Inspiration for Writers:** Honest feedback helps authors grow and refine their craft for future books.
- **Community Building:** Your review sparks conversations, connecting readers worldwide.

We'd love it if you could share your thoughts on your favorite platforms, such as Goodreads or Amazon. Your feedback will help this book reach more readers who might cherish it as much as you do.

Thank you for sharing this journey with us. We hope this story captivates you as much as it did us.

Happy reading,

The Silver River Publishing Team

ACKNOWLEDGMENTS

From the bottom of my heart, thank you for giving your time, passion, and imagination to this story. Without readers, stories would remain only dreams. Your support enables me to bring this world to life on the page.

If this book resonated with you, I'd be deeply grateful if you could leave a rating or review on Amazon, Goodreads, or even your favorite social platform. Reviews are a small act with a huge impact—they help stories like this one stand out in the vast sea of books published every year. More than that, they help connect new readers to the tale you've just walked through.

Writing this book has been both a joy and a challenge, but if I had to begin again, I wouldn't change a thing. For years, Kharis lived only in my imagination, and sharing her story with you now is an indescribable gift. Thank you for being part of their journey—and mine.

But... equally important:

Although writing is technically a solitary endeavor, it rarely happens in a vacuum. I'm forever indebted to my parents, Ana and Carlos, who instilled a love of reading from a very young age and nurtured my endless curiosity and mischief.

I want to thank my sister, Pilar, one of my greatest supporters. But above all, I want to thank my daughter, who was instrumental in the development of this story. Night after night, I'd shared with her the tale of a girl not so different from herself, and I watched the way her eyes lit up.

In that moment, I knew I had to write it—so that one day, she could pass it on to her own children. As my daughter grew, so did the story, and the 12-year-old Kharis we first imagined together became the woman who now lives in these pages.

I'm deeply grateful for Michelle, my chosen sister, who walked this path with me. A dear friend, lunch provider, coffee-bringer, and the one who kept me on the straight and narrow when I felt like giving up on the idea of being a published author.

I also want to thank Alice Creswell, Ana, Deborah, Noelle, Nick, Margaret, and Robin, who beta-read the series and provided invaluable feedback that improved the story. I'm grateful to Poppy Kuroki from Kuroki Books and Sophie Huhn from Silver River Publishing for their thorough editing and proofreading.

To everyone who read *A Land of Mist and Loss*, you've made my world shine brighter.

We write to share our stories with the world; you discovered mine. I'm forever grateful for your support and encouragement.

A.S.R. Gelpi

A Land of Shadows and Moss

A sublime introduction to exotic lands full of alluring characters and extraordinary magic.

— KIRKUS REVIEWS

A Land of Shadow and Moss is a beautifully written fantasy of spellbinding suspense and the powerful ties of sisterly love.

— POPPY KUROKI, AUTHOR, GATE TO
KAGOSHIMA

The Dandelion Tree, Part One

An extraordinary hero energizes a measured but absorbing fantasy.

— KIRKUS REVIEWS

"The Dandelion Tree: Part One" is a spellbinding meditation on power, grief, and the quiet defiance of a cursed soul. Kharis's journey unfolds like poetry etched in shadow—layered, deliberate, and full of aching humanity. With every choice, the stakes deepen, not just for the world she inhabits, but for the woman she's struggling to become. Darkly lyrical and emotionally fierce, this is fantasy for those who crave soul-deep stakes over spectacle, and strength that looks like survival.

— NEWINBOOKS.COM

"Destiny rarely asks for permission; it arrives dressed as duty and leaves with your heart." The Dandelion Tree, Part One, by A.S.R. Gelpi, is a fantastic novel that harnesses its fantasy elements to the truly complicated emotions of guilt, grief, and love. Kharis is and has always been portrayed authentically, but her reconciling of trauma and the desire for redemption feels so much more strikingly real here.

— READERS' FAVORITE

Once again, ASR Gelpi has woven a mesmerizing tale of magic, adventure, political intrigue, forbidden love, and powerful heroines. From the very first page, I was completely enthralled, and I cannot wait for the next installment!

— ERIKA SAPPIA, NETGALLEY ARC REVIEWER
@ERIKAREADSNOVELS

A beautifully crafted fantasy that weaves together magic, destiny, and an unbreakable sisterly bond.

— R. VRÁBELOVÁ, NETGALLEY REVIEWER

Spectacular world-building and wonderful character development.

A beautifully depicted world with exceptionally well-done characters and rich storytelling that is so immersive.

The Dandelion Tree, Part Two

Dazzling characters navigate this magic-infused tale of gallantry and resolve.

This series still stands as one of my favorites. I absolutely love the way Gelpi writes emotions and relationships! The richness and depth of the characters is absolutely beautiful and the way the story just seems to unfold while completely enveloping the reader is just something that must be experienced.

If you want an immersive, emotional, and highly engaging story - this is the one for you.

I absolutely love Gelpi's work–her storytelling is powerful, layered, and emotionally rich. The first two books were incredible, and Part Two only deepens the magic. Her world-building is vivid and grounded in a kind of mythology that feels both ancient and intimate. The character development continues to shine. Kharis's internal growth mirrors the epic scale of the story.

— ERIKA SAPPIA, NETGALLEY

Flew through this one. The Dandelion Tree, Part Two completely delivered on everything I hoped for—intense stakes, emotional resonance, and characters who feel heartbreakingly real.

— HOLLY COLE, NETGALLEY

This book was incredible. From the first chapter, I was completely hooked and couldn't put it down. The writing is beautiful and emotional, and the twist genuinely surprised me.

Kharis is a powerful and relatable character. Her struggle with the curse, her grief, and the choices she faces kept me fully invested. The world feels dark and mythic, but it's the emotional depth that really stands out.

If you love character-driven fantasy with rich writing and real stakes, I highly recommend reading this. I'm already looking forward to the next one.

— RACHEL CATER, NETGALLEY

ABOUT THE AUTHOR

A.S.R. Gelpi began writing fantastical tales to entertain classmates (and occasionally terrify teachers—sorry again, Mr. Cumbie). In college, storytelling became her favorite distraction during long lectures (*what if a monster burst through that door right now?*) and while waiting for the bus in 35°F weather (*a unicorn would've been handy*).

Her dreams of dragons and doomed heroes eventually gave way to academia—earning an M.A. from Stony Brook University and a Ph.D. from the University of Southern California (go, Trojans!). But the magic never truly disappeared; it merely hid behind a mountain of grading, endless meetings, and that elusive quest for tenure (she got it!).

After years of scholarly pursuits and caffeine-fueled conferences, Gelpi returned to her first love: weaving worlds. The result? **The Dandelion Chronicles**—an epic fantasy saga brimming with intricate characters, lush mythology, and just the right amount of chaos.

These aren't merely books—they're what happens when a linguist with too many ideas finally lets the monsters out again.

When she's not lost in her literary worlds, A.S.R. Gelpi can be found devouring books, sketching out new story ideas (*do not give her more coffee*), indulging in anime, exploring hiking trails, battling the occasional dragon (aka grading), or soaking in the sweeping vistas of Yosemite National Park.

Join her on this enchanting journey—where every page invites you to dream.

ALSO BY A.S.R. GELPI

A Land of Shadows and Moss

The Dandelion Tree, Part One

The Dandelion Tree, Part Two

Kharis's journey is just beginning—stay tuned for upcoming books!

A Land of Mist and Loss (February 2026)

A Land of Fire and Ash (May 2026)

A Land of Salt and Mirth (August 2026)

A Land of Wind and Thunder (November 2026)

Curious? Scan the QR code to browse the books in the series, grab your free samples, and even bonus chapters!